Her REVOLUTION

GEMMA JACKSON

POOLBEG

Published 2019
by Poolbeg Press Ltd.
123 Grange Hill, Baldoyle,
Dublin 13, Ireland
Email: poolbeg@poolbeg.com

A catalogue record for this book is available from the British Library.

ISBN 978178199-3316

www.poolbeg.com

About the Author

Gemma Jackson was born in the tenements of Dublin. She is the fifth child of Rose and Paddy Jackson. Gemma has travelled extensively and experienced life from a viewpoint of wealth as well as extreme poverty. She freely admits she preferred being wealthy.

She grew up listening to and being fascinated by storytellers. The radio was a large part of her growing-up years – back in the days of the dinosaurs – when stories were read aloud on the radio to the delight of millions. She has never lost her love of stories. To open a book and escape into an unknown world still delights her. To be able to share her world with her readers is a great joy.

Also by Gemma Jackson

Through Streets Broad and Narrow
Ha'penny Chance
The Ha'penny Place
Ha'penny Schemes
Impossible Dream
Dare to Dream

Published by Poolbeg

Acknowledgements

Thank you – two little words with so much meaning attached. Thank you to the people who buy my books. Thank you to those who take the time to comment on reader forums. Thank you to all the amazing people who have populated my life.

I could fill the page with grateful mention of so many people. It is humbling when you really think about all of the people who touch your life in big and small ways. I have a lot to be thankful for.

The ladies of Poolbeg. Paula Campbell for giving me the chance to fulfil my dream of being a published author. What a thrill even to write those two words – published author. Gaye Shortland who takes every word of my wittering and turns them into pearls. The woman deserves a medal.

Kate Nash my agent – it's nice to have someone fighting your corner.

My daughter Astrid for the river of tea she serves while I work away. If I didn't have her to remind me to 'stand away from the computer' I might well be found hunched over my desk unable to move. I do love writing and escaping into other worlds.

Finally, the people at Newry computer who jump to help when I've once more blown up the computer and crippled the keyboard. No, I am not exaggerating!

Rathmines, Dublin, Ireland
June 1998

Chapter 1

Finn walked into her kitchen, thrilled the work on the house was finally completed. The house was free of what at times had felt like hordes of workmen. She had cleaned and polished this area last night before falling into bed in a state of self-satisfied exhaustion. The wide smile on her face almost hurt. She couldn't wait to put her mark on this – her domain. She looked around at the seeming miles of countertop. She gave a fond pat of her hand to the kitchen island as she passed. It was time to put on the kettle and make her first pot of tea of the day.

She leaned against the unit that hid the kitchen sink, her back to the window overlooking the long wide stretch of garden to the rear of the old house. The golden sunshine streaming into the kitchen delighted her. Ireland was enjoying an unusual spat of sun-filled days. She couldn't bear to darken the glass of the kitchen window with blinds to keep light out. She sipped her first cup of tea of the day, filled with pleasure. It was done – after years of planning and hard physical labour on her part – the house was finished. She would refuse to take part in any more updates. The house was perfection. She allowed herself to bask in her own accomplishments for a moment.

She loved the early-morning hours when she was the only one awake in the house. When her two boys were small she had

1

almost held her breath, praying they would remain asleep while she crept around. She needed this precious time to herself. She did miss the company of their old dog. She didn't miss sweeping up dog hair or the heated disputes over whose turn it was to pick up the dog poop. She smiled sadly at the sweet memories of a loving companion. It was time to get the day started. First order of the morning: get a pot of coffee on for her menfolk.

She touched the sensor pad on the worktop and watched the very expensive coffee machine rise up from its hidden location. It stood proudly, all bells and whistles, ready for action. She wanted to laugh aloud as a vision from one of the old movies her father loved appeared in her mind's eye – Esther Williams, Olympic-medal-winning swimmer turned movie star – rising from the sea – sparkles, make-up and diamonds glittering. Perhaps she should have musical accompaniments to the sudden appearance of her kitchen appliances. She'd have to remember to share that idea with her father. It would tickle his funny bone.

"*Nuala, I hope you haven't forgotten I plan to arrange a photo shoot for the house.*"

The disembodied voice caused Finn to start in surprise. She hadn't turned on the communication system. Wasn't she supposed to do that? Surely his voice had echoed around the house – what button had he pressed – what command had he given?

Finn turned to look at the screen that appeared when the clever tile wall-adornment cleared – wasn't technology wonderful? Once upon a time the gentry rang for their servants. These days, with this newfangled computer system, the demands came with pictures and an on-screen glare.

"*That kitchen needs to remain immaculate. I hope you are not planning to indulge in one of your ridiculous baking marathons.*" Her husband's beautifully modulated voice echoed around the kitchen. Patrick Brennan – the Voice of Dublin – beloved of housewives around the country.

"*Mother, where is my blue shirt?*" Ronan's voice barked out as the screen split to reveal his image. "*I expressly stated that I would need it this morning.*"

"*Mother,*" Oisín's face joined the others on screen, "*my shoes haven't been cleaned.*'

She stepped back as three visions of male displeasure glared at her.

"*I'll be down for my coffee presently.*" Patrick Brennan, looking camera-ready, glared at his wife.

In spite of the fact that he had made his mark on radio, Patrick insisted they should all be groomed to perfection before coming downstairs. No messy hanging around the kitchen in your PJ's – not in this house – not anymore. His image didn't frown – the Botox injections didn't allow it.

"*I want fruit salad and yogurt. I hope you have completed that project on those women's protection schemes I asked for?*" He didn't wait for a response but snapped off his side of the connection.

"*Mother, are you even listening to me?*" Ronan, his image on the screen a blue-eyed blond copy of his father, frowned fiercely. At twenty he didn't have to worry about frown lines. "*I need that shirt today. What have you done with it? I expected it to be laid out. I can't be late to the studio.*"

Finn took the remote control from the pocket of her beige knee-length walking shorts and, aiming it like a gun, switched off the screen. She could have done it with a touch but there was something very satisfying about holding the power in your hand. Sighing deeply, she turned to the recessed fridge freezer and began to pull ingredients from its depths. How dare her son speak to her as if she were an underling? What had happened to the blue-eyed little cherub who would jump laughing from his bed into her arms first thing in the morning for a kiss and a cuddle? She should never have agreed to turning their home into a computer-dominated space – 'smart home' indeed.

"I hope there are no grapes in my fruit salad?"

Patrick Brennan, his long lean body beautifully attired in a silver-grey tailored suit and one of the white shirts she sent to the laundry after he complained she was not ironing them to a high enough standard, stood in the open kitchen doorway allowing her to admire his perfection – not a blond hair out of place. He entered the kitchen, sure of his own place in the

Universe. He walked with ground-eating strides over to the kitchen island and took a seat.

"Coffee!" He snapped his fingers, impatient at any delay in his workday. "Really, Nuala," he said with a longsuffering sigh, "I did tell you I'd be down." He didn't raise his eyes from his yogurt and fresh fruit salad while she stood pouring the coffee into the mug she'd had ready. "And sweep those peelings away immediately. Really, Nuala, you must keep this kitchen clean at all times. We are in the modern world now – try and remember that – this is not one of your father's mobile homes. We have standards to maintain."

Finn wondered when her name had become 'Really, Nuala?'. She tried to ignore the hurt that lodged beneath her breastbone. Patrick unknowingly used his beautiful voice as a weapon. He didn't realise his words were hurtful. The poor man was under a great deal of pressure. The disappointment of failing – yet again – to get a television slot had put him in a foul mood recently.

Patrick clicked his fingers and the screen appeared. "If you boys expect to travel to the studio with me, you had better get down here now." He checked his image on screen, pleased with what he saw.

Finn stiffened at the sound of Patrick's voice echoing around the house. He had activated all screens again it would appear. The sound of running feet sounded over her head. The two boys certainly jumped at their master's voice. They didn't react like that when she screamed at them to get ready.

"Coffee." Oisín dropped into a chair across from his father. He grunted and inhaled the delicious scent of fresh coffee Finn poured from the carafe in her hand.

"Did you not bake this morning?" Ronan stood in the kitchen doorway, glancing around in expectation of the usual morning treats his mother provided.

"I don't want your mother turning this kitchen into a French bakery for you two." Patrick hadn't removed his eyes from his own image on screen. He was perfect for television and he knew it. Why couldn't those bloody-minded producers see that? "Time and past you grew up. Sit down."

Finn served the three men, her heart galloping in her chest. They were such pranksters. Honestly, ignoring her like that – did they think she wouldn't see through their game? She glanced around the kitchen, searching for anything out of place. What would it be? She had been dropping hints for months. Had the boys hidden it in the garden? Oh, she couldn't wait for her surprise. She did love special days.

"I'll have that report now." Patrick snapped his fingers in her general direction.

The surprise must be in her home office. She almost ran from the kitchen, wanting to know what they had bought for her. She stood in the doorway of the office. looking around. She didn't see anything out of place. Oh, they did like to tease her!

She picked the thick folder of facts and figures from her desk. She had already downloaded the information to Patrick's computer but he did like to have the information in black and white. It had been a fascinating and disturbing project. So many women and young children in need of protection – it had made her appreciate her own lot in life, gladdened her heart to know she was one of the lucky ones. She had written a detailed and amusing speech for Patrick to deliver to his colleagues. She hoped he liked it. It thrilled her to be able to help him in his work.

Back in the kitchen, she saw Patrick had stood up, his impatience obvious.

"It took you long enough."

The boys hastily gulped the last of their coffee, knowing their father meant it when he said he wouldn't wait for them.

"It's a shame your speaking voice is so unpleasant." Patrick took the folder from her fingers. "It would be far more convenient for me to listen to your findings as I drive to work. These old-fashioned written reports are a thing of the past. Still, it spares me having to listen to you, I suppose." He hit the folder against his grey-suited thigh and walked from the kitchen.

Their two sons jumped to their feet and ran after him.

Finn listened to the sounds they made walking away from her to the front of the house. She had left Patrick's Mercedes

5

parked and facing the street on the driveway as she did every morning. It saved him having to take the time to back the car out of the garage.

"*Clean that mess up immediately.*"

Finn almost jumped out of her skin.

"*Those juices could stain the worktop!*" Patrick's voice barked into the kitchen and echoed around the house. "*The boys have just informed me they will not be home this evening – nor will I.*"

Finn stood for a moment, frozen in shock. Her green eyes took in the mess left for her to clear up. When had they stopped picking up after themselves? Once upon a time they had picked up their dishes and put them in the dishwasher – hadn't they? She fell onto one of the chairs at the kitchen island, tears flowing from her eyes.

"Happy Birthday, Finn," she whispered into the silence. "Happy Anniversary too. We love you, Mum, see you." She put her head in her hands and sobbed.

Chapter 2

"Right, Finn, enough feeling sorry for yourself."

She restored order to the kitchen. She'd spent so many hours designing this space. Keeping the old-world charm while adding all the up-to-date fixtures and fittings hadn't been easy but, looking around, she thought she'd succeeded.

She'd been looking forward to a day baking. Her boys loved her hazelnut cheesecake – always a birthday treat. She had the ingredients for one of her deluxe meals in the fridge. What was the point? They would not be home for dinner.

"This place looks like nobody lives here." She didn't care that talking aloud to yourself was considered one of the first signs of madness. It was an inveterate habit of hers. Who was it who justified speaking to yourself with the words 'When I speak I know there is an intelligent person speaking and when I listen I know there is an intelligent person listening'? She thought it might be Oscar Wilde. Anyway, that was her excuse and she was sticking to it.

"Today is my birthday!" She slapped the worktop and almost cursed when an appliance appeared. She took the remote control from her pocket and with an experienced flick of her fingers shut the system down. She didn't want to live in a bloody computer. This was supposed to be a home for goodness' sake! "If no one else is going to mark the day *I* am – it's my day." She pulled open the door from the kitchen to the wide stretch of garden. "How often do we get sun-filled days in Dublin?"

She marched out onto the tiled patio and looked around, wild-eyed. "I am going to spend the day in the garden and to hell with the rest of the world." She began pulling an old-fashioned deck chair from one of the garden sheds onto the trimmed green lawn. She wasn't foolish – as a natural redhead underneath the blonde she had to be careful – she set the chair up in the shade.

She looked down at the outfit she was wearing. Patrick picked her clothes. It had started early in their marriage. She had not dressed in a fashion suitable for the wife of an up-and-coming TV and radio presenter. The family had an image to project. She sighed and shrugged. That was fine and dandy but she was alone in the garden. Who was going to see her? She spun on the heels of her brown loafers and almost ran into the kitchen and up the stairs to the master bedroom.

"No." She stared into the depths of the wardrobe. The interior revealed a veritable sea of beige. No colour dared to peek through the row of hanging garments. "I don't want beige today. It is my day." She ran out of the bedroom into the long beautifully decorated hallway. She ran to the back of the house and the servants' stairway leading to the attic. "There are no cameras and speakers up there, thank God!" She ran up the stairs, mentally making a search of the cupboards that she'd put up here.

She walked carefully across the wooden floor and with a laugh pulled open the door of what she thought of as her holiday wardrobe. She fell to her knees and with a smile pulled a brightly coloured swimsuit from the drawer at the bottom of the wardrobe. A matching cover-up and a pair of her much-loved embroidered espadrilles joined her pile.

"Not bad for an old broad," she said when she stood in front of the wall of mirrors in the bathroom.

Patrick insisted she was fat. Finn turned to look at her own back. She didn't think so but then – she sighed – everyone in the media seemed to be stick-thin – each to his own, she supposed. Maybe her breasts were bigger than they needed to be but what could you do? She knew she could afford to lose twenty pounds, but the darn fat seemed to come and go at will. You got the body you got in this life. The swimsuit had a built-in bra and she thought it was flattering.

"What am I doing inside looking at myself?" She turned from the image and with impatient hands pulled her shoulder-length hair up into a ponytail. She didn't want to examine her hair. Patrick had been strongly reminding her for ages to get her roots touched up. She hadn't taken the time. There had been so much dirty, dusty work to be done around the house when those men were putting in the computer system. You couldn't keep your hair in a glamorous style when it was pressed under a hard hat most of the day. It was all she could do some days to keep her hair clean.

Back in the kitchen it didn't take her long to squeeze oranges into a tall glass jug. She pulled the bottle of champagne she'd kept on ice for this special day out of the fridge. She pressed a tall glass against the lip of the icemaker and watched the ice cubes fall into the glass.

"Mimosas in the garden!" She made a generous glass of the drink for herself then placed the champagne and juice back in the fridge and began to return order to the kitchen. "What more could you want?"

"*Finn, Finn Brennan, where are you?*"

The female voice calling her name jerked Finn from the light doze she had fallen into – the sunshine and buzzing bees had relaxed her. She sat up in the chair, used her bare feet to search for her shoes on the grass and reached for the multi-coloured filmy cover-up. She stood when her feet were in her shoes, pushed her hands into the floating material of the cover-up and started to walk across the lawn.

"*I'm here, Angie!*" she called out, stepping onto the paved patio as her long-time friend and cleaning lady appeared around the corner of the house.

"Happy Birthday, Finn!" Angie Lawrence, a whirling dervish of a woman, threw her arms wide open. "Isn't this day too gorgeous for words? Happy Birthday!" She hugged the much taller Finn close to her ample figure.

"What are you doing here, Angie? Today isn't one of your days, is it?" She didn't think she would have made a cleaning date on her birthday.

"I couldn't let the day pass without wishing you a Happy Birthday." Angie was looking around her. "Where is that son of mine?" She turned her head and shouted, "*Diarmuid Lawrence, where are you in the name of God?*"

"*I'm coming, Ma, keep your hair on!*" a male voice barked.

"Diarmuid is with you?" Finn touched her hair and wondered if she was all sweaty.

"I had to have someone push your present – your new wheelbarrow!"

"You didn't!" said Finn, delighted.

Angie's son appeared around the corner of the house pushing a fire-engine-red wheelbarrow. "I don't know why we couldn't have just loaded all of this into my van," he grumbled.

"I don't want you getting fat and lazy," Angie said with a grin. "Besides, calling that wheeled palace you drive a van is ridiculous. I'd be terrified of scratching the paintwork."

"Hello, Finn." Diarmuid stood upright, groaning and pressing his hands to his back in mock pain. "Happy Birthday."

She tried not to let her eyes devour his long-muscled figure, clad in tight jeans and a T-shirt that hugged his abs. She felt heat rush to her face. It would seem she wasn't dead from the neck down after all as Patrick claimed. "Thanks, Diarmuid, long time no see." She gestured to the table and chairs set out on the patio. "I thought you were in America."

"The big fella is coming home to live!" Angie almost bounced with excitement.

"I was sorry to hear about Jane, Diarmuid," Finn said softly. "She was a lovely woman and much too young to die." He had lost his wife of many years to breast cancer.

"Thank you." Diarmuid looked at his feet. "Yes, she was." He looked around him for a moment. "Where do you want this stuff?" He pointed to the wheelbarrow and the misshapen wrapped goods it held.

"Leave it there and sit down a minute," Finn invited. "I can have a pitcher of mimosas and nibbles out here in minutes."

Diarmuid looked as if he was going to refuse but Angie slyly kicked his ankles while Finn wasn't looking.

"That would be lovely." Angie didn't think it was right to spend your birthday all alone in your garden. "I have the two da's' birthday gift too. Those two men never know where they're going to be from one day to the next – well for them. They sent your present to my place ages ago so you'd be sure to get it on your birthday."

"Lovely!" Finn almost clapped her hands with glee. The da's always sent something wonderful. "Look, sit down." She pulled out one of the heavy wrought-iron chairs that surrounded the circular table. "I won't be a minute."

She stepped into the kitchen, pulling the door closed behind her. She did it automatically after years of trying to keep a dirty dog outdoors.

"Jesus, Ma," Diarmuid joined his mother at the table, looking around the expanse of lawn, "I had no idea houses like this still existed in Rathmines." He gave a nod of his head to the rows of houses and towering blocks of flats, not quite hidden by the high curtain wall that surrounded this oasis. "A big house like this sitting in its own grounds – the place must be worth millions. I can't believe developers haven't snapped it up years ago." He admired the view of the old house and the well-tended lawns and garden. It was like stepping into a slice of the past.

Before Angie could comment, Finn returned carrying a tray.

Diarmuid jumped to his feet to take the tray and carry it to the table.

"Thanks, Diarmuid." Finn looked around, wondering what else was needed. She had arranged a selection of cheese and crackers to nibble with the pitcher of mimosas. The tall glasses were filled with ice cubes.

"Could you call me Dare, please?" he said with a smile. "After listening to the Americans calling me 'Dear Mud' for a while I had to settle on a name that didn't hurt my ears. So 'Dare' I became and I'm used to it now."

"Fine, Dare." Finn was on her knees, examining the wheelbarrow with delight. She was longing to tear open the packages sitting in its belly. "Thank you for wheeling my barrow around from your mother's house."

"Strange kind of birthday present if you ask me." Dare looked at the thing. "I thought me aul' ma had run mad."

"Less of the aul' if you don't mind, son of mine, and besides no one asked yeh." Angie gave her son a gentle cuff. "It's ideal for this one." She gave a jerk of her head towards Finn.

"If you say so, Ma."

"The wheel fell off my old barrow!" Finn's laughter pealed out. "I was desperate for a new one. I love it. I can't imagine where you found an old-fashioned heavy barrow and not one of those new lightweight fibreglass things." She had searched for one herself. She hated the new thin barrows which were all that seemed to be in the shops. She turned away from the wrapped packets reluctantly and joined them at the table, accepting a glass from Dare.

"I was just saying to me ma that I didn't know places like this existed anymore."

"As you see, they do."

Dare spread Boursin thickly on a cracker and popped it into his mouth. He chewed before saying, "Your husband was lucky to find something like this untouched. I can't imagine how you've escaped the developers but I'm glad you did. This place is wonderful." Radio presenters must earn a lot more than he'd ever believed, he thought, looking at the prime real estate.

"That's just from the outside," Angie said. "You should see what Finn has done with the inside. The woman is a maniac when it comes to pulling down stuff and building it back up again."

Dare would have loved a look around the inside but didn't like to ask – not today anyway. "I hear you have joined me in the big Four-Oh Club – although I've been a member for a while." He let his glance travel down her long lean legs in admiration. She was an attractive woman – and not one of the surgically enhanced types he had become accustomed to seeing.

"I have," Finn beamed. "I am forty today." She picked up her glass and saluted him with it. "I have to say – it feels a bit strange – almost like being a grown-up for the first time."

Angie sat back and sipped at her drink, enjoying watching two people she loved getting on like a house on fire.

"Turning forty is a shock to the system." Dare laughed. "I stood on the veranda of our home in Malibu, wondering how the heck it had happened. I didn't feel much older than sixteen." He shrugged, inviting her to enjoy the joke on himself.

"Try turning sixty-five," Angie put in.

"We've a while yet for that, Ma." Dare took his eyes from a smiling Finn. She was married, he reminded himself.

Angie watched Finn slice into a wheel of Camembert and started to giggle. "Do you remember the time you gave me a snack with that cheese, Finn?" Her eyes were brimming with laughter at her own expense. She didn't wait for Finn to respond but turned to share the joke with her son. "It was on my very first days here." She gestured over her shoulder at the house. "Ronan was only a few days old." She closed her eyes and her generous belly shook with laughter. "I kept telling your one here that the baby needed to be changed." She roared with laughter.

"I remember," Finn said when Angie was almost choking on her own glee. "We were in the kitchen." She turned to explain to Dare and felt a shock almost like electricity run through her. She forced her eyes away from his. She smiled widely. "It seems to your mother Camembert smells very much like something a baby would dump in its nappy."

"It may well stink, Ma, but you can't deny it's delicious." Dare cut a triangle of the cheese under discussion to put on his cracker. He stared around the garden while the two women calmed down.

Then he pushed to his feet suddenly and walked over to examine a metal figurine almost hidden in a niche in the long wall that surrounded the garden.

"Sorry, I don't mean to be rude." He realised he'd left the table without a word. His mother would box his ears. "I needed a closer look at this little gem. It's been calling to me ever since we sat down." He spotted another and walked over to admire it too. "Me ma has something like this over the taps in her kitchen." He'd admired it but she'd refused to say where she got it. "I love steampunk art – it appeals to the child in me." He noticed a metal face peeking through the branches of an apple tree and walked over to have a closer look.

"*Leave them alone!*" Angie shouted but inwardly she was bouncing with happiness. She'd been hoping he would notice the charming metal figures that were dotted around the lawn and garden.

"It's a little wonderland." Dare turned to smile back at the women watching his every move. "My kids would love these – where did you get them? I must have some." He strolled back over to join them, his face alight with pleasure.

"Meet the artist!" Angie gestured towards Finn.

"They're just a little pastime," she protested. Patrick would kill her. He hated her figures – didn't want anyone to know his wife passed her time beating metal like some kind of unstable hippie. He had tried for years to stop her making them – she couldn't. "I've always made little fantasy figures out of discards. I started with cardboard, feathers, fluff, anything I could find really and gallons of glue." She didn't meet their eyes. "Comes from being an only child, I suppose." It used to pass the time on long journeys in the camper van. Then she started working with metal when the boys were little, and turned one of the garden sheds into a workshop.

"Finn," Dare couldn't believe that this woman was embarrassed by her talent – all signs to the contrary, "those figures are works of art. The humour you captured on the face of that little boy," he pointed to the first figure he'd admired, "the way you used a broken branch of that tree to place a winged figure. There is magic in your garden, Finn. I love everything I've seen and I know many people who would want to own one of these figures – more than one."

"Don't be silly!" Finn was sure he was pulling her leg.

"Finn –"

"Do you want to see the present from your da's?" Angie felt they had pushed Finn enough for one day. Her son had planted the seed. Maybe now the woman would believe the figures were genius. God knows she had been trying to tell her that for years.

"I'd love to." Finn was glad of the change of subject. She was mortified that someone had paid attention to her little 'doodles' as Patrick called them. She put her empty glass back on the table. She would have to switch to tea for a while. She felt lightheaded.

Dare opened his mouth to continue asking about the figures. He really did want to see more of her artwork. A swift kick under the table and a shake of his ma's head shut him up. He had time. He'd question her when they got home. He wasn't going to let this go – he wanted to own some of those delightful whimsical figures – price no object.

"This is my contribution to your artwork." Angie walked over to the wheelbarrow and pulled a well-filled hessian sack from its bed. "Pots and pans!" She held the sack up and shook it – discarded kitchen utensils rattled loudly. She ignored Finn's embarrassment. The woman needed to stop hiding her head in the sand. She had talent. She seemed to be the only one who didn't know it. Her bloody husband did, for all he put her down constantly – it wouldn't do for his wife to become more successful than him – that wouldn't suit the man at all. He liked to keep her under his thumb.

"This," Angie bent and took a wrapped rectangular object out of the barrow, "is from the two da's."

Dare wondered again what she meant by 'your da's' but didn't ask. His mother had her own way of expressing things. Better to keep his mouth shut. He would watch and listen.

Finn pushed to her feet and took the package from Angie's hands. She removed the brown paper, revealing a painting. Putting the painting onto one of the chairs, she stepped back to see it more clearly. She stood for a moment, staring at the image. She sensed the other two coming to stand by her side and stare.

"That's powerful." Dare looked from one woman to the other, wondering if he was reading the message in the painting correctly.

"If that had come to me, I'd say that black umbrella represented my old man." Angie pointed at the large colourful canvas.

The scene depicted was of a crowd of laughing people on a sandy beach. The colours almost hurt your eyes – sunlight blazed from the canvas. Except for one little figure in the foreground. The beige figure looked burdened down by troubles. A large black umbrella covered the cowering figure. The vibrant colours in the painting splashed in a rainbow against the black umbrella but failed to touch the figure. She alone remained outside of all the joy in the painting.

"My da-ma painted this." Finn wanted to clutch her stomach and bend over to ease the pain. She understood the message being sent. It couldn't be true. She wasn't like that. She had everything she had ever wanted.

Dare wondered what the hell a 'da-ma' was and opened his mouth to ask. A glare from his mother stopped him. Jesus, it seemed this woman his mother thought so much of was crippled by secrets and questions that couldn't be asked.

"They say a picture paints a thousand words," he said. "I'd say that painting was screaming its message to the world." It was a bloody uncomfortable image – brilliant – but he wouldn't hang it.

"We need to be going." Angie prayed that Finn would spend some time studying the image. She needed to wake up before it was too late.

"Thanks for my presents." Finn tore her eyes away from the painting. "It was lovely to see you again, Dare." She sucked in a breath, turning on her hostess self. She had to hide how much that painting had upset her. "I will probably see more of you if you really are returning to live here. Will you live with your mother?" She wasn't really aware of what she was saying. She needed them to leave.

"I'm a bit old to live with me mammy." Dare got the distinct impression it was 'here's your hat, what's your hurry' so in the spirit of good neighbourliness he took his mother by the elbow and began to walk towards the gap in the curtain wall at the end of the driveway.

"We would kill each other." Angie laughed over her shoulder. "Besides, your man here made his fortune in America. My house wouldn't be fancy enough for him and his kids."

"Now, Ma," Dare towed her along with him, "my kids would drive you around the bend and you know it."

Finn stood listening to them laugh and joke as they walked away. She stood alone for a moment in the sunshine – surrounded by the beauty of her garden – reluctant to return and look at that painting again.

She returned to the patio and stood over the painting for uncounted moments, unable to tear her eyes away. Her da-ma – her father's long-time partner Rolf – had painted a powerful image. Last year's painting had been a science-fiction image of an ostrich. Her da likened Finn to an ostrich often enough – head in sand – arse in air – positioned for kicking. She tried to smile and dismiss the painting, carry on with her private celebration, but she didn't quite manage it. That painting seemed to mock her belief in her secure little world. She imagined she was bleeding from the wounds that poor beige figure in the painting had inflicted on herself. She wasn't like that – she insisted over and over to herself – she wasn't.

Finn turned away from the disturbing image. She put the sack back in the barrow and, with tears dripping unnoticed down her ashen face, she pushed the wheelbarrow towards her little hideaway. The long high cement block building hidden in her garden housed her little metal figures and workshop. She would think about the message in that painting – she wouldn't be able to stop herself.

Chapter 3

"I am not doing it," Finn bit out through throbbing teeth when her alarm sounded. "This is the first day of the rest of my life and all that other horseshit I ranted and raved about last night. It's time to stand up and be counted. I have to start sometime and today is 'D' day." She turned over in the king-size bed. She had slept alone again. What a surprise.

"What idiot ordered a king-size bed?" she yelled, punching the pillow. *"What lunatic thought we needed a bed this big? We could host a party for six in this bed and still have room to spare!"* She was on a roll now. To hell with it – who wanted to sleep when it was the first day of the rest of your life?

She hurried into the en-suite shower. The weather people had promised another lovely day. She pulled a floral cotton-glaze long dress down her damp body. The dress was another item from her holiday wardrobe – she'd raided that wardrobe last night while under the influence of very many champagne cocktails. The elasticised top of the dress and wide straps would support her breasts. No need of constricting underwear in such hot weather. She shoved her feet into her espadrilles and left the bedroom.

A quick rap on two tightly shut bedroom doors was all she was willing to do this morning. She refused to indulge in the usual round of shouts, threats and mayhem. She'd been tempted

18

to put a computer program in place to frighten the life out of them this morning.

A pot of lifesaving tea was called for – urgently. The bottle of Dom she'd finished off by herself last night had not settled as well as it had in the past. She felt lousy – but determined. She locked the screen in the kitchen down – when she'd agreed to have the latest computer system put into the house, she hadn't realised how easy it would be for the men in her life to order her around. Well, not today!

Ronan, her beautiful tall blond son was the first to show.

"Mother, what in the name of God is going on? Why is there no coffee prepared? Do you know what time it is? How could you have failed to wake me? I'm going to be late."

Had he always sounded as pompous as his father? She remembered her little boy with heart-breaking fondness. She didn't like this man in the making, speaking to her as if she were a slightly dull-witted secretary.

Finn sat silently back and watched her son, all six feet two inches of him – no, they didn't measure like that anymore, did they? She had been home-schooled by her father. He had taught her the modern methods but in their home they still used the old-fashioned terms. Wasn't that typical of her life? She didn't even know what her son measured in metres. There was a time when she'd celebrated every additional inch with him.

He threw his elegant body into a kitchen chair and waited. Thank goodness she had put her foot down and chosen sturdy chairs for the kitchen. They would have been sitting on the floor now if they had gone ahead and picked the stylish set Patrick had so admired.

"*Does anyone in this house know what bloody time it is?*" a highly irate voice barked from the top of the stairs. "*I'm going to be late. How could you have allowed me to sleep in? I left a memo asking you to wake me, didn't I?*"

Oisín was awake then. It strengthened her resolve that he hadn't addressed any of his remarks to her personally. Even when talking to their old dog, her sons gave the animal a name – but not her – she was just the one who made sure their lives were without fuss or bother.

Finn Brennan, housemother, chef, chauffeur, chambermaid

and general bloody dogsbody. That's who I have been in the past – but no more. Finn was determined to change.

Sitting at the kitchen table sipping at the first lifegiving cup of tea of the morning, she had to physically force herself not to move. She was programmed to jump and provide at the first sign of the males in her life.

"Mother?" Ronan stared across the empty expanse of kitchen table. The table was normally set and overflowing with good things to eat at this hour of the morning. Their father wasn't home so she had no excuse for not providing the delicious treats she normally had waiting for them. "Mother, it's getting late. Where is breakfast?"

Ronan, my little alien, ninety-nine-point-nine per cent of the mothers in Ireland are called Ma or Mam or Mum. Nevertheless, her sons called her 'Mother'. Little aliens – where had her blond cherubs gone?

"What is going on now?" Oisín's entrance into the kitchen was its usual noisy announcement of his supreme presence. His voice echoed a world-weary fatigue.

Was she expected to bow down before him now?

Finn studied these two prime examples of Irish manhood. Both over six feet tall, they were very handsome. They had for years found work as extras on the many television programmes being produced in Ireland. They wore their straight long blond hair to their shoulder blades. Ronan with his blue eyes and almost white-blond hair and Oisín with his strawberry-blond mane and green eyes – they were definitely eye candy. Their images were striking and much in demand on screen. She wasn't the only one to think her sons gorgeous. Young girls and older women who should know better, in the neighbourhood and farther afield, had been throwing themselves at these two for years. At twenty and eighteen years of age they were wonderfully conscious of their importance in the Universe.

"Where's breakfast?" Oisín stared at the empty table in disbelief. "Do you realise that I'll be late?"

Of her two sons Oisín was the most impatient – but it was Ronan you had to watch. Ronan was like his father and oozed charm to get his way in life.

"Mother, is something the matter?" Ronan said. "You know we have to be on set. We need to eat before we leave the house. How often have you told us that?"

Oh, he was good. Ronan threw her own words back at her with a skill his father would envy.

"Gentlemen," Finn stood to refill her teacup, "allow me to introduce myself. My name is Finn. As of this morning I am resigning from my position as your mother and domestic slave."

"*What?*" they sang out in perfect unison, looking at her as if she'd grown an extra head.

At least she had their attention. That was something.

"Mother, I'm beginning to worry – what's the matter with you?" Ronan was looking at the time displayed on the kitchen screen. "Should we call Father?" He looked at Oisín as if she were incapable of answering.

"There is no need to disturb your father. I'm sure he and his latest secretary are still in bed in whatever hotel they landed in last night." She refused to pretend she didn't know what was going on any longer. "Or does this one have her own apartment?" She looked at her sons with a question in her eyes. They would know what Patrick was up to if anyone would. When had the three of them formed their gentlemen's club?

Oisín had the grace to appear uncomfortable – it didn't turn a hair on Ronan's perfectly groomed head. Ronan was his father's son in every way that mattered. She had failed the women of Ireland. How could she have nurtured a son like this? That she should raise a young man with no idea of the value of the female of the species – shame on her!

"Is it the menopause?" Oisín asked, blushing. "Is that what's the matter with you?"

Ah, he knew about the menopause. Perhaps she wasn't as big a failure as she'd thought.

"My God, Oisín, please! I haven't even had a cup of coffee yet this morning." Ronan looked uncomfortable now.

"You are – both of you – considered adults by the law of the land. I think you are capable of getting your own breakfast. You had better put on a bit of speed. You will be taking public transport today. I have had enough of your complaints about folding your length into my little car. I'm sure you can figure out between you how to find the coffee pot and toaster."

She swept majestically from the kitchen out into the garden, carrying her cup of tea. She resisted, with admirable restraint, watching their reaction on the computer screen in the kitchen on her handheld unit. She'd allow them their privacy.

Finn, the new woman, took a seat at the patio table and stared out into her garden. They said a picture painted a thousand words. She was still reeling from the dagger-stroke of that painting she'd received for her birthday. The beige figure in the painting had been her. She could not deny it even to herself. She had carried the painting into her home office and hung it where she could see it whenever she looked up from her desk.

Before going to bed alone and lonely after a day that should have been one of celebration, she had stood examining the contents of her built-in wardrobe. When had she become the Queen of Beige, she'd wondered in despair? Her wardrobe appeared to consist entirely of brown and beige garments. How had that happened? When had she turned into a frumpy old biddy? Rip Van Winkle had only slept for twenty years – it would appear she had him beat by a year.

A gentle breeze blew her unbound hair around her face. She looked at the strands for a moment – blonde hair? She'd been refusing to admit that the shade was more beige than blonde. When had she started to dye her natural red hair? Who had chosen this colour? How long had it taken for the constant gentle hints to work on her? "It's so vulgar a colour, darling," Patrick had said not long after the wedding. Had she complained? Never. She thought the man hung the moon. So, to surprise her darling she had dyed her hair blonde. He had been so enthusiastic, so complimentary.

In a reflex action Finn started to put her hair into its usual sedate bun and stopped. It was tragic – even trying to be a new woman she automatically started to put her hair in a bun. Nope – not going to happen – not today. She might fall back into bad habits – but she could catch herself. She would improve – starting now.

Sometime later Oisín, a bad-tempered scowl on his face,

joined her on the patio, "Mother, we believe you owe us an explanation," he stated in all seriousness.

"An explanation? What a novel concept in this house!" Finn pretended to think about it.

She got up and walked back into the kitchen, Oisín following in her wake.

The formerly pristine area looked as if a gang of unruly children had been let loose in it.

She began to make a fresh pot of tea. It gave her something to do and tea never went to waste with her around.

"Yesterday, gentlemen," she bit out, staring over her shoulder at her two sons, "I celebrated my fortieth birthday and my twenty-first wedding anniversary." She didn't even pause to see if they winced. "I spent the day and evening alone and completely unacknowledged." She waited in vain for them to say something, anything. Even a mumbled apology would help her feel marginally less worthless.

"We'll be late." Ronan stood abruptly.

"Got to go." Oisín joined his brother. "We can talk later."

The two young men she had loved and raised practically ran from the kitchen. Neither even tried to offer an excuse. They left the house with a loud bang of the front door.

Finn sat down at the untidy table and fought back tears. She had cried an ocean last night. Enough tears had flowed to last most people a lifetime. She refused to cry today. It was a new dawn, she was a new woman. She was going to kickstart her life today. She would change or by God she would know the reason why.

Chapter 4

Finn stared into her wardrobe, trying to find an outfit she could wear into the village. She needed to get out of the house. She refused to wear the clothes of her old self. The clothes belonging to the woman Patrick had turned her into could rot as far as she was concerned. Miss Town and Country, perfect beige casuals with pearls no less – well, no more.

She riffled through her make-up. Beige, no thanks. She couldn't believe she'd been brought to this place in her life. Yesterday had been a kick in the teeth, a rude wake-up call, and not before time.

Finn looked into her own eyes, feeling guilty. She could have dropped the boys off this morning. But she had wanted them to realise how seriously upset she was. How hurt. She had to start her new life somewhere. Twenty-one years of waiting hand and foot on other people had earned her exactly nothing. It was time to think about Finn. What did she want and need out of life? She had paid her dues, her boys were legally men. They could bloody well prove it.

Finn reached over to turn the radio on then jerked her hand back when she realised what she'd been about to do. Who wanted to listen to Patrick Brennan crowing about family values in his early-morning radio programme? The man was a hypocrite.

In the early days of their marriage Finn had faithfully listened to every word uttered in every programme Patrick hosted. He had wanted and needed her input into his professional life, he had told her. Sure he did: as a young housewife and mother she was his target audience. Naïve as she was, she had found her husband's interest in her day-to-day life so loving.

She cringed, remembering the women who hung around the school gates either dropping off or waiting for their children – they had sung the praises of Patrick Brennan and envied Finn her involved concerned husband. She had been his chief cheerleader in those days, singing her husband's praises, boasting to the other women. How many times and in how many ways was she going to have to kick herself?

She sighed. The worst part of all this soul-searching was the one glaring fact that had to be faced. She had no one to blame but herself. No one had given her blinders with orders to put them on. She had willingly put thick black, or maybe that should be beige-coloured, blinders on and then left her brain in idle for over twenty years.

At the local bus stop Oisín and Ronan didn't speak. They hunched into their lightweight jackets and waited. It was no big deal taking public transport. They lived in Rathmines – at a pinch they could walk into town. They boarded the bus when it came, still without exchanging a word, and made their way to the back seats. Two poor, abused, misunderstood young men.

"You should never have allowed her to watch that bloody DVD – you know the one – *Shirley Valentine*, that was it," Ronan muttered between clenched teeth. "This is your fault."

"Don't be more of a prick then you can help, bro." Oisín wanted to punch something. He hadn't enjoyed this morning at all. "I was writing a paper on Willie Russell at the time. The man's a genius. I wanted to watch his work on film. I couldn't help it that Mother joined us on the sofa."

"I'm telling you, she hasn't been the same since she watched that film. She cried when she was watching it, remember? It wasn't normal crying – she howled like a banshee." Ronan was satisfied that he'd discovered the cause of his mother's unhappiness. It had nothing to do with him. It was all the fault of a bloody DVD and some kind of woman's problem.

"Did you remember it was her birthday and wedding anniversary yesterday?" Oisín felt bad about that. They could have bought her some flowers or something. She wasn't a bad aul' skin as mothers went.

"Don't be stupid. If I'd remembered, I'd have made a point to be home for dinner last night. She usually makes a fabulous meal for special occasions – hate to have missed that."

"Jaysus, you're as self-centred as he is!" Oisín said in the tone of one who has just been granted a major revelation.

The brothers bumped shoulders and said nothing further. Everything that needed to be said had been said. They felt satisfied that they had solved the problem. She'd be fine this evening. They'd grovel a little – send her a bunch of flowers – that should fix whatever was wrong with her. Ronan gave Oisín twenty pounds and told him to add to it and pick a gift. Problem solved.

While her sons were congratulating themselves, Finn came to a decision. There were no clothes in her bedroom wardrobe that she was willing to go out in. She took a deep breath and decided to wear one of her light summer dresses. Patrick would hate to know she was appearing in public in less than a classic outfit. She tried not to care. She had made an appointment to have her hair cut and styled.

"I'm sorry, Mrs Brennan." The ultra-modern, stick-thin young stylist met her customer's eyes in the mirror. "I can't cut your hair in the style you asked for."

"I beg your pardon?" Finn wanted the beige strands shorn from her head.

Eve played with the dried-out dyed strands. They could do with a good cut but she wasn't willing to get into Patrick's bad books. He liked his wife's hair to look a certain way.

"Your husband has mentioned on his programme how pleased he is with the service we offer to his wife. It's been good for our business." She blushed with the lie she told. "I think you need to discuss such a drastic change with him. He does have an image to uphold, you know." The last time she'd been with Patrick he'd bitched about this woman's hair and a lot of other things. That was when she decided to give him the old heave-ho. "I have the dye you prefer on hand, all ready to mix."

"Thank you, Eve." Finn removed the hairdressing cape from her shoulders. "I don't think so." She avoided looking at the other woman. She hadn't known she was one of Patrick's bedmates – not before today. "I'll find someone who will do what I want."

"It's *my* hair!"

Finn pulled her phone out of her bag, intending to look up another hairdresser in the area and make an appointment. She had her mind set on it. It was the first step for the new her.

But before she could do anything the phone in her hand signalled. She looked at the screen in surprise. The smart house was telling her that someone was in it. She stepped out of the crowd of hurrying people into a nearby laneway to watch her screen for a moment. Had her sons decided to return home? She watched the screen, surprised to see her husband Patrick step into the hallway. Why was he there at this time of day? Was he looking for her? Had the boys called him? He was followed into the house by a thickset man she didn't recognise. A slender young girl, electronic notepad in hand, brought up the rear.

"*I'll give you the royal tour.*" Patrick's voice came out of her telephone speaker. Finn looked around to see if anyone was nearby – spotting no one, she leaned against a nearby wall and prepared to watch and listen. He had engaged all screens again as he seemed to prefer. Why did he continue to do that? Surely the boys had shown him how to use the system properly?

"*This is a fabulous space you have here,*" the unknown male said as Patrick made much of showing the pair around the downstairs rooms. "*How many bedrooms do you have?*"

Ha, Finn thought – answer that if you can – she'd bet he didn't know.

"*I have ten doubles and eight bathrooms that are finished and fit for habitation.*" Patrick astonished her with his knowledge. "*In a house this big the work of keeping up with repairs and such is a full-time job.*" He smiled winningly and led the way upstairs. "*I sometimes think I'll never finish all the work needed.*"

Finn watched and listened open-mouthed as Patrick quoted facts and figures. She'd have paid good money to bet he knew nothing of the work she'd carried out on the house.

She waited for him to say that the house belonged to his father-in-law. The house was Finn's ancestral home. Patrick only rented the property from her father, at a reduced rent. The longer she listened the more confused she became. She took her eyes away from the small screen for a moment – her brain felt as if it were going to explode. What was going on here? Patrick never did a tap of work in the house – that was always Finn's domain.

"*Wow, this must belong to the Queen of Beige!*"

Finn returned her attention to the screen and watched in horror as the Morticia wannabe stood in front of the open doors of her wardrobe and stared.

"*My wife doesn't like to draw attention to herself.*"

Patrick gave the girl a smile Finn recognised. He was on the hunt. This young woman had not yet shared his bed.

"*This place is a real hidden gem. The way you have managed to meld the old with the new is stunning.*" The man stood looking around with interest. "*If you should ever divorce,*" he looked at the young woman and gave Patrick a man-to-man smirk, "*your wife could take you to the cleaners on the value of this place.*"

"*Will never happen.*" Patrick laughed and led the way out of the master suite. "*Nuala is an excellent housekeeper and social secretary. She is content to deal with the day-to-day matters that would bore me. My wife is devoted to me.*" He admired his own smug image in the nearby screen. "*This place was an old wreck when I took it on. The previous owners had let it go to rack and ruin.*" He shook his head sadly.

Finn looked at the image on the screen, wondering why she had never noticed how much Patrick enjoyed looking at himself.

"*I have details of the amount of sheer slog it took me to turn this house into the desired modern residence you see now,*" he said.

"*It's a real shame you didn't call me in sooner.*" The other man continued to examine the details of the updates that had been carried out. "*The television programme I make likes to follow people who bring these old houses back to life. I can tell you have done a great job here, Patrick, and hats off to you. But my programme can't make use of your house, I'm afraid. The work has all been carried out. We would have no programme content. Sorry to disappoint you.*"

Finn leaned against the wall, shocked at hearing her husband make it sound as if every inch of the house was a result of work carried out by him alone. What was he up to? She didn't turn off her phone until Patrick and company had left the house.

It was a while before she began to pay attention to her surroundings. She couldn't remain standing in this alley. Where was she anyway? She looked around for landmarks. Then she saw where she was – it seemed the Universe was trying to send her a message. She used her shoulders to push her shaking body upright and began to walk towards a set of traffic lights. She needed to cross the road. If they were home, she would take it as a sign.

"Finn Brennan, as I live and breathe! What in the name of God are you doing at my door?" The laughing figure of Scott Halpin stood in the open doorway staring down at her.

"I know your salon is closed today – but will you cut my hair anyway?"

"Come in!" Scott held the door open and stepped back to allow her entrance.

"I need a radical new haircut and my stylist refused to do it."

Finn had known Scott and his partner Paul for years.

"I was hoping you were coming to have your eyebrows tattooed on." He'd suggested at their first meeting that she have her eyebrows and eyeliner tattooed on. As a natural redhead Finn had very light-coloured eyebrows and lashes.

"I could be persuaded." Finn followed him inside and up the stairs.

Chapter 5

"Take a deep breath." Scott had refused to allow Finn see what he was doing. He'd turned her back to the mirror in his salon and ignored the panicked sounds she made as long strands of hair fell to the floor at her feet.

"Would you like a cup of tea, love?" Paul put his head into the salon to ask.

The two men lived in the flat on the top floor of the lovely old building. They ran a tattoo parlour and hairdressing salon on the lower floors.

"I think I need it intravenously at this stage."

"Looking good, love." Paul walked over to stand by Scott's shoulder and stare down at the work he himself had done. "I used a special paint for your eyebrows and eyeliner. It will wash off – eventually." He laughed at the look she sent him and grabbed at his heart. "Oh, shot through the heart with arrows of green fire!" He staggered back.

"Go make the tea you offered her, you fool!" Scott hid a smile.

Poor Finn looked terrified, he thought. She'd been a brave soldier, allowing them to do whatever they wanted to her face and hair. The poor woman must be desperate for change – not that he blamed her. The style, colour and shape of her old

30

hairstyle did nothing for her. He'd been itching to get his hands on her hair ever since he met her.

"You look stunning," Paul leaned down to say in all seriousness. "A new Finn – ready to take on the world."

"That's what we were trying for," Scott said.

As Paul left to fetch the tea, Scott spun the chair around and allowed Finn to get a first look at her new image.

"Dear God!" She leaned forward, unable to believe that the woman in the mirror was her.

"I couldn't cut away all of the beige hair as you wanted. You'd have been bald. I had to dye your hair as close as I could get to your natural colour." Scott held his breath. Was she going to cry? The change was extreme. He ran his hands through the boyishly short red cap that fluttered around Finn's face. "The dye job for your lashes and Paul's artwork on your eyebrows and eyeliner look amazing with this new style. What do you think?"

There was silence in the salon while Finn simply sat and stared at the woman in the mirror. She was vaguely aware of Paul returning with a cup of tea which he put on the workstation in front of her. He stood back and the two men waited. They exchanged uneasy glances when the silence continued.

"Hello, Finn Emerson." Tears flowed freely down Finn's face. The woman in the mirror was vaguely familiar. "Welcome back – it's been a while."

The wide smile she turned on the two men had them clutching at each other in relief.

"Thank God the salon is closed today." Paul gave her trembling hands a quick squeeze. "Poor Scott will need a lie-down after this."

"It's going to take me a while to get used to the new me." Finn, for perhaps the first time in her life, ignored the tea and stood up to join the two men. "I can't thank you two enough for all of the attention you gave me at a moment's notice. I don't think I'd have been brave enough to make an appointment for this work." She gestured towards her head. "I'd have chickened out if you hadn't taken me straight away – so – thank you." She pushed up onto her toes and gave each man a kiss on the cheek.

"You're going to need a new wardrobe, love." Paul had a camera in his hand and was recording the change in image. He'd already taken a great number of photographs before they started work on her. The before and after images would be a great advertisement for their business – thank God Finn had agreed to record the change.

"That will come." Finn opened her purse to pay.

"We really shouldn't charge you." Scott looked at Paul. The pictures of this woman in their street front windows would excite interest and bring in clients.

"I insist." Finn knew these two were struggling to get established.

The thought of Patrick's absolute horror at the idea of his wife's pictures appearing on a tattoo-parlour storefront gave her a moment's pause. She raised her chin and reminded herself that she was done with pleasing everyone else in her life.

Finn walked along the busy streets of Rathmines village almost unnoticed. The feel of the warm air blowing around her head surprised her – catching sight of her image in the shop windows she passed gave her another shock.

Back at the house she didn't stop to examine her new image. There was something she had to do. She hurried into her office and grabbed her laptop off her desk.

She glared at the painting featured prominently on the wall facing her desk. "*I am no longer that beige figure!*" she practically roared. "*I can and will change!*"

With the laptop under her arm, she turned towards the door. She hurried back to collect several blank DVDs from her desk drawer. She would need them.

In the garage she plugged her laptop into the house-computer control system. She simply could not understand why Patrick insisted on turning on all of the security screens every time he was in the house. Surely the man knew he was being recorded. He had been the one to insist on the installation of the system and smart-house hardware. Patrick wasn't a great fan of computers, true – but he must be aware of how the system worked. One of the boys would have explained it to him. She needed to clear the memory of the old Finn but only after she had made a copy of his visit to the house with those two strangers.

She pressed a control on her laptop and prepared to be bored rigid as she checked to be certain she was not erasing anything worth keeping.

As the first image appeared on screen Finn lost the use of her legs. She slid down the breeze-block wall and with a thump landed on the floor, still holding the laptop. She watched in frozen horror as her husband – the man she had given her all to – led one of his young floozies up the servants' stairway. She froze the screen and examined the woman's face – her hair-stylist Eve.

Finn clapped a hand to her mouth as her stomach tried to empty the little she had eaten today from her system.

The images continued to scroll across her screen – she had shut off the sound. She didn't want to hear as well as see her husband betray her. The man was lost to every shred of decency. How could he? He had turned their home into his own knocking shop.

She folded over in pain when an image of Patrick – leading yet another one of his young things – out this time – passed their son Oisín on the stairs. Finn froze that image. Oisín didn't seem surprised to see his father with a woman not his wife. In fact, the boy gave a nod of recognition to the girl. How could he?

She sat on the floor of the garage until her butt almost froze. She sat bleeding from wounds that would never heal. She watched her husband and sons betray everything she held dear. She checked the dates on screen. She'd made it so easy for them. Tuesday and Thursday, the evenings she spent with Paul and Scott. Paul was a skilled welder – he'd trained in the trade. She had spent years studying with him improving her imaging and welding skills.

"*No! Enough.*" The word was forced through numb lips as Patrick and a woman Finn had thought was her friend appeared on screen – fornicating in the garage no less. Patrick had the stupidity to smile into the computer screen. Had he no sense?

The women surely didn't know they were being filmed.

Finn put the first of the DVDs into the port and with a heart hardened by the pain of betrayal she started to record. She tried not to put a name to the many faces that passed through her house and her husband's bed – well, at least he had the decency to take the women to one of the guest bedrooms.

"I don't understand." Finn pushed to her feet suddenly, feeling a thousand years old. She ached in every limb. "He insisted on putting in the bloody system. Why would he do that? Surely he knows that unless you command it otherwise the system records the comings and goings in the house?" She stumbled towards the door leading out of the garage and into the house. She was glad she didn't have to step out of the concealment of the house. She couldn't bear to face anyone right now.

She put the laptop carefully onto the desktop and almost fell into her office chair. Her eyes once more went to the painting her two da's had sent to her. Did they know? Was she the only unsuspecting fool left on the planet?

Her eyes dropped away from the painting to the desktop – it was too uncomfortable to look at that colourful scene right now. She noticed her copy of the report she had compiled for Patrick. She had given him a copy – was it only yesterday? Surely that morning was a lifetime away.

"They say life begins at forty – it would appear mine ended." She hated the sob that shook her voice. "I have to think." She absentmindedly patted the folder cover. "I interviewed those women and children. I listened to their horror stories." She closed her eyes against the tears that continued to stream down her face. "He was betraying me even while I did his work for him."

She couldn't take any more. She put her head onto her folded arms on the desktop and wailed her despair to an uncaring world.

"Enough!" After what felt like aeons later Finn pushed herself into a sitting position. She pulled the folder towards her and prepared to read it with new eyes – eyes forced open. She couldn't react in a kneejerk fashion. She had to think, plan. All of the women she had talked to regretted walking away from their marriage with nothing. She had no income of her own. She had never worked outside the home. What would she do for money? A bitter laugh rang around the office. Who would believe that Finn Brennan in her fancy house was worried about money?

"Dear God, what am I going to do?" She was sick of her own misery. She needed to think – not sit around beating her breast. She pushed her hands through her hair, shocked to feel the short strands – so much for a new image.

She stood, avoiding any surfaces that might reflect her image back to her. She needed to allow herself to absorb the shocks that had been delivered to her body that day.

Chapter 6

Finn walked around her home, trying to see it as others saw it. The work on updating it had begun in the early days of her marriage. She'd loved every dirty dusty minute of it. She walked through the four reception rooms, admiring what she had revealed hidden behind the dread plasterboard. The plasterboard walls had been ugly but they had protected the beautiful panels hidden behind their bland surface.

She pushed open the beautiful stained-glass doors that separated two of the reception rooms. She stood remembering all of the parties she had hosted. She had gone out of her way to impress Patrick's work colleagues – an invitation to one of Patrick Brennan's bashes was much sought after.

She made her way to the back of the house, pushing open doors that led into bathrooms. She had kept many of the original features – to save money – but also because she found the outdated fixtures and fittings beautiful. She had endured the disdain of some people but the laugh was on them – these old features were bang up-to-date now and worth a fortune. She continued to examine her home, remembering the work she'd put into every inch of the place. The delight when she completed one room and the sheer joy of beginning the next.

She had been so happy with the boys running around her

feet getting into everything – the dog causing mayhem – Patrick's voice in her ear from the radio.

She stood in the mudroom she'd turned into a wet room to wash down boys and dog. She could almost hear the giggles of her sons and the frantic barking of the dog as she'd tried to get them all clean and dry. She pushed away from the wall and closed the door gently at her back.

Her kitchen – her pride and joy – the place where she loved to work creating tempting meals and titbits for her menfolk.

The ring of the front doorbell gave her an excuse to turn away from the stabbing pain in her heart.

"Flowers, missus." A grinning delivery boy stood behind an enormous bouquet of flowers.

Finn accepted them from his arms with a smile she had to force to her lips. She stepped back into the house, closing the door at her back. She examined the card – her sons it seemed – no apology – no belated birthday greetings – simply 'From your sons'. Too little too late, she thought, carrying the bouquet towards the kitchen. The flowers needed to be put in water. She filled a vase with water and left the beautiful arrangement sitting in the middle of the kitchen island before walking out of the room.

She went back upstairs.

"My sons still don't seem to understand that fairies no longer pick up after them and make the bed."

She closed the two doors, having to practically force herself not to jump into action and restore order.

"I wonder if I should have a sign posted on this door?" She stood in the open doorway of the green guest room, staring at the rumpled bed.

There were no sheets on the bed. She'd watched Patrick cover it with one of her expensive thick bath towels before lowering his woman of the moment down onto it. To add insult to injury she'd laundered those bloody towels. She pressed trembling fingers against the pain in her stomach.

"Patrick's love nest," she sobbed on a laugh. "I should have it printed up and framed and put it on the door."

She wandered dazed around the rooms and hallways of what

she had thought was her home. It wasn't – it hadn't been for some time. She'd been too blind to see – it was a way station – somewhere to wait for her men to return.

"I live in a ghost house."

She walked down the long elegant central staircase, her fingers caressing the highly polished wood of the rail.

"I have given a whole new meaning to the term housewife – I was married to a bloody house and didn't even know."

She walked towards her office, her steps dragging.

"I am beginning to bore myself. Time to administer a swift kick in my own arse – I have a life to plan."

She sat at her desk, staring at the painting she had begun to think of as 'The Beige Lady'. It was all very well to say she was resigning as a wife and mother – but how would she survive?

She looked at the laptop on her desk with a sigh deep enough to shake her body. She needed to pay attention to what she had discovered in sound and image. The video of Patrick and his love interests could remain frozen forever as far as she was concerned – however, she might need it in the future.

She set the visit of the two strangers to play. She needed to study it, now that she was sitting down and had no fear of discovery.

"I need a pot of tea before I can watch that again."

She paused the image and stood – she knew she was procrastinating – but she was still reeling from the shocks of the day. The sight of her own image passing a long art deco mirror in the hallway almost gave her a heart attack. It took her a moment to recognise her own changed reflection.

She put the kettle on to boil. "I don't care what time of the day or night it is, I'm putting a dash of whiskey in my tea. I need something to put fire in my belly."

With a cup of the whiskey-laced tea close to hand, Finn pressed play and sat back to examine the scene being played out before her. She had been astonished at the facts and figures Patrick reeled off to impress his company – but this time of viewing she noticed that Patrick consulted his electronic notepad a few times before giving a figure. What was that all about? She watched the scene twice more before shutting the video down.

She began to pull files from her drawers and put them with care on the surface of her desk. The brown file jackets were dated to the first days of her work on the house. She had taken pride in documenting every step of the refurbishment. She'd sent dozens of photographs to her father and Rolf. She had copies of those photos in the relevant files. She had a collection of computer disks that were filled with a pictorial history of the house changes she had instigated over the years.

"So why did Patrick claim he had done the work?" She stood back and looked at the small mountain of paperwork that covered her desk. "Why did he claim he paid for all the work done – and where did he get the exact figures – what the hell is going on – and who was that man with him?"

She sat at her computer again and opened her banking files. She kept exact figures – she always had. She scrolled through years of expenses, studying the debit and credit columns she'd updated religiously. What was she missing?

She went to her file-cabinet and opened the bottom one. Patrick threw his paperwork all over the house – she picked it up and filed it – he never asked what happened to it.

Back at her desk, she began to study the documents. Dear God – he'd been borrowing large sums of money for years – money he claimed he needed for restoring this house – it had been going on since the early days of their marriage. What did he do with the money? She'd never seen any of it. Her father had paid for the work done on his ancestral home.

"How much of a blind fool can one woman be?" She stared at the beige figure in the painting as if expecting an answer. "He paid back the money over time. But what did he do with such large amounts? He can't have spent it all – surely to God I would have noticed."

When no answer was forthcoming from the Beige Lady, she stood. She needed to process the information she had discovered.

"I'm going into my workshop and I am going to beat out my frustrations on helpless pieces of metal. I'll have to do that – I'm sorely tempted to beat Mr Patrick Brennan senseless. I have to get control of my rage and disappointment. The workshop is the safest place for me right now."

She carefully locked away all of the documents. She would need to put a file together but had no idea what she would need – or indeed how she would or could use the information. She had to think and beating metal into fun figures had been her escape for years.

She unlocked her garden workshop and stepped inside. She felt like a madwoman – her brain simply would not stop running in circles. She put her protective clothing over her body and in minutes was lost in the mindless action of beating metal. She pulled the safety goggles over her eyes and applied flame to her welding torch. She began to melt metal.

Chapter 7

Finn picked at the flowers in the bouquet her sons had sent her. The leaves were beginning to dry out and drop from the huge bouquet. The fine weather had broken the day after what she had come to think of as her World's End. She had spent the last week escaping to her workshop, beating out her frustration on the metal figures she created. The sound of the rain falling against the metal roof of her shed suited her mood. She hadn't spoken to her sons or her husband in days. She hadn't even seen them. She crept out of her bed early. She had a kettle in her workshop. She used the hand-held computer controls to creep around the house unseen. It might be childish and slightly ridiculous but she couldn't bear to see any of them until she had her head on straight.

She had taken time out of her self-imposed exile to contact a lawyer. That had been a joke – one on her.

"Sit back – keep your head down – shut your eyes – shut your mouth and count your blessings." Finn sucked the blood from her finger. She had stabbed herself on one of the long-stemmed yellow roses in the bouquet. "I paid good money – money I can ill afford for that crap advice. Do men like him take courses in abusing women verbally?"

She had asked the man, a local lawyer, for an emergency meeting – just for a talk. Talking – that was a joke, more like being talked down to by that twit. She needed advice and guidance. She'd wanted to know her legal position if she chose to kick Patrick out. She'd given her name as Finn Emerson – with the change in her appearance she had hoped the man wouldn't recognise her. It hadn't made much of a difference. She'd needed a basic idea of the problems in front of her. She'd supplied a brief verbal history of their marriage. She'd worked long and hard on her presentation. She'd gone so far as to practise every point she wanted to make. She'd made notes about what she wanted to say. While beating the crap out of what felt like a ton of old pots, Finn had listened to her own arguments. She'd thought she was prepared.

"A woman of your years cannot expect to catch another husband." The twit of a lawyer had looked at her over his glasses and smirked.

She'd wanted to punch his lights out. She wasn't looking for another husband. She already had one too many.

"You state that your husband has provided a luxurious home for you and your family." He'd given her another look over the glasses, examining her clothing. "You claim you did the manual work on the house." He'd smirked again. "I hardly think choosing wallpaper and paint colour can be considered manual labour."

His attitude, while seriously riling Finn, made her realise she needed proof to back up her words.

She needed to spend time sorting out the many albums of pictures that recorded her work on the house. Finn had inherited her Uncle Rolf's habit of filming everything. She had mountains of photos of her looking filthy and delighted, with a smartly suited grimacing Patrick. She'd gather that information together for when she needed it: one more piece of evidence for her side of the argument.

The lawyer had talked down to her – had given her a totally unnecessary potted history of marriage laws while she'd sat grinding her teeth, thinking about how much he was charging her. He had thrown out the name of several lawyer colleagues who handled domestic disputes, in order to impress her with his intimate knowledge of the system.

He'd only mentioned one woman. Orla Mountjoy. An easy name for Finn to make a mental note of. She'd intended to name any daughter she might have 'Orla' and Mountjoy was a jail. Easy. She'd scribbled the name down as soon as she'd left the twit's office.

The experience infuriated Finn. Did every woman have to put up with this kind of attitude? She paid the large bill before leaving the office. She would not be returning under any circumstances.

She would ask around about the woman he'd mentioned but actually talking to Orla Mountjoy in person would have to wait.

She had a date – at least she thought she did – with her two sons.

"It's coming to something when a woman has to send a message to her sons and make a date to see them." She wiped the beads of sweat from her brow. Thank God for short hair. The rain had stopped and the weatherman was promising the return of sunshine – in the meantime, it was muggy and close. "I suppose I should be glad they both agreed to turn up."

The potato salad was under cling film in the fridge. God forbid she'd serve a meal without potatoes. The barbecued pork was slow-roasting in the mammoth gas barbeque unit that sat in silver splendour on the patio. She'd opened cans of baked beans and added her own barbeque sauce with extra treacle just as her boys loved. The beans were keeping warm in the oven section of the barbeque unit – corn on the cob was ready – she'd even made their favourite French bread. Her famous hazelnut cheesecake was sitting on a glass stand in the cool room. She knew her men – the way to their hearts might not be through their stomachs but a mountain of food would guarantee they remain seated at the table – and she needed to talk to them. A huge pitcher of Sangria sat ready in the fridge.

She ran up the stairs. She needed a shower and it was time to dress.

"Looking good." Finn examined her image in the steamy bathroom mirror. She looked closely at her eyebrows and eyeliner. She had to be careful not to get them wet for a while longer. She'd returned to Paul to have them tattooed on. The peeling she'd been warned about was gone, thank goodness. She'd waited to talk to her sons until she didn't look like something the cat dragged in.

"Who knew I was vain?" she asked her own image and left the bathroom.

She had a cotton shirtwaist dress ready on the bed. It had been a gift from her da-ma. The green was almost the exact colour of her eyes. She pulled underwear out of her drawer, wishing she could go braless. She pulled the dress over her moist skin before turning to examine her image.

"Why have I never worn this dress – it's gorgeous – and it suits me."

She remembered Patrick's reaction to this dress. He hadn't approved of it – surprise – surprise.

A sound from the computer screen she'd aimed towards the driveway caught her attention. She felt her heart sink. It was Patrick's Mercedes arriving. She didn't want him here this evening. She wanted to talk to their sons on her own. Perhaps she should have waited. Patrick was leaving to begin a demanding tour of outside broadcasts. She had packed his bags already. They were standing on the floor just inside the bedroom door, waiting for him. She had thought he'd use this time to visit his mistress. Once the very thought of a mistress would have brought tears to her eyes – now she just felt relief.

She felt the air leave her body when Patrick's voice came through the speaker. "*You two boys need to think about getting your own cars. Your old man won't always be available to drive you home.*"

"*We were going to take the bus,*" Oisín said.

"*I was coming this way anyway. I have things to take care of before I leave to record those outdoor broadcasts. You can tell your mother I have a business meeting – remember, tell me everything she says. I really think she's losing the plot – shame the days of a man committing his batty wife to the asylum have long gone.*" With a loud laugh and a toot of the car horn he reversed out into the street.

Finn sank onto her bed. She took a deep breath and forced herself back to her feet. She slipped her feet into her open-toed sandals and walked to the door.

She walked slowly down the stairs to greet her children. She tried to look at her sons with fresh eyes – she needed to see them for the young men they were, not her mental image of little boys.

"Mother!" Ronan stared open-mouthed at the woman walking down the stairs. What the hell had happened to her?

Finn continued down the stairs, smiling at her boys who were staring in astonishment.

"You probably want a shower," she said. "Don't be too long. We're eating on the patio."

"Jesus!" Oisín said and ducked, expecting a slap for swearing as she walked past them towards the kitchen.

But Finn didn't react.

"I've got to tell you, bro," Oisín said, "I feel like someone in a body-snatcher movie. Who was that and what the hell has happened to our mother?"

"I know what you mean, bro." Ronan stood for a moment, staring after the redheaded woman. "Come on, we'd better get showered and changed. I can't wait for a homecooked meal. I'm sick and tired of sandwiches and salads."

"I hear yeh."

The two young men ran up the stairs, eager to sit down to one of their mother's offerings.

"You are both very angry with me, aren't you?"

Finn had waited until they had shovelled in enough food to keep a small army on its feet.

"I don't know what you mean, Mother." Ronan almost licked his lips. God, the woman could cook.

"We will never get anywhere if we continue to lie to each other." Finn was determined to get these two to talk to her. She refused to lose her sons. "We need to talk – have an adult conversation."

"Oh, for God's sake, Mother!" Oisín bit back the words he wanted to spew.

"We need to talk about the changes taking place in this house, don't you think?" she said.

She waited to see if they would say anything.

When they remained silent, she said, "I plan to visit my father and Uncle Rolf for a few days. I'd like to leave with no unresolved issues between us. What do you think?" She leaned forward to stare at them, mutely begging.

"I notice you didn't think to ask us to accompany you." Ronan patted his mouth with his linen napkin. "We haven't seen Grandfather in some years. We could have arranged time off."

"You've made a point of keeping good old Uncle Rolf and Grandfather Emmet away from Ronan and me." Oisín desperately tried to keep the words back but they poured from him. "What's the problem? Are you ashamed of us or do you have something to hide?"

"I don't understand." Finn stared at her sons. She hadn't expected the conversation to turn in this direction. They complained bitterly when she drove them anywhere in her little car. They had never mentioned a desire to visit her father before. "Why on earth would you think I am ashamed of you or have something to hide?"

Oisín didn't understand what was going on with his family. Once they'd been a picture-perfect family – a happy father, mother, two children – now they were all adrift. Their mother had become a stranger creeping in and out of the house like a thief in the night. Their father was busy chasing skirts young enough to be his daughters. Ronan and he were being abandoned – left to their own devices – it wasn't fair.

"What exactly do you two imagine is going on?" Finn asked.

"I don't have a bloody clue what's going on!" Oisín didn't know what he wanted. Yes, he did. He wanted his life back the way it was before his mother had lost her mind. They forgot her birthday and suddenly she didn't want to be their mother anymore.

"Nor do I," Ronan said. "What the hell is going on inside your head?" He was trying not to shout. "Just because we forgot your birthday?"

"How many of your birthdays have I ever forgotten or ignored?" Finn asked sadly.

"It was a simple oversight on our part!" Ronan snapped. "I can't believe that was enough to make you practically disappear from our lives. You've been avoiding us."

"I needed time to think about my place in this family. To you two I'm there simply to wait on you hand and foot. Someone you take for granted and abuse."

"*Abuse?*" said Ronan.

"We never!" Oisín objected.

She didn't respond, just allowed the silence to linger.

"Mum ..." said Oisín.

Finn stared at him. "Oisín, you called me 'Mum'. I hate being called 'Mother'. I don't know why you two ever started calling me that – I find it cold and distancing."

"See, that's typical!" Oisín jumped to his feet. He began to pace, shoving his hands into his jeans pockets.

"We never talk as a family," Ronan said. "It's a cosmic joke. Our father, the head of the family, is known for opening up topics of conversation that no one else will touch. His radio programme has supposedly helped millions of people improve their lives. The great Patrick Brennan has helped the entire nation of Ireland to express its emotions. But what do we do as a family? Nothing!"

"We have all been living alone." Finn had felt separated from her family for such a long time – now she discovered her sons felt the same way. She was the parent here – she had to try and save what remained of the family she had created. "I'm sorry but I'm not a mind-reader. I don't understand what's going on inside your heads. There was a time when you ran to me and whispered your secrets in my ear." She smiled sadly. "Those times are long gone. If you two don't speak to me, don't tell me what you're feeling, how am I supposed to know?"

"We need to know what you want from us." Oisín was pleased with himself. He thought that had sounded just right.

"I want us to be able to talk to each other – express our opinions." She wanted her sons back.

"In the spirit of this open discussion you seek," Ronan

straightened his shoulders and raised his chin, "I have a question to ask and I'd like an honest answer." He and Oisín had whispered about this for years. Did he really want to know? He was only going to make things worse by opening a can of worms. But, faced with this new mother – this stranger wearing his mother's face – he seemed incapable of censoring his own words.

Finn waited, aware of Oisín moving to stand at his brother's shoulder.

"I have to know – is Rolf my biological father?" Ronan stared at his mother, watching the colour drain from her face.

"*What?*" She seemed to sway.

Oisín was afraid she was going to faint. He reached out to grab her elbow.

"I think you heard me, Mother," Ronan said. His mother might look pathetic but he'd come too far now to back down. "I asked if Rolf, your adored Uncle Rolf, the man you are running to – is that man my biological father?"

"Where in the name of God did that rubbish come from?" Finn could only stare. The two squirmed but said nothing.

"Let me see if I have this straight." She pushed her fingers through what little hair she had. "You both believe I married your father then immediately turned around and had an affair. I gave birth to this other man's baby and passed that child off as belonging to Patrick Brennan. Have I got my facts right?"

"That's not what I said," Ronan objected. It sounded a lot worse when you put it like that.

"That is most certainly what you implied, young man." Finn wasn't willing to let him off the hook.

"I didn't really think about that part of it." Ronan's shoulders were up around his burning red ears. The thought of his mother having sex with anyone was obscene. It didn't matter who it was, it wasn't something he was comfortable thinking about.

"For your information, Patrick Brennan is the only man I've ever been intimate with. He has the singular honour of being sire to both of you. Is that understood? I trust you don't need an explanation of the workings of sexual intimacy?" Finn blew air through her lips, fluttering the red hair on her forehead.

"How do you explain Ronan's uncanny resemblance to Rolf then?" Oisín jumped in to support his bro. 'If you look at old pictures of Rolf you can see the resemblance. Except for the clothes you could be looking at Ronan. If there is no blood connection between them," he wasn't going to let the subject drop now they had come this far, "how come Ronan looks as if Rolf spat him?"

He and Ronan had spent years staring at old black-and-white photos they'd found of his mother's Uncle Rolf. Ronan was convinced Patrick Brennan was not his biological father and his feeling of guilt about – and gratitude to – a man he believed raised a child that wasn't his was ruining his life.

"I've always thought Ronan was a carbon copy of Patrick." Finn was shocked to her toes by the direction of this conversation. "When did the two of you decide that I was a slut and had been lying through my teeth for years?"

"We didn't really think of it as you lying, exactly," Oisín replied for both of them. "It's just that you never seemed to mind when Father played around. You turned a blind eye and said nothing. We figured it was because you played away first."

"Charming, that is absolutely a delightful way of looking at your mother!" Finn reminded herself she couldn't box their ears. "I repeat, Patrick Brennan is the only man I have ever been intimate with. I have never 'played away' as you so delicately put it. I did mind – very much – when Patrick broke his marriage vows." How was a woman supposed to discuss something of that nature with her sons? They'd been toddlers the first time she'd learned Patrick had betrayed her. She'd been reeling, sick with grief, crippled by the bruising shock. When she confronted Patrick, he cried in her arms. He swore to her it would never happen again.

"What did you two expect me to do? Discuss the matter with you? Tell you how I felt about your father's infidelities? You were children. I thought I was protecting you."

"Talking to us, telling us how you were feeling might have helped us understand what was going on around here," Ronan said.

"You were babies the first time – protecting you both was all I could think about." Was there a manual somewhere that explained what to do when your sons looked at you with disappointment in their eyes. Oisín's sad green eyes – her father's eyes – hurt.

"Look, can we take a break?" Ronan felt wrung out emotionally – the elephant in the room had finally been exposed.

"I'll put on a pot of coffee." Finn pushed her chair back.

"Coffee?" they said together.

"Not tea?" said Ronan. "The world has come to an end."

With their slightly strained laughter ringing in her ears Finn went to make a pot of coffee.

"So you two believed Rolf was Ronan's father?" Finn asked after serving coffee and cake. She had a hard time accepting her boys thought she'd had an affair with Rolf. Lord, it was incestuous.

"Yeah." Oisín buried his face in his coffee mug.

"Mum, do you have any idea how many times we saw our grandfather when we were growing up?" Ronan asked. "The visits to exciting places to see him stopped completely before we were teenagers."

"What has that got to do with anything?"

"We didn't get to see Emmet very much, or spend much time with him, did we? But it seemed to us that Rolf was always around when we went to visit him. We thought it was to give Rolf a chance to see Ronan."

"Go on," Finn prompted.

"Well, no one ever thought of explaining to us who he was. What he was doing in our family gatherings. Father never came with us, not once. We always went with you alone and when we returned from our holidays Father would be in a pig's mood for days." Ronan shrugged. "We thought we had it all figured out."

Finn fought against the desire to laugh madly. She felt her lips twitch and resisted. She couldn't go off into gales of laughter. It would hurt their feelings.

"How to put this delicately?" she said. "Rolf and your grandfather are lovers – life partners. They have been in a solid committed relationship for more than fifty years."

Finn lost the battle then. She roared with laughter. The totally stunned look on their faces – it was priceless!

"*No way!*" they said together.

"*Way!* Right back at you, boys. If you want to comment you'd better come up with something better than that."

Finn wiped the tears of mirth from her eyes. This was really priceless. She couldn't wait to tell her fathers. They'd enjoy the humour of the situation. She couldn't see the resemblance herself. How could the boys not see the likeness when they looked at Ronan and Patrick together?

"You can't just leave it at that!" Oisín stared at his laughing mother as if he'd never seen her before. How could she tell them something like that and expect them to have no problem understanding?

"What do you want to know?" Finn really didn't see what the problem was. Rolf had always been in her life. He was her 'da-ma', a father and mother combined. He was as much if not more of a parent to her than Emmet.

"Everything, anything. Jeez, I don't know – you've sort of knocked our socks off. I never expected this answer, never!" Oisín was shaking his head.

"OK, your grandfather is gay, clear?" Finn waited for their nod before she continued. "Rolf and he are, in a sense, married. They have been for over fifty years."

"There's a surprise." Ronan was reeling.

"Patrick is very uncomfortable with the entire situation and never wanted to be around my 'fathers'. He fought exposing his delicate boys to the 'den of iniquity' that was my home life. His words – 'den of iniquity'."

"But you ... how did you ... what did they ...?"

Oisín obviously didn't know quite how to phrase the question but Finn understood. She'd been answering this question in some form or another most of her life.

"They paid some woman to agree to give birth to me," she said softly, saving her sons further embarrassment. "It was illegal to be gay, you know. My father and Rolf have suffered all of their lives for being different. I know both you and Ronan studied the life of Oscar Wilde in school?"

Ronan nodded, feeling as if he'd fallen off the edge of the world. This was a lot stranger than his mother playing around. God, his grandfather was gay. That was going to take some getting used to.

"Do you know ... your mother?" he asked.

"We never really talked about it and honestly I never asked." Finn shrugged. It was just a fact of her life.

"Give me a break! How on earth could you not talk about it?" Oisín was indignant on her behalf. What kind of life had she had, for god's sake?

"I was very young when I married your father. I wasn't much older than you are now, Oisín." Finn hadn't ever thought of the situation in these terms. Oisín was her son, her baby. He wasn't ready for marriage! How had her father and Rolf allowed her to marry Patrick? They must have thought she'd lost her mind.

"How can you bear knowing nothing about your own mother?" Ronan was having a hard time accepting his mother's acceptance of her unusual situation.

"I don't think of the woman who gave birth to me as my mother." Finn smiled at the look of horror on her sons' faces. "The woman was paid a lot of money to have my father's child. Rolf is my mother in every way that counts. That may be hard for you to understand but to me it's how things have always been."

Oisín put his arm around his mother's shoulders. "It's not exactly a picture-perfect family, is it?"

"It's my life, the only one I knew. I was surrounded by love and laughter. How was I to know it wasn't normal? What the hell is normal anyway? The life I had with your father?"

That silenced them. They concentrated on drinking coffee and eating cake – from time to time she'd catch them looking at her – they asked no more questions. She tried not to laugh – they were looking at her as if they had never seen her before.

Chapter 8

"Morning, Mum." Oisín stepped into the kitchen, thrilled to smell coffee and cinnamon. He examined his mother from head to toe. It was going to be hard to get used to her new look. "I don't think I've ever seen you decked out in jeans before." He bent and pressed a kiss into her cheek.

They had discussed her distress at the loss of their affectionate embraces last night. Oisín too had missed their closeness.

"That shirt looks familiar." Ronan walked into the kitchen. He too pressed a kiss on his mother's cheek. "Did Father get away?" He'd heard him return in the early hours of the morning.

"He left very early. He wanted the chance to rest up before going on air. You know your father likes to appear at his best at these outside broadcasts. It's a chance for his listening public to see him." He'd made enough noise coming into the bedroom but she'd pretended to be asleep. She'd heard enough insults out of him about the change in her appearance. "And, the clothes I'm wearing belong to you two."

Finn felt she'd won the Lotto. Patrick would be away for weeks. Her sons were willing to try and change how they behaved. She wanted to dance around the kitchen.

"I could never bear to throw out anything belonging to you two. The shirt, jeans and sneakers came out of your old things that I had put to one side."

"Well," Oisín accepted a mug of coffee and a cinnamon bun with a wide smile, "they will never fit us again, Short Stuff."

"I will have you know, young man, that I am considered tall for a woman." She poured Ronan's coffee. "I think Ronan wore these jeans when he was about thirteen."

"What are you planning to do today, Mum?" Ronan asked when the batch of hot fresh buns had disappeared from the platter.

"Paperwork." Finn was going to pull the office apart putting the history of her marriage together – as much as she could anyway. She wanted facts and figures at her fingertips before she started anything. Twenty-one years of marriage was a lot to give up, she was finding.

"Rather you than me." Ronan began to push his chair back.

"Before you go –" Finn put her hand on his arm and stopped him from moving. She poured more coffee and waited until she had their attention. "I planned to discuss something with you two last night – but we got side-tracked by talk of my lurid past."

"Ah, Mum!" the two objected and moved uneasily.

"I wanted to discuss the computer system we've had installed in the house." She glanced from one to the other. "I was surprised when your father suggested it. He is not known as a computer person." She waited to see if they would say anything.

They exchanged uneasy glances.

"Which of you put the idea in his head – and why?"

Oisín glared at his brother. Ronan could step up to the plate on this one. It had been his idea after all.

"I suggested the system." Ronan swallowed visibly. "It's cutting edge, Mum. I heard about it from one of the technicians visiting the studios. Computers are the way of the future. I paid for it too."

"My God, son, the cost of that system ran into thousands – tens of thousands. Where did you get that kind of money?"

"We are not extras in the films and TV shows anymore, Mum," Oisín jumped in. "I know you don't watch much TV but your little boys, Mrs Brennan, are fast becoming sex symbols."

"We can talk more about that later." Finn used the flat of her hand to push gently at his face. "I'm delighted for you two if that's what you want out of life. However, I want to know the true purpose behind that system." She noticed them cringe. "I noticed your father lights up every screen in the house when he uses it." She caught the guilty exchange of glances.

"Mum …" Ronan was almost in tears. How could he tell her that he'd put the system in place to spy on his own parents? He'd been heartily sick of what he saw as their cheating and lying. He'd never explained the perils of using the system to Patrick. He'd wanted to get back at them both for the mess he thought they'd made of his life. "I was fascinated by the concept – computers are the way of the future."

"I don't think so, son." She'd spent a lot of time thinking about that computer system. "You were using the system to spy on this household. And you didn't bother to explain the system completely to your father. That is why he records himself into the system memory every time he turns on the house system." She made no mention of what she had discovered about Patrick on that system. She would make every effort to keep them both out of her upcoming battle with their father.

"Yes, I was so angry with both of you, with what I believed you were doing to this family, that I acted without thinking about the consequences," Ronan said.

"And you were hoping to catch me in the act – so to speak." She ignored their cringing. "You must have been bored out of your skulls watching me run around the house like a madwoman keeping order."

"It was a surprise to see how hard you worked." Ronan hoped they could leave it at that.

"Where do you go on Tuesday and Thursday evenings?" Oisín knew Ronan wanted to know. He didn't care one way or the other.

She'd wondered if they would dare to question her. "I've been studying with my friend Paul. The man's a genius with a blowtorch. I've been improving my welding skills, learning to turn metal – for my nutjobs."

"Has he taught you to turn elbows and knees?" Ronan knew his mother had found bending the metal without breaking it difficult.

"He has." Finn was thrilled they even thought about her little nutjobs.

"Good for you," Oisín stood up, "and now we must get off."

She walked to the door with her sons.

"That's a good way to get mugged, missus," Dare Lawrence said when the door opened before he could knock.

Finn and two young men stood in the hallway.

"What are you doing here?" Finn accepted the quick kisses and goodbyes from her sons. They stepped around her and her visitor, but she couldn't tear her eyes away from the man standing on her doorstep.

"In the name of God, woman," Dare felt his jaw drop, "what have you done to yourself?" He didn't wait for a reply before stating, "You look fabulous."

"Thank you." Finn stood frozen in the open doorway. Her heart was fluttering in an unfamiliar fashion – her knees went weak – was this her first hot flush? "What brings you to my door?"

"What?" Dare felt blindsided – he'd thought she was attractive before but now she was breath-taking. "Oh, yes." He pushed his fingers through hair longer than Finn's now. "I have to return to the States. I've a lot to tie up before I can move."

"Yes." Finn didn't see what that had to do with her.

"I wanted to try and buy some of your amazing steampunk artwork." He could see the refusal on her lips. What was wrong with the woman? "I want to give them as gifts to friends in the States – people who helped me when Jane was sick."

"I don't sell my nutjobs." Finn felt sick to her stomach at the thought of exposing her tinkering to others.

"Your what?"

"That's what I call my tinkering." She shrugged. "My nutjobs."

"I love it," Dare grinned. "Please, would you let me see what you have? I really want some."

"On your own head be it."

Finn had to take firm control of her nerves. She wanted to change her life. Here was a chance to prove she could, to herself if to no-one else. She never showed anyone her nutjobs. She stepped out of the house to join him on the front porch.

"Follow me."

She led the way around the house to the back garden.

Dare tried not to laugh. You'd think she was heading for the guillotine.

Finn removed the large lock from the door of a long cement-block building that was partially hidden by the fruit trees in the garden.

She pushed open the well-oiled door and pulled a cord to turn on the overhead lights. The interior of the room was suddenly exposed.

Dare staggered into the workshop, staring around him at the walls of human figures made out of odd-shaped pieces of metal. There were a great many of them, even some up under the exposed beams of the roof.

"These are my 'nutjobs'." Finn pointed around at the stacked figures.

"How long have you been making these little beauties?" Dare stood in front of what was obviously a female figure. The body was made out of two large silver-coloured metal cooking pots – the lids, he noticed when he tipped the figure forward, had been soldered on making a well-rounded bottom and top for the figure. A smaller pot with the handle split to resemble a hair-bow was the head. If he wasn't mistaken empty baked-bean cans formed the neck and the female breasts. Two long legs, with one foot stamping, were made out of some kind of piping. It was bloody brilliant and this woman had it hidden away.

"I started making my nutjobs out here when the boys were little. I'm not overly fond of television and I couldn't work on renovating the house when the boys were in bed." She smiled, remembering. "They woke at every little sound." Besides,

Patrick had complained at the smell of paint and sealant wafting around. "And, since it gets bright early in summer and I'm always up before everyone else, I'd come out here." She shoved her hands deep into the pockets of her jeans. It was difficult to stand here while he strolled around her hidden world – touching things.

She waited for him to say something and, when he didn't, she rushed into speech.

"I used a baby monitor." She didn't want anyone to think she neglected her children. "I was always close if the boys needed me." She stood just inside the door, almost twitching with nerves.

"Why do you call them 'nutjobs'?" Dare moved to a smaller figure, a little boy. He didn't want Finn to see his face. She had created whole families out of metal. He wanted to curse Patrick Brennan to the sky and back. How many lonely nights had she spent in this room creating metal people?

"I use bolt nuts for the mouth and eyes," she shrugged, "so I call them 'nutjobs'."

"Why don't you allow anyone to see these, Finn?" Dare had moved to yet another figure, this one a man. She'd used an old-fashioned black kettle for the bottom half of the male figure. The spout stood to attention in a rather eye-catching way. He didn't compliment her work, sensing that she would be uncomfortable with any suggestion that she was a gifted artist.

"I don't work on these when I have company." Finn waved her hands around. "Tinkering is a way to pass time, beat out my frustrations."

Dare was impossibly moved by all that he saw. Finn hadn't a clue how revealing her work was. She'd used kitchen utensils almost exclusively. Fingers, eyelashes, hair, were all fashioned out of knives, forks and spoons. The bodies were pots and pans. They were devilishly clever. The staggering amount of hours this woman had spent alone was clearly outlined in the volume of work on show.

"Who in the name of God ate all the cans of beans?" Dare could safely turn to face Finn now he had his emotions under control.

"Patrick and the boys, mostly Patrick." Finn laughed. "I'd prepare some terribly exotic dish for Patrick and me to share when he came home in the evening. I don't know why I bothered – more than half the time Patrick would take one look at what I'd prepared and ask for beans on toast. He is not an adventurous eater but I couldn't stop trying to change his mind."

"So you'd come out here and turn the empty cans into necks and breasts. You made them into sleeves for shirts and dresses. You even made seaside buckets for little boys to carry." Dare wanted to find Patrick Brennan and kick the ever-lovin' shit out of the man.

"It seemed to me I should do something with all the empty cans. I had so many of them." Finn walked over to stand with Dare. It felt strange to talk about the world she had created out here. Dare was admiring the seaside buckets she'd made for several of her little figures to carry. "I played around with those bloody cans, making fun items for the boys. It grew from there. I started to use old pots and pans I'd find abandoned or in charity shops." She looked around her at the room filled with a metal world. "Your mother brings me any metal she finds around the place."

"I want to buy some of these figures." Dare had friends in the art world. These figures needed to be shown to people who would appreciate them. He was suddenly determined to see that the figures went on show. If he had to rent an art gallery himself they were going to be shown because that's what they were. Art.

"I wouldn't know what to charge you for them." She gestured around. "Take what you want. I can make more."

Dare wanted to take Finn by the shoulders and shake her until her bones rattled. The woman had an amazing gift for seeing the ridiculous in the everyday. He'd pay good money for any one of these figures.

Dare stopped before the figure of a small boy hanging upside down from a rail.

"I modelled that on my son Oisín. I'm afraid he didn't like having all of his bits on display like that." Finn gestured towards the bolt and nuts she'd used to model childish sexual equipment.

"We need to think about shipping," Dare said. He'd consult his friends about pricing – no way was she giving this stuff away.

59

Chapter 9

"Yoo hoo! It's only me!" a bright cheerful voice called after the ringing of the doorbell and the sound of a key turning in the lock.

"Angie, thanks for coming. I'm in the kitchen! I have the kettle on and a quiche made."

"Oh my God!" Angie stared at the woman in front of her.

Finn hadn't seen Angie for a few weeks. She'd been hiding from the world in her workshop. Angie knew not to disturb her there. She and her crew had done the twice-weekly cleaning and left without seeing or talking to Finn.

"I love it. Let me look at you. You've had a haircut obviously – but what else have you had done?" Angie lowered her overweight body into a chair.

"I went to my usual hairdresser, but the stylist refused to cut my hair. I had to go elsewhere." Finn still found herself from time to time during the day wanting to put her hand to the back of her neck. She felt naked with all of her hair gone – exposed.

"She did not – the cheek of her!" Angie gasped. "Although – looking at you – it's just as well. That cut is fabulous – *trés gamine*, as yer da would say. It really brings out the bones of your face and the green of your eyes." She stared intently for a moment. "You've had something else done though … what?" She couldn't put her finger on the change.

"I had my eyelashes dyed and my eyebrows and eyeliner tattooed on."

"Tattoo! Jesus, you're turning into a wild woman." Angie pushed to her feet and stepped closer. "G'is a look – that's fab. I might go in for that meself." She stared into her friend's face a moment before asking, "What's brought this on then?"

"Angie, I think I'm losing my mind. I've taken a good long look at my life and I don't like what I'm seeing. I want to kick my own arse ... run through the streets screaming ..."

Angie listened to her younger friend's tale of woe while enjoying the excellent quiche and garden salad Finn had prepared. None of what she heard was a surprise to her. She'd often longed to give Finn a swift kick herself and tell her to 'wake up'. Still, she hated to see her so upset.

"Do you think it has anything to do with turning forty?" Finn looked at Angie as if the older woman held all the answers.

"Well, to speak the God's honest truth, this reminds me of a time in my own life." She helped herself to another slice of the quiche sitting on the table in front of her. It would be a shame to waste it and Finn was only picking at her food. "I was past forty – my children had left home and my husband was out the door with a one twenty years his junior behind them."

"What did you do?"

"I went for a job interview. I had to earn money. The job was close to my house. I was willing to accept anything. I was shaking in me shoes, I can tell yeh – me knees were knocking. I made an eejit of meself at the interview." She looked across the table at a wide-eyed Finn. "I poured out all me troubles to the young one looking for a cleaner. Then this young woman in her falling-down house had the gall – the sheer nerve – to tell me to quit complaining and get on with my life."

"Me," Finn said, pointing at her own chest. "I remember. Jesus, Angie, why didn't you deck me?"

"Because you talked a lot of sense. You were younger than my daughters but so full of ideas and plans. You took the time to listen to me and offer advice. I needed that at the time."

"I had a cheek telling you what to do."

"You let me talk, Finn. You listened to my problems then offered well-meaning advice. I would never have thought of starting up my own business. Magic Brooms would never have been born without you. The thought of being my own boss would never have occurred to me. I have a comfortable income now from my cleaning business." Angie was justifiably proud. "I enjoy working with the other women I employ. You started that ball rolling for me. That's why I still lead the teams that clean your place though I don't do much of the cleaning anymore."

"I'm not as brave as you, Angie," Finn sighed. "I've spent the last twenty-one years catering to the men in my life. I don't regret that – I loved being a wife and mother. But, now," she pushed shaking fingers through her hair, "Jesus, Angie, I feel like the invisible woman!"

"You've reached a point where you need a new life plan – at one time, that would have filled you with excitement."

"Angie, I can truthfully say I'm scared spitless," Finn whispered.

Angie wondered if Finn would mention Diarmuid's purchase of her little figures. The man was driving her nuts calling shipping companies. He was worried the figures would get damaged in transit, for God's sake. They were metal figures – what could hurt them?

"Think about what you can do. That's what you told me. Let yourself dream, plan. Remember how you would make miles of lists? You must have used up a forest making lists of things to do, plans for the future. You stopped doing that. Maybe it's time you started again." The woman had the skill at her fingertips if she'd only wake up to her own talent.

The two women sat for a while enjoying their snack.

"I've been out in my workshop beating metal while my mind has been running around in circles. I feel like one of those poor hamsters on a wheel – running miles and getting nowhere." Finn gulped the last of her tea. "I've made some decisions. I don't know if they are right or wrong but I have to do something. First off, I'd like your help moving Patrick's things into the green bedroom." Finn couldn't bear to lie alongside Patrick on the rare nights he showed himself.

"Are you sure you want to do that?" Angie had seen this woman take a lot of verbal abuse over the years and turn a blind eye to things that would have had Angie reaching for the rolling pin to beat a man bloody. "It's a very big step pushing him out of your bedroom."

"I'm not sure of anything. But I've got to start somewhere. The man I married – if he ever really existed and was not a figment of my imagination – has been gone a long time, Angie. I was just too stupid to notice," Finn said sadly. "Patrick only comes here to fetch clean clothes and get a decent meal. He uses this place like a lodging house." Her shoulders shook but she refused to give in to the despair that threatened to cripple her. It was hard to give up on twenty-one years of your life.

"Come on then." Angie wasn't going to let her change her mind. "I'll make a few phone calls while you tidy the kitchen." She needed to check in with her cleaning crews – make sure no unforeseen problems had cropped up.

The two women, working together in silence, removed all traces of Patrick Brennan from the master suite. Angie was afraid to open her mouth in case she said the wrong thing. When all traces of male had been removed, Finn started on her own side of the wardrobe.

"What are you doing now?" Angie asked.

"All these have got to go."

Angie watched Finn remove almost everything she owned from the wardrobe. There was soon a pile of articles in the middle of the stripped-down bed.

"Do you have a key for this lock?" Angie examined the bedroom door. She didn't think Patrick Brennan would take this lying down. The man had never been violent as far as she knew but his tongue was lethal.

"I do and a spare I've hidden." Finn took pleasure ripping things from hangers and flinging them towards the bed. Some lightweight articles slipped from the bed to lie on the floor. "I'm going to be a new woman, Angie. I'll lock my door, never worry. The new me is never going to wear any of this wallpaper stuff again." She stood regarding the mayhem she'd created with satisfaction.

Angie looked at the mess Finn had made and shook her head. It would have been easier to pack all of the stuff away as they removed it from the wardrobe. But she understood Finn's need to grab and throw. She'd often felt like doing the same thing herself.

"The hardest part of all of this, Angie," Finn gestured wildly around, "is that I did it to myself. No-one forced me to become the woman I am now. I wanted a normal life. The kind of normal life I'd never had – a husband, kids, and a dog kind of normal. Well, by God I worked hard at achieving what I believed to be normal."

Angie shook her head. The woman was coming apart at the seams.

"I'm going to give all of this crap to the local charity shop," Finn said, brushing her hands together.

"Don't be ridiculous!" Angie snapped. For a woman left alone with no money coming in, giving away an entire wardrobe because she didn't like the colour was not a good idea. "Have you never heard of fabric dye?"

"I hate these clothes!" Finn kicked out at the pile of beige on the carpet.

"Pity about yeh!" Angie wouldn't let her do something that she couldn't take back. The charity shops didn't do returns.

"I've been wearing my sons' old clothes." Finn gestured towards her jean-clad figure. "I've always bought them the best. They fling it everywhere and don't even know what they have. I have a ticket to France booked and paid for – I'm going to hunt up the boys' old tent and take off. I'll pack up my car with whatever I need and drive away."

"In the name of God, Finn, what are you thinking of? You can't just jump in your car and run away from home." Angie was shocked down to her toes.

"Angie, I can do any bloody thing I like."

"*You cannot just run away!*" Angie was almost shouting.

"Watch me." Finn hugged the woman who had been a friend to her for over twenty years. "Now where did I put that tent the last time the boys used it?" She started out of the room.

"Wait a second!" Angie called before she could leave. "Give me a hand picking up this mess."

"But –"

"I don't want to hear another word about charity shops, Ms Rich Bitch." Angie knew that would get to Finn. She hated how everyone thought she was rich while Patrick Brennan kept his family on a very tight budget. "We can pack this stuff up in the attic for the time being – so, come on – let's be havin' yeh!"

Finn agreed without a word. She ran down to the kitchen and was soon back with black garbage bags. The two women pushed the clothes any old how into the bags.

Angie could only shake her head and follow the younger woman's lead. She had often felt like running away from home herself. She had never had the nerve to do it. It seemed that Finn not only had the nerve but she was going to do it. Well, not without her help. The two women grabbed the bulging plastic bags by the necks. They dragged them behind them out of the room.

"I don't know why we're bothering to do this," Finn complained.

"You will thank me someday!" Angie panted.

The two women bumped along the long corridor towards the stairs leading up to the attic. They stored the bags of clothing before searching out the camping equipment and clothing needed to get Finn started on her journey.

Chapter 10

Finn felt her heart sink when she heard the drone of an expensive car engine behind her. It was early evening. She'd been packing the items she would need into her car. She planned to sail to France tomorrow or the next day. She'd wanted to discuss her plans with her sons before Patrick's return. She had to fight the urge to hunch her shoulders at the sound of Patrick's car pulling into the driveway behind her. Why on earth did he have to choose today to return?

"Nuala, what the hell is going on?" Patrick Brennan, tall, blond, beautifully groomed as always, stood glowering at Finn. His beautifully modulated tones were hushed. He wouldn't take the risk that anyone might overhear.

Ronan and Oisín stepped out of their father's car and stood behind him – silent witnesses.

Finn wanted to disappear – could feel her shoulders bending inward – she forced herself to stand erect and turn to face him.

"Have you lost what little mind you have?" Patrick demanded, grabbing Finn by the arm. Then he waved and shouted a gracious hello to a woman passing the end of their driveway.

"Patrick, dear," Finn said in tones dripping sweetness as she was towed towards her own front door, "how nice to see you."

They were all in the hallway now behind a slammed closed door.

Ronan and Oisín looked like they wanted to be anywhere but there. Finn didn't blame them.

"Look at you," Patrick bit out, pointing a disparaging hand at Finn. "I left strict instruction before I left that you were to purchase a wig. Your hair is shorter than mine!"

In jeans, sneakers and a T-shirt, Finn was feeling like a new woman. The clothes were so comfortable.

"Your regular hair stylist was good enough to call me. I couldn't believe what she told me. There are photographs of you – my wife – pasted up in the windows of a tattoo parlour for God's sake! What the hell is wrong with you?" He'd made his displeasure with her new look very plain before he left. He'd ordered her to change back into the Nuala Brennan he'd created. How dare she disobey him! "What if someone we knew had seen you looking like that?" The gesture with his hand was meant to bring her to her knees in mortification.

"I love my new haircut." Finn pushed her hand through the short soft feathers of red hair on her head. She thought Patrick would have a heart attack. There was practically steam coming out of his nose.

"*I have a position in the community to uphold, you know that!*" Patrick was shouting now, his voice not quite so wonderful, no one to impress here. "*While I've been touring the country working my fingers to the bone for this family you've been letting the side down. I cannot believe you could be so selfish. You know how something like this could reflect badly on me?*"

One of the things the new Finn planned to learn was how to be selfish – and here standing in front of her was the very person to take selfishness lessons from. Why hadn't she realised she'd been living with an expert for years? She didn't have to wonder about how to live life for herself. She would copy Patrick – after all, he'd been selfish all of his life.

Starting as she meant to go on, Finn ignored Patrick. She walked around him and made for the stairs.

"Ronan, you boys are probably hungry – use your fingers

and telephone for some Chinese take-out," she said calmly over her shoulder. "Order enough for everyone. You can use your father's credit card. I'm sure he'll be delighted to pay for the meal." She ignored the clearing of a throat and outraged muttering. "I'll be down directly." She fought the urge to stick out her tongue.

She had a quick shower, knowing the nearby Chinese take-out would have the food delivered quickly. She was hungry and would enjoy food prepared by someone else. She examined the clothes inside the wardrobe. She had packed very lightly for her time away, hoping to live in shorts and T-shirts. She'd discovered a lilac dress she'd never worn, because Patrick disliked it, stashed at the back of one of the attic wardrobes. She pulled that dress on now. The glazed cotton dress was long, down to her feet, and flowed like water down her body. The computer screen showed Ronan accepting the delivery of Chinese food. She shoved her feet into purple crocs and started downstairs.

Patrick, Ronan, and Oisín stood like three lost lambs in the dining room. The table wasn't set, she noticed. This was her fault. She had completely spoiled them. They would never think of setting the table. That was her job. She felt their eyes boring into her back while she took utensils and dishes from the dining-room sideboard and set one place only at the table. She was determined to prove to her sons at least that she meant what she said. She was not their servant. She turned back for ebony chopsticks and still in silence set them by her plate. When everything was in place, she walked past them to fetch a bottle of white wine from the chill box. She took out a single glass and poured white wine for herself. She could almost feel their indignation on her skin.

"Am I the only one eating?" She sat at the table, raised her glass and sipped.

"Oh, for God's sake Nuala, how childish can you be?" Patrick spat out before beginning to set the table for himself and the boys.

"See, I knew you could do it if you tried. It's not at all difficult, is it?" Finn asked sweetly.

Her two sons began to help their father. Finn gave them a

slow handclap. She couldn't remember the last time any one of them had even offered to set the table.

"OK, tell us what the hell is going on, Nuala?" Patrick demanded as soon as the meal had been served. He tried to keep his eyes away from her. That hairstyle was a disgrace, as was a woman of her age wearing jeans and hippy dresses. Who did she think she was?

"There is not a great deal going on as far as I know," Finn said.

"Nuala, I am not in the best of moods!" Patrick spat out. "I don't have the time for any of your stupid games."

"My name is Finn," she said calmly, using her chopsticks with expert ease. "It was Finn when you met me and that is still my name."

"Is it the menopause – do we need to take you to see a doctor?" Patrick looked at her as if she were a bug that crawled out from his prawn salad. How dare she age? She was over ten years younger than he. He wasn't old. He was a man in his prime.

"I doubt it's the menopause although I'm no expert." She wasn't really sure, but no way was she admitting that.

"*Will you tell me what in the name of God is going on?*" Patrick roared.

"It's not complicated." Finn was tired of this situation. She supposed she owed him an explanation. She hadn't explained how she felt to him. "I have resigned as a wife and mother. I have had the thankless job for over twenty years and feel I need a change."

Ronan and Oisín were ploughing the food into their mouths as if they hadn't eaten in months. Their ears were wagging though. They didn't want to miss a word of this conversation. They had known their mother planned a trip but they had not expected to be present when she told their father of her plans. It was uncomfortable but they wouldn't miss it for the world. Their mother was really taking a firm stand this time.

"You're an idiot!" Patrick bit out over his king prawn salad. "Resigning from the job for God's sake! What is that supposed to mean?"

"Exactly what it sounds like, Patrick. I have moved your belongings to the green guest bedroom. You pass through this house like a lodger anyway. I am going on a short vacation. If you want Angie's company to clean for you, you need to contact her." Finn waited for the storm to break over her head.

It wasn't long in coming. She couldn't continue to eat as she listened to her husband rain abuse on her head.

A piercing whistle broke through the shouting. It was Oisín. The boy could really make a noise when he wanted to.

"So you're determined to go, Mum?" She had told them she was going to visit her father – well, he supposed that would be fathers, wouldn't it – oh, to hell with it, who cared.

"I am. I'm going to take the ferry to France. I talked to my dad this morning, but I didn't tell him I'm coming to see him. It's been a while since I visited him. I plan to surprise him, spend time with him." Finn was careful not to mention her two fathers in front of Patrick. She'd learned to keep the peace in that area of her life. She looked at her sons. "I need to step outside of my role as a wife and mother." She was terrified that she'd step back into her role of unthinking slave if she stayed here. "I have discussed with you how I resent the way you both have treated me. I realise that you have both followed your father's example. You are both young adults now and must admit he is not the greatest of husbands. I don't think he's been a very good father either. But it is up to you two to judge his efforts in that role."

"*I object!*" Patrick was red about the gills now. "Nuala, how can you possibly say that I'm not a good father? I love the boys and they love me!"

She noticed he made no mention of his standard as a husband.

"Is this about your birthday still?" Patrick demanded. "All this fuss because we forgot a stupid birthday?"

"It was also our wedding anniversary." She had thought it so romantic when he insisted they marry on her birthday. To celebrate the two greatest events of his life in one magical day. Oh, God, this was more painful then she'd ever imagined.

There was an awkward moment of silence which Oisín broke.

"This is getting us nowhere."

Finn noticed that the conversation was not putting anyone off their food.

"It really is very simple. I've already said I am going to visit my father and think about my future. When I return we will continue to share a roof. However, I will not wait on you three hand and foot as in the past. You are all responsible for yourselves. At no time need you be concerned about me or what I'm doing. Since we have been living in this fashion for years anyway, the only change will be that you no longer have a free, willing domestic slave. Talk among yourselves about that and figure out what you want to do."

Chapter 11

"Nuala …"

The tone was definitely Patrick at his most beguiling. Shit – she'd forgotten to lock the bedroom door. He probably thought a few words from his talented lips would change her mind. The man himself followed his dulcet tones into the bathroom.

In the past she would have been mortified, wondering how her sagging breasts and child-scarred abdomen could be hidden – now she didn't give a damn. She'd earned her wrinkles and scars. She accepted herself, wrinkles and all. If he didn't like it, he could look away. This was her bath and no-one had invited him in here.

"You always did like a bath 'to soak your troubles away'." He took a seat on the closed toilet. "We need to talk. I deserve more of an explanation than your mythical resignation, don't you think?"

He really did misunderstood male very well. She should never have given him the advantage of the bathroom – all of those mirrors for him to admire himself.

"Patrick, dear, first let me congratulate you," she said, running the natural sponge over her raised arm. "That makes it several times in one evening that you've managed to call me by name – albeit a name not my own. How sweet."

"There is no need to be sarcastic. I have always called you Nuala. We agreed from the beginning that Finn was a ridiculous name for a woman. Why are you only objecting now?"

"I thought it was wonderful when you coined a special name for me. I was young and foolish. I even thought it was sweet when you constantly referred to me by a term of endearment. That was until I realised that you did it in order to keep the females in your bed straight – pet names eliminated the possibility of calling one of us by the wrong name." She continued to sponge her skin, not even bothering to look at him.

"You are being ridiculous," Patrick blustered.

"Could we, for once, have an honest conversation?" she bit out, wishing she'd thought to bring a strong drink into the bath with her. "Our marriage is over – no, don't interrupt." She held up one wet hand as he seemed ready to rise in righteous indignation. "I asked for honesty. Is that too much to request?"

"I have always been honest in my dealings with you, my dear, you know that."

He was all bruised male dignity now. How long had she been letting him get away with this posturing? Did he really believe all he had to do was smirk his way out of this?

"God," she groaned, looking at him now with eyes wide open, "the tragedy is that you probably have, in your own way." Why had she never realised that he believed his own lies?

She wanted to cry – the end of her life as a wife and mother was about to come about with a damp splash – no fire, even in this.

"I want to get out now," she said, standing and reaching for her towelling robe. "If you insist on having this conversation, go and get a bottle of wine. We can at least toast the end of our life together. That seems fair. It will be the first time in years you've actually taken the time to listen to anything I have to say."

Patrick checked his watch impatiently. "I'd love to, really, but I have a previous engagement. It's business, you understand."

He left the steamy bathroom.

"Of course I understand." She watched him almost run from the room. "Haven't I always been an understanding wife?"

The pain under her ribs would go away eventually. It was hard to bury an ideal. Her dream had been dead for a very long time. She had just not noticed.

"*Where the hell are my clothes?*"

The roar came from the bedroom. Why was she surprised he hadn't listened to a word she'd said to him downstairs?

"I told you." She walked into the bedroom, belting the robe around her waist. "I moved you into the green room. You should be very familiar with that room as it seems to be a favourite of yours for your little rendezvous with the slappers you've been bringing into our home."

"I have no idea what you are talking about." He pushed her none too gently out of his way and hurried from the room.

"*I would appreciate it if you found somewhere else to fornicate!*" she shouted after his disappearing back.

She was going to have to do something about Patrick's little love nest. She would not tolerate the insult to her.

"Right, no more wallowing in self-pity – I swore I was going to take charge of my own life and by God I am going to!"

She started when she saw Ronan and Oisín standing in the open door of the bedroom. They didn't speak – their faces said everything. They knew this was serious – the first time she had ever removed their father from the bedroom.

"Are you two going out this evening?" she asked.

"We ..." Oisín looked at Ronan and, getting a nod, he continued. "We would like to talk to you. If you have time?"

When was the last time, if ever, they had asked for her company?

"Let me put some clothes on and I'll join you downstairs," she said over the sound of Patrick cursing and kicking from the green room. "Please put the kettle on, Oisín. Ronan, see if you can find something to nibble on. That Chinese food doesn't stay long with you, does it?" She would not allow anyone or anything to change her mind.

Finn joined her sons in the kitchen. They were beginning to accept the fact that their world was changing more than they had thought possible. From the looks of them, they weren't happy about the situation.

"I hope you enjoy your time with Grandfather and Uncle Rolf." Oisín brought the teapot to the table, which was already set. "Give them our best."

"It's been years since you took us with you to visit them." Ronan had put cheese and crackers out.

"You two grew too tall to fit into my little car." Finn was fighting tears. Patrick had bought the little run-around for her – better for town driving, he'd said. By doing so, he'd achieved his aim of keeping her sons from her fathers – and she'd never noticed. "You both complain bitterly whenever I drop you off at the studio. You have to almost fold your legs into the space available." Patrick refused to allow her to use his expensive model.

"I'd like to do more travelling." Oisin passed her a cup of tea. "I'd love to see the world."

"It must be in the blood." Finn accepted the cup.

"Was the start of all of this really because we forgot your –"

She saw the word *stupid* form on Ronan's lips before he bit it back.

"– birthday and anniversary."

"Being ignored and alone on my special day was simply the straw that broke the camel's back."

Oisín was staring at his mother as if seeing her for the first time.

"I won't be away long." Finn watched them flinch. In spite of the conversation they had shared, they were still astonished that she hadn't changed her mind on the spot because they were unhappy. She decided not to prolong this conversation. "I'll be leaving very early in the morning before you're awake so I'll say goodbye now."

She left them staring at her back while she walked from the kitchen. She could feel their eyes follow her from the room. It was the first time in years that she knew she had their full attention.

Before sleeping, Finn doublechecked her papers. She had everything she needed: passport, driver's licence, credit cards, reference number to pick up the tickets she'd booked. It occurred to her that Patrick could cancel her line of credit. If he thought of doing that she was in big trouble. The ticket was paid for, but she would need cash for unexpected expenses. She'd stop at a cash machine in the morning and get Irish money. Then, as soon as she arrived in France she'd find a cash point and draw out enough French francs to see her safely over the holiday. She didn't think Patrick would stop her credit but it never hurt to be prepared.

Chapter 12

Finally on the road, Finn began her journey to Rosslare. She planned to stop along the way for something to eat. She rolled down the car window and prepared to enjoy the drive. She had done it often in the past. This time she actually missed the little voices screaming from the back seat. She had forgotten about the battles fought over every little thing. There was no one kicking the back of her seat demanding attention. She was nuts to miss all of that – wasn't she? This was her time. She was on her way, alone, off on an adventure. She wished she could say it felt great, but truthfully, she was more scared then she'd ever been before in her life.

"I wonder if this really is a mid-life crisis?" Finn said aloud to the empty car. "Is all of this because I turned forty? I don't think so. Life is so strange." She hoped any passing motorist would think she was talking on her mobile phone. No need to advertise the fact that she was losing the plot. "I spent my early life being envious of people who had secure homes. I never knew where I was going to wake up. Dad would load me into his van and away we would go. He did that all the time and I hated it. I felt so deprived, so alone. I envied the kids we drove past. They had everything I thought I wanted. Those kids had houses and school and friends. I had Dad and Uncle Rolf. I longed for a normal life." Finn shook her head in sorrow over her old self. "I never appreciated the love and attention that was showered on me. I never appreciated the adventure of it all. I was too busy feeling sorry for myself. Some things never change." She laughed. "I'm even talking to myself, how tragic is that? I don't have a friend to call and cry on her shoulder. Is that my fault? Of course it is. I made Patrick and the boys my entire world."

When she met Patrick Brennan he'd seemed the answer to so many of her prayers. He'd offered her the one thing she found irresistible: stability. Come to think of it, that was sad, an eighteen-year-old searching for stability.

Patrick and Finn had a whirlwind romance and marriage. The babies had come quickly after. She had finally been living the kind of life she had only dreamed of before. A big rambling fixer-upper of a house, two kids, a dog and a good-looking husband – what more could anyone want? She'd wallowed in her safe, secure, unexciting life. It was no one's fault but her own if that life had been more of a mirage then actual fact.

Finn felt oddly liberated as she drove along talking to herself. The road was much improved from the first time she had taken it. Talking aloud was great therapy. It was good to listen to yourself every now and again.

She stopped in Gorey for lunch before getting back on the road to Rosslare.

She joined the line of cars waiting to board the ferry. The crossing would take almost twenty-four hours. She'd booked a berth in a cabin and prayed it wouldn't be in the bowels of the ship. She hated being below the water line. But she loved travelling by sea – the sensation of being cast adrift. Strange, she had always thought she hated travelling but somehow ships were different – they were special. There had been no problem picking up the ticket but actually driving onto the ship was a little scary. There were so many trucks and camper vans travelling. She felt a bit overwhelmed in her little car.

A sinking feeling in her stomach was becoming familiar. She was scared. This was the second time in her life when she stepped away from everything familiar. The first time she had been running to a life she desperately wanted. She wanted to marry Patrick and settle down so much that she hadn't even thought of being scared. Maybe it was because she'd been eighteen and thought she knew everything. Whatever, this time she needed to carefully plan every move. She couldn't sit idly waiting for life to happen to her. She had been doing that for too long already, not even knowing that was what she'd been doing.

"Oh, wow, you're so old! I can't believe you're taking this trip all by yourself. That is so brave. I wish my mother would do something like that instead of sitting around the house all day." These were the first words of greeting from a brown-haired young minx called Natalie.

They met in the cabin they would be sharing on the trip. At the moment they were the only people in the four-berth cabin. Finn could hardly wait to meet the other two strangers who would be sharing the cabin if this was the reception she could expect.

"I'm just going to drop my stuff here. I want to get out and see what's happening. This is going to be so much fun," Natalie said as she quickly stuffed her backpack onto the lower bunk of a pair and turned to run off. "Watch my stuff for me, OK?" She didn't wait for an answer.

"Sorry, I've given up playing mum," Finn bit out between clenched teeth. She had a key to the room and would lock the door as she left. Natalie should have her own key.

Finn strolled around the deck. She didn't belong with the teenagers backpacking around Europe. She didn't belong with the young mothers struggling to keep toddlers under control. She didn't belong with the golden oldies enjoying their freedom. In fact, she had no idea where she belonged anymore.

She struggled to her favourite spot at the back of the ship. She loved the stormy white froth that roared out behind. It seemed filled with magic promise. They were leaving their problems behind, rushing towards adventure and couldn't wait to get there. At least that's how it had always appeared to her. Now it seemed like everyone else on the ship had a place and a plan. She was adrift and scared.

The rest of the trip was an education. She had been living in a cocoon of her own making for so long. The lines of her life were murky, not as clearly defined as she'd thought. It was up to her now. She had to draw new lines for herself – could she do it? It was a rude awakening to realise that she didn't even know her own taste anymore. She had ceased to exist as an individual. How could she find herself again?

She wanted to talk to her dad. He had always been so free-spirited, never needing roots. He loved to travel – never met a stranger. Her father should be able to help her or at least point her in the right direction.

The reaction of the other two females sharing the cabin had been similar to Natalie's. They had looked at Finn like she was an old fogey who didn't belong in the same cabin as three bright young things. They had asked fascinated questions, all dealing with the shock of discovering someone of her age who was brave enough to strike out on her own. Their remarks about Finn's age and the fact that she was the same age as their parents became a little tiring. She could have done without the constant reminders of her great age.

The crowning glory came that evening when the girls invited her to join them in the bar. A young waiter, giving Natalie the eye, remarked on how nice it was for her to have her mother with her. Finn might have been old enough to be the mother of all of the girls but she didn't need the fact rubbed constantly in her face.

Once in France Finn made good time on the motorway. She had forgotten – if she had ever known – how much fun it was to speed along with the windows open, wind in her hair.

Her father – an experienced and talented chef – usually took a job in Deauville, along the coast. She couldn't wait to surprise him. She knew the campsite where he was staying. His camper van would be parked close by the water. He stopped in the same campsites every time he was in an area. For all his crazy ways, he had a routine. It surprised her to realise that her father was a creature of habit. She would have argued if someone had tried to point it out to her, but he really was predictable to a certain extent.

The van was where she expected to find it. There was no-one around so Finn parked her car and pitched her tent. With luck she would have it up and in place before her dad or Rolf arrived.

With the speed of long practice, she soon had everything set up. She changed into shorts and a T-shirt before stretching out on a towel on her tummy, facing the sea. It was wonderful taking time out to do absolutely nothing – just watch the waves foam.

"Here, you, what the bloody hell do you think you're doing? This is a private site – don't you know anything about the rules of camping?"

The angry voice still had a touch of Ireland in it even after all these years.

Finn, still lying face down, turned her head slightly. Emmet Emerson, large as life and twice as handsome, was glaring down at her, his hands fisted on slim hips.

"Hey, handsome, give us a kiss!" she said.

"Finn, is that you?" Emmet shouted, dropping down onto the grass by her side. He flipped her over before enveloping her in a fierce hug, rocking her close to his chest as if she were still a little girl. "Let me look at you." He pushed her away from his chest but didn't release her. "What have you done to yourself," he asked with his large hands clamped around her head. "You look bloody fantastic." He kissed her roughly, his bristles scratching her face.

"Finn! Get out of my way, Emmet." This time the voice was clipped and had a German accent – Uncle Rolf. He tried to grab Finn away from Emmet. They struggled good-naturedly, pulling Finn between them like a rag doll. She roared with laughter, kissing and hugging them back.

"Da-ma, I've missed you so much."

"What are you doing here? Why didn't you let us know you were coming? What's wrong?" Emmet was standing over Rolf and Finn now as he demanded answers. Tightly wrapped in Rolf's loving embrace, Finn stared up at her dad. He was so tall. His green eyes drilled a hole through her. Grey-haired now that the red had faded from his thick mop, he was so handsome and vigorous at seventy.

"You look *wonderbar*, sweetling!" Rolf was examining the changes in her appearance with keen eyes.

Finn brushed a kiss across his cheek and stood.

"I don't know what I'm doing here."

"Have you finally woken up and left your Ken doll?" Emmet demanded. He never liked Patrick and the feeling was mutual. Emmet claimed that Finn and Patrick were like Barbie and Ken dolls, all plastic and hair.

"I want to spend some time with you two, is that OK?"

"Of course it is, sweetling." Rolf stared at Emmet, his blue eyes glaring a warning. It was obvious to him at least that something was not as it should be with their darling girl.

"You know you are always welcome," Emmet said, heeding the warning Rolf was giving him. "Come on, you can help gather shellfish – tonight is one of our open houses." He grabbed Finn's hand and with his other picked up some gathering buckets. He started pulling her towards the ocean. "You coming with us?" he called back at Rolf, knowing he wouldn't want to be left behind. He might miss something.

The three of them, gathering buckets in hand, headed towards the rocks that dotted the beach. Finn felt six years old again. Her dad had always held open house at his campsite. Emmet was a fabulous chef. He'd taught her everything she knew about cooking. His open-house evenings were the stuff of legend. He would gather from the nearby beach and make an enormous fish stew. Rolf was in charge of putting together a salad. With fresh bread from the nearest bakery, it was a feast fit for kings.

"It's lucky I caught you on one of your days off, Dad." Finn searched the rocks for mussels and whelks.

"I only work when I feel like it these days." Emmet pulled shellfish off the rocks.

"Sometimes not even that," Rolf remarked slyly. He was such a contrast to Emmet, shorter and portly. He claimed Emmet's cooking had ruined his figure. Rolf's grey streaked-blond hair was thinning but his blue eyes still sparkled with love when he looked at Finn and her father. Finn thought Rolf looked like Santa Claus in shorts.

"Really?" Finn had never known Emmet to rest. Her earliest memories were all of Rolf taking care of her, her dad working constantly.

"I want to take it easy," Emmet said, not looking at Finn. "Thanks to Brainbox there," he pointed towards Rolf, "I can afford to please myself."

Finn let the subject drop – now was not the time to get into a heavy conversation. She'd wait until later. It would appear her father was making changes in his life. They could discuss everything sitting around a table with a glass of wine. When the sea was blowing salt spray and sand all over you was not the time for heart-searching. They were hunting dinner and that was the important thing right now.

Emmet Emerson's open houses attracted people from all over the campsite. Some people from the village came along to enjoy the evening as well. The food was superb. The wine was plentiful – this was France after all – the music lively and the conversation interesting. Finn's earliest memories of her father were of him standing over a large cauldron of boiling ingredients, laughing and sipping at a glass of wine.

Emmet charged a small fee for the food served. The evening was fun and profit for him.

Finn sat back and watched her father and Rolf work their magic. She had no responsibilities – a child again for this moment. Rolf and Emmet had the whole thing down to a fine art. People sat on the grass or on towels they'd brought with them, eating and laughing, shouting across to each other as jokes and ideas were cast back and forth and translated into whatever language was needed.

Each person brought their own dishes, so the only washing-up at the end of the evening for Emmet and Rolf was the large pot and a few serving dishes.

Finn knew she would have no chance to talk to her father this evening. She could wait and mercifully he didn't host an open house every evening.

She crawled away long before the party ended. It was galling to realise that she still couldn't keep up with her father and Rolf – men in their seventies. They would party all night then bounce out of bed bright and early in the morning. It had always been that way.

Chapter 13

Finn was up and about early the next day. Rolf and her father had plans they couldn't change because she had turned up unexpectedly. She toured Deauville on foot. She had forgotten so much about this famous little Normandy jewel. It was a part of Northern France she had visited many times as a child. It seemed that there were a great many more tourists here than ever before. Deauville had been attracting tourists since the 1800's. She remembered as a child watching the movie *Gigi* and giggling when Gigi begged to be taken to Deauville. She doubted Emmet would be coming to this area for much longer. He wasn't fond of places that attracted hordes of tourists.

She returned to the campsite in the late afternoon, laden down with goodies she hadn't been able to resist from the local boulangerie. The low cost of the vast selection of cheese tempted her to pick up what she knew was too much – but who cared – she was on her holidays.

"Have you enjoyed yourself, sweetling?" Rolf greeted her when she reached their site.

"The place has changed a lot."

"Do not get your father started," Rolf said with a laugh. "I beg you."

"Started on what?" Emmet came up from the beach. He

threw one arm around Finn's neck and hugged her close.

"I bought a load of goodies for us to try." Finn rattled the bags she held. She didn't want to start her father on one of his infamous rants.

"Some of these camper vans are bigger than houses." Finn, linking arms with the two men, was strolling around the camp site examining the different vehicles parked there. It was a favourite pastime of theirs – a holdover from her childhood. They had always visited what Emmet called their neighbours before going to bed.

"It is getting ridiculous," Emmet waved when someone called his name but didn't stop. "Look at the size of these things!" He waved at a huge recreational vehicle. "They bring their satellite dishes for heaven's sake. Everyone has to be connected to a computer service and their television. That's not camping." He waited a minute and very much tongue-in-cheek added, "The Germans are the worse of the lot."

"*Ja,*" Rolf agreed mildly. "We will blame the Germans."

All three laughed and continued their stroll around the entire site. Finn couldn't believe the changes in the type of vehicles parked around the site. She stood open-mouthed watching one family use an old-fashioned crank to make rooms appear on the side of their caravan.

"If you think that's something, look over there," Emmet said with a jerk of his head, giving her a sly nudge.

"In the name of God!" Finn had to force her mouth shut while she watched a man back his car down a ramp out of the interior of his van. "I ask your sacred pardon!"

"That's not what I call camping," Emmet moaned and started walking again.

They continued on their tour, each lost in memories of the past.

One morning – almost a week later – Finn was paddling along the beach. She kicked at the waves foaming around her feet. The whole area was bathed in sunshine and mostly deserted. Finn had been secretly hoping to hear the voice of God, or at least meet an angel holding out a scroll with a detailed plan for her life clearly written with step-by-step instructions. Ah well, she thought – may as well dream here as in bed.

The tide was going out and she watched water gather in the indentations made by her bare feet. The ocean stretched for miles towards the far horizon. It was difficult to tell where the sea ended and the sky began – a lot like her life at the moment. What was past and where was her future? The sun was a big yellow balloon in the sky. The sea sparkled and danced.

Finn in her cut-off boy's jeans and oversize T-shirt felt detached from life.

"Finn, Finn, for the love of God will you wait up!"

She turned to see her father and Rolf hurry down the beach towards her. Emmet carried a cooler while Rolf had a blanket over one shoulder and a baguette under his arm.

How many times had she watched these two appear just like this? They were the kindest, most loving parents in the world. Had she ever told them how much she appreciated them? Just as well she hadn't met that all-knowing angel on the sand. She would have received the swift kick she so richly deserved.

"We wondered where you disappeared to," Emmet said when they reached her. He wasn't even out of breath but poor Rolf was panting like a dog. "You might have thought to leave a note."

"Sorry, Da, Uncle Rolf, I didn't think." How long had it been since anyone cared about her comings and goings? Jesus, she was beginning to bore herself.

"If you ask me that's your problem, right there in a nutshell: you don't think." Emmet glared at her.

Rolf chose a grassy spot away from the water and wet sand to spread the blanket and collapse.

"Emmet, that is not how we agreed to start this conversation," he called softly, his German accent making the words a gentle rebuke. He sat among the stalks of burned grass staring at the two fiery redheads in his life. He loved both of them but he didn't always understand them.

Emmet strode over to Rolf and dumped the cooler on the blanket beside him. He was grinding his teeth, angry with himself. Rolf and he had discussed this situation at length. They had agreed on how they should approach Finn but as usual his temper had got the better of him. How many times through the years had Rolf stood between Finn and him as they battled? Only now it seemed that Finn had lost her fire somewhere. He hated to see his only child acting like a kicked dog.

"Finn," Rolf gently patted the blanket in invitation, "come and join us. It is time we discussed what brought you to us, *ja?*"

Finn sat and waited while Rolf unpacked the big cooler they used as a carryall – a thermos of coffee for the men, one of tea for Finn. There would be pain au chocolate and croissants from the bakery. Rolf loved to cater to his family and never overlooked anyone's preference. Was that where she got her nurturing instincts from?

It was like old times, the three of them sitting and listening to the sound of the ocean in the background. The whispers of Emmet and Rolf as they carried on a soft-voiced argument in German was very familiar to her. She knew these two would wait until she was ready to discuss whatever was bothering her.

"It began on my birthday ..."

For the next while Finn's was the only voice heard over the screaming of the gulls and the whisper of the ocean. She held nothing back. She shared everything she had discovered about her own life since that disastrous birthday when she'd been forced to open her eyes. She truly believed she was guilty of allowing herself to be treated like a doormat. All anyone had to do to let that happen was lie down and allow people to wipe their feet on you. She'd done that – all unknowingly.

A sea breeze chased the sand onto their food and the blanket but they ignored it. The men sat comfortably on the blanket, shoulders touching, giving her their time and complete attention. They didn't interrupt her but she was aware of them exchanging glances as she told her tale of woe.

"My boys are being affected by the poisonous atmosphere in the house – I won't allow that," she at last concluded. She tried, she really did, not to sound self-pitying but she could hear the whine in her voice.

"What are you planning to do now?" Emmet asked the question while Rolf refilled their cups. They had almost emptied the flasks. The delicious fare from the bakery was only crumbs now. They had eaten everything Rolf had brought with him.

"That's just it. I have no idea." Could she make anyone understand how lost and alone she felt? She couldn't return to her childhood and hide behind these two men. They would allow her – but she had to stand on her own two feet – she was an adult for heaven's sake. But the world seemed a big cold place to her.

"Did you want to travel with us for a while?" Emmet asked, knowing the answer before the question left his lips.

"No – thank you – but I think not."

"We have a suggestion," Rolf said, touching Emmet's arm gently to keep him quiet for the moment. Rolf knew how much it hurt Emmet that Finn rejected the life they had given her. Emmet had never been able to understand how his only child could long for the life he had run away from.

"Suggestions welcome. I have to make some kind of decision about my future. I need a plan for my life and where I want to go from here." She smiled at the two men. They sat comfortably on the blanket, shoulders touching, giving her their time and complete attention.

"That's because you insist on planning too far ahead!" Emmet felt he'd been silent long enough. "You were the same as a little kid. We would barely have survived the New Year and you were demanding our plans for Christmas. Jesus, you could never take life one day at a time. What is the point of planning every little step of your life? Where is the surprise – the wonder – the adventure in that?"

"I'm not like you, Da. We know that," Finn said softly. "I want a normal life. Is that too much to ask? I can't be like the pair of you constantly on the move – always looking for the next adventure – curious about what's over the horizon. I'm sorry, but I can't live like that."

"*Not can't, won't!*" Emmet shouted. "There's a bloody big difference, you know!"

"Now, now, you two, this will get us nowhere." Rolf stepped in to stop these two saying something they would both regret later.

"I'm sorry, Rolf." Emmet jumped up and paced around the blanket. "You're right, as usual." He shoved his hands through his hair, staring down at the two on the blanket. "It burns me up to hear her harping on the same oul' song. She wants a normal life, she says – well," he threw back his head and roared towards the sky, *"would you mind telling me, miss, what the bloody hell is normal?"* He was frustrated with Finn's blindness to everything life had to offer except her imagined 'normal'.

"Finn, as I see it," Rolf ignored Emmet's outburst, "you are at a crossroad in your life. You made a decision when you were very young – too young we believed at the time – anyway, that's neither here nor there – the decision was made."

He looked towards the sea, trying to gather his thoughts so that his words would reach Finn's stubborn head. He sighed deeply. He should be used to the high drama of life with these two by now, surely.

"Finn, you wanted what you insist on calling a normal life and went after it with single-minded determination. You lived that life for over twenty years and appeared to be blissfully happy. Yet now you come to us and tell us you no longer want that life. What are we to think? How can we help you? You never listened to us in the past, never believed we knew anything about 'normal' but we are the place you come for answers."

Emmet dropped down on his knees. "Let's pack up here and return to the campsite. I fancy making a delicious lunch. We'll walk back to the campsite and continue this conversation in comfort. I'm getting too old to be sitting for hours on a blanket on the beach."

They gathered up their belongings and let the subject drop for the moment.

As soon as they arrived back at the campsite Emmet took over. He ordered the other two around like a sergeant major. They prepared a slap-up meal for three. Emmet was never willing to compromise when it came to food. Finn talked about her trip around the area and mentioned some of her surprise discoveries while they ate the delicious meal of seafood, salad and pasta that Emmet had seemingly thrown together. The other two made suggestions about things to see and do. It was all very civilized but underneath there was tension.

"I don't know what I want," Finn finally admitted as they sipped orange-flavoured liqueur from tiny glasses. The campsite had been tidied and they were sitting relaxing. "The first eighteen years of my life I spent with you two living like a nomad." Finn was trying to get her thoughts straight in her own head. "I was always jealous of the people who lived in the places we passed. I dreamed of a settled life. Patrick Brennan offered me that and I grabbed at it with both hands. I know I hurt you both by wanting something different from all that you gave me. I felt so grown up at eighteen, ready to make my own way." Looking back as an adult she could see how she had hurt these two. "I'm sorry that it hurt you but it was a choice I had to make, for me, and I can't regret that decision. I have two sons that I love. I lived the dream life I wanted for twenty-one years. The time has come for me to make a new decision. I can't begin to make any plans until I have some idea of where I am going from here. I feel like one of those hamsters running around on a wheel in a cage. I keep running madly but I'm getting nowhere."

"We have not told you the reason we chased after you this morning," Rolf said, taking her hand in his and squeezing it. He looked at Emmet, waiting to see if he wanted to open the discussion.

"Yes, old Brainbox here," Emmet lightly punched Rolf's shoulder, "has a master plan. You can't beat Rolf when it comes to financial planning. You know that, daughter."

"Finn," Rolf decided he'd better be the one to explain – you never knew what Emmet would say next, "when you moved into the house in Rathmines it was a wreck. Sad and neglected from years of abuse – you totally remodelled the building. You dragged that house back to life. You selected the designs and did all of the decoration. You even did some of the plastering, plumbing and electrical work yourself. I remember how impressed we both were with your skills."

"We never did figure out how you learned to do all of that stuff. You certainly hadn't learned any of it from us." Emmet remembered the pictures she had sent them during that time, a faithful record of the before-and-after transformation of her home.

"I learned from books and asking people for help." Finn still kept her hand in every time anything needed repairing or work needed to be done on the house.

"Yes, but you did all the manual labour, Finn," Rolf said. "Patrick never helped with that end of things. In time you had two small children underfoot and a home to run, yet you still worked like a Trojan turning that house into what it is today."

"I enjoyed every second of it. Do you think I should hire myself out as a painter and decorator?" Finn was being facetious.

"Exactly!" Rolf slapped the wooden picnic table and almost giggled he was so pleased with himself.

The two men roared with laughter at the stunned look on Finn's face.

"But ... but ..." Finn stared at the two men as if they had lost their minds.

"Listen, please listen," Rolf said. "It's not as crazy as it sounds." He waited until Finn had caught her breath and was giving him her full attention. "We," he shook a thumb between Emmet and himself, "own two old railway cottages on the seafront in Bray, County Wicklow."

"On the advice of Brainbox here," Emmet put his two-cents-worth in, "we bought the cottages many years ago."

"Yes, it was one of those deals whereby you buy the property at a reduced price but allow the former owner to live out their natural lives in it." Rolf looked at Finn to see if she was following along. "It was a very popular system in the seventies – you will have heard of such a thing?"

Finn had heard of the scheme. When she was about fourteen or fifteen a young French lawyer had bought a house from an old lady – one of the first under the scheme. The lady had lived to one hundred and twenty years of age. She had outlived the much younger lawyer by at least twenty years. Every year on the woman's birthday the media ran jokey articles about the woman and the lawyer. Finn had never known that Emmet and Rolf were involved in the scheme, nor had she known they owned property in Ireland.

"The old dear I bought the house from died after a full and happy life." Emmet shrugged. He would not pretend a sadness he didn't feel. He hadn't known the woman on a personal level.

"The family I purchased the neighbouring house from have all moved away and now the last living member wishes to leave the house," Rolf said. "He wishes to move into an old folks' community. He is very old and his family have become concerned for his safety. So – soon the two cottages will be empty and they are in dire need of a makeover." He almost bounced on his seat he was so excited. Everything was coming together. They would be able to help out their little one and offer her a lifeline at the same time.

"And what has this to do with me?" she asked, but she could see where the conversation was heading.

"We think you should go and work on the two cottages. They are adjoining properties. We would like them made into one large property. We admired what you did with the house in Rathmines. We know and trust you. We believe you can do this."

"We will of course pay you a salary and cover the cost of contractors and supplies," Emmet said. "We want you to oversee the project. Be our eyes and ears on site, so to speak."

"But I have no idea of your taste when it comes to houses or what you would want done to the properties," Finn said. "And I can't see you settling down in a cottage in Bray, Da. No matter how big a cottage it might be when you've finished turning two properties into one."

"As far as we can recollect, the properties are wrecks by modern standards," said Rolf. "We need you to first see what needs to be done. You should do a walk-through and get an idea of the work involved before we can talk about anything else. Take some digital photos and email them to us. We can discuss all of this in greater detail later. But first tell us – are you interested?"

"I would love to do it," Finn said, feeling the blood move through her body in a rush. "But have you two any idea of the cost involved? It's not cheap doing over two houses."

"We have money." Emmet dismissed that problem with a laugh. "Thanks to old Brainbox." He pushed lightly at Rolf. "He has been investing our money for years – all of your life and more. Rolf was a computer nerd long before such a thing was world-famous."

"This would give you the breathing space you need and let you decide what you want to do with your life." Rolf smiled at the dawning pleasure on Finn's face. It was good to see their little beauty light up from within with a glowing smile. He had missed that look on her face.

Finn had a hard time sleeping that night. She could not believe that Emmet and Rolf had managed to save her life, yet again. She tossed and turned in her sleeping bag, listening to the sound of the campground settling down for the night. Her mind buzzed with so many plans.

Giving up on sleep, she crawled out of her tent when the sun was just peeking over the horizon. She had the shower block to herself. It was too early for anyone else to be up and about. She took a long hot shower in the spotlessly clean building then stood combing out her wet hair in front of one of a group of mirrors over the hand-basins – short hair was so much easier to manage.

When Emmet and Rolf roused themselves it was still early. Finn was waiting for them with a selection of mouth-watering breads from the bakery. While the coffee scented the morning air, she waited for the two men to exit their camper van.

They took the coffee from her with words of gratitude. They examined her closely without saying a word. Finn had changed in some subtle fashion. She looked and acted years younger and lighter of heart.

Talk turned again to the cottages in Bray. It took hours and oceans of tea and coffee but finally they put together a tentative plan for the cottages. It was impossible to make detailed plans without her first viewing the properties in question but Emmet

93

and Rolf gave her a general idea of what they wanted and she agreed to oversee the project. She had a plan now and a place to start. She was excited to see what she could do with the opportunity given her. She couldn't wait to get started.

Emmet stood with Finn on the driver side of the car. She was leaving.

"Finn, that house in Rathmines belongs to my family. Patrick Brennan is my tenant. I can give him notice to quit if you want." He saw the look of dawning realisation on her face. "He has lived in my ancestral home paying a ridiculously low rent for twenty-one years." He hit the hood of the car with his open hand. "That is something you need to think on as you drive home." He opened the driver's door and waited while Finn seated herself. "Keep in touch, kid. I love you even when you drive me nuts." He stepped away from the car and Rolf came to take his place.

"Your visit was a lovely surprise." Rolf bent and kissed Finn's cheek, his fingers running in a gentle caress over her short red hair. "Drive safely, let us know when you reach home."

The two men watched her drive away, both hoping that they had done the right thing for her. All they could do now was stand back and wait to see what she would do with this new beginning. They had done all they could do. The rest was up to her.

Chapter 14

Finn let herself into the house in Rathmines. No one rushed out to meet the returning traveller. There was someone in the kitchen, she thought with a sigh. She'd talk to them after her shower.

Finn ached in places she hadn't even been aware of before. It was a long drive from Rosslare to Dublin. She had planned to stop in Bray – it was on the way after all – but she'd changed her mind – she needed home.

She carried her overnight bag upstairs. She could unpack the car tomorrow. A knock on the bedroom door surprised her.

Finn's mouth dropped open at the sight that greeted her when she opened the door. Patrick Brennan stood, smiling charmingly and carrying a tea tray. This must be an alternate universe she'd wandered into. He'd never prepared a tray in his life, much less delivered one.

Finn saw Oisín's fine hand in this little gesture. It amused her that at least one of the men in her life knew her so well. She opened the door wider and gestured to Patrick to enter. He put the tray he carried on top of her dressing table.

"How are you, dear?" Patrick poured the tea. "Did you have a good trip?"

He was using his radio voice on her, Finn noticed. It had

been a long time since Patrick had tried to charm her with his trust-me-I'm-your-friend voice.

"I'm fine, thank you. The tea is a lovely gesture." Oh God, were they reduced to this?

"Damn it, Nuala, how long is this ridiculous state of affairs going to continue?" Patrick shoved his hands through his expertly cut hair. "I have missed you." He started to touch her but the blazing fury directed at him stopped him in his tracks. She'd never looked at him like that before.

"Get out, Patrick." Finn had been curious about the position he would take. "As for this situation as you call it – it's permanent." She practically pushed him out of the room, slamming the door behind him.

She pulled the door open again when someone knocked. If this was Patrick again she wouldn't be responsible for her actions.

"Good to have you home, Mum." Oisín hugged his mother close. "You know why I've been sent in?"

"I imagine your mission, should you decide to accept it," Finn smiled at her son, watching the grin form first in his eyes as she quoted from one of his favourite spy movies, "is to talk sense into the nutty old dear that is your mother."

"Sit down and drink your tea."

Oisín sat on the unmade bed while Finn sat at the dressing-table chair. They had seen her return on the kitchen monitor. It had hurt his heart that she had not called out to tell them she was home. Instead she had almost crept up here like a stranger in her own home. His father was almost foaming at the mouth over this situation. He'd been ranting and raving about his problems constantly. It hadn't stopped him chasing skirts though.

"What are your plans, have you any idea?" He watched his mother close her eyes in bliss at her first sip of tea. He listened, trying not to let his jaw drop to the floor as she spoke of her plans. This was going to cause ructions when he passed on the information. "You really think you can turn yourself into some kind of super building contractor?" Oisín held up his hands when he saw the hurt in his mother's eyes. "I'm not saying you can't, Mother. I'm just trying to understand."

Finn sipped her tea. "Oisín, do you have no memories of living in a building site when you were little?"

"I vaguely remember following you around begging to be allowed paint a wall or something." Oisín shrugged.

"That will do for a start." Finn yawned. "Oisín, I'm really tired – can we continue this conversation another time?"

"Sure thing, Mum."

Oisín left, feeling slightly hurt at the abrupt dismissal.

Finn waited to see if Ronan would be sent in to question her. When no knock came to her door, she went into the corridor to collect fresh linen for her bed. It took a great deal of effort on her part not to turn on the computer system and spy on her menfolk.

"Have either of you boys seen my white shirts?" Patrick was standing directly outside the locked master-bedroom door. "I've an interview with someone from the *RTÉ Guide* this morning. I need to look my best." He grinned and waited. Nuala would never to be able to resist that. She'd run out and put her hand on his clean shirts, showing her superiority in all things domestic. He didn't care, she could be as superior as she liked about her skill at domestic chores. Just so long as she did the bloody chores.

Finn rolled over, looking at her bedside clock. Seven in the morning. Patrick had never been very considerate about others' sleeping habits.

"Have you checked your wardrobe, Father?" Ronan stood at the bottom of the stairs, staring up at Patrick. He knew what his father was trying to do. After the talk Ronan had held with Oisín late into the night he didn't think his father was going to win this round.

"Of course I've checked my wardrobe! But who can ever find anything your mother puts away?" Patrick made his voice shake with sorrow as he projected towards the bedroom door. His voice was his fortune. He knew how to use it to great effect.

"I suggest you look again, Father." Oisín appeared in his bedroom doorway. He crossed his arms and glared at his father.

How could the man not know how serious this situation was? Had he always been so totally self-obsessed?

"You should both be up and dressed. You need to have breakfast before leaving the house." That would shift Nuala. Patrick smirked. She was a fanatic about a well-cooked breakfast in the morning. She'd soon be up and jumping, if not for his sake then for her children.

To Patrick's amazement there was no sound of hurrying feet behind the bedroom door. Was the woman really going to lie in bed while the men in the house got ready for work?

Finn ran the water in the shower. She would not leave her bedroom until Patrick left the house.

Patrick slammed the door so hard behind him as he left the house that he was vaguely surprised the glass didn't shatter. His sons had left to get the bus into town. He didn't have the time to drive them around. That was Nuala's job.

Finn almost fell to her knees and kissed the carpet when Patrick's car drove away. Remaining in her room this morning had been one of the hardest things she'd ever done. The temptation to jump back into being a domestic drone had been tremendous.

She unlocked her bedroom door and almost crept out onto the landing. Her breath was being forced in and out of her lungs like a bellows. She pushed sweat-dampened hair out of her face.

She'd done it. She'd held firm against outrageous temptation.

The breadbin held only stale crusts. She'd have cereal this morning. She opened the kitchen cupboard – two boxes of cereal stood on the bottom shelf. She took a box in each hand and almost screamed. They were both empty. Why did men do that? Why did they return empty boxes to the cupboard?

She opened the fridge. There was milk at least. The kettle boiled while Finn tried to find something to eat. Surely Patrick and the boys had shopped while she'd been away?

She kept bread in the freezer for emergencies. She walked into the utility room, trying not to notice how untidy it was. Boots and coats were thrown over every surface and some had fallen to the floor. For the first time in her life she stepped over the clutter.

The storage freezer was covered in discarded damp clothing. Finn swept it off and onto the floor. Someone needed to start taking better care of their stuff. She gritted her teeth and pulled up the freezer cover. Here was the answer to at least one of her questions.

The freezer was empty of all of her carefully prepared meals. How on earth had they managed to eat all of that food in ten days? The frozen pork products she kept on hand for preparing an emergency full Irish breakfast were gone. Not a sausage remained. A lone loaf of sliced bread sat in the bottom of the freezer. Finn pulled it out and let the lid drop back into place. She wondered if she should unplug the freezer. She wasn't going to fill it anymore.

She put two pieces of bread into the toaster.

She opened her preserves cupboard only to discover that her men had depleted her store of homemade jams and preserves too. The cupboard that had been stuffed looked miserable with only a few richly coloured jars sitting around. She grabbed a jar, not needing to look at the label.

"OK." She'd discovered the benefit of her habit of talking aloud to herself over the last few weeks. Somehow hearing things said aloud made everything clearer. "I need to make a list of things I want to get done – I have to check out those houses in Bray."

Finn sipped her tea. She couldn't take another morning like this one. Not without giving into the temptation to jump right back into her old ways. Tomorrow she might even manage to get to Bray in time to watch the sun come up over the ocean. She'd enjoy that. She hurried into her home office to fetch a pen and pad. She wanted to make a list of things she needed to achieve.

"First and foremost: money." She dropped back into her kitchen chair, pen poised. She wanted to open an account in her own name. She needed to take charge of her own finances. *Finn Emerson, Businesswoman*, she wrote on top of the page with a sad smile. If only she could turn herself into that person with a stroke of the pen.

She didn't feel good about taking money from Patrick's accounts. She wasn't fulfilling her role as a wife and mother. But she had no choice at the moment. She needed her own funds. How long did it take to open a bank account? She didn't know. There was a great deal she didn't know. She'd been a housewife and proud of it. Sad to finally understand that she'd been married to the house, not the man.

"What was it they said in the old days? 'My pockets are to let'? That was it. Well, all I've got in my pocket now is dust. I'll need money for petrol and DART fares. I need to get ready to go to the bank."

Finn stood, refusing to wallow in negative shite anymore.

She rinsed her own dishes and put them in the dishwasher. She firmly avoided looking at the small pile of dishes sitting on the work surface. She needed to make a list of rules for this house. She would not be the slave anymore nor was she willing to live in a tip. It was time everyone living here learned to lend a hand in the everyday chores of life.

Chapter 15

"Do you have identification?" The bored bank clerk was trying very hard not to allow her opinion of the customer in front of her show on her face. How many times and in how many ways would she have to explain the same thing to the woman before she understood and moved along.

"I have my driver's licence and the credit cards I've already shown you." Finn wanted to sink through the floor. She didn't exist as a person. She had no credit record in her own name. She was a Mrs and only that.

"Your papers are in the name of Mrs. Patrick Brennan." The clerk had said the same thing twenty times. The woman was married to Patrick Brennan off the television and radio. What had she to complain about? She should try sitting here having to deal with idiots all day. "You want to open an account in the name of – Finn Emerson."

Finn was Patrick Brennan's wife. Every piece of paper she had was in the name of Mrs. Patrick Brennan. She hadn't even bothered to keep her own Christian name.

The clerk sighed. The queue behind this awkward customer was growing. The floor manager was glaring at her from behind the glass walls of her office. Let her come out and deal with this woman.

"Thank you." Finn had been aware of the crowd of frustrated bank customers lengthening behind her.

What an idiot she was. She needed to stop and make a realistic examination of her circumstances. She didn't have the price of a cup of coffee saved anywhere under her own name. She was a non-person, no name, no address, no credit record, no money. She needed time to absorb the change in her status. The shock of being treated as a non-person by the bank clerk had left Finn reeling.

"I'm terribly sorry!" Finn exclaimed as she bumped up against another person in the local café where she'd gone for a pot of tea.

"It's OK – no harm done."

"I am sorry." Finn raised her eyes to look at the other woman. "Nuala? Nuala Brennan?"

"Yes." Well, she'd been that woman for an awfully long time. She couldn't refuse to answer to that name overnight.

"It's Maggie, Maggie Spencer." The younger woman waited to be recognised.

"I'm sorry?" Finn had never met this woman. It wasn't unusual for people to approach her when they knew she was married to Patrick Brennan but this woman seemed to expect Finn to know her.

"Perhaps I should have said Margaret Upton?"

"Oh, yes, of course! You were married to Charles Upton for a time." Finn almost bit her tongue in half. Was she looking at her own future? Charles Upton was a producer on several of Patrick's programmes. The woman in front of her was younger than Finn but she looked worn and tired. She had deep dark bruises under her eyes. Her hair was badly cut and her clothes were hanging on her body.

"We're blocking traffic," Maggie said. "We should find a table?"

"Yes, of course."

A minute later they were unloading their trays onto a corner table.

"How have you been, Margaret?" Finn asked politely when they were seated.

"I prefer to be called Maggie these days."

"And I'm Finn!"

Maggie smiled and leaned forward, pushing her untidy hair out of her face. "Finn, if I'm being nosy and rude please tell me to butt out." Her elfin features were sincere, her caramel-coloured eyes staring into Finn's. "I've seen the pictures in the tattoo-parlour window. I've heard the gossip running around the village. You look like a woman who has lost herself or perhaps I should say a woman trying to find herself?"

Finn was dismayed to realise that she was so obviously a woman in crisis. "I think lost is the right word."

She would never have talked to a relative stranger like this in the past. She'd always been terribly aware of Patrick's celebrity status. Patrick had impressed upon her that anything she said or did could be used against him. But if she didn't open up she was going to drown. She needed help and Margaret Upton – no, Maggie Spencer – seemed to be the answer to her prayers.

"I seem to be floundering."

"I can see the change in you – hard to miss." Maggie smiled. Nuala Brennan with an almost shaved head of red hair and an outfit she wouldn't normally be caught dead in was a strange sight. Even if Patrick Brennan had not been broadcasting his marital problems to all of Ireland, she would have known something was very different in Nuala's – no, Finn's – life.

"I refuse to wear beige and pearls anymore." Finn was wearing what were skinny jeans on her. They had belonged to Ronan when he was about thirteen. Thank heavens her two boys had had their growth spurt early, otherwise she would be walking around in jeans that only reached her knees. A dress shirt of Patrick's hung loose over the jeans, cinched in at the waist with one of Patrick's more colourful neckties. Her own stylish black boots completed the outfit. She'd felt good when she examined her image in the bedroom mirror.

"I like the new look." Maggie laughed.

"Thank you." Finn pushed her red fringe away from her forehead. "I'm struggling to find my way."

"One does in this situation." Maggie glanced at her watch. Her children were with her parents, she had time. "As a woman who has been there and has the scars to prove it, can I help you?"

"I've discovered I'm nobody!" Finn almost wailed. "I don't exist."

"Tough, isn't it?" Maggie Spencer wished she'd taken a pound for every time she'd seen this reaction in a newly separated woman.

"You know?" Finn was desperately trying to remember anything she'd ever known about Margaret Upton now Maggie Spencer.

"Let me refresh your memory." Maggie knew Finn would have very little knowledge of her own situation. "I stormed away from Charles Upton, leaving the family home with the clothes on my back and my twin girls on my hips." She shrugged, remembering her younger self-righteous self.

"What had happened?" Finn asked.

"I caught Charles with his pants down one too many times. He was having fun with the girls' nanny if you can believe such a cliché." Maggie sipped her cooling coffee. "I left the family home that very moment, full of righteous indignation."

"What else could you do?"

"If I'd known how tough it is to be a single mother I might have thought twice about walking away." Maggie wondered how much she should tell the woman staring at her with lost hurting eyes. "I know now I should have made the cheating snake leave the house. Hindsight is a wonderful thing."

"I'm so sorry, Maggie." Finn hadn't even been aware of the situation with Maggie and her children. Charles Upton was still a welcome guest in her own home. She was ashamed of her ignorance of the world around her.

"I'm afraid it's a common enough story." Maggie shrugged. "I, too, quickly discovered I was no-one. I'd never worked outside the home. I married Charles far too young. I was in love and wanted to be with the only man in the world for me. I refused to listen to anyone trying to give me advice. They were all jealous of my good fortune, I reckoned." She shook her head over her own hard-headedness. "So, I had no one to blame but myself. When I left Charles I had no home, no income, no credit record, no money and no rights. I've had to fight for everything I needed to survive. The twins have suffered a great deal because of my actions."

"Charles' actions surely," Finn snapped.

"Yeah, but we women are great at taking the blame for everything that goes wrong in our world." Maggie picked up her empty cup. "I need more coffee. Can I get you another pot of tea?"

"I'll get them."

Finn hurried over to the counter. Maggie had information she needed. The younger woman seemed prepared to share what she knew and God knows Finn desperately needed all the help she could get. A cup of coffee was a small price to pay.

Back at the table, Maggie took both of Finn's hands in hers. "Finn, the situation you are in right now makes a liar and a thief out of a person." Then she sat back, waiting for Finn's reaction.

"I beg your pardon?" She had never lied or stolen anything in her life. What on earth would cause her to start now?

"You will learn that if you follow all the unwritten and written rules and regulations honestly, you'll be back as Patrick's obedient wife before you can blink. The good advice of friends and family will practically push you back into your place." Maggie sipped her fresh coffee.

Fin thought of Emmet and Rolf. "Maybe I'm luckier than most in that respect. I'm just back from France. My father and his partner live there. They were very supportive. But, then, they're not conventional people, I guess."

Maggie looked at her. "So you've been away for a while?"

"In recent weeks, yes."

"Oh." Maggie seemed to hesitate. "So, do you know that Patrick has been broadcasting your domestic problems to all and sundry?"

That came as a shock. "No. I didn't know.

"Well, you need to know." Maggie began to tell her about Patrick's daily discussions on his radio programme concerning women going through the menopause. He had been getting more airtime than he'd ever received by telling the world and its mother all about 'his' problems. He'd been a guest on one of the afternoon shows on television several times in the past weeks. Women were lapping up his opinion of 'their feminine problems'. Patrick was playing the poor suffering misunderstood male to the hilt and Irish audiences loved it.

"I can't care," Finn said when Maggie had filled her in. She wondered why she was surprised. Patrick had used their home life in his broadcasts for years. Why should this be any different?

"No, you can't care, not if you want to truly find your own feet," Maggie agreed. "So do you want to tell me what had you looking like a kicked pup just now when we met?"

Finn related her wasted morning at the local bank. She'd been made to feel two inches tall and a nuisance. She knew she wasn't stupid – she could learn how to function in this new world. The woman in front of her had experience and advice. Finn was darned well going to take note of everything Maggie said.

"I have to pick my children up from my mother's house," Maggie said when Finn had explained her difficulty. "I don't have time to go into everything you need to know right now." She checked her watch. She was really pushed for time.

"Of course, you need to get about your business." Finn swallowed her disappointment.

"No," Maggie smiled. "I'm not dumping you to drown." She gathered up her belongings. "Angie Lawrence cleans for you, doesn't she?"

"Yes." Finn wondered what Angie had to do with anything.

"Angie is the woman you really need to talk to."

"Really?" Finn was genuinely surprised.

"Angie employs a lot of women who suddenly find themselves alone and penniless." Maggie shrugged. "She's great. I don't think I could have survived without her."

"You work for Angie?"

"Three days a week. My parents pick the girls up from school and look after them until I can pick them up. I'll give you my phone number." She put the bags back down on the floor and, opening her handbag, retrieved a pen. Writing her number on a napkin she gave it to Finn. "Finn, I've probably been through most of the situations you're about to face, and if I can help you I will. If I can't, chances are Angie can or we know someone else who can."

"You're being incredibly kind. I'm very grateful." She was amazed at Maggie's generosity. After all, they were practically strangers.

"People helped me a great deal when I was in the same situation. They asked for no return except that I'd pass the knowledge along. When you're on your feet I'll ask the same of you. We have to help each other in this world, Finn, or what's the point?"

Finn knew what it was like trying to organise two children after school. The pace was frantic. The last thing you needed was a stranger delaying you. "I'll program your number into my phone. Perhaps you could find the time to talk to me after your children are in bed?"

"Sure thing."

Chapter 16

"Yes, Mother?" Ronan's voice was longsuffering when he answered his mobile.

"I need you home this evening," Finn said simply.

"Why?" Ronan had a sort of date. He could break it but why should he?

"I thought you might like to be included in a conversation that affects your life." Finn refused to say more. "I'm calling Oisín next. I'll cook a family meal but I need to know if you'll be home to eat it."

"I can't give an exact time. I have a few scenes to appear in but I'll be home as soon as I can. Gotta go." Ronan hung up.

Finn needed to shop first then clean the kitchen before starting the meal. She assured herself she wasn't regressing. It was simply that she knew the promise of a homecooked meal could move her menfolk faster than anything else. You had to use the weapons to hand.

"Are we to assume you've come to your senses?" Patrick demanded when he slid into his place at the head of the table in the dining room. This was how it was supposed to be. Mother, father, children sitting down to a well-cooked carefully presented meal. It was about time everything was back to normal. Nuala had been sulking long enough.

"Wait." Finn was willing to cook and serve this meal, but she had a purpose and they could bloody wait until she was seated before asking questions.

"Do either of you know what is going on?" Patrick looked at his sons seated on either side of him.

"I only know what I told you earlier on the phone." Ronan had called his father directly after speaking to his mother. He hoped that hadn't been a mistake.

"Why don't we wait until we've eaten to find out more?" Oisín suggested. The smells coming from the kitchen were making him dizzy. It seemed like years instead of weeks since he'd had one of his mother's homecooked meals.

Finn carried the meal to the table. Roast beef, Yorkshire pudding, roast potatoes, vegetables and gravy. She considered the meal her own heavy artillery – a man's meal.

She watched the men dive into the meal as if they were starving. It broke her heart to think this might be the last meal of its type eaten at this table, but she had to remain strong.

"We need to discuss the division of labour in this house." Finn opened the conversation when the men had served themselves second helpings of everything. She'd barely picked at her food.

"Don't be bloody ridiculous!" Patrick snapped. "We are out of the house all day. I work hard to provide for my family. The boys are on set all day every day during the summer, then they return to college. Your job is to see that we have everything we need to function in our everyday lives. That is the role of a wife and mother."

"Father!" Ronan wanted to kick Patrick.

"I resigned from my position as wife and mother, Patrick. Remember?" Finn cut the beef on her plate into bite-size pieces.

"*Not that bloody rubbish again!*" Patrick roared.

Ronan and Oisín frantically tried to catch his eye. They needed to find out what their mother wanted of them. It was the least they could do. They wanted their mother at home and taking care of them again.

"Patrick, I've stated my case. I refuse to allow you three to abuse me any longer." Finn was almost whispering.

"You are being ridiculous. No one in this house has ever abused you. How dare you even suggest such a thing?" Patrick wasn't put off his food by this conversation. He was shovelling the food rapidly into his mouth. He had a rendezvous with a buxom young blonde later.

"We will agree to disagree on that point." Finn pushed her plate away. "I asked everyone to be home for this meal for a reason."

"The boys will fill me in later." Patrick stood and pushed his chair back into the table. "I have to go out, business." He threw his napkin on the table and walked swiftly from the room. The boys could listen to Nuala's rubbish. He had better things to do with his time.

"That went well." Finn stood to clear the table. "Do either of you want dessert?" Silly question – when had her sons ever refused food?

"I have to leave." Ronan began to push away from the table.

"I haven't talked to you yet, Ronan." Finn stood and stared at the boy who was rapidly becoming almost a clone of his father. She'd allowed Patrick Brennan to walk all over her for years. She'd be damned if she'd allow that crap with her own son.

"Will this take long?" Ronan sat back down, heaving a longsuffering sigh.

"That depends on you two." Finn hurried from the dining room. She had an apple-pie cooling and cream whipped.

The apple-pie served, Finn proceeded.

"I think we need to discuss the changes that need to be made in the running of the house." She had actually written down what she wanted to say. She'd learned it off by heart in case she was in danger of allowing herself to slip back into bad habits.

Oisín and Ronan ate the apple-pie and whipped cream as if they hadn't consumed the vast amount of food she'd seen them inhale.

"You boys need to decide on a division of labour around here." She waited for them to make some kind of remark on her statement. Express some kind of interest, anything. "I refuse to live in a tip. This house demands a lot of work. I refuse to do all of it alone any longer."

Ronan sipped the coffee. She was making a big deal out of very little as far as he was concerned. The house didn't take much looking after for God's sake.

"The house is looking neglected," Finn stated.

"So?" Ronan didn't understand what his mother was trying to say. He wanted to leave. All this talk of household chores had nothing to do with him. He didn't make a mess.

"I'm trying to treat you both as adults." She could see that the matter of taking care of themselves was going over both of their heads. They would learn. "I'll clean up here. This will be the very last meal I'll prepare alone and clean up afterwards alone."

"That's terribly dramatic, Mother." Ronan stood, dropping his linen napkin on the table.

"Is it?" Finn watched her sons hurry from the room – so much for having an adult conversation about the division of labour.

"What was that all about?" Ronan demanded of Oisín while they hurried down the road. They were meeting a bunch of friends at the pub.

"I'm not sure." Oisín shrugged.

"She'll never change – we just have to wait for a while and things will get back to normal." Ronan was sure he had everything in hand. They had to give the woman enough rope to hang herself.

"Jesus, bro, you've got your head so far up your own arse your eyes are turning brown." Oisín punched lightly on his brother's arm. "Did you not see the look in her eyes? Things are going to change around here and we'd better get ready for it."

"Father will take her in hand." Ronan shrugged. "He has before. She'll be back to her old self in no time." He pushed open the pub door.

Oisín followed his brother, wondering if he were the only one who'd noticed the change in his mother. Not the haircut and clothes, there was a much deeper change going on.

Finn cleaned the dining room and kitchen after the boys left. She then hurried into her home office where she watched the clock carefully, and phoned Maggie when she felt the time was right.

"Where does trust stop and stupidity start?" Maggie queried when Finn explained her confusion about the situation she found herself in.

"That's what I keep asking myself," Finn responded.

They talked on for ages, with Finn taking reams of notes and instructions.

"You have everything you need at your fingertips from what you've told me," Maggie concluded. "You need to get the paperwork out of the house and somewhere safe. Patrick Brennan is riding the crest of a wave right now. You need to think smart."

"I'll do that, Maggie." Finn's head was reeling.

"I've got to go now, Finn. Talk again soon."

With the list of Maggie's suggestions firmly in hand, Finn started to put together the information she'd need. First and foremost, she had to establish her own identity. With that in hand she could open a bank account. She'd have to take money from the family account but she would consider that money payment for the work she was doing keeping order in the house.

Ronan and Oisín returned from the pub late. They found their mother standing over the computer printer, pulling pages off as fast as they appeared.

They said nothing – simply stood in the doorway of the home office staring at their mother. She always told them what she'd been doing when they came in. She'd ask after their evening, wanting to know who they'd met – where they'd been – what they'd done.

Finn smiled sweetly and waited. They didn't have to know her teeth were locked against the questions she longed to ask.

"Would you like a cup of tea, Mother?" Oisín broke the uncomfortable silence.

"That would be very nice, thank you." My, aren't we polite all of a sudden, Finn thought as he left.

"I'm going to bed – I have an early start in the morning."

Ronan waited, convinced his mother would want all the details.

"Goodnight," Finn said simply.

Ronan took the stairs to his room, wondering what the hell was going on with his life. His mother always wanted to know every little thing about her sons. He'd resented it in the past and hidden things from her but now she'd stopped asking he wasn't sure how he felt.

Oisín arrived back.

"I'll be gone by the time you boys get out of bed tomorrow," Finn said, accepting the cup of tea from him. She planned to remove herself from the house. If she didn't she would just drift back into her old habits. "I don't know what time I'll return in the evening."

"OK," Oisín said. Really, what could he say? "Goodnight, Mum." He turned away, feeling lost and alone.

"Goodnight, son, sleep tight."

Finn didn't watch Oisín leave – she was too busy reading the reams of information she'd printed off the computer. She had papers she needed to study carefully.

Finn turned off the light in her office. Maybe she should just check to see if Oisín remembered to turn everything off in the kitchen.

Finn gasped at the mess Oisín had left behind him. She checked that all electrical appliances were turned off. There was no point in allowing a fire to start just to prove a point. With a shudder she turned away from her kitchen. They could clean up their own mess from now on. She almost wanted to delay leaving the house in the morning. She'd enjoy seeing their faces when they discovered that the fairies didn't come in at night and clean up their mess.

Chapter 17

"That car is going to die on you one of these days, missus."
Barry Ryan shook his grey head sadly. "You need one of those
fancy big cars your husband buys for himself."

"Chance would be a fine thing, Barry." She had taken her
car to the mechanic a short distance from the house. The car
had been making unsettling noises. She didn't want to break
down on a busy road. "Do what you can with her – please."

"I can't raise something from the dead, missus. The last fella
that tried that walked on water." He sucked energetically on his
cigarette.

"Do the best you can." Finn turned to leave.

"Here, missus, before you go – I have a load of metal to shift
– do you want it?"

"I'd love it." Finn took metal sight unseen. She never knew
what she might receive. It amused her to make something out of
nothing. "I got a new wheelbarrow for my birthday. If it's not
in your way I'll come and shift it myself one of these days."

"It's not a bloody new wheelbarrow you need, missus – it's a
new car." Barry wouldn't let any of his relatives drive that car,
he didn't care if it was considered a classic. Patrick bloody
Brennan should be ashamed of himself. "I'll have one of the
lads put it to one side for you. Pick it up when you can."

"Thanks. I'll see you later." Finn left, laughing.

She travelled on the bus and DART out to Bray. The DART train hugged the cliffs and coastline around Dublin, passing magnificent scenery that delighted her. When the sun shone – which admittedly was rare – you couldn't beat Ireland for beauty.

Rolf had said the cottages were within easy walking distance of the DART station. She walked along the Victorian promenade in Bray, searching. She thought she knew the area fairly well. It was one of her son's favourite places to visit when they were little. Ronan and Oisín had consumed mountains of candyfloss and oceans of whipped ice cream while chasing each other in and out of the freezing cold waves. She stopped walking to stand with her back to the ocean and stare across the street at the amusements. She remained standing with her back to the iron railings, elbows resting on the waist-high balustrade, and simply stared, remembering times past.

How many rainy days had she spent standing on the sidelines in that amusement arcade? The boys had driven the dodgems, climbed the twister and pulled frantically on the handle of one-arm bandits while the Irish summer bucketed down outside. Finn pushed off the railings with a smile. Happy days.

According to the directions she held, the amusements were past the address she was looking for. She turned and started back the way she'd come, blind and deaf to the screams of the children playing on the pebble-strewn beach. She'd have to ask someone for directions.

"Railway Parade?" said the man frying chips behind the serving window that opened onto the street. "You're not far from it." The man prepared the fish and chips Finn ordered, took orders shouted to him from the waitresses in his busy restaurant and still smiled while giving her directions.

Finn was thankful she'd noticed the serving window up a side street from the bustling restaurant sitting on the seafront. The place was packed with hungry families enjoying their day out. It was a happy accident she'd happened to look up this side street and seen the line of people picking up their white paper-wrapped meals. Munching happily on her fish and chips, Finn turned to follow the man's directions.

The directions had been sound. She stood in front of the railway cottages and groaned. Emmet said the cottages were on the seafront. He'd stretched the truth a bit. He'd made no mention of the four-storey Victorian Bed and Breakfast places that blocked the view of the sea completely. The tall granite buildings overshadowed Railway Parade, preventing light from reaching the row of eleven attached cottages. Her father would never be happy living without sunlight.

Opening the door of number three with the key Emmet had provided, Finn stepped into a time warp. She tried to remember what Emmet had told her about the woman who'd lived in this time capsule. She knew the woman died but from the looks of this place the house hadn't been touched in decades, maybe even centuries.

She touched a hand to the banister of the worn staircase directly in front and to the right of the doorway. The old thing was an accident waiting to happen. The naked wooden steps were bent and worn with age and use.

"The place stinks." She kicked years of junk mail out of her way. "What this place needs is a wrecking ball." She pulled her phone out of her pocket and pressed the number one option. She had brought her camera with her to take pictures but this place was beyond her direst imaginings.

"*Ja*, sweetling, what is it?"

"Rolf, engage your screen please. I am going to walk you visually around this place."

"One moment." His smiling face appeared on the screen of her phone.

"This place, Rolf, has been sadly neglected."

Finn aimed her phone around the hallway, allowing the pictures to speak for her. She walked into the small front room on her left. The room had a fabulous fireplace but the torn and peeling thick layers of wallpaper revealed cracked plaster and mouldering finish. A naked light bulb hung from the fungus-mottled ceiling. The place was dark and musty.

"Emmet could fry the fungus growing in here," she said.

"That is bad." Rolf's voice covered the sound of Finn's footsteps.

"It stinks too."

The second small downstairs room which she assumed was a dining room of sorts was in a similar condition. No light came into this room either. Finn was afraid to try the light switch. The Lord only knew what condition the wiring was in. She preferred not to risk touching anything until she'd had a better look around the property.

"Oh my God!" she said.

The German translation came over the phone at the same time.

The long back room was a rude shock, even though a great black range stove built into what she assumed was a chimneybreast was a delightful treasure to Finn's eyes. This couldn't be the kitchen, could it? There was a cold-water tap, a tap that in her opinion that was better suited for outdoor use, since no sink but a mouldy tin bucket sat under its dripping spout.

Two old decrepit easy chairs were parked in front of the cold range. The old lady must have spent most of her time sitting in this room. There was nothing here that would be recognised as a kitchen in today's world. A small window off to the side opened onto a narrow walkway. Here too the lack of light made the place dark and depressing.

"I didn't know places like this still existed." Finn's arm was beginning to ache from holding her phone out in front of her.

There was no indoor plumbing that she could see. How had the old dear lived with no toilet, no bathroom and no heating system other than the open fireplace in every room? She was wondering about her family. How could they have allowed their elderly relation to continue to exist in such an out-dated, uncomfortable house? Would it have cost that much to put in a toilet for the poor woman?

"This is a bit more than updating an old house, Da-ma."

Finn opened the door off the back room. A small step out and she was facing a wall which obviously separated the back yards. She sighed, walking down the cobbled path, wondering what she could do to drag this property into the present day.

She found the toilet down the back of the cottage in a small yard. Two old buildings stood holding each other up. The coal and rubbish were in one building. The antique toilet stood gloriously alone in the building nearest the kitchen. Finn stared at the overhead cistern with its long pull-chain. She was half expecting to see old newspaper on the floor instead of the modern loo roll. She couldn't believe her eyes – an outdoor loo in this day and age – amazing.

"It is a slice of history – frozen," Rolf whispered. "We bought the cottages at a ridiculously low price. It is never a mistake to invest in property."

She stared at an enormous wall that cut along the back of every cottage in the row, trying to understand what exactly she was looking at. The wall was at least forty feet high and solid grey stone. It was when she heard a train whistle that she understood.

The wall was part of the railway system that crossed this row of cottages with two bridges over the roads on either end. It appeared to lead directly into the railway shunting yard.

Talk about dismal, the B&Bs blocked the light in the front and this monstrosity blocked all light in the back. A way would have to be found to overcome that problem. No one wanted to live in a dark and gloomy house.

Finn continued her tour of the house. She found three good-sized bedrooms and a box room upstairs. Every room was in the same dilapidated condition. Here too a Victorian fireplace graced every room. The box room was the only room in the house without a grate. How had the poor woman managed to live in this place? Had no one cared what happened to her?

She was glad she'd decided to take this look around. She could never in her wildest dreams have imagined these cottages – it was astounding. The second railway cottage was a carbon copy of the first. How had the old people been left to live in these buildings? Surely they had children and grandchildren, people who knew of the improvements that could be made? Perhaps they'd resented the fact that someone else actually owned the cottages. Someone else would benefit from any improvements made? It was something to think about.

"I think you and Da need to come over to Ireland and see this for yourself. The cost of updating these cottages will be prohibitive. I can do nothing until we have walked around these places together."

"*Ja, ja,* they are *wonderbar!*" Rolf sounded excited about what to Finn looked like a nightmare. "I will talk with your father." He clicked off before she could comment.

Finn locked the two cottages and left, very much aware of the twitching of lace curtains as she passed along the pathway. She wished someone would be brave enough to come out and face her but they remained behind locked doors. Finn would have liked to knock on doors and talk to people. What would the neighbours on this quite street think of having a crowd of builders and a lot of noisy machines on their street for months? That is – if Rolf went ahead. Using the film in her phone she would put together a list of changes that must be made – then they would see.

She returned to the DART station. She had things to do in Rathmines. Dragging those buildings up to date would be a time-consuming task. The cost of the refurbishing would be enormous. Would they be worth the investment?

Chapter 18

Noise was the first thing to hit her when she entered her house. The blaring music was coming from two directions. Sweet classical strings poured from upstairs and thumping rap shook the doorframes of the living room. Obviously the people in the house at the moment were hard of hearing.

"Ronan, did you want a snack, bro?" Oisín appeared in the hallway. "Hi, Mum! We thought you had gone to your metalwork class. It is Thursday."

"Where is your father? That's his music entertaining the neighborhood."

The look of horror on the face of her son answered her question without words. She pulled her phone out of her pocket and tuned the computer system into the upstairs rooms. How dare he – what in the name of God did the man think he was doing? She engaged the camera and began recording under her son's horrified gaze. Without a word she turned towards the stairs. Silently she crept up the staircase, avoiding the stair that creaked.

Right, no more Mrs. Nice Guy. She pushed the door to the bedroom open. Patrick's trousers were lying just inside the door. She bent down and grabbed them from the floor without disturbing the fornicating couple writhing on the bed. They never noticed their audience.

She returned downstairs, the trousers held high like a trophy of war. Ronan and Oisín stood frozen at the foot of the stairs – a look of identical horror and fear on both their faces.

"Right!" Finn snapped. "Ronan, get into your father's car. I want you to go to the bank and withdraw the maximum amount of cash you can on all of his credit cards." She pulled car keys and a wallet out of the trousers and threw them at him. "I know you know his pin numbers so don't even try to tell me you don't. You can leave your father's car in the driveway when you return. Oisín, you need to go with your brother – parking is a bitch around here. One of you stay with the car while the other runs to the cash point. Be as quick as you can, both of you."

Was this what Maggie meant about turning into a thief?

The two young men stood completely still, staring at their mother in frozen shock. Finn practically pushed them out the door.

She headed towards the room that was her sanctuary – her kitchen.

The smell of tobacco drifted down the stairs. The couple had obviously reached a resting point. At least she hoped it was only tobacco. With the way Patrick was carrying on, who knew? She hadn't looked at the face of his partner. She'd no intention of tuning into the screen to check. She'd no idea who he was bonking but by God it was the final straw.

She heard the boys returning and hurried to join them. With a quick jerk of her head she walked towards the kitchen, confident they would follow her.

"Right, how much cash did you score?" she asked, holding out her hand to Ronan.

"Mum," Ronan said, "I'm not happy about this." He reluctantly handed over a wad of twenty-pound notes.

"Objection noted and understood!" Finn snapped. "Who is with your father?"

"Brenda Green from down the road." Ronan shuffled his feet.

"What on earth is that girl thinking of – a family pack?" Finn stared at her two mortified sons

Finn was reeling – had that young madam or God forbid Patrick – left the bedroom door ajar in anticipation of Ronan joining them? Was her home turning into a bonk shop with Brenda Green as the star attraction?

Brenda Green had been a problem in the Brennan household from a very young age. She had chased after the boys with single-minded determination. She'd climbed in their bedroom windows to screw them. Finn refused to call it making love. Now she was bonking Patrick.

"Stay in the kitchen, boys," Finn bit out. "I'll be back soon," She stormed from the room, heading for the stairs.

Without stopping to knock, she shoved the door to the bedroom open.

"I would have served a drink but didn't know what you'd like," Finn bit out to the startled couple on the bed.

From her bird's-eye view Patrick's dimpled white rear end looked as if it were gearing up for action. They'd been on the point of starting again. Finn was not about to let this continue. The room screen captured Patrick's long white naked body, primed for action over his young lover. She'd download and delete that before his sons saw it.

"*What the hell? What's the meaning of this?*" Patrick roared, grabbing for a sheet to cover his sagging bits. "Nuala, what are you doing here? I thought this was one of your evenings to be out!" He jumped from the bed. "What the hell are you doing here?" He stood tall and naked, trying to intimidate Finn with his majestic presence.

"I live here, which is more than you can say." Finn threw his trousers at him. "Get dressed, Patrick, and get out. You can continue this 'business' meeting elsewhere."

"You can't throw him out of his own house!" Brenda Green glared at Finn with black smudged eyes.

She'd hoped for this when she'd begged Patrick to bang her in his wife's house. This was better than she could have hoped. She hated the frigid cow, Mrs. bloody Brennan. The old bitch had all the things she wanted and deserved. But that was all going to change now. Brenda was in control here. The bitch would be the one leaving. Brenda was moving into this house that she'd always coveted and there was nothing this stuck-up cow could do about it.

Finn couldn't bear to look at Brenda Green. God knows it wasn't the first time she had seen the hussy naked in bed – fresh from being serviced by one of Finn's menfolk – but it was the very last time.

"*Patrick, you tell her!*" Brenda roared, furious at being ignored. She was more important than anyone else here. She'd show the bitch. "*Patrick is going to marry me!*" Her eyes gleamed with almost manic hatred as she glared at Finn.

"Well, that will certainly make you a very close-knit family unit," Finn remarked softly. "You should get dressed, Brenda, or leave naked again, it's up to you."

"*You can't talk to me like that!*" Brenda screamed "*Patrick, you tell her, tell her right now!*"

Brenda jumped out of bed, put clenched fists on her naked hips and glared at the man jumping around on one foot trying to get his trousers on.

Finn had become aware of her children standing like stone behind her. What a wonderful education they were receiving. Damn Patrick Brennan.

"Boys, help your future stepmother find her clothes and throw her out of my house if you please."

Patrick didn't even turn when his two sons entered the room. Had he always been such a wimp? Couldn't he try and communicate with the boys – say something – anything? Although what could be said in a situation like this? Next?

It was Ronan who forced Brenda into her skimpy skirt and top, no underwear. Oisín picked those up from where they were thrown around the room. He put the small pieces of lingerie into Brenda's shoes and, with an abrupt nod of his head to Ronan, started to walk from the room.

Brenda's screams for Patrick to do something were ignored by all. When she tried to grab onto the door in order to stay, Ronan picked her up and threw her over his shoulder. With her bare arse up to the public, he carried the little madam from the house and dropped her – barefoot and bare-arsed on the driveway.

Brenda's screams and torrent of verbal abuse continued in the street. It was better than television. Neighbours stuck their heads out to see what was going on. Brenda gave them both an eyeful and an earful. She enjoyed being the centre of attention, showing that old cow Nuala Brennan up for the jealous bitch she was.

"Get out, Patrick," Finn said, holding the bedroom door open.

"I really can't see what the problem is, Nuala. It was just a momentary temptation. She was there, you weren't." He was the wronged one here. She'd walked away from their marriage and their bed, not him.

"Have you always been this stupid? Do you even know what you're dealing with here? Did you ever listen when I explained the problems I was having keeping young Miss Green away from your sons? That girl's biggest ambition in life is to get pregnant by one of the males in this house. She's not fussy about which man fathers her child – any one of you will do." Finn was pushing Patrick in front of her. She couldn't believe what had taken place under her roof. It was worse than a French farce. "*Get out!*"

"You're obviously overwrought." Patrick couldn't take his eyes off the furious woman glaring retribution at him. He'd never seen her like this. "Why don't we go downstairs and discuss this like adults?"

"There is only one adult here, Patrick, and it's not you. Now for the last time *get the hell out of my house!*" She was practically pushing him down the stairs. She wanted him gone before she gave in to the temptation to beat him stupid.

Patrick resisted. He could hear young what's-her-name screaming in the street. He didn't want to have to face her on top of everything else.

"*Ronan!*" Finn yelled. "*Open the front door – your father is leaving!*"

Ronan did as ordered. Finn gave an almighty heave and pushed Patrick from the house. She quickly closed the door and leaned against it. She could hear Brenda still screaming abuse and crying, loudly entertaining the neighbourhood.

It was a shame she'd told the boys to leave Patrick's car in the driveway. She would have enjoyed his embarrassment as he had to remove his car from the garage. Still, he was gone and she was left with two young men who had seen a great deal more than was good for them.

"That vasectomy Father had after Oisín's birth is proving a blessing," Ronan said, following his mother into the living room. He grimaced when the colour drained from his mother's face.

Finn reeled where she stood. Ronan jumped forward to catch her before she could fall to the floor.

The ocean was covering Finn's ears. She couldn't hear. She could see his mouth moving but the words weren't making it through. Her eyesight was fading. Finn – for the first time in her life – fainted.

"We should call a doctor." Ronan stood with his mother clasped in his arms. He was shaking like a leaf. He lowered her gently to the sofa.

"What did you say that made her do this?" Oisín snapped. The sight of his mother's pale white face hurt something deep inside him.

Finn groaned and tried to sit upright.

"Perhaps you should wait a minute before trying to get up." Ronan was trying to appear in control. His mother's faint had frightened the life out of him.

Finn thought of all the months and years of trying to get pregnant. The tears each month her period arrived on time. The desperate visits to the doctor, being poked and prodded in incredibly intimate places, trying to discover the reason why she couldn't conceive the child she longed for. Years of feeling like a failure as a woman while Patrick assured her that eventually she would conceive. He'd been so sympathetic, so understanding of her failure. She should have guessed then that something wasn't quite right. He'd held her when she cried, patting her back, telling her they should be thankful for the blessing of two healthy sons. She'd been so grateful for his gentle understanding. The bastard, the rotten lying deceiving bastard! He'd had a vasectomy.

"Mum, what happened?" Ronan asked.

"I want a pot of tea." Finn croaked out. She refused to discuss this betrayal with her sons.

Oisín was glad of something to do. "I'll make it."

Chapter 19

Sunday morning, after nights spent tossing and cursing in the blue guest bedroom, Finn walked down the main staircase determined to lock the pain she felt deep inside.

It was Sunday and a traditional breakfast was called for. She and her sons worked as a team to get a full Irish breakfast on the table. They laughed and joked, bumping hips preparing the mountain of food.

"I know they say silence is a compliment to the chef but that was ridiculous." Finn pushed her empty plate away.

"Father telephoned. He needs clothes for work tomorrow." Ronan shuffled his feet uncomfortably. "He ah ... asked if you had calmed down any."

"First order of business then," Finn said, standing. "You two give me a hand picking out enough to get your father through a couple of weeks. We can do a major pack-up later."

In the green guest bedroom Finn pulled suits from hangers and passed them to Oisín. Ronan was sorting through mountains of underwear and accessories. How on earth could one man have so many clothes?

Finn packed a couple of suitcases. She was fighting the urge to tear Patrick's business suits to shreds. She was so angry and had no way of expressing her fury. She wanted to burn the rotten bastard in effigy.

She'd been trying so hard to handle this difficult situation in a civilized manner. Now she wanted to rant and rave, tell his children what she really thought of the lying, cheating, low scumbag. Leaving aside what he had done to her, how dare he behave so badly in front of their sons?

"You two carry the bags down and I'll put on a pot of coffee." Finn patted herself on the back for not suggesting that they pour petrol over the lot and strike a match.

"*Coffee!*" both voices sang out in pretend astonishment.

Ronan smiled. "By God, things must be serious when you start making coffee, Mother. The world must be coming to an end."

"Smart mouth!" Finn laughed, starting down the stairs. "Come on, I'll make coffee and rustle up a few scones." She knew her sons. They were always hungry. "We can put the suitcases in the hallway. I won't give in to the temptation to just dump them in the driveway."

"My da's will be visiting soon." Finn offered. "I need them to check out the properties in Bray." She had told her sons about the cottages and shown them photographs. She dared to think that they were rediscovering their old closeness.

"It will be nice to see Grandfather and Rolf – but it's going to be weird," Ronan muttered into his coffee mug. "It's strange having a gay couple as grandparents."

"My father's sex life is none of your business," she stated and considered herself a saint in the making for not bringing up Patrick's clear disregard for any rules of moral behavior. "If there was a grandmother in the picture, would you two be wondering how often they made love or even how?" The subject died a natural death then.

Finn went to refill the mugs, leaving Ronan and Oisín whispering and murmuring together. She returned with three mugs of coffee and a platter of hot scones. The first batch of scones had disappeared in seconds.

"I don't know if I can afford to keep living in this house," she said when they were all sitting comfortably. "I can't cover the overheads."

Ronan sat up – shocked. "I don't want to lose my home. I love this house."

"We need to put our heads together." Oisín wanted to travel – but only with the certain knowledge that he had a home to come back to.

"That is one of the many things I want to discuss with my dad." Finn didn't want the responsibility of this big house any longer.

It was noon when Patrick arrived to pick up his clothes. He appeared to be amazed to discover that all had not been forgiven. Finn couldn't believe his gall. He really believed all he had to do was grin and stroll back into this house.

"This nonsense has gone far enough, Nuala. You are married to me and have a duty to behave in a certain fashion." He pulled a business card from his jacket pocket. "I've made an appointment for you to speak with this woman." He pushed the card into Finn's hand. "You are obviously suffering from some kind of mental imbalance."

Finn stared at the card. The man took the biscuit. The female psychologist, Lacey Elliot, was one of his on-again off-again lovers. She held the card with white-knuckled force. Without speaking, she gestured towards the packed suitcases.

"This is my home", he said. "I've spent years and a small fortune updating this house. My sons are here. Where do you expect me to go?" He smirked, sure of his advantage.

"I have a few suggestions as to *your* eventual destination, Patrick." Finn smiled coolly. "I am, however, too much of a lady to use such language."

"I want to see the boys." Patrick sniffed elegantly. "This entire situation is ridiculous, Nuala. I cannot believe the way you've been carrying on. Have you thought of the effect all this madness is having on my sons?"

Finn almost bit her tongue through on that one. With herculean effort she remained calm and gestured him towards the lounge where the boys were. She stood by the front door, her hand on the latch. She didn't want him to get the impression that he was welcome to stay for any length of time.

Patrick returned with his sons almost forming an honour guard as they escorted him to the front door. The look of disbelief on his face was worth the price of admission. It would appear that he really hadn't realised how his behaviour had damaged his relationship with his sons.

"Maggie, do you have time for a chat?" Finn needed to talk to someone who had experience of this nightmare situation. She'd waited until the boys left to visit friends before contacting Maggie Spencer.

"I can try to talk but my twins have no respect for my private moments."

"Would you like to bring them over here?" Maggie lived on a nearby council estate. "I have a large garden they can run wild in while we talk."

"I give you fair warning – my mum calls the girls the Demolition Derby," Maggie said as soon as Finn opened her front door.

"Do you gots kids?" a brown-haired little angel lisped. "I don't want to play with *her.*"

The girls were identical.

"I have two big boys." Finn held the door open wide, gesturing the frazzled woman and her children to come inside.

"I've got the name of a lawyer." Finn collapsed onto a chair pulled away from the patio table. She'd forgotten how much energy looking after two little people burned up.

"Lawyers!" Maggie stood watching her daughters run around the walled garden, hiding behind fruit trees – examining the metal figures – and stopping to blow bubbles from time to time.

"I've never had anything to do with the law or lawyers," Finn admitted. "I wasn't impressed by the first lawyer I spoke with."

"Most people are unaware of law courts unfortunately." Maggie joined Finn at the table.

"Did you have a bad experience?"

"I was completely out of my depth," Maggie didn't like to

get into details about her time in court. It always put her into a deep depression for days afterwards. "It was like visiting a country where you are the only one who doesn't speak the language." She wanted to prepare Finn for the shocks ahead.

"What do you mean?"

"I can't explain it very well. *Stop that, you two!*" Maggie shouted at her girls without losing her place in the conversation. The twins stopped pulling each other's hair.

"Come inside – there's something I want to do." Finn got up and made for the kitchen.

"*We'll be inside, girls!*"

Inside, Finn began pulling the makings for 'play dough' from the cupboards. It had kept her boys quiet for hours. The girls were getting tired of the garden.

Maggie stood at the window, watching. She wondered what Finn was baking. The girls wouldn't eat home cooking.

"It seemed to me – but this is my opinion only," she said, "that lawyers forget they're dealing with people – us, I mean – their paying clients. They seem to be having so much fun proving how clever they are to each other." She had to bite her lips to stop them trembling.

"Take a minute." Finn could see how much this was upsetting her.

"The lawyers seemed to belong to an exclusive club of clever fellows who play together and try to outsmart each other. You, as their client, don't come into it. It's a game they play and each one tries to prove he's the smartest. It was like watching very erudite talking heads playing at one-upmanship – they play to win." Maggie fought off the bitter memories.

"I have the name of a female lawyer – do you think that might make a difference?" Finn was alarmed to see how upset Maggie was, just thinking of her experience in the law courts.

"I don't know – it would be nice to think so."

"I want to be as prepared as possible. Here!" Finn threw a towel to Maggie and armed herself with another. "The girls will be soaked from spilling the bubble liquid all over each other." They opened the kitchen door and each woman grabbed a squirming little girl.

"Tell me, by any chance has Lacey Elliot, that renowned radio personality and psychologist, put her b-with-an-itch nose into your life?"

"Patrick suggested I talk to her."

"I guessed he would. That ... woman ..." Maggie was conscious of 'little ears', "almost cost me my children." Charles Upton hadn't wanted custody of the twins. That was the only thing that had saved Maggie's sanity. "She gave a written profile of me that had me wondering who she was talking about. Stay well away from her. She's poison."

"I have no intention of keeping the appointment." Finn had the girls, wearing old T-shirts belonging to her sons to protect their fresh outfits, kneeling at the kitchen table. She was showing them ways to play with the multicoloured balls of play dough she'd made.

"Good for you."

Maggie and the girls watched figures appear under Finn's busy fingers. She showed the girls how to work the salt dough. Maggie watched her children play quietly in amazement.

"All I can suggest about lawyers is shop around," she said. "Try to find one you can work with. Get as much paperwork together to back up your claims as possible. Bury them in written and photographic evidence. You're going to need it."

"I'm scared, Maggie."

"Good – you need to be."

"Maggie, that's not helping me."

"It is, in fact. You need to watch your back." She didn't want Finn to underestimate the difficulties ahead. "I went into court with a smile on my face – my head held high – full of righteous indignation. I crawled out with my tail between my legs."

"How about we make hair for your dolls?" Finn willingly sacrificed two garlic presses to show the girls how to force the dough through and make squiggles of colourful dough. It gave Maggie a moment to pull herself together.

"I discovered I'd been married to a penniless man who could not afford to support two households apparently. Charles had done some creative bookwork. He'd managed to make his money disappear. The house I know he owns free and clear was now a rented property. He'd rented the large property at my insistence the court was told. I sat in that court listening to his manufactured lies. It was better than reading a book of Myths and Legends but the court bought it all – every lying word."

Finn couldn't believe what she was hearing.

"Watch your back," said Maggie. "That's the best advice I can give you."

Finn closed the door behind Maggie and her tired little girls. Then, with Maggie's warning in mind, she turned into a whirling dervish. She had photographs, cards, memories stored in boxes all around the house. Finn threw nothing out.

"What else?" She rested on her heels at last, staring at the small mountain of files she'd compiled. She'd recorded – to the best of her ability – all of her dealings for the last twenty-one years. She'd kept annual diaries that she'd stored. Leafing through them reminded her of everything she'd done for Patrick and his career.

It was an impressive body of work if she did say so herself. She'd worked for twenty-one years without a break. Finn had created a financial chart for the work she'd done, using a paid housekeeper's salary scale. The amount she'd never earned was staggering.

Chapter 20

Finn pushed her red wheelbarrow along the street, thrilled with what she had found at the local junk yard. Barry, her mechanic, had passed along old car exhaust systems and the tall heavy-duty springs from car suspensions. She couldn't wait to see what treasure she could turn this trash into. The fat body of the exhaust was her favourite body type for her nutjobs.

She wanted to spend days in her workshop beating metal. She had a desperate longing to turn her brain off. The six weeks since she threw Patrick out had been a time of constant learning and doing. She wanted the world to stop for a while. She'd opened a bank account in her own name. Following Angie's advice she'd mailed letters and cards in her own name to her home address – getting her sons to address the envelopes had been fun. She'd found an old identity card with a photograph attached to use as ID. She'd used the money she'd taken from Patrick to open the account. It had been time-consuming but the paperwork was under way. Just one of the many things she had to take care of – but it was done.

The pace of the last weeks had been frantic – amassing proof of her part in her marriage broke her heart and putting evidence together to justify her existence was painful – and she still hadn't made any firm decisions. Her da would say she was hiding her head in the sand again. She wasn't. She hoped she had learned that lesson well – head in sand, arse in air, perfect for kicking. She felt sore from the kicks she'd been receiving lately.

Her da and Rolf were on their way to Ireland. Taking the slow route if she knew them – her da could never resist driving down unknown roads.

"*I can see you're enjoying your birthday present!*" the male voice calling out to her put a hitch in Finn's stride.

Dare Lawrence – she'd thought he'd gone back to America. She wanted to curse. She ran a frantic mental check over her own figure. She'd have to do – the jeans and boots she wore were becoming almost a uniform. If he'd given her warning she'd have tried to present a better image. What are you thinking, woman, she silently berated herself. She raised her eyes to the two figures waiting outside her house. The man didn't care what she looked like.

"Hello, Finn."

"Dare, I thought you were in America!" She almost closed her eyes at her own stupid words.

"I've been to America and back since I last saw yeh, Missus." Dare didn't want to talk about the problems he was facing in the States. He smiled and put his arm around the woman at his side. "You know my niece Chloe. She says she used to babysit your kids. She's our Nathan's girl."

"Isn't it great the way we give seed, breed and generation?" Chloe was nervous. She wanted something from this woman but her grandma and uncle had warned her not to gush.

"Good to see you, Chloe," said Finn.

"I wanted to talk to you about your nutjobs," Dare said, aware he was walking on eggshells. "Were you on your way to your workshop?" He gave a nod to her packed wheelbarrow resting on the road.

"I gave that fellow you sent all of the ones you selected," she said. "He packed them all very carefully. I watched."

"Yes, but ..." Dare looked around. "Look, do you really want to discuss this out here?"

"You're welcome to come inside." She picked up the handles

of her barrow. "Prepare to be bored out of your mind, Chloe." She started to push the barrow forward. "You can blame your uncle."

"I'll be fine." Chloe had to remind herself not to run ahead. She had seen the photographs of this woman's artwork and she wanted some of it.

Finn looked over her shoulder while unlocking the shed. "We've lost Chloe."

"She'll find us – she's making a tour of the figures in your garden." Dare pushed the door of the shed open wide. "I wanted to talk to you."

"Talk away." Finn started to unload the barrow.

"Can I help?"

"No, I'm OK." She had a system of storage and didn't like anyone to disturb it.

Dare pushed his hands into the pockets of his tailored trousers. He longed to push all of the figures out into the sunlight. It was a crime to hide such art in a dark garden shed.

"I might have mentioned that I was moving back to Ireland."

"Yes." Finn was lost in the placement of her finds. She had to be able to put her hand on them as required.

"I got a bit ahead of myself."

"How so?" Finn turned to pay attention to what he was saying.

"I suppose being home and spending time around my mother and the rest of the family made me homesick." He shrugged. "I thought I had nothing to hold me in the States anymore. I'm ready for a change of lifestyle – but my kids don't agree."

"Oh dear." Finn smiled in sympathy. She knew through Angie that Dare had four children.

"Yeah, I was made to feel like the worst parent in the world when I told my kids we were moving to Ireland." He took his hands from his pockets to shove them through his inky black hair. "I thought they would be thrilled. They are always asking about their Irish family."

"It's not easy packing up a life." She ought to know.

"Yeah, it's going to take me a lot longer than I thought.

That's why I'm here." He paused, almost holding his breath. "The nutjobs I had packed up and mailed were chosen as gifts."

"Yes, I remember," she prompted when he seemed to be lost for words.

"I want some of the larger figures for myself," Dare said in a hurry. He didn't want to lose the chance of owning the figures he so admired.

"Well, help yourself!" Finn flung her arms out, wondering what the man saw in her tinkering. They were her nutjobs and she loved them – but really – they were just something to keep her sane. Still, she supposed if he took more away it would free up space in her shed.

"Since you refuse to put a price on your art what I suggest is that I ask a friend of mine in the art world to put a price on the items I've already taken." He'd met with a friend who owned a very trendy art gallery in LA on his last quick visit to the States.

"If you insist." She didn't understand what the problem was. She'd given him the nutjobs he'd asked for. "It's just scrap metal for goodness' sake. I get most of it for nothing."

"Finn, you will drive me to drink!"

"Have you asked her?" Chloe had been listening outside. She thought it better to step in now before her Uncle Dare totally lost his temper.

"Asked me what?" Finn said.

"Chloe is a landscape artist." Dare glared at his niece. He wanted to talk money with Finn. The figures could make her fortune if the stubborn woman would only wake up and smell the roses.

"I'm putting together a garden to appear in the Bloom festival of flowers." Chloe didn't mention that the making of the garden and the event would be televised daily on RTÉ. "I was hoping you would loan me some of your figures to put in my design." She couldn't afford to buy one – not at the prices her uncle was quoting for the little wonders. "I'd take very good care of them and get them back to you as soon as possible."

"What is it with you Lawrences – are you all doolally? They are just tinkering for the good Lord's sake." Finn looked from one to the other, expecting them to admit they were pulling her leg.

"You need to put a price on your nutjobs, Finn." Dare had people asking about the figures since the ones he sent reached his friends in America. He'd known they would bring pleasure to his friends but it seemed everyone who saw them wanted one. She had to be made to see what she had.

"I can't think about this right now." Finn had enough to think about. "Just take what you want, Dare. You can send someone to pack them up. I'll trust you to put a price you think fair on them if you must."

"Finn ..." Dare closed his eyes and gritted his teeth.

Chloe kicked him on the ankle before he could get them thrown out. She knew what it was like to be asked to put a price on your God-given talents. It was difficult to see your efforts – particularly when it was something you loved – as others saw them.

"Look, Dare –" Finn really wanted to start beating metal into shapes. She was tired of thinking. She just wanted to turn the trash around her shed into little figures. "Take what you like – you're Angie's son – I trust you."

"In the name of ..." Dare actually put his hands out to grab her shoulders when Chloe stepped in the way.

"Do you have a bank account?" she asked.

"The paperwork to open an account in my own name is under way. I'll let you have the details as soon as I can." If Dare did decide to pay a little something for the nutjobs, she wanted the money to go into the account that was hers alone.

"You can talk about a fair price for the nutjobs when you have your own bank account." Chloe knew about this woman's problems. How could you not? Patrick Brennan was turning his marriage problems into media gold. She didn't want her uncle causing problems. She wanted two of the big figures for her garden – and as many of the little ones as she could get – she would design the landscape around them – they were magical.

"You can't have that one." Dare noticed where his niece was looking. He wanted that male for his own collection.

"What do you mean I can't?"

Finn stood to one side watching two people actually fight over her nutjobs. She was beginning to think it was Angie's relatives that were nuts. She wished they would just make a choice and leave. She wanted to get started on the figure she could see in her mind's eye. That battered exhaust was almost calling her name. She walked around the shouting couple and began to pull out the items she wanted. It didn't look as if those two would be finished anytime soon.

Finn waved goodbye to her visitors – they were still arguing – but at least she wouldn't have to listen. Chloe had fought with her uncle over several of the figures but they had reached an agreement, finally. Dare had said he'd be back – promise or threat, she didn't know.

She put everything out of her mind and with a sigh of satisfaction locked her shed door with the world outside. She put her head through the straps of her heavy rubber apron – she needed protection against sparks – and was soon bent over her worktable turning trash into her little treasures. The world outside could wait. She'd had enough of it.

She spent hours heating and beating metal. The tines of old forks turned into long curling eyelashes that she placed with care around bolt nuts to make eyes for the female she was assembling using one of the exhausts for the torso. A large nut gave the figure an open-mouth expression of surprise. She bent metal to make arms that crossed across the female's chest. She beat out all of her anger and frustration, turning the problems of her life into whimsical figures of fun. The light outside turned to evening and still she remained bent over her work, unaware of the world around her.

"I'm starving." She stepped away from the almost completed figure in surprise. She stretched, putting both hands to her back, and slowly straightened from her bent position. "I'm surprised the boys didn't come looking for me demanding to be fed. Maybe they're learning."

She restored order to her little world and carefully checked that everything was turned off. She stepped out into an inky star-studded night. It was much later than she had thought.

Chapter 21

"In the name of God, daughter, could you not have warned us?" Emmet jumped down from the driver's seat of his camper van.

"Warned you about what, Da?" Finn ran into her father's open arms.

Emmet was never happier then when he had something to moan about.

"The enormous changes taking place in the countryside. The buildings erupting like poisonous mushrooms all over the place. Surely to God there are more houses then people in this country now? What happened to my poor sleepy Ireland?" Emmet swung Finn in his arms and whirled her around.

"It must have woken up when you were off gallivanting," Finn said. "I can't believe the entire country didn't first ask your permission before implementing any of the changes wanted and needed in the country."

"You always were a cheeky little thing." Emmet was thrilled to see the change in his daughter. She fairly sparkled, no more miserable greyness about her at all.

"Emmet, let someone else say hello," said Rolf.

Ronan and Oisín were standing back, watching their mother greeted with a great deal of love and affection.

"Sweetling, you look *wonderbar*!" Rolf whispered into Finn's ear as he hugged her close to his chest.

Finn was aware of her sons staring in fascination.

"Come say hello to the boys," she said.

"Good to see you, Emmet, Rolf," said Ronan as he shook their hands. He was examining every feature of Rolf's face. There was a strong resemblance there, no matter how much his mother might deny it.

"Great you made it," said Oisín, "but are we going to stand out here all night starving to death? Would yez for God's sake come in so we can sit down and attack the food? The smell has been driving me mad."

Everyone laughed and pushed through the doorway.

"I didn't know what time you would get here, so I prepared a coddle," said Finn. "It's one of those meals that tastes better the longer it cooks." She wanted to wrap this memory around her. Everyone she loved, happy and laughing under the one roof. Why had she allowed Patrick's displeasure to keep her da's from visiting?

"A coddle?" Emmet wrinkled his nose in feigned disgust. "Is that what you serve to starving men, daughter? A coddle?"

"Don't be such a food snob, Da. There is nothing better on a chilly evening then a good coddle." Finn nudged her father. "I'm not serving a French meal so a good Dublin coddle it is – like it or lump it."

"What is this coddle?" Rolf asked, hating to be left out.

"It's what we'll be getting instead of a cuddle from this one!" Emmet laughed at Rolf's frown. "It's a Dublin dish peculiar to the region and peculiar is what it is."

"Give me five minutes and I'll have it on the table." Finn led the way.

"I'd like a chance to wash my face and hands," Emmet said.

"Boys, take your grandparents to the master bedroom," said Finn.

"I thought we would stay in the camper." Emmet was having difficulty stepping into this house that held so many memories for him. He'd like the chance to walk around the old place on his own. He had ghosts to lay.

"I know you love that camper, Da, but please stay in the house."

"We would be delighted," Rolf said.

"The smell of that coddle has me salivating, daughter." Emmet led the posse of her menfolk into the kitchen. "I haven't had a coddle in years." He lifted the lid off the oversized pot Finn had simmering on the hob. He sniffed appreciatively and almost groaned at the memories that smell evoked. Jesus, it whipped him right back to his youth.

"Leave my food alone!" Finn rapped Emmet's knuckles lightly with the wooden spoon. "Go sit down in the dining room and I'll bring the food through."

"What are we, guests?" Emmet moaned.

"Just for tonight, yes." Finn shoved him towards the dining room. "Now do as you're told for once in your life and go sit down, out from under my feet."

"It comes to some –" Emmet started before Rolf stepped in.

Rolf knew these two could keep up their comic moaning-and-groaning routine for hours. "Let us obey the cook," he said softly. "Especially as this cook is armed and dangerous."

Finn began to spoon the rich coddle into her large flower-sprigged soup tureen. There was enough to fill the tureen several times.

"Ronan, carry the tureen to the table for me, please."

"Finn, sweetling, I love it." Rolf stood in the centre of the dining room slowly turning as he tried to take in all of the little touches that made the dining room look so inviting. "You have made this room a work of art."

"I learned about presentation from you, Uncle Rolf." Finn was happy to have one man in her life who noticed the effort she'd taken to make the room look festive.

"What are you two yakking about? It's a crying shame the girl doesn't have a matching set of dishes." Emmet examined the mismatched tableware.

"I don't mean to be rude, Grandpop, Uncle Rolf," Oisín's voice was a pathetic moan, "but could we please eat?"

"The lad is making a great deal of sense." Emmet laughed and ruffled Oisín's head of strawberry-blond hair.

Finn took her place at the head of the table and gestured to her father and Rolf to take the chairs on either side of her. She placed Ronan beside Emmet and Oisín beside Rolf.

"This is good." Rolf tasted the coddle. "Is it not, Emmet? Why have you never made this?"

"I'm having a religious experience here, Rolf." Emmet swallowed the delicious broth. What was it about food that evoked so many memories at the first taste? "My grandmother – my mother's mother – the poor one – made this every Saturday." His green eyes glistened. "I haven't tasted it in years. You can't get bacon products like this anywhere else – that's why I never try to make it." He shook his head of thick greying hair, continuing to enjoy this trip down Memory Lane.

"The food is of course very good." Rolf smiled at Finn, allowing Emmet to wallow in sentiment. "Emmet taught you very well, sweetling."

"Da taught me how to cook, you taught me how to make my surroundings beautiful." Finn touched Rolf's hand. It must be difficult for him to be surrounded by Emmet's family and Emmet's memories of a time he didn't share.

"If that is true, sweetling, you have taken anything I might have taught and made it your own."

"Any more of this coddle, Mum?" Oisín liked to keep the mood light and entertaining.

"Good idea, Oisín." She forced herself to remain seated. "You can refill the tureen."

Oisín grabbed the tureen without complaint.

There was silence for a moment as they all simply enjoyed being together.

"I left the hob on, Mum." Oisín returned, carrying the brimming tureen. "I have a feeling that I'll be filling this thing up again."

"You are probably right, Oisín." Emmet served himself from the tureen. "I can't seem to get enough. We didn't stop to eat on the way here – old Misery Guts insisted that Finn would have prepared something special." Emmet gave a jerk of his head in Rolf's direction. "I hate it when he's right. It makes him unbearable."

Rolf ignored him and buttered the strange-looking bread Finn had prepared. "When do you return to school, Oisín?"

"I'm not sure that I'll be returning." Oisín didn't mind having his college education referred to as school. His mother did the same thing.

"How is this?"

"I want to travel –" Oisín began, only to be interrupted by his grandfather sniggering.

"That apple didn't fall far from the tree!" Emmet gave Ronan a hearty nudge.

"Emmet, please." Rolf rapped Emmet over the knuckles with his butter knife. "I wish to understand. Your mother has told us that you were enrolled to study this year, Oisín."

"No, I don't know what I want to study. I'd like to see a bit of the world before I make any decisions about the rest of my life."

"What do you think, Finn?" Rolf knew the importance Finn placed on a college education for her sons.

"I've been trying to persuade both of my sons to get further education," Finn answered. "Without a great deal of success."

"What do you think, Ronan?" Emmet asked the young man shovelling food into his mouth.

"I agree with Oisín. I'd like to see what I can do with my music."

"Music!" Emmet laughed. "Jesus, there is no fighting genetics is there? Music and travel."

"I'm glad you find this amusing, Da."

"Why not be amused by fate?" Emmet gave a quick glance around – everyone seemed to have finished eating. "Why don't we let the boys clear the table?"

Ronan and Oisín jumped to obey their grandfather.

"Should I make a pot of coffee, Mother?" Oisín asked.

"Leave that till later," Emmet answered. "We'll relax a little and just wallow in our greed."

"So, Finn, what's been happening?" Emmet had been served with a glass of Glenfiddich.

They were all seated in one of the smaller drawing rooms.

Finn had illuminated the electric-fire-effect screen. It gave no heat but she thought it added to the cosy atmosphere of the room.

"I evicted Patrick." Finn didn't mention the vasectomy. Emmet would have offered to cut off Patrick's equipment without the use of anaesthetic. She might be tempted to let him.

"I know a lawyer, well, he's a judge now – Harry Bailey – he's an old friend of mine," said Emmet. "He may be able give you advice about what you need to do."

"That would be great. I've been feeling a bit lost to tell the truth. I never expected to find myself in this situation." Finn bit her lip and looked at her two sons.

"I'll call Harry and see what he thinks needs to be done." Emmet stared into his glass. Finn should have seen this situation coming from a mile off. God knows he had, almost from the moment he'd reluctantly walked Finn down the aisle.

Rolf had become aware of Oisín making head signals in Rolf's direction and rolling his eyes at Ronan.

"Now, about the houses in Bray ..." Finn began.

"Before we verbally visit Bray perhaps Ronan and Oisín have something to add to this conversation?" Rolf enquired. "They seem to have something they wish to say to me."

"Not me." Oisín waited for Ronan to pick up the conversational ball and run with it.

Ronan sat staring miserably at his clenched fists.

"Ronan has a question." Oisín nudged his brother with his foot.

"You have something you need to know, Ronan?" Rolf waited. It was difficult to believe this one was Emmet's grandson. He was obviously a watching and wondering kind of person.

"For God's sake, Ronan, will you ask your bloody question?" Oisín exploded. "I'm sick and tired of listening to you bellyache about this. Now is the time, ask the bloody question. You can get the answer direct from the horse's mouth."

"Perhaps you should ask this question, Oisín, since Ronan does not appear ready to speak." Rolf smiled. Oisín had inherited his grandfather's quickfire temper.

Finn and Emmet decided to be the audience to this

conversation. While in France Finn had told both her da's of the boys' belief that Rolf was Ronan's biological father.

"This is very difficult for me." Ronan pushed shaking fingers through his mane of blond hair. "But I need to know." His blue eyes were almost manic.

"You may ask me anything you like," Rolf said softly when Ronan seemed unable to continue.

Ronan drew a much-handled black-and-white photograph out of his rear pocket. He put it on the coffee table that stood in front of the loveseat Finn and Rolf occupied.

"Please explain to me," he pointed at the picture, "if I have no relation to you at all, why does the man in that old picture look just like me?"

"Good Lord, where did that come from?" Emmet walked to stand behind the loveseat occupied by Finn and Rolf. "That's an old photograph of you, Rolf. You were about eighteen. I don't remember seeing this before." He squinted his green eyes, trying to bring the old photo into focus.

"*Ja, sein ich*," Rolf shook his head. "That is me but so long ago. Where did you get this picture?"

Ronan waved the question away. "Could you please explain the resemblance?"

"Finally, someone has the guts to ask." Emmet gave Ronan a hearty thump.

"You mean there is something to this?" Finn gasped.

"The evidence is right in front of you." Emmet pointed at the photo. "I thought you were going to stop hiding your head in the sand?"

"Emmet!" Rolf reprimanded him.

"I know, Rolf, but sometimes she makes me so mad."

"Is this going to be a long dramatic revelation?" Oisín broke into the uncomfortable situation. "I want coffee and some of that apple-pie Mum made before we get buried in sentiment."

"Oisín, you're a man after my own heart," Emmet said. "I've something to fetch from the camper van that will help this conversation along. You set things up in the dining room." He hurried from the house to the camper van parked on the driveway.

Finn had the old picture in her hand, staring from the photograph to her son. "Uncle Rolf ..."

"Just wait, sweetling. Let us all return to the dining room and sit around the table like civilised humans and all, as they say, will be revealed."

"It seems I've opened a can of worms," Ronan said.

"No, you have not," Rolf said. "This is a matter that Emmet and I thought would come under discussion years ago. We thought our Finn would be the person asking the questions."

The tantalising smell of percolating coffee began to filter through the house.

Finn sat like a statue, staring at Ronan.

"Are you alright, Mum?" Ronan bent across the coffee table and offered his hand.

Finn allowed herself to be helped from her seat. Ronan put his arm around her shoulders and led her into the dining room. He pulled out the chair at the head of the table and practically pushed Finn into the seat. "I'll be right back."

"Well, bro, it looks like you've put the cat among the pigeons," Oisín said when Ronan appeared in the kitchen. "It seems there really is some big dark secret in our family."

"Oisín, I think our mother is going into shock," Ronan plugged the electric kettle into the socket almost absentmindedly. He watched Oisín take the apple-pie from the oven. "How on earth can you think of food at a time like this?"

"Look, bro, it's obvious we're about to discover a whole world of family history. It seems to me that we would all be better sitting around the table with something to shove down our gobs." Oisín shrugged his shoulders. "That's all."

"Trust you to think that having food will make everything better." Ronan rinsed the teapot with boiling water.

"Just you wait and see." Oisín began to slice the apple-pie. "Everything is more civilised when you're sitting around a table with food to eat. I'm telling you, bro, it makes a world of difference."

Ronan put the teapot on the hob. His mother wouldn't drink tepid tea.

Finn sat and watched as Oisín and Ronan carried in the

desert and coffee after they had set the table with dishes and cups taken from the sideboard.

Then Emmet walked into the room, carrying a dust-covered box. He put the box on the sideboard and hurried to the downstairs toilet to wash his hands.

"Any of that tea going?" Emmet asked when he returned to the dining room. "I drink coffee when I'm away from home but as soon as I set foot in Ireland I want a good strong cup of tea."

Everyone waited while tea and coffee was poured.

"Right, is everyone sitting comfortably? Then I'll begin," Emmet then said, parodying an old-time radio announcer.

"Emmet, you are not helping matters!" Rolf objected.

"Just trying to introduce a little levity into the situation."

"Get on with it, please," Rolf ordered.

"You two know I'm gay?" Emmet waited for Ronan and Oisín to nod.

Ronan was glad he had the pie to shove into his mouth, giving him an excuse not to respond verbally. He would have to thank Oisín for his brilliant idea.

"I know it's become fashionable nowadays to declare you're gay but believe me in our time," Emmet gave a nod across the table towards Rolf, "we could have been imprisoned or battered to death. Being Irish, I'm sure you know what happened to Oscar Wilde –"

"Don't start," Rolf ordered.

"Sorry, mustn't get side-tracked." Emmet shrugged. "Anyway, Rolf and I met at college where I was majoring in parties and Brainbox over there was studying like mad. Mathematics of all things – Rolf was a computer nerd, you know, long before such a thing was even heard of."

"I knew it was a mistake to give you the floor." Rolf glared at Emmet. "They don't want our life stories, you old fool!"

"But it pertains –"

"You never got your law degree so quit talking like a lawyer and explain everything to these people, our family," Rolf insisted.

"I'm sorry. I've been waiting for this day for a very long time." Emmet sipped his tea. "The truth of the matter is that

Rolf and I have been partners for more than fifty years. We began to travel together because it was safer than staying in one place." Emmet tried not to think of the years he had spent feeling like a hunted animal, terrified of making a mistake and risking arrest. "Rolf and I had been together for years travelling like gypsies, afraid to stay anywhere for any length of time, when we received a letter from Rolf's youngest sister Ingrid."

"We were in France when the letter caught up with us. It had taken time to reach us as we were of 'no fixed abode'," Rolf said.

"Ingrid wrote that her husband Pieter died in a farm accident. She had been left with two young sons to rear," Emmet continued. "We had no idea how we could help but even then we were all right for money. Rolf has always had a knack for keeping us in funds. To cut a long story short, we travelled to Dresden to see Ingrid. The woman had a proposition to put to us that fairly knocked me off my feet." Emmet looked around the table. "She knew how much Rolf longed for a child – the lack of a family of his own was breaking his heart."

"Ingrid was one of the very few people I could talk to about my life with Emmet," said Rolf. "She was and is my good friend and sister."

"Ingrid suggested that she should have a child with me," said Emmet. "The baby would be my natural child and Rolf's niece or nephew. The baby would be born with pieces of both of us in its little body. That baby was you, Finn." He had to stop to blow his nose.

"You never told me." Finn stared at her father and Rolf. "Not once, all the times I said Uncle Rolf was not really my uncle but a friend of the family. How could you allow me to hurt him like that?"

"You didn't want to know, Finn. You never wanted to know."

"Right, you did it – that's why I look so much like Rolf." Ronan sighed. "He is my great-uncle by blood."

Emmet wanted to put his head on the table and bawl like a baby. So much pain and soul-searching reduced to a few simple words. He remembered the sick terror he'd felt at Ingrid's suggestion – the world of desperate longing in Rolf's eyes.

"Could I have some more tea?" he asked. "My throat feels like a desert." This was hard. He never spoke of that time. He refused to ever return to visit Ingrid or her farm from hell.

Emmet took the 'memory' box from the sideboard and set it in the middle of the table.

"Right," he said when everyone was in place. He pulled out a fistful of old photographs. "This is Ingrid." He was proud of himself for not adding a nasty comment about the woman. "Pass the pictures along."

Ronan stared at the image of the woman who was, in a very real sense, his grandmother.

"She looks a great deal like Rolf." Oisín looked at the photograph. "That must have helped."

"It did." Emmet wanted to get to know this grandson of his better. "Truer words were never spoken."

"Why have I never seen any of these before?" Finn stared at the woman who had given birth to her.

"Rolf and I put this 'memory box' together years ago, planning for the day you would ask us about your heritage. To our amazement you never bothered to ask."

"I had a da and Uncle Rolf was always a great mother." Finn touched Rolf's hand. "Perhaps if I had gone to school with other children instead of being home-schooled by you two it might have been different. Life with you two was all I knew."

"Then you ran away and married that twit while you were still wet behind the ears!" Emmet declared.

"Emmet, you are speaking of the boys' father." Rolf needed to stop Emmet expressing his slanderous opinion of Patrick Brennan.

"We're getting a bit off track here," said Oisín.

"You are correct, Oisín." Rolf agreed. "Tell them everything." he ordered Emmet.

"We stayed on the farm with Ingrid and her boys for eighteen months." Emmet had to do hard physical labour. Work he hated and had no skill or talent for. Then the nights – oh Lord – the nights. Emmet had almost fallen to his knees when Ingrid reported after two months of torture that they had been successful. He had gone to the bathroom and vomited what felt like his intestines away in a rush of incredible relief.

"We left that farm a showplace." Emmet smiled at Rolf. "His nibs over there worked like a dog while running around waiting on his sister hand and foot. I don't think there has been a pregnant woman in the world spoiled as Rolf spoiled his sister during her pregnancy." The entire experience had felt like a prison sentence to Emmet.

"In all the ways that counted Ingrid was carrying *my* baby." Rolf beat his fist against his chest. Ingrid gave him a gift beyond price. The child of the man he loved.

Emmet had been biting his tongue for years. They never mentioned the small fortune they had paid Ingrid for the use of her womb. He tried very hard not to even think about it because he was afraid his rash temper would get the better of him someday and he would say the unforgivable.

"If you think you look like Rolf, kid," Emmet said, "check out these two."

"Who are they?" Ronan stared wide-eyed at the photograph.

"Ingrid's two sons, Pieter and Dieter. They were in their twenties, your age, when that photograph was taken."

"Wow, bro," Oisín said. "Quite the family resemblance going on here – although they appear a lot shorter than you – unless that's the fault of the photo?"

"No, they get their height from their mother." Rolf passed the photograph to Finn. "You two take your height from Emmet and your father."

Finn stared at the two young men in the photograph.

Emmet continued to pass photographs.

"Why did you stay eighteen months in Dresden?" Oisín glanced at each photograph. After the first few the resemblance to his brother was less of a shock.

"I wanted Ingrid to breastfeed the baby for six months." Rolf shrugged. "I read this would give the infant the best start. I needed instruction in the care of a baby. Ingrid taught me a lot that was very useful when I had full responsibility for the little one."

"You were a wonderful parent." Emmet had wanted to run away from that farm and the woman who reigned over it as soon as the umbilical cord was cut.

"That's true. You were always the best of mothers." Finn stood slightly and kissed Rolf on his blushing cheek. "I never lacked for anything in my life with you two."

"So, we have uncles and I suppose cousins, in Dresden." Ronan continued to study the photographs. "Do they know about our mother?"

"Of course they do," Rolf said. "My sister didn't hide her pregnancy from them. Dieter was six years old at the time and Pieter was five. They understood slightly. Ingrid has never been one to hide her head in the sand. She explained everything to them."

"A woman of vision unlike the girl she gave birth to," Emmet murmured.

"So that explains the resemblance, bro. Are you happy now, content?" Oisín demanded of his brother.

"Do you have any up-to-date photographs?" Ronan was fascinated.

"Photographs!" Emmet exclaimed. "Are you serious? Please, the man has complete movies on his computer."

"I'd really like to see them," Ronan said.

"I would be delighted to share these things with you," Rolf said with a smile.

"Will we get to meet this branch of our family?" Ronan asked.

In his delight Rolf went into rhapsodies in German. He was delighted that Finn's children should be open to meeting his family.

Emmet sat back and listened to Rolf rave about his family. He wondered if he should start to translate or if the sheer joy on Rolf's face was explanation enough.

"You need to take a deep breath, Uncle Rolf," Oisín said in fluent German which had the effect of stopping Rolf in mid-sentence.

"*You speak my language!*" Rolf shouted.

"Our mother insisted. We spoke German at home on Wednesday and Saturday. French was the language we spoke on Monday and Tuesday. Gaelic on Sunday at our father's demand and English whenever we could." Ronan explained in his crisp, precise German.

"That's what we did with you." Emmet stared at Finn.

"It worked."

Chapter 22

"Prepare yourselves?" Finn said as her menfolk followed her into the first of the Bray houses.

This morning, after several days spent playing tourist in the Rathmines area, Emmet had insisted on loading everyone into his camper van and making the journey out to Bray.

Emmet stared in dismay after they entered the house. "Mother of God, daughter, you have your work cut out." The place was a tip. He would pull everything down.

"These old fireplaces are fabulous, Mum." Ronan was caressing one of the Victorian mantelpieces. "It looks as if this mantelpiece is original. Is it, do you know?"

Finn could only nod her head.

"It would be kind of cool to have a fire burning in every room," Oisín said.

"Only if you have servants to clean and light every one of them before you put your foot out of bed," Emmet quipped.

"This is *wonderbar*, Emmet!" Rolf was almost dancing on his heels. "I want to record all of this." He clapped his hands in delight. "It is our duty to record the history of these houses before we change them forever. I will go get my camera. Do not move from this spot." Rolf hurried from the house.

"You've done it now, daughter. That man won't let you

move a muscle until he has recorded everything in these houses for posterity." Emmet sighed, knowing Rolf would not move from here until he had enough film to smother a mountain. Thank God for digital cameras and computers.

Emmet had been so grateful when the first digital camera had come on the market that he'd bought shares in the company. After years of searching for 'dark rooms' that Rolf could use to develop his film the digital camera had seemed a gift from the gods.

"It's a good idea, Da. These old houses are amazing." Finn had grown up with Rolf's camera following her every movement. She'd reason to be grateful for Rolf's obsession with recording everything. She had continued the habit. Thanks to Rolf, she had a picture history of her married life to back up her claims for the law court should it become necessary.

"Don't you start – I have to listen to that kind of bullshit from Rolf. I'm not taking it from my own flesh and blood."

"I am back. I am here." Rolf hurried inside. He had a camera bag around his neck and was fiddling with his expensive digital recorder. "Finn, lead the way, show me everything!"

"The houses are stuck in a time warp." Finn was able to ignore Rolf and his muttering as she led the men from room to room.

"This old range belongs in a museum." Emmet ran his hands along the cold blackened stove in the bare kitchen. "I remember my grandmother on her knees once a week polishing one of these monsters. It was a matter of pride to have the blackest one. A woman was judged by how black her range and how red her front doorstep was." Unlike his father, his mother had not come from money.

"We should bulldoze the whole place down. Start fresh." Emmet loved to put the cat among the pigeons. He waited for the cries of outrage.

"Emmet, you are without heart – how could you think of such a thing?" Rolf hit Emmet with his camera bag.

Emmet laughed while fighting off Rolf's attack.

Ronan and Oisín watched two men they considered ancient

act like children. They were waiting for their mum to say she'd bang their heads together – then they would know they'd fallen down the rabbit hole.

"The outdoor loo is down this path." Finn led the way out the back door, not checking to see if anyone followed her. There was a great deal to show them and decisions needed to be made.

"Everyone in these places must have been constipated. Imagine having to haul your arse down here in the freezing cold every time you wanted to shit?"

"Emmet, there are young people present!" Rolf barked.

"Good to know where you get your loose tongue from, bro." Ronan nudged Oisín.

"I suppose they had their po in the house." Emmet stared into the cold loo.

"What's a po?" Oisín asked.

"One of those porcelain things that everyone kept under the bed for use at night." Emmet shuddered. "I still have nightmares about those things."

"That's gross." Oisín was enjoying being part of this strange group.

"I'm surprised that they are not still using newspaper cut into squares and tied on a piece of string," said Emmet.

"*What?*" said Oisín and Ronan.

"Didn't you know?" Emmet shrugged, still checking out the outhouses. "That's what people used before commercial toilet paper. Old newspapers." He laughed at the look of complete horror that came over his grandsons' faces. He was discovering it was a lot of fun having these boys to tease.

Finn ignored the conversation. "I don't know if I have to seek the permission of the railroad before removing the dividing wall. The dividing walls between these houses hardly support that monster." She threw her hand in the direction of the wall towering over them. "It's something that needs to be checked out."

"There is a lot more to this work than I thought." Ronan bent his head as far back as he could. He could hear a train but he couldn't see it.

Pulling the door of the first house she'd shown them closed

behind her group, Finn stepped out onto Railway Parade. She turned her head at Rolf's command, hardly noticing the camera. All through her childhood Rolf had always had a camera in hand.

"The biggest drawback with these houses is the lack of natural light," she said.

"We noticed," the others agreed.

"I've been in touch with a firm in Germany about the problem." She walked towards the second house.

"*Yoo-hoo, missus!*"

They all swung around.

A woman was beckoning to them. "*You might want to join us. We're having elevenses and a meeting!*" she called out. "*We're going to talk about the Parade!*"

Finn and others stared in surprise.

A crowd of women were seated around a table placed in the middle of the Parade. A few men stood off to the side, holding mugs of tea in their hands and watching the action.

Nellie McGinn had organised her neighbours into a team. The men had pulled the heavy table and loads of chairs out. The women had supplied sandwiches, pies and cakes. A teapot the size of a child held pride of place. A veritable feast had been laid on.

"*Larry Jameson called this meeting!*" Nellie loudly announced to the gathering, beaming.

Larry Jameson, a childhood friend of Nellie's eldest son, blushed. He hadn't expected a crowd when he'd promised to talk about his idea.

"It's like this, folks," he said. "I'm talking to Mr. Kelly about buying his house."

Everyone shouted an opinion, none of which could be clearly heard.

"I've noticed this lane is a prime spot for vandalism. I'm not willing to put up with that."

Larry was shouted down as every person there told of an incident of vandalism against them personally.

"*I've talked to your local councillor!*" Larry shouted, quelling the noise. "You should have told him what was going on here."

"*We did!*" Liam Carr shouted. "It didn't do us a blind bit of good. What do they care that some yahoo is shoving his private parts in our letterboxes and pissing like a racehorse?"

"*Liam, there are ladies present!*" someone shouted.

No one disputed Liam's words. A new trick was rags and matches. It made a body afraid to fall asleep.

"*I've heard the stories!*" Larry shouted to stop the flow of horrors being listed. "*Your councilman is coming to talk to all of you! I want you to tell him what you've told me.*" They were all listening now so he lowered his voice. "We might be able to get a grant to put gates up at either end of the Parade. Turn this into a private walkway."

"I've never got something for nothing from the government in my life," Liam Carr grumbled.

"Just tell the man what's been going on here for years. He can't know unless you tell him." Larry Jameson wanted to protect his investment. He would not buy the property without securing a promise of gates to keep out the drunks. It was constant abuse – drunks performed disgusting acts that turned the lives of the people living on the Parade into a nightmare.

Finn stood back and watched the speaker being skilfully interrogated. Nellie and her cronies drew every bit of information they could manage out of Larry. Rolf was having a ball recording the occasion. Her sons were being petted and stuffed with homemade goodies. The women were flirting madly with the two older gentlemen. Everyone, except Larry Jameson, was having a great time.

"Have another cup of tea." Nellie held the heavy teapot over Emmet's mug and beamed. He was such a handsome man and unmarried, he said.

"I think my daughter has more to show us." Emmet gulped the hot tea. He gave the crowd of old biddies staring at him a regretful smile. He needed to get away before they had the shirt off his back.

"Mother of God, daughter, those women could give lessons to the Spanish Inquisition." Emmet had his back pressed to the tightly locked door of the second house they had come to see. "The men were almost afraid to open their mouths. Probably terrified of saying something they shouldn't."

"It's nice to see neighbours looking out for each other." Finn kicked rubble out from underfoot. "This house is almost an exact copy of the first one. You have seen the state they are in. So tell me – do you want me to update them for resale?"

"No, that was never the plan." Rolf put his camera away.

"I think we should knock these old horrors down," Emmet said.

"You two need to make a decision." Finn said. "What did you have in mind when you bought these houses?

"A good investment." Rolf looked around at the little gems of history.

Finn shoved her hands through her hair. "What do you want from these buildings?"

"You're asking us to make snap decisions?" Rolf wanted to enjoy these old buildings before Finn pulled them apart.

"You two have owned these buildings for over forty years – there is nothing quick about this."

"I want to film these monuments to a bygone era. I will never have a chance like this again." Rolf smiled. "I will employ my two nephews to assist me in this endeavour. Can you allow me this time?"

"You're the boss." Finn should have known that Rolf would not be able to resist recording a vanishing way of life.

"Old Sobersides there is right." Emmet rubbed his hands together. "We don't have to decide everything in one sitting."

"I will spend a lot of time here getting the pictures I want," said Rolf. "I have new equipment I want to play with. These old buildings give me such possibilities. The boys will be my helpers and my stars. The buildings will not be abandoned." Rolf was already planning the mini-movie he would make here. His brother Dolph would love to see these buildings as they were now before they disappeared forever under a facelift of modernisation. Rolf couldn't wait to get started.

"Let's go now –I need to pick up something to cook." Emmet wanted out of these dark rooms – they depressed him.

"I'm thinking of renting a car." Emmet wiped his mouth with his linen napkin. "These three want to make a 'major motion picture' of the houses in Bray." He pointed around the table. "Rolf has corrupted them. I have no interest in making movies so I thought I'd have a drive down Memory Lane on my own."

"Great idea, Dad," said Finn.

Back home, it had been party time all the way as the four males laughed and joked in the kitchen while Finn was relegated to the living room, wishing she could escape to her workshop.

"By the way, I talked to my old mate Harry Bailey," said Emmet. "He'll check out that female lawyer you mentioned. I gave him her name."

"That's nice of Harry." Finn needed to begin the process of legal separation. She seemed to be the only one feeling any pain. Her sons didn't seem to be thinking of their parents' marriage break-up at all.

"I'm sure Harry will be glad to help you."

"Thanks." Finn dreaded the process to come.

"It would help to make a list of everything you want to cover before you visit with the lawyer, sweetling." Rolf gave Finn one of his sweetest smiles. He knew how she hated to be rushed or pushed.

"Are you the one we have to thank for all the lists Mum makes?" Oisín pointed his fork at Rolf in accusation. "Those bloomin' lists were the bane of our childhood."

"Oh, the horror of those endless lists!" Emmet roared with laughter. "What I've suffered over the years."

Ronan shuddered. "Every time we turned around Mum had a new and updated list of something or other."

"It's all his fault." Emmet pointed at Rolf. "The man's a menace."

"*Ja*, everything is my fault," Rolf agreed good-naturedly.

Finn sat and watched her family laugh and joke with each other. It did her heart good to see how much her sons were enjoying this time with their grandparents. They might not be the ideal nuclear family but there was a lot of love and laughter at this table. The pain of loss was being assuaged slightly by the introduction of these two exotic men into her boys' lives.

"Right – you guys can clean up after yourselves. I'm going to bed." Finn got to her feet. She was an early bird, she always had been. Right now she got the impression that the men in her life were waiting for her to 'flake out' so they could really get the conversational ball rolling. She decided to give them a break.

Chapter 23

Finn sat in her silent kitchen, her heart hurting. Her boys and the da's were up and gone. Her sons had refused to continue with their studies. What could she do? She couldn't force them but she wasn't happy with the situation. Patrick had been no help. He refused to become involved. She didn't know why she was surprised.

The days were closing in but the darkness suited her mood. She was alone and feeling useless. Her father had bought a luxury car, having decided the loss when he resold it would be less than the price and bother of a long-term rental. The men in her life were up and out every morning with plans that didn't include her. Her father had taken over her kitchen. He ruled her boys with a firm hand. They jumped to obey his every command. She felt like a child again waiting for life to happen to her.

The ringing of the phone interrupted her pity party.

"Nuala, Nuala, are you there?"

"What do you want, Patrick?"

"I'm calling to remind you of your appointment with the psychologist," Patrick snapped. "The woman was kind enough to cut out a slice of time for you today. It's a compliment to me that she's willing to meet with you. You don't want to be late –

it wouldn't reflect well on me. I'm preparing to go on air. Try and get yourself organised and for God's sake dress properly!"

"I can't make the appointment. Sorry." Finn refused to allow her temper to escape. Patrick could be taping the call. The man was underhand enough. She laid the phone very gently in its cradle.

She felt as if she were running in place. She wanted to get started on the homes in Bray but Rolf and the boys were knee-deep in something or other there. She'd been in email conversation again with the German building firm who specialised in innovative lighting ideas. They had been more helpful than she could ever have imagined. Nothing seemed to be too much trouble for them – and all without her being a client. She was impressed.

She stood up with a tired sigh. She'd spend the day in her workroom beating her frustration out – again.

Days later Finn sat, not really listening, to the chatter going on around her. She was feeling proud of herself. She managed to wave goodbye to her menfolk every morning with a smile on her face. She spent the days working on her nutjobs. She was trying a new process.

"You have things to tell Finn, Emmet." Rolf sat back and watched the two young men clear the dining-room table after breakfast.

"Finn, Finn!" Emmet knew that look. The girl was off in a world of her own.

"Sorry, I was miles away."

"I've asked Harry Bailey to come here this morning. He and I are having a great time catching up on all the news that's fit to print. I thought if he came here that would be better for you. All the paperwork you've gathered is here. You can show Harry everything you have and he can advise you on which pieces are the most important."

"That's fine," Finn said.

"You've gathered a mountain of information together, Finn. I've no clue what you'll need. There's more to winning an argument then being in the right."

There was an uncomfortable silence while the two men exchanged glares.

"There's something else?" Finn knew her fathers. They were hiding something.

Emmet looked at Rolf to see if he wanted to take it from here. At his partner's glare he shrugged and said, "That company you've contacted in Germany – the one Rolf suggested?"

"What about it?"

"It's run by Ingrid's son Pieter, your half-brother, and a few more of your German blood kin."

"Shit! So that's why they've been so helpful!"

"He would like to meet you." Rolf held his breath, waiting for her reaction.

While Finn was still reeling from the shock, her sons decided now was the time to tell her what they had planned.

Oisín and Ronan stood in the open door.

"Mum, we have something to tell you."

"You men decided to give me all my blows at once." Once more she was the lone female outside the gentlemen's club.

Ronan took the lead. "When Granddad and Uncle Rolf leave we're going with them."

"I want to travel." Oisín was excited about the possibilities. "Granddad is going to show me the ropes while Rolf and Ronan visit the German relations."

"Well, isn't it well for you all!" Finn was trying not to let her bitterness show. "Have you discussed any of this with your father?"

"We haven't told him anything," Ronan assured her. "We haven't seen him in a while." He was sick of his father calling and blaming every wrong in his life on their mother.

"Well, gentlemen, you've certainly given me a great deal to think about." Finn was at a loss for words. She glared at Emmet, green eyes locking with green eyes.

The ringing of the doorbell shattered the uneasy atmosphere in the room.

"That'll be Harry." Emmet jumped to his feet with relief. Saved by the bell!

"*Come in, Harry, save me!*" he roared dramatically when he flung open the door.

"You always were an old ham." Judge Harry Bailey walked into the house.

Emmet led him into the dining rom.

"Let me make the introductions," he said, "before everyone rushes off." He knew the lads and Rolf had things to do, places to be.

There was a round of introductions and polite conversation before leavetaking.

"I hear you have need of advice from this old man," Harry said when only he and Finn remained. Emmet was in the kitchen rattling dishes. Harry hadn't seen Finn Emerson since she was a tiny infant. She'd grown into a beautiful woman.

"Before we start picking your brain . . ." Finn smiled at the distinguished, charming older man. It wasn't his fault her father had blindsided her with his sudden appearance. "How do you want to be addressed? Judge, sir, Your Honour, Mr. Bailey or simply Harry?"

"Let's keep it simple. I'm Harry." His brown eyes were sparkling with good humour.

There was also a spark in the judge's eyes that told her he thought she was an attractive woman.

"Well, Harry, can I get you anything before we become buried in dusty papers?" Finn was nervous.

"Tea would be welcome." Harry Bailey liked surprises and having Emmet pop up out of the blue had done him a power of good. He hoped he'd be able to help his old friend's daughter.

In the next few hours Harry drank an ocean of tea and nibbled on the snacks Emmet supplied. He sat at the dining-room table, carefully studying all of the papers Finn presented to him.

Finn pointed to the papers she'd presented that showed her careful working within budget through the years. She'd been proud of keeping the family debt-free.

"You've amassed a mountain of paper and that can only be a good thing." Harry sat back and stared at the woman before him. He'd handled all the legal documents concerning her unusual birth. It was quite a surprise to see how she'd turned out.

"I have a feeling I need to protect myself," she said.

"Yes, you do." Harry agreed. "The law of the land is still not very clear when it comes to legal separation, I'm ashamed to say."

"So I've discovered from talking to other women."

"What I suggest ..." Harry pulled his bottom lip away from his mouth as he thought the situation through, "is this. You make an appointment with Orla Mountjoy. That young lady is well known in the lower courts and has the reputation of being something of a shark. I can act as an advisor if you like but this is not my area of expertise."

"That's very generous of you, Harry." Emmet had come in on the end of that offer.

"I'm hoping I get a meal out of it at least." Harry Bailey stood and stretched. "The smells coming out of that kitchen have been killing me for hours."

"I was coming in to shift you two along so I could get this table laid but I was afraid to interrupt you – really afraid!" Emmet said with a grin.

"I'll take this stuff away." Finn began to gather up her papers.

When she left to go to her office Emmet leaned towards Harry and whispered, "What are her chances of getting a legal separation?" He'd had to stop himself from eavesdropping, to hear what was going on in here.

"Her paperwork is very impressive." Harry felt a sinking feeling in his stomach as he met Emmet's eyes. He realised his friend's daughter might well be facing a legal nightmare. "I liked her graph showing earnings she should have received. It'll never stand up in a court of law but it will make people think."

"Finn's always had a head for figures. She gets that from Rolf's side of the family." Emmet didn't like the look on his friend's face. "They have this house wired up like something out of the future." He didn't want Finn to be able to listen to their conversation and he had no clue how all the gadgets in this house worked. "Why don't we have a cigar outside on the patio?"

"Right," Emmet puffed on a fat Cuban cigar. "Now tell me what has you looking like a man with an ulcer."

"Jesus, Emmet," Harry looked around him, "how many years has it been since I've visited this house?"

"What has that got to do with anything?"

"Everything." Harry shook his cigar in Emmet's face. "This place was falling apart the last time I saw it – now it's a bloody show home. Do you have any idea of its worth in today's market?"

"Millions if I wanted to sell it."

"Only you could shrug away millions, Emmet." Harry closed his eyes in horror. "I can bloody guarantee that Mr Patrick Brennan will not be so casual about money. You should have warned me."

"About what?" Emmet threw his hands up in the air.

"This is a nightmare. I'm going to have to consult people," Harry waved his cigar in the air, "and I'm going to bloody charge you for their fees."

"OK."

"This isn't my area of expertise. Legal separations for the most part go through family court – the lower courts – I have nothing to do with them. But, because of the value of this property the lawyers are going to wet themselves, seeing fat fees in their future. Your girl could be in serious trouble if we don't handle this right."

"This house and I suppose everything in it belongs to me – not my daughter." Emmet really couldn't see the problem. "To all intents and purposes my girl is penniless."

"I'm afraid the courts may not agree with you." Harry sighed. "We have to document everything. Finn has gathered enough paperwork to choke a horse but we need more. We need details, facts, figures."

"You need to talk to Rolf." Emmet was beginning to worry. "He's the man when it comes to finances."

"We will have to put our heads together."

"Finn, is there any way we can talk this old reprobate into returning to Ireland?" Harry Bailey asked as they sat drinking coffee after a very fine meal.

"It's impossible to talk the man into anything. You should know that."

"I'm going to try." Harry sighed. "I've missed the old goat."

"That old goat is sitting right here!" Emmet snapped.

"I really do want you to think about coming back to Ireland to live," Harry said.

"I'm not ready to settle down yet," Emmet growled.

"For God's sake, man, none of us is getting any younger. You've been travelling for fifty years – how much more of the world do you need to see?"

"I like my life."

"I'm not saying you don't but surely you could give some thought to moving back home."

"You'd want me to learn to play golf," Emmet moaned. "That's for old folks."

"I've news for you, Emmet – we are old."

"I am not," Emmet insisted.

"Stay around a while. Give your daughter some support. She's going to need it."

"I promised Oisín I'd take him around Europe in the camper," Emmet snapped.

Finn stood and began clearing the dishes. She couldn't add anything to this argument. She'd love her father to stay longer but she refused to hold anyone back from following their dreams.

"Gentlemen, I think you would be more comfortable in the lounge." She wanted to clear the table and tidy the room. "Emmet knows where I keep the booze. Why don't you go in there and talk in comfort?" Finn didn't feel guilty deserting her guest. These old friends didn't need her sitting in on their conversation.

Chapter 24

"I'm sorry – it's completely unprofessional I know, but I am so excited." Orla Mountjoy couldn't conceal her glee. They were in the lobby of the building on Merrion Square that housed the law office of Bailey, Shuster, and Byrne.

Finn had met with the dark-haired, frighteningly efficient lawyer several times to discuss this meeting. She'd never seen the other woman so energetic. You would think she was going to a pop concert to see her favourite star.

"I cannot believe Judge Bailey is going to sit in on this meeting. The man's a legend in the legal profession. I've never had the honour of coming before him in court. To have him sit in on one of my meetings is blowing my mind." Orla Mountjoy was practically bouncing in her black court shoes.

Harry had offered the use of his office for this first meeting between Finn and Patrick Brennan and their lawyers.

Finn had been impressed with Orla Mountjoy from their first meeting with the lawyer. Orla, after careful questioning, had reduced Finn's mountain of paperwork to five pages of notes. She'd practically stripped Finn's brain of information before agreeing to this meeting with Patrick and his lawyer.

Orla led Finn up the richly carpeted stairs towards the top floor of the building. They could have taken the lift, but they were early. Besides, Orla said, she wanted to take in every feature of this enclave of the top tier of the legal profession. One day she would be a judge. She'd need to know how she wanted to set up her rooms. This was a big moment for her.

Finn listened to her lawyer gush. Maggie had been accurate in her judgement of lawyers. Orla Mountjoy was enjoying the chance to show off in front of her peers. Patrick's lawyer happened to be an old classmate of hers. Finn had no cause for complaint yet, but the feeling of being on the sidelines of her own life was not pleasant.

They reached Harry's office and entered. His secretary announced their presence to the Judge through the intercom.

The door to the inner office was flung open.

"Ah! Come on in!" Harry ushered them inside.

"Harry, thanks for letting us have this meeting here." Finn knew she was being a bitch referring to the judge as Harry, but she wanted every advantage she could get.

She introduced the suddenly solemnly professional Orla Mountjoy to the judge who offered coffee while they waited.

But before they could accept, a disembodied voice spoke from the intercom on Harry's desk: "*Mr. Brennan and Mr. Coyle have arrived, Judge.*"

"Send them in."

Harry walked over to stand behind Finn as she and Orla turned to face the door. He pressed her shoulder, apparently in sympathy, but the force of his grip helped Finn fight back the nerves. She had to hold it together.

The door opened and Patrick Brennan and his lawyer entered.

"Nuala, this is ridiculous." Patrick Brennan, beautifully groomed as always, spread his arms around to encompass everyone in the room. "I'm afraid my wife is having a very difficult time right now. Perhaps you listen to my daily radio programme?" No one made any response to this piece of self-advertisement. "I've been interviewing experts on the distressing subject of the menopause, hoping to find someone who could help my wife deal with her delusions."

Finn opened her mouth to blast the man but the force of the

Judge's hand on her shoulder shut her up. She was paying Ms. Mountjoy to be her mouthpiece, better let her do the talking.

"Gentlemen, you're welcome," said Harry in an effort to establish civilities. "Come and sit down." He led the way to a grouping of comfortable chairs set around a circular table.

They all sat.

"I am here as an impartial observer of these proceedings," Harry said then. "I hope you are all clear on that?" He wanted to hear right from the horse's mouth what Patrick and his lawyer had planned. This could get ugly.

Patrick was suddenly on his feet again and addressing the room. "My wife is falling apart. Look at her, for goodness' sake. She looks terrible. She needs medical attention."

"Mr. Coyle, you need to ask your client to sit down," Orla Mountjoy practically whispered.

"Patrick, take a seat." Declan Coyle had given Patrick advice on how to behave in this meeting. He'd warned the man against trying to play the room.

Patrick sat and leaned forward, appearing distraught. "We have had a long and happy marriage – two wonderful sons – it is breaking my heart that it has come to this – my wife needs help." His beautiful voice quivered – tears appeared in his lake-blue eyes.

"We are meeting today to set up the ground rules for a legal separation." Orla Mountjoy smiled in Patrick Brennan's direction. The man was a fool and a liar. Declan Coyle would be worried if he knew the facts.

"I will never agree. I take my marriage vows seriously." Patrick jumped to his feet. His lawyer yanked him back down.

Finn waited for lightning to strike him at that blatant lie. Nothing happened. He continued to deliver what was obviously a prepared outpouring.

"Nuala, darling, I know you've been difficult to live with lately, but I'm sure we can work through this difficult time in your life – together." Patrick was using his voice to express deep emotion. "You are not the first woman to lose her sanity because of the menopause and tragically you won't be the last."

"My client prefers to keep your transgressions private, Mr. Brennan. However, if you insist in this behaviour I will be forced to list my client's grievances against you." Orla Mountjoy would enjoy nothing more than wiping the floor with the smug grandstander.

"I'm unaware of any transgressions," Declan Coyle said, wanting to drag Patrick Brennan out of this office and beat the truth out of the man. Orla Mountjoy was behaving like a cat that swallowed the canary. He did not appreciate being made to look a fool in front of Judge Harry Bailey.

"Mr. Brennan turned the family home into an unhealthy environment for his growing sons." Orla had decided to use that little stinger as her opening shot. She had plenty.

"Nuala, how can you sit listening to these lies? I love my sons, you know that," Patrick objected. "You'll have to forgive my wife – she's been under a great deal of strain lately. I made an appointment for her with a renowned psychologist which she refused to attend. I'm frankly at the end of my tether trying to guide her through this difficult time in her life."

"I am not aware that my client created an 'unhealthy environment', Ms. Mountjoy," Declan Coyle said, "whatever you may mean by that."

"Well, let me tell you ..."

Finn sat back while the lawyers indulged themselves in extensive argument, using her private life like a rubber ball. She was mortified by the private matters being discussed openly in this office. Ms. Mountjoy and Mr. Coyle were like children showing off in front of a teacher. It did not impress Finn but even so she knew her lawyer was winning.

"Nuala, say something for God's sake!" Patrick exploded. "I can't believe you can allow these people to slander me like this. You love me, you always have."

Finn was numb. She'd gone to a great deal of effort to appear cool and sophisticated for this meeting. Now she wanted to beat her breast and pull her hair out. These people had discussed things openly here she wouldn't discuss with a priest.

"Nuala!" Patrick's voice was at its most beseeching.

"My name is Finn." Finn dragged herself back, becoming aware Patrick was standing over her.

"I don't want this, any of it." Patrick was finally beginning to realise that he couldn't charm himself back into her good graces. "We've been married for twenty years. Don't throw our happy marriage away in a moment of anger."

Finn looked around, wondering how the others were reacting to this. All three lawyers were in a huddle. Finn didn't get the impression the talk was related to her case. The two younger lawyers were sucking up to the judge. Nothing that had taken place in this room affected them. She was a miserable wreck.

"Our marriage lasted twenty-one years, Patrick, but only because I was willing to turn a blind eye to all your shit." Finn smiled sadly. "Guess what? I'm not doing that anymore. It's over, Patrick, let's end the thing with dignity."

"Patrick." Declan Coyle approached Patrick. "We should go now."

"Go? What do you mean 'go'? I'm not giving up fighting for my marriage!"

The lawyer tried to lead his client from the room. There was a brief struggle but shortly both men left the room, arguing in low voices.

"Finn, my dear, are you alright?" Harry Bailey pulled Finn from the chair into his arms as soon as the door closed behind her husband and his lawyer. He was sure that wasn't the last they would hear from the man. There was a great deal of money involved in this case – he'd been surprised that matter wasn't raised here today. But it would be. Of that he was certain. Patrick Brennan was a fool. He'd had a good life he'd thrown away. Finn was an attractive woman – if she had not also been the daughter of a good friend, he'd try his chances with her. After all they did say 'the older the fiddle the sweeter the tune' – he wasn't past it yet.

Orla Mountjoy's eyebrows were in her hair. Finn Emmerson was obviously held in great esteem by the Judge. She'd have to make sure the woman's case was handled only by herself. She wouldn't pass this one along to her assistants.

Finn walked around Dublin in a daze. She'd refused lunch with the Judge, wanting to be alone. She felt bruised by the meeting with Patrick and the lawyers. It was an effort to put one foot in front of the other. She felt as if she walked along enclosed in a plastic bubble that rendered her invisible to all who passed her. Was that really the beginning of the end of her marriage? Shouldn't there be a great deal more fanfare than this?

"God, Angie, it was a nightmare. I still can't believe it happened." Finn shivered, clutching a mug of whiskey-laced tea while she sobbed. "You would not believe how clueless Patrick appeared. The man really thought if he gave me enough time I'd change my mind."

"Don't keep doing this to yourself, Finn." Angie was sitting on the ground holding Finn's hands. She had rushed over to Finn's house, knowing the meeting would have been difficult. Maggie Spenser had warned her. Maggie wanted to be here herself but her twins made that kind of gesture on her part impossible, so she'd asked Angie to be available for Finn.

"Where is everyone?" Angie thought Finn's family would be here with her.

"They're shooting in Bray." Finn hadn't wanted her family here. They were men and at this moment in time men were not her favourite people. "I asked my da and Rolf to keep the boys busy." She fought her tears. She had to get control of herself.

Angie sat back and stared at Finn. She had no advice to hand out in this situation. When her husband left her she'd buried the pain and carried on. Of course, she had no money and no property which simplified things.

"Want me to make another pot of tea?" Angie was gagging for a cup of tea. They had talked and cried themselves dry.

"Great idea, Angie, a straight cup of tea sounds like heaven right now. I left some sandwich makings and dip in the fridge. With any luck there is still something left. I would swear I had kitchen gremlins except I know that the men in my life are like a shower of locusts where that fridge is concerned. Thankfully my da is having a blast discovering favourite foods from his youth. He cooks up a storm almost every day and that is keeping us all going at the moment."

"Some people have all the luck. I can't imagine the wonder

of having a man around the house who can cook. I'll root around in the fridge and cupboards. I'll put something together for us to eat. I'm starving." Angie pushed up from her position on the floor.

"I knew there was a good reason I kept you around. Thanks for reminding me." Finn laughed as she watched Angie hurry towards the kitchen. She squared her shoulders, unconsciously heaving a sigh that seemed to come from her toes. She had to put this behind her and get on with her life.

Chapter 25

"Ronan, clear the table – Oisín, serve fresh tea and coffee."

Finn sat at the head of the table in her dining room, staring around at her men. The table was covered in the remains of the breakfast Emmet had prepared and served. In the two weeks since her meeting with the lawyers, this was the first time she'd had a chance for a serious conversation with her menfolk. She'd taken time to nurse her wounds but now it was time to act.

"I want to talk to you all."

"We need to get going," Emmet objected.

"I need to talk to all of you," Finn insisted. "I had thought to ask Rolf to take my sons out of the firing line while I pinned your ears to the ground, Da, but I changed my mind. They can hear what I have to say." She stood up and moved away from the table. "I need a pad and pencil." Making notes on an electric notebook just wasn't the same. She opened a drawer in the sideboard and removed what she needed.

She swung around at a noise behind her.

Emmet was on his feet.

"I'm serious, Da." She strode over and, putting her hand on his shoulder, she pushed him back into his seat. "I'll have the boys sit on you if I have to, but by God you are going to talk to me."

"I was going to give the lads a hand clearing the table," Emmet objected.

"My eye." Finn had the bit firmly between her teeth.

"No, seriously. Let's clear first. Then we can give you our full attention"

"Very well. Go ahead. I'm waiting."

The table was cleared – the dishwasher in the kitchen was turning – they had all settled down around the table – coffee and tea had been served.

"OK, missus," Emmet sulked. "We're all here – what's this about?"

"First item on the agenda – this house."

"We've a bloody agenda now," Emmet muttered.

"Emmet!" Rolf tapped his partner's knuckles with his teaspoon.

"You need to decide what you are going to do with this house, Da." Finn glared at her sulking parent. "I cannot afford to run it. The taxes are killing. You lot," she waved around the table, "are having a rare old time, making plans but no-one has thought to ask me what I'm going to be doing. You all seem to expect me to sit here like Penelope and wait for my men to come home. Well, guess what – *yez can all go fuck yerselves!*" She hadn't realised how angry and hurt she was by their total disregard for her thoughts and feelings.

"What is it you want to know?" Emmet finally broke the uncomfortable silence that had fallen.

"This house is yours, Da. I've spent the last twenty-one years of my life being married to the bloody thing." She held up her hands to stop the objections she saw coming. "I was happy to take care of the changes that needed to be made. I loved raising my children in this house – but times have changed. I'm not willing to be a house servant anymore. I have no money to put into this estate. A decision has to be made and you are the only one who can do it, Da."

"Do you want me to sell the place?" Emmet had been astonished by the changes in the house. Patrick Brennan had not welcomed his company so to keep the peace for his daughter he had stayed away. He'd seen photographs through the years but nothing had prepared him for the changes his daughter had made to the family home. It was a little palace and worth a fortune. "I could sell the place and give you your inheritance now."

"If my opinion matters," Ronan raised his hand like a child, "I love this place. I don't want to lose it. I'd hate to see it go out of the family. I'm proud to live in a house that has been in my family for generations."

"To add to what my bro said," Oisín couldn't stay silent, "I love this place as well. We had a great childhood here – the house is full of love and happy memories for me. Yeah, I want to travel but only knowing I have a home to come back to."

"That's lovely, lads," Finn clenched her teeth on the words she really wanted to say. "Would yez care to discuss how such a thing might be achieved? I am deadly serious when I say I will no longer spend every morning of my life cleaning up this house – that makes no mention of the work in the garden. The house eats my time and a great deal of money. I'm no longer willing to give my time and I have no money." She sat back, almost panting at the effort it took not to scream at them. "Talk among yourselves."

"Mum," Oisín sat forward, "do you have any idea how much we earn from our work at the studios?"

"No. You have never discussed it with me." She knew Patrick had stopped giving the boys pocket money but had no idea how much they earned. They were mostly in teenage angst programs which held no interest for her. She was proud to know they were doing something they enjoyed, but sitting watching rubbish in case her sons' faces might pop up on screen was not her idea of a good way to pass time.

Oisín and Ronan exchanged glances.

"It works out at about five thousand pounds a week," Ronan said after thinking about it for a minute. "Each."

"That's obscene!" Finn gasped.

"That's why we don't want to continue with our education," Oisín leaned forward to say. "There doesn't seem to be any point to it – after all, who knows how long this gravy train will last for?" He was very much aware they could be out of a job tomorrow.

"What in the name of God do you do for that kind of money?" Finn stared at her sons as if she'd never seen them before. It was monopoly money they were talking surely.

"I've been investing the money for us." Ronan said. "We are heavily into computers and their future." Surely his mother had seen news articles about the number of young millionaires sprouting up all around the world. The dot.com millionaires they were calling them.

"You can be very proud of your children," Rolf said. "You have raised two fine young men. But you also need to watch them on television, sweetling." He held up his hands at the glare she sent him. "I know, I know, this is not the time. We must stay with your agenda – the house – that is what we must discuss."

"Thank you, Da-ma. So, if I'm understanding correctly, I am the only penniless one at this table." Finn didn't think she could take many more shocks.

"We wouldn't see you go short, Mum," Ronan and Oisín said almost as one.

"Good of you boys to look after your old mother." Finn didn't know whether to laugh or cry but she couldn't be dealing with that now. She was determined to get some kind of decision about the house from her father. "Da, would you never think of moving back to Ireland and living in this house? I'm sorry but you and Rolf are not getting any younger. I worry about you both. This house would be ideal for the kind of lifestyle you both enjoy. You just wouldn't have wheels on your heels anymore."

"Before you answer, Emmet ..." Rolf sat forward and covered one of Emmet's hands with his own. He could speak freely here – they were all his family. "I would like to have a home. I have enjoyed living in this house very much. I would love to have somewhere to invite my extended family. I believe it is time we settle down and enjoy what we have together. The years are passing too quickly."

"Look what you started now, daughter!" Emmet looked at Rolf, his heart softening at the appeal in his blue eyes.

"Will you think about it, Da?" Finn knew her two da's

would have to discuss it in great detail – but she'd put the matter on the table – it was up to them now.

"We have much to discuss, sweetling." Rolf felt his heart catch at the thought of finally having somewhere to call home. "If you wanted to speak your dreams aloud – as we have been doing at great length – what would they be?"

"I'd like you and Da to live in this house," Finn had dreamed many dreams when she couldn't sleep at night. "I don't want the housework involved in running a house this large – it's more like a bloody hotel – if I'm dreaming then I'd like to own one of the German module homes I've admired so much on the television – I'd live in that at the bottom of the garden and be able to keep an eye on my two da's. My sons would have a home to visit their grandparents." She threw her hands out. "You did ask!"

"None of this can be decided in minutes, daughter," Emmet said.

"I know that, but I've been listening to you lot discussing your plans – more power to you – but none of you have thought of what needs to be done around here before you all run away from home."

"What needs doing, Mum?" Oisín asked.

"Before you lot sail off into the wild blue yonder, I want to put the gates back up." She had removed the tall iron gates from the entryway some time ago. They were in her workshop. She'd mended the gates and painted them. If she was going to be living here alone, she wanted those gates back in place. "The gates are in my workshop. You two can get them and hang them for me. I don't have the muscles needed." She held up her arms jokingly.

"We'll have to get a few of our friends to help us. Those gates are heavy." Ronan thought about who he could ask to help. "Come on, bro, we can get started on that now."

Emmet watched his grandsons hurry from the room, wishing he could go with them. "There must be money in the house maintenance account."

"The total was very healthy last time I checked," Rolf said.

"What are you two talking about?" Finn asked.

"The rent Patrick paid on this place over the years has been lodged in a special account. That money has paid for the repairs and updates you made, Finn," Emmet said. "We never touch the money – it covers any costs you might meet in the maintenance of this house – did you know that?"

"No." Finn stared at him.

"I did not tell you, sweetling," Rolf said. "I did not want Patrick to know he was contributing to the upkeep of the house." He'd been surprised the marriage had lasted as long as it had.

"The rent Patrick paid for this place was piddling in comparison to the prices old Harry quoted to me," Emmet said. "Do you know the rent on a one-bedroom apartment in Dublin goes up from 1,000 pounds a month? Patrick knew when he was well off."

"Mum!" Oisín almost exploded back into the room before she could react. "I found some of my old peekaboos – look!" He held out cupped hands and smiled with delight. "I'd forgotten them – could you make them into belt buckles for me? I'd love to wear them."

"What about the gates?"

"The lads are putting them up." Ronan walked into the room. "I promised to treat them all to a drink down the pub later. They look great, Mum – you did a marvellous job of repairing them."

"What do you have, Oisín?" Rolf was glad of the change of subject.

"Peekaboos." Oisín opened his hands and let the little metal figures fall onto the table. "Mum used to make these for me and Ronan." He tried to put a figure over his finger but it wouldn't fit. "She would make up stories to go with them." He turned to his mother. "Remember?"

"I remember." Finn looked at her first attempts at metal figures.

"Could you make them into belt buckles?" Oisín was excited at the thought. "I'd love some metal armbands as well." They were being asked to appear shirtless in the show more and more. He'd love to be able to wear his own accessories. He and

Ronan were being picked out for special appearances because of the long hair. This would add to their camera appeal. Every little helped and it was all money in his travel kitty.

"I've never made a belt buckle." Finn fingered the little figures, remembering her two sons hanging onto her every word as they used the finger-figures to make her stories come alive – happy times.

"Finn," Emmet examined the figures, "you made these?"

"Mum makes all kinds of weird and wacky shit out in her workshop." Ronan too was examining the little peekaboos. He'd forgotten all about them.

"I want to see this workshop," Emmet said.

"Me too." Rolf wouldn't be left out.

"It's nothing special. I just like to tinker around with metal."

"Lead the way, daughter." Emmet wouldn't be put off.

Chapter 26

"Someone needs to cut this grass," Ronan said while they all walked through the garden in the direction of Finn's workshop. "It's getting very overgrown."

"Guess what, son?" Finn snapped. "You're 'someone' and *this* 'someone'," she pointed both of her thumbs towards her chest. "has quit."

"I'd forgotten there were sheds down here." Emmet ignored the other two. He wasn't in the mood for more disagreements. Finn was right, her sons were old enough to help her in the maintenance of the property they claimed to love so much.

"This is my workshop." Finn patted the cement blocks fondly. "I hope you are not expecting too much. I come in here to tinker and beat out my frustrations on metal." She unlocked and pushed open the double doors. She pulled the string that turned on the lights.

Ronan held back. She wasn't surprised. He'd never been that interested in her tinkering.

"Jesus!" Emmet reached out for Rolf's hand without thinking.

The two stood in the open doorway staring around. There was so much to take in – the room was filled with wonderful figures of whimsy – and their girl had done this!

"Mum, where's the figure of me with my bits hanging out?"

Oisín was grinning widely. He'd always thought his mother's figures wonderful no matter what their father might say. They made him smile and that could only be a good thing.

"Angie's granddaughter borrowed it." Finn was almost hyperventilating. What would they think? She valued her parents' opinions.

"Finn …" Emmet was trying to speak past the lump in his throat. That she should have hidden her talent away like this! What had been done to his daughter? He wanted to punch Patrick Brennan until his knuckles bled.

"These are *wonderbar*, sweetling!" Rolf knew what Emmet was thinking and feeling. "I want that little one." He pointed to a small figure with the biggest ears and smile he'd ever seen. It was captivating. "I will put it in the camper – show it to my friends – my daughter, the artist!"

"Take it." Finn was flattered.

"What's Angie's granddaughter's name, Mum?" Something was tickling at the back of Oisín's brain. Hadn't he heard or seen something about this – what was it?

"Chloe Lawrence," Finn answered absentmindedly while taking the small figure Rolf wanted from the shelf. The figure was covered in dust. Her workroom was her escape. She refused to keep it neat and tidy. She dusted the little figure and gave it a quick polish.

Emmet wanted to take his time admiring every figure in the workshop. Each one was different but all were a delight to the eye. He wanted to own one. He wanted to be able to puff out his chest and show what his talented daughter was capable of. "Rolf – I cannot believe I have to say this to you of all people – but we need your camera."

"*Ja!*" Rolf slapped his own head. "I was admiring and forgot. I will get it." He hurried from the workshop.

"What's the hold-up?" Ronan put his head into the workshop. He hadn't thought it would take them long to look around the place.

Emmet put his hand to his heart. "My grandson – it breaks my heart to say this – you, my grandson, are a philistine – can you not see the wonders before you?"

"What?" Ronan stepped inside and looked around with eyes that didn't see. "This stuff – Father was ashamed of it – told us to never tell anyone."

"Typical." Emmet could well imagine Patrick Brennan wanting nothing to take the attention away from himself. "You need to form your own opinions." He put his hand on Ronan's shoulder. "If you can look at these marvellous figures and tell me that you can see nothing special about them – that is your opinion and you're entitled to it – just as I can call you a blind fool – but for God's sake," he shook the shoulder he held, "look!"

"Mum, you need to see this." Oisín held out his phone – an extremely expensive model and more of a mini-computer. "I get several newspapers downloaded daily."

"What?" Finn glanced at the small screen. "What am I looking at?"

"Your interpretation of your favourite son," Oisín said, very much tongue in cheek.

"Name of God!" Finn stared at a photograph of one of her figures. "What's that doing there?"

"A judge's enquiry is under way." Oisín knew he'd seen something about this. There was a great deal of sitting around on set – reading through the download service he paid for helped to pass the time.

"Why?"

"It seems Chloe Lawrence wishes to use the creations of a well-known artist in her Blooms garden. Someone objected, claiming a garden with these figures in it would be too expensive for the average man to create."

"What has that to do with anything?" Ronan took his own phone from his pocket to read the article.

"It means, it is being claimed, that our mother's whimsical figures command a five-figure sum." Oisín laughed. "It sounds to me like one of the gardeners is trying to make trouble for Chloe Lawrence."

"If someone discovers which of my figures fetched a five-figure sum, for pity's sake tell me – I'd like to know about it." Finn laughed off the article. Here she was without a pot to piss in and people thought she was rich – chance would be a fine thing.

"Mum!" Ronan was gaping at the phone in his hand. He held the phone out to his mother. "It would appear that Tim Liner," he named the world-renowned actor, "has put in a bid of an undisclosed sum – claimed to be in the high five figures – to purchase one of your figures." How had this actor who lived in America and was a Hollywood darling even seen one of his mother's little figures?

"Someone's been smoking funny weed." Finn shrugged off the two stories.

"How would anyone in America see your figures?" Ronan wasn't willing to leave it there.

"Dare Lawrence – Angie's son – sent a bunch of my smaller nutjobs to friends of his in the States as presents," Finn said. "I suppose this fella-me-lad could have seen them there."

"How much did you get for them?" Ronan couldn't see anyone paying good money for a bunch of reused metal.

"He's Angie's son – I couldn't charge him – besides I haven't a clue what kind of price you could put on something like these." She dismissed her body of work with a wave of her hand.

"I am back." Rolf had his video camera in hand and metaphorically his director's hat on. "Boys – I want you to help your mother carry these figures out into the garden. The outdoor light isn't really good enough, but I will do what I can. Finn, please, you will dust the cobwebs off. We will use what light there is and have the boys show them off. I want film. I want to send this film to my brother Dolph. He will love them, I know."

"Have you seen the fairy in the apple tree?" Oisín stopped what he was doing for a moment to mention one of his favourite little figures. The branch had broken in a fascinating shape and his mum had made metal wings to create a tree fairy.

"I do not have the equipment I need here," Rolf fretted. "I am not capturing the essence of my sweetling's work. I need Klieg lights. I have what I need in Bray." He moved around the figures, trying to capture an image from different angles. "I have Klieg lights I rented from Ardmore Studios. Maybe I should talk to my brother's friend at the RTÉ film studios." He muttered in German, lost to his audience. "I must call him. I want to light the workshop and show off everything."

Finn sidled over to join Emmet who was standing off to one side. "Da, what's he doing?"

"Leave him to it, daughter." Emmet was delighted that Rolf wanted to show Finn's work to a wider audience. "What did you call these little sculptures?"

"Honest to God, Da, they're not sculptures – they can't be called that. I call them 'nutjobs' because I use so many bolt nuts."

"She calls them nutjobs, Rolf."

"*Ja, ja!*" Rolf was directing Ronan in the best way to present the figure he held in his hands, berating him in rapid German for his lack of enthusiasm.

"So, Mum," Oisín walked over to join them, "about turning my peekaboos into belt buckles – can you do it?" He was going to ask his Uncle Rolf to allow him to use the photographs. He'd pin them up on the notice boards that were becoming popular with computer nerds – he'd seen similar items pinned under Steampunk Art. His mum had been ahead of the crowd with her art.

"I can try but do you really want to have those little gargoyle figures on your belt?" She had made the figures with gargoyles in mind. The two little boys had loved them.

"Please!" Oisín wanted to share his mother's talent with his fans. "And armbands as well." He pointed to his biceps. "Something that will go around the top of my arm and stand out against my skin," He had the milk-white skin of the redhead – very popular in vampire stories.

"Leave me one of your belts and I'll see what I can do," Finn would enjoy the challenge of turning her nutjobs into other forms. She mentally ran through a list of items she'd need to create the armbands Oisín wanted.

"Finn," Rolf walked over to join them, "I want to take some of your figures out to Bray with me. I will place them around the houses. I must spend more time in your workshop too please. I need time and more equipment to light the wonderful nutjobs. I will want to try different ways of presenting them. This is good?"

"Fine with me, Da-ma." Finn didn't care what they did out here. As long as they didn't interfere when she was making something, they could do what they liked.

"I have people waiting for me in Bray." Rolf, the camera back in its case and slung over his shoulder, was almost bouncing on his toes. He did love to be busy. "I would rather stay," he looked towards the workshop with regret, "but I have not time now – I must not be late to Bray – I will plan the best way to do this." He clapped his hands, ordering Ronan and Oisín to load up the figures he pointed to.

It amused Finn to watch her sons jump to obey.

"I'm going to put the kettle on," she said. "You can leave the workshop doors open. I'll be back in a minute. Oisín, I'll need one of your belts before you go. Rolf, I'll fill your flask with coffee."

"She has no idea of the power of her talent, does she?" Emmet said to his grandsons after she left.

"Father spent a lot of time denigrating her 'tinkering' as he called it," Oisín said. "Wouldn't have them in the house."

"The man is no fool when it comes to looking after his own best interests," Emmet bit out.

"What are you talking about?" Ronan still couldn't see what the big deal was.

"These figures," Emmet closed his eyes against the blank look on his grandson's face, "they are works of genius. My daughter – our daughter," he looked at Rolf, "the woman who gave birth to you two, is a bloody brilliant artist! I'm so proud of her talent that my chest feels twice the size it normally does. Rolf and I created a genius and we are only just finding out."

"It must not be left locked away." Rolf looked around at the sheer scale of the work completed.

"I think I'll have a word with Angie about this son of hers." Emmet wanted more information about the man.

"I'll have a word in Chloe Lawrence's ear." Oisín remembered Chloe now. She babysat for them from time to time when they were growing up.

"This must be handled correctly," Emmet put in. "We don't want Finn to turn into a mule and refuse to allow anyone to see her work. The bloody woman is capable of that."

"I'm going to go and give her a hand with the tea and coffee," Ronan said, walking away. "Because I don't have a clue what you lot are talking about!"

"My brother is his father's son." Oisín had tried to tell Ronan how talented their mother was – he hadn't wanted to hear. "I'm going to run upstairs and get a couple of my belts for Mum to use. I can't wait to see what she'll create. I love her work and can't wait to wear it."

"From what your mother has told me Ronan has tried all of his life to please Patrick. He'll grow out of that, if God is good," Emmet said.

"What a wonderful day!" Rolf beamed.

Chapter 27

"Do you mind if I root around out here?" Emmet had waved Rolf and his grandsons off. He wasn't needed in Bray. Rolf was in his element out there, ordering everyone about. He planned to pull his daughter's workshop apart. "Will having someone around put you off your work?"

"I've never had anyone out here with me before." Finn was rooting through her supplies, searching for something she knew she had. She didn't see the effect of her words on her father.

"Jaysuz, you have a potbellied stove out here, daughter." Emmet clenched his fists and refused to allow the curses he longed to heap on Patrick Brennan's head to pass his lips. "Does it work?"

"Yeah." Finn was hunkered down searching the bottom shelf of one of her units. "I found it in a junk yard and repaired it." She continued searching, not paying attention to her words. "I love a real fire. Those phony things in the house might keep the place clean and look good but you can't beat a real fire. You can light it if you want. It's getting chilly. I don't know what Oisín is thinking of starting his camping trip as we move into winter."

"What are you looking for, daughter?" Emmet watched her hunt amongst the piles of rubbish stacked around the place.

"I know I have some of those long-handled spoons people

use for ice-cream sundaes. They would be ideal for what I have in mind." She spotted what she'd been searching for at the back of the shelf. "I never found a use for them before and I hated to break the handles. I knew I'd find something to do with them someday." She stood clutching a handful of long metal objects.

"What are you going to do?" Emmet was fascinated with this new aspect of the woman his daughter had become. He had despaired of her life as Patrick Brennan's willing handmaiden – but look at her now. An artist, by God – he'd made this wonder.

"I'm going to make an openwork Celtic-knot armband." She dusted the long-handled spoons. "I've seen people with tattoos of the design. I'll melt and weave the spoon handles. The armbands will clasp tight around Oisín's bicep." She could see it in her mind's eye. "I don't know how to cut metal to make a band someone could wear but the spoons are already smooth and without sharp edges – so won't cut when worn."

"Have you enough to make some for Ronan?" Emmet loved how she mentioned heating and weaving metal in a way other people would say 'I'll peel an apple'.

"Ronan wouldn't wear anything I made," she replied without thinking.

"I'll get the fire going and let you get on with it." Emmet was going to have words with his eldest grandson. "Why peekaboos?" he asked while rolling old newspapers into balls for the fire.

Finn put the spoons on her work top, running her fingers over the metal to get the feel for the material used. "Oh, I'd make up stories. The boys each had little gargoyle shapes that fit over their fingers. They'd make a fist." She smiled remembering their eager little faces hanging on her every word. "When I reached a point in the story they didn't like they would reveal a gargoyle – shout *peekaboo!* – and then they would have to finish the story."

"We did that with you." Emmet had tears in his eyes at the memories she had invoked. "There were no gargoyles involved but you put your little hands over our eyes." He laughed. "When the story we were telling got in any way off the fairy-tale path you would stop us."

"It was the opposite for the boys." Finn set her anvil up close to her work bench. She handled the heavy equipment without a second thought – over the years she had learned ways of dealing with items difficult to shift – she'd had to. "The more ugly creatures with bad breath the better."

They were silent while each got busy. Emmet had a fire going and stood back to admire his work. Finn was right – you couldn't beat a real fire. The smell of turf whipped him back to his childhood. He continued to pull her work from the shelves and looked around for a ladder so he could reach the figures he could barely see under the rafters. He grunted with satisfaction when he found a folding metal ladder stashed under one of the shelving units. He climbed up and dusted and polished each figure big or small, laboriously shoving the ladder along from time to time.

His breath caught at the talent displayed. It would be difficult to pick a favourite. He loved them all.

Finn ignored her father until she turned off her welding torch and carefully placed it on her work surface. She stepped back from the anvil, pressing her fingers into her back to release the tension. "Da?"

"Yes?" He turned from the gamine figure he was polishing to stare over at her. She was standing like some figure from history, her goggles pushed to the top of her head – heavy rubber apron wrapped around her.

"Make a pot of tea, will you?" She replaced her goggles and bent back to her work.

"In a minute." Emmet came to stand at her shoulder, admiring the form she was creating as she used her welding torch to melt the spoons. He held his breath, hoping his presence didn't put her off her work. He wanted to watch. He had struggled for so long to accept that his daughter – his only child – had rejected everything he and Rolf tried to give her. By God – look at her now – bent over her art – creating magic with her fingers. He fought the tears that filled his eyes, not wanting to miss a second of this wonder.

"Thanks." Finn had to move fast before the metal cooled and hardened, using forceps to shift the soft metal into the form she wanted. She'd never tried weaving metal before. She stepped back for a moment to examine the Celtic knot that lay on the worktable. Into a bucket of water now to cool, enjoying the sizzling hiss of the hot metal.

She pulled the cooled item from the bucket and examined it in detail. "What do you think?" She held the forceps clenched around the Celtic knot up for him to view. The metal was folded over to form an open circle.

"It's –" Emmet gulped back the words of astonishment and pleasure he wanted to pour over her. She'd retreat into a shell if he praised her work to the skies. It was bloody brilliant. "Will it break when he bends it to put it on?" he contented himself with asking.

"No, it should work like the torques of old. He can put his arm into the opening and tighten it around his biceps."

"Do you have enough of those spoons to make two?" My God – spoons into wearable art – it was a privilege to be here to see it.

"Why would he want two?"

"Daughter," Emmet closed his eyes for a moment, not wanting to shout at her and spoil the moment, "I despair of you. You have two sons running around half-dressed on TV and you seem to be the only one who hasn't seen them."

"I don't like vampires and scary things – you know that."

"Yeah – Walt Disney or nothing – how the hell did I create such a bloody Pollyanna of a child, I ask you?" He looked towards the sky as if begging an all-seeing God for answers.

"So, why two?" Finn ignored him. She'd heard it all before.

"The lads are usually half naked no matter what they are playing – vampires or Vikings – they are mostly oiled up and shirtless. If you make two of those things," he pointed at the armband sitting on the workbench, "then Oisín will really stand out from the crowd. Which is what the lad wants if I am any judge. That is if and when they are employed on another project. It's an iffy business they are in."

"OK." She turned to make another armband. This one would be quicker. She had the feel of the metal now.

Emmet opened and closed cupboards in the little area she had set aside for teamaking.

"Da," Finn turned to him again, "I don't know what to say or do when Rolf talks about yer one Ingrid. If I didn't know better I'd think yer one walked on water." She shoved her hands through her hair, knocking her safety goggles off her head. She bent to pick them up. "If you read between the lines of what he says the woman is no saint."

Emmet bit his lips on quipping 'kettle, black'. Look how long it took her to see through that plastic man she'd married.

"Da, he keeps insisting on referring to the woman as my mother – she's not – I have the best mother – even if my mother is a man."

"Just listen and smile, daughter. That's all any of us can do." Emmet was glad his back was turned. "The woman gave us the most precious gift in the world. As gay men we would never have been allowed to adopt. It is difficult enough for a regular couple. Having said that – Ingrid is poison. She has milked Rolf for years because of her great suffering." Emmet put the metal teapot on top of the potbelly stove. "I've spent years biting my tongue until it bled rather than say what I think about that woman."

"Rolf is crazy happy at the thought of moving in here." She waved in the direction of the house. "I know he sent her film and photographs of it."

"So?" It was like pulling teeth.

"Da, anyone looking at that house sees a mansion." Finn had spent years listening to people tell her how lucky she was to live there. It looked wonderful but no-one ever mentioned the cost of upkeep on the darn place. The sheer hard labour it took to keep the place looking good. The house was built in the days of a cheap servant workforce. "I'm afraid Ingrid might look at the house and what she thinks is our lifestyle and want a bit of the action." She took one of his hands in hers. "Am I wrong to worry?"

"No," Emmet sighed, "and now you have me at it."

"Did Rolf ever learn Irish?"

"No, why would he?"

"You will have to be extra careful in Germany."

"What?"

"My boys will be no match for a woman like Ingrid. She'll be able to suck them dry of any knowledge they might have."

"Jaysus, you're getting very dramatic." Everything she said could just as easily be said about Patrick Brennan. Didn't she realise that? Perhaps worrying about Ingrid kept her from worrying about her own problems.

"I've been thinking and worrying about this." Finn turned her attention back to the spoons waiting to be turned into an armband. "You need to step back, Da." She pulled her goggles back over her eyes. She was aware of him stepping well away from the workbench. She turned on her welding torch.

"It will be no use warning the boys about Ingrid!" She shouted over the tap-tap of her hammer on the melting metal. *"If you are on the spot you can cut them off in Irish. No one will know what you're saying."*

Emmet stood back and watched his daughter. She'd given him a lot to think about. He despised Ingrid. The woman quite literally made his flesh crawl. She sucked the life out of all around her and Rolf couldn't see it – had never been able to see it – wouldn't hear a word against her. What was he going to do? Finn was right about the two lads. They'd be no match for a woman like Ingrid. He wanted to howl at the moon. There was no way he wanted to put himself back within reach of her grasping clutches again. But how could he leave Rolf to her tender mercies?

He turned to pour the tea. He felt chilled to his bones. He had a sinking feeling the chill had nothing to do with the temperature outside.

Chapter 28

Finn rolled over in the bed, waking to a new day. The silence of the house around her was almost painful to her ears. How many mornings had she wallowed in the silence before the storm? Now she was bemoaning her lot. The blue guest bedroom seemed to suit her mood lately.

"Rise and shine, Finn!"

She was proud of herself. She'd stood in her driveway smiling and shouting teasing remarks as the men in her life drove away. She'd been determined they wouldn't leave her standing snivelling in the driveway. She'd helped her sons get ready for their big adventure with a smile on her face. She'd waved them away with a laugh. She deserved a medal.

She was being paid a stipend from the bank account that covered house maintenance. She didn't feel she was taking money for nothing – she earned it – keeping the house and grounds ticking over. Rolf had set the weekly payment up. It would show up in her bank account which was a positive thing. It wasn't much but it kept the wolf from the door – if she was careful.

She was living alone for the first time in her life and sometimes it felt like she'd been alone for an eternity. The house was big and empty around her. She'd walked through the halls like a ghost of the past, weeping and wailing. Finn was glad no one could see her kicking walls and shouting. She escaped the loneliness by disappearing into her workshop, losing herself for hours beating metal, trying to release the pain.

She sat down to her first pot of tea of the day, her stomach tied in painful knots. She had a guest arriving this morning.

She practically jumped out of her skin when the doorbell sounded through the house.

"Finn?" was all the man standing on her doorstep seemed capable of saying.

They stared at each other for a long moment while Finn tried to find her voice.

"You look so much like Rolf," Finn finally managed to say with a shy smile. "Come in, please."

"Thank you for agreeing to meet with me." Pieter Buckmeister had been hoping for this day for so long. Now he was here, his hands trembling, his nerves shot.

She'd thought long and hard before agreeing to this visit. "Are you hungry?"

"I would like a cup of tea, please."

"Tea?" Finn's eyebrows went up.

"Rolf told me to ask for tea. He said it would please you," Pieter admitted with a familiar grin.

"Tea it is!"

She showed him to a guest bedroom, trying not to trip over her own tongue. They had agreed he would stay for one night at least before returning home. She was terribly nervous.

"I don't know what to say to you, what you expect from me," she said when she had served him tea in the kitchen.

"I do not expect anything. I wish only the chance to get to know you. I am hopeful you will wish to get to know me. We cannot meet after all these years as brother and sister, I know this, Finn. I do not wish you to be uncomfortable in my presence. I ask only for the chance to get to know you. Can we not try to form a friendship?"

"I can use all the friends I can get." Finn smiled at the man who was a younger copy of her Uncle Rolf. The man was her half-brother. She had to put that fact into the back of her mind and accept the man for himself. She didn't know how to act as anyone's sister, didn't know how to behave around a brother. She'd try for friendship and see how that went.

She smiled when he grimaced over the tea. She had to hand it to the man, he was willing to try. She stood and began to prepare a pot of coffee.

"Did you have the chance to meet my sons before you left home?" Finn knew Emmet planned to drop Ronan and Rolf in the heart of their German family before he and Oisín continued travelling. The few quick text messages and phone calls she'd received hadn't been enough for her mother's heart.

"Oh, your boys – they are such a hit." Pieter grinned "Frieda, my daughter, is having the time of her life introducing her Irish cousins to everyone in sight."

"Both boys are in Dresden?"

"No, no – Emmet, he can never bear to stay very long around our mother."

"*Your* mother." Finn was determined to establish that fact straight away.

"As you say," Pieter shrugged. "Your boys came to visit me and my family in Munich. We enjoyed meeting them very much. They were such a success with everybody – and their German language skills, what a surprise!"

"You didn't want to live on the farm?" Finn knew nothing about Rolf's family. She'd never asked, never needed to know. Was that wrong of her?

"I left the farm early with Uncle Rolf's blessing and financial help." Pieter stared at this strange woman who was his sister. The tiny baby he remembered all grown up. "The farm will pass to Dieter as the eldest son. That is right, how it should be. I did not wish to spend my life working for my brother, needing to ask his permission for every little action. That is not the kind of life I wish to live." Pieter pushed the tea away when he smelled the coffee brewing.

"Uncle Rolf gave me the name of your company." Finn felt she needed to get that fact out in the open straight away. "I wouldn't say he tricked me – exactly. I contacted you because you were listed as one of the most innovative companies."

"So Rolf assured me." Pieter leaned back in his chair, wondering what he could say that would make this tense woman relax. He wanted nothing from her. He simply wanted to know about her. "I am what you might call 'a big noise'." He grinned with a shrug.

"So I'm talking to the top dog?" Finn was willing to go along with Pieter's attempt to lighten the moment.

"Very much top dog." Pieter struck a pose. "I am almost famous."

Finn told herself to relax. She was being too suspicious. She'd agreed to meet this man and now it was up to her to treat him with the manners her fathers had drilled into her.

"My Uncle Dolph works behind the scenes as an adviser on many programmes on German television," he went on. "A building programme is very popular. Uncle Dolph uses my products a great deal in this programme. He does not do this because we are related but because of the quality of my firm's products." Pieter was sorry he'd started this now. He sounded as if he were boasting which was the last thing he wanted to do. "I am sorry. I am talking too much. I am nervous."

Finn could see Pieter was desperately trying not to upset her in any way. "Let's try and be open and honest with each other," she said. "If one of us is having a problem we will say so, OK?"

"OK."

"In the meantime, are you hungry?"

"I am starving." Pieter laughed. "My stomach was tied in so many knots I have not eaten for a long time."

"I'll going to make you an Irish Breakfast. You'll like it." Finn had everything ready to hand.

Pieter watched her set the kitchen island for breakfast. "You did not wish to visit Germany with your family?"

"No, I am not ready to make that trip." Finn was beginning to see this man less as a copy of Rolf and more his own man.

"What do you enjoy doing? Rolf showed me photographs of your improvements – your plastering and painting work on this house." He'd been warned not to mention her artwork too early in this their first meeting.

"I enjoyed learning how to do many different things when I

remodelled this house. I love plastering – it reminds me of icing a cake."

While Finn watched over the food cooking, they discussed different architectural styles they admired, finding their tastes remarkably similar.

Finn put the food on the table then sat down to join him. "Pieter, why are you here?" Talking over food was the best way she knew.

"It is time, *ja*?" Pieter picked up his knife and fork. "I have no words to explain why I am here. When I accepted your phone calls to my company I knew who you were. I treated you as a potential customer but you are family to me. I remember the baby sister that was taken away never to return."

"Pieter –"

"No, let me tell it, please." Pieter had tried to practise what he should say. "I have a need for family. Yes, there is a mother and a brother but we are not close. I have many uncles and cousins yet always I think and wonder about the sister I don't know. You, Finn, have always been a missing part of my life. I can explain it no better than that. I have a wonderful wife and four children I love. I am a happy lucky man. Perhaps I need to share this happiness. I don't know."

Finn didn't know what to say.

"Our mother, Ingrid," he shrugged when she went to interrupt, "is a hard woman. I do not know if the loss of her husband made her this way but it is fact. I love and respect my mother but I do not like her. It is so with Dieter my brother – we have never been as close as I would wish." Pieter didn't want to prejudice her against her close relations. He wanted only to make her understand his point of view. "I liked farming. I love the countryside and the animals, but I could not support Dieter's treatment of me. I had to leave. Dieter forced my leaving, yet he has never forgiven me for deserting the family farm." He shrugged.

"Do your children visit the farm?" Finn offered Pieter more coffee and poured.

"Yes, I did not cut ties to my family. My children visit out of duty but it will not continue. They are not treated with kindness." Pieter tried to make Finn understand. "My wife does not like to visit the family farm. Gerta does not like my mother or Dieter – she takes my part."

"Ronan desperately wants family." Finn worried her son might be disappointed.

"Ronan is being treated with great kindness. He is visiting royalty. He came with Rolf. Rolf is my mother's favourite big brother – he lives to give – Ingrid lives to take. They get on well together. She would never allow Rolf to see her for the woman she really is. Emmet sees this and stays away." He looked down at the table. "I am ashamed to speak so of my mother."

"Well, they say you can choose your friends but not your relatives." Finn didn't know what to add. She didn't know the people he was talking about.

"This is true." Pieter hoped he hadn't given too bad an impression of his family. He wanted there to be truth between Finn and himself. He hadn't been sleeping well, terrified and excited about this trip to see the sister he'd never known. He'd kept her memory alive through the years, hoping for this moment.

Chapter 29

Pieter tried to catch his breath. The wind off the sea was strong and cold. The salt particles in the moisture-driven wind stung exposed flesh. "So this is Bray and those are the houses you contacted me about – they present a great challenge."

"Yes, they do." Finn hadn't known what to do with this stranger. They couldn't sit around the house looking at each other. She had brought him to Bray on the DART. The coastal train journey was breathtakingly beautiful. She'd thought to give him a chance to see a little of Ireland and at the same time see the dark dingy cottages belonging to Rolf and her da.

"When I contacted your firm I believed I would start work immediately." She put her arm through his when he offered his bent elbow even though he was slightly shorter than her. They had bonded over those dilapidated cottages. The man was so knowledgeable. "Then Rolf fell in love and wanted them recorded for posterity."

"I have seen the many films he has shot." Pieter didn't care about the custom he might get from those buildings. It had been a pleasure to watch his sister relax in his company as she had sought his opinion.

"I enjoy a brisk walk," Finn said as they bent almost double to fight the strength of the wind pushing against them. "I thought you might like some fresh air after being in airports, a plane and those dark and dusty cottages."

"I too enjoy walking. This is a beautiful place."

They turned to lean against the Victorian rail that ran along the seafront. It gave them a moment to catch their breath. They stood enjoying the view out over the white-capped waves of the Irish Sea.

"You must tell me when you have had enough," she said. "We can turn back at any time."

They continued walking along the Victorian promenade towards the cliffs. Finn knew that after a short climb the road they were on straightened out, following the cliffs over the sea in a magnificent walk. She loved it and had taken it many times with little fingers holding tight to her skirts. She dragged in great deep breaths of the fresh sea-scented air. The path, cut into the cliffs high over the ocean, was beaten bare by the many feet that passed over it.

"Will you show me your nutjobs?" Pieter stared down at the seagulls making their homes in the cliffs beneath their feet – the birds wheeled and swooped, white against the blue sky.

"What do you know about my nutjobs?" That was the last thing she'd expected him to say.

"I too like to work with metal." Pieter had seen many images of the figures his longed-for sister had produced. He wanted to own one. He wanted to share his knowledge of metalwork with her. Would she allow him to visit her workshop? Was it too soon to ask?

"I might pick your brain on that subject too," she responded.

They walked along in silence for a while, each enjoying the natural beauty that surrounded them. The fields stretched out on one side of them. Goats clambered and ran around fleetly on the bare rocks on the higher ground. Sheep and horses grazed the green, green grass on the lower cliff. Birds twittered madly in the bushes. It was soul food.

"I am sorry I am not as Uncle Rolf – always a camera to hand." Pieter took deep breaths of the salt laden air. "I thought the train journey beautiful. I was afraid to blink my eyes in case I missed something. How will I ever be able to describe this to my Gerta?"

Finn loved the way he spoke of his wife. She stepped off the path to allow people going in the opposite direction to pass. Then she dropped down onto the wide grass verge, inviting Pieter to join her. It was cold but they were both well wrapped up. They sat in silence and watched the antics of the waves and the screeching gulls that wheeled over them. People out for a walk strolled past with a casual nod in their direction. She allowed the silence to deepen. It was not uncomfortable. She had no idea what to say at this point. She lay back on the grass and stared unblinking at the sky. She watched big fat white clouds chase each other.

Then a dark cloud crossed over the sky, darkening the day and threatening rain.

"We'd better start back." Finn stood, brushing off the seat of her jeans. She held out a hand and pulled Pieter to his feet.

"I have enjoyed this very much." He fell into step beside her.

"I think you will also enjoy visiting an Irish pub." Finn shivered. "I can feel an Irish coffee calling my name."

"You have coffee that speaks?"

She laughed and put her arm through his offered elbow. "On a day like today an Irish coffee is perfect for blowing the chill away. That is only my opinion – we will see what you think."

They retraced their steps. They hadn't reached Greystones, the final destination of the walk they'd been on, which she thought a shame. She'd been looking forward to sharing the train journey from Greystones to Bray – another beautiful coastline railway trip. Ah well – perhaps another time.

Finn pushed open the door to one of the many pubs close to Railway Parade and across the green from the sea. She enjoyed Pieter's exclamation of delight. In no time they were sitting on comfortable chairs in front of a roaring fire. Pieter's eyes were everywhere. He couldn't seem to take enough in.

"I must bring my Gerta here." He picked up the stemmed glass, holding the Irish coffee Finn ordered. He took a sip through the thick cream that formed a crown over the black coffee. His eyes widened at the first sip. "This is *wonderbar!*"

He sounded so much like Rolf with his 'vonnderbar' that Finn laughed aloud. "What is it?" he asked.

"Coffee and cream."

"There is more." He took another sip and licked his lips to remove the moustache of thick cream that had formed on his upper lip.

"A good dollop of Irish whiskey," she said. "And a little sugar."

"You know how to make this?" He held up the half-empty glass.

"Yes."

"You will teach me?"

"Yes."

"Gerta –" he closed his eyes in ecstasy, "I will make this for her. She will love me even more." He jumped to his feet. "We will have more! They are small."

Finn sat back in her fireside chair and smiled. The whiskey was strong – more than two and they'd be rolling her out of the place. They had the pub almost to themselves. There were not many people about on a dark cold afternoon.

It was easy to sit here with this man who was a stranger yet related to her by blood. The surroundings allowed them to feel free perhaps? She didn't know. She only knew she was enjoying his company.

Pieter was being skillfully interrogated by the barman. She closed her eyes and put her head back, listening to the two men laugh and joke, enjoying the blazing log fire.

"Finn," Pieter was standing over her, thinking she was asleep.

She snapped open sparkling green eyes to ask, "Have you given the man your seed, breed and generation?"

"*Bitte?*"

"Sorry!" He looked so much like Rolf that she had assumed he would know the phrases her da used all the time. "It means that you have been interrogated in a nice Irish way."

"*Ja*, I tell him everything. He will bring the drinks." He sat down and with a worried frown bent forward. "Finn, I would like to ask …"

"Yes?"

"I need to telephone my wife – my Gerta – she is worried I will not be welcome here." He'd had to promise to telephone as soon as he knew what his reception would be. He had delayed – Gerta would be worried. She had wanted to accompany him but he had wanted this first meeting with his sister alone. She had understood.

"Oh, the poor woman!" Finn knew what it was to worry about people you love travelling away from you. "Call her this instant." Then she put her hand on his knee to stop him for a moment. "You do know I speak fluent German?" They had been conversing exclusively in English. She would not like him to think he was having a private conversation with his wife when she could understand every word said.

"*Wonderbar!*" His smile almost split his face. "You can talk with my Gerta – she will be so pleased. She was worried her English was not good enough."

It was a happy man who telephoned Germany. He didn't bother to lower his voice as he told his wife of all the wonders he had seen so far. He promised faithfully that the next time he came to Ireland his family would come with him.

Finn sat listening with half an ear. She didn't want to be rude. His almost childish delight in everything he had seen and done was wonderful or 'vonnderbar' as he would say.

"Finn has promised she will teach me to make the Irish Coffee, Gerta." He passed the phone to Finn. "My Gerta, she wishes to speak to you."

Finn took the phone.

"*Danke – vielen Dank, Finn,*" Gerta said with tears in her voice. She switched to English. "You have made him so very happy. I was so afraid. He is a wonderful man. Thank you."

"I look forward to meeting you and your family one day in the near future," Finn said in her practically perfect German.

"What will you two do now?"

"We will have fish and chips from the local chip shop and walk along the seafront fighting the breeze and the gulls for our food! We are getting to know each other, Gerta. I will look after him for you."

"*Vielen Dank, Finn.*"

Finn passed the phone back to Pieter just as the barman brought the fresh drinks.

It had been a surprising visit so far. It seemed she might have found a brother.

Chapter 30

Finn walked along the stalls of the local weekend market, searching for what she didn't know. She was proud of herself. She was surviving, putting one foot in front of the other, and it felt like a triumph some days. Today she was feeling slightly adrift. In past years the time leading up to Christmas would have been frantic. She'd have been buried under the details of staging events and selecting gifts. This year she decided to ignore the holiday.

There would be no presents to worry and fuss over. She'd not bother decorating the house. She wouldn't spend her holiday period in the kitchen preparing mountains of food. There would be no drunken fools to entertain for Patrick. The relief at that thought surprised her. The house would remain clean without constant effort on her part – her Christmas alone would be a time of peace and joy.

"*Finn!*" a voice called out. "*Finn – Mrs Brennan!*"

She turned at the sound of her name.

"You look away with the fairies, Finn!"

"Maggie! I didn't know you had a stall here!" She stepped over to stand in front of a stall piled high with colourful fabric.

"Charles or my parents take the twins while I man the stall at weekends." Maggie waved a hand over the many items displayed on the waist-high table in front of her. She leaned closer to whisper. "This time of year I hope to make enough to pay Santa."

"I love these patchwork baby blankets." Finn fingered one of the charming items. "Is all of your work patchwork?"

"I can turn my hand to most things to do with sewing." Maggie smiled at a woman examining the items on the stall. She allowed the woman to look – she didn't like to jump on people as soon as they stopped at her stall.

"I could make you a brace to go along the back of the stall," Finn looked at the bare area behind Maggie's head. "You could hang your work – really show it off – it's beautiful."

"Thank you." Maggie blushed. "What have you been doing with yourself? I haven't heard from you in a while." The people around her stall started calling for information. "But, look, we can't talk here. Why don't you meet me at the Silver Swan later and we'll have a chat?" Maggie needed to pay attention to the potential customers right now.

"Oh, I can't – I must get home – I'd better let you get back to work." She was in the way of paying customers.

She walked away from the stall, wondering why she'd refused a drink. She could go out in the evening. There was no one waiting for her. She could stay out without asking permission or planning for someone to take care of her family. When would that penny finally drop? She was free to do as she pleased.

"*You should be ashamed of yourself!*"

An older woman suddenly confronted Finn.

"You took your vows before a priest, the same as the rest of us!" There were murmurs of agreement from around. "Marriage is for life – not something you walk away from – you hussy!"

Finn was afraid the woman was going to hit her with her handbag. She hurried away without responding, losing the woman in the crowd.

That's all I need, she thought. I can't even go out for a walk now without someone verbally attacking me.

She pushed her gloved hands into the pockets of the heavy

coat she wore and lowered her chin into the scarf wrapped around her face and neck.

She'd been invited to join her menfolk and celebrate the holidays in Germany. Pieter wanted her to meet his family. She'd refused gently. She wasn't ready for all that family togetherness just yet – as hippy-dippy as it sounded – she was working on finding herself. She was spending time exploring her own wants and needs. She'd started simply, by choosing music she thought she'd like. She'd checked self-help books out of the Rathmines library, faithfully completing each exercise given. She'd compiled lists of questions she'd never have thought of without the aid of those books. Lists of questions about herself that needed to be asked and answered.

Lost in thought, she didn't notice the car parked outside the locked double gates of her house.

"Nuala, why are these gates locked? I couldn't get in!" Patrick Brennan was shouting while he pushed open the car door and stepped out onto the pavement. He slammed the door shut and stood with his hands braced on his hips, glaring at the scruffy stranger. Where was the woman who'd catered to his every need for over twenty years? He wanted his wife back.

"Patrick, lovely to see you."

"I want you to agree to see a marriage counsellor." Patrick hadn't time to waste on social pleasantries. He gave her one of his most charming smiles, guaranteed to make her agree to anything he wanted. He'd had enough of living as a single swinger. The lifestyle didn't suit him at all. He needed someone to take care of him.

"I have no wish to discuss my life with anyone at this point."

"I've been discussing your problems on my show. Have you been listening?" He waited but when she didn't reply continued. "I've got an expert coming in next week. I thought we could speak with the man in private before the programme goes out."

"You're having a male consultant discuss female issues, are you?"

"I wanted to speak to someone who would understand my point of view." Patrick wanted her to agree to talk with his guest. It would give the programme more bite.

"Of course you did." She wondered what Patrick really wanted? It wasn't like him to stand in the street talking.

Finn began to walk towards the wooden door set into the curtain wall that surrounded the estate. The heavy gates that she'd put back in place and locked were proving a blessing right now.

"*Nuala, I need you to have a word with Mrs. Green!*" he almost shouted.

"About?" she asked over her shoulder – curious.

"I want you to ask her to speak to her daughter. That young lady is completely out of control." He was being stalked by Brenda Green. The stupid girl was demanding she move into the very expensive apartment he'd been forced to rent. That was the last thing he wanted. He needed a woman who thought only of him – someone like Nuala.

She opened the door in the wall – jumped inside and bolted the door at her back.

"*Nuala!*" Patrick rapped against the door, unable to believe she wouldn't help him. She had to get Brenda Green off his back. He was suffering financially – paying out good money to cover his living expenses. The cleaning woman wouldn't take care of his laundry for a smile and a pinch. The woman insisted on charging him extra to take care of his laundry. "*Nuala!*" Patrick used the side of his fist to beat on the door. This was outrageous – how dare she bar the entrance to him! "*Nuala, let me in!*"

"Go away. We have nothing to say to each other." Finn leaned against the door.

"Patrick? Having problems?"

Brenda Green appeared in the street at Patrick's back. This man was her ticket to the big time. She deserved the high life. She'd earned it sweating under Patrick Brennan, putting up with his fumbling. You would think a man of his years would be a better lover, having had years of practice. The Sunday papers might be interested in her revealing story. There was more than one way to make money off a man.

"Why don't I come home with you – help you get rid of that tension?" Brenda strolled towards the cowering Patrick.

"*Nuala!*" Patrick shook the door with his blows.

He pulled at the hem of his jacket, feeling like a hunted animal. He didn't need this friction in his life. He wanted peace and care so he could be there for his listeners. They needed him at his best.

"I'll talk to you later, Nuala!" Patrick pushed past Brenda, holding his breath against the heavy perfume she wore. He jumped into his luxury car and drove away with a squeal of tires.

"Hey, bitch!" Brenda ran her fingernails along the paintwork of Finn's little run-around. "You forgot to put your 'classic car' away."

"Go home, Brenda. I've had quite enough drama for one day." Finn walked into her home. She turned on the computer system to watch what was happening in the street. She sighed. She'd never used the garage. That was kept for Patrick's car of the moment and the ride-on lawnmower.

"*Make me!*" Brenda shouted loudly, unaware that Finn could watch her every movement.

"*I'm calling the police!*" Finn opened the door to shout. She closed her eyes in disgust at her own actions.

Brenda sniggered and shouted, "*You're too much of a toe-rag to call the police.*"

Finn sighed and rang Mrs. Green.

"Mrs. Green. Mrs Brennan here. Your daughter is causing a scene in front of my home. Please remove her or I'm calling the police." Finn knew the woman was aware of the situation over here. Mrs. Green spent her life spying on her neighbours.

"There is no need to make that kind of threat." Nellie Green had hoped her daughter could trap one of the Brennan men. The good Lord knew it was easy enough to trap a man. She'd told her daughter how to do it but had she listened? No. The girl thought she knew everything. The Brennan men would be a good catch for any girl but talk of calling the police made her nervous. She needed to have a long talk with young Brenda. They needed to come up with a different plan.

"Get your daughter away from my property and keep her away," Finn demanded. "The next time this happens I'm calling the police and pressing charges." She stood with her eyes fixed on the screen.

"I'll be right over – give me time to put me shoes on." She was going to knock that daughter of hers into next week. She didn't need these problems.

"I'm calling the police now to discuss the charges that can be brought against you both." She knew the Greens didn't want any dealings with the police. They had too much to hide.

Finn stood in front of the screen, watching mother and daughter almost come to blows in the street. She was so angry – steaming – with herself – with Patrick – the man who made the problem then ran away leaving Finn to clean up after him.

Chapter 31

"Thanks for coming over, Maggie." Finn had telephoned Maggie and invited her over for a meal and a chat. "I've invited Angie over. I thought we could have a ladies' evening."

"I was surprised you called." Maggie sat and watched Finn buzz around her kitchen. "When you refused to come out for a drink, I thought you might have had plans."

"Nope." Finn sniffed the aroma of the coq-au-vin she had simmering in the oven. It was one of her favourite meals to prepare. It was a complicated and boozy recipe but she enjoying preparing and eating it. "I'm afraid my refusal to meet you for a drink was a kneejerk reaction. There was no reason I couldn't have met you but I've lost the habit of spending the evening in company – if I ever had it."

"You didn't have to go to all this trouble for me." Maggie sipped at the glass of red wine Finn had poured for her. She didn't know one wine from another but whatever this was it was very pleasant.

"I enjoy cooking and there is something I want to talk to you about."

"Only you would consider cooking 'fun'. It's an awful lot of hard thankless work as far as I'm concerned." Maggie threw frozen meals into the microwave and she resented having to do that much.

"That's what makes us all individuals. I wouldn't want to work with fabric the way you do. I'd rather eat the material with a knife and fork. I'm discovering lots of things about myself I never knew. I'm on a learning curve, throwing out the things I don't like and concentrating on my delights. Does that sound very 'hippy-dippy'?"

"Not in the least, if one of your delights is serving me fabulous meals. Well, we can put eating your meals in my plus column." Maggie had begun to make lists of her own potential. "Is Angie late?"

"No, I asked you to come a little earlier because I want to talk to you about something." Finn hoped she wasn't going to insult her friend.

"For another glass of wine you can ask me anything." Maggie held out her empty glass.

Finn refilled Maggie's glass and poured a glass for herself. She sat down at the table and spent a moment looking at Maggie.

"Well ... I wanted to throw out every stitch of clothing I wore when I was Mrs Patrick Brennan." She pulled a face at the memory. "Angie wouldn't let me."

"I should think not – trying to keep clothes on your back eats up a lot of money." Maggie shook her head. "I spend what money I have on the girls – finding clothes for myself comes a long way down on the list of things I need."

"The clothes are all in the attic." Finn needed something to wear besides her sons' castoffs. "I was wondering if I could pay you to dye the fabric – rip the old-lady outfits apart – and refashion them into something the new me could wear?"

"A challenge!" Maggie spent most nights when the twins were tucked up in their bed huddled over her sewing machine. She bought clothes from the many charity shops in and around Rathmines and turned them into patchwork. She'd do anything to try and make a bit of extra cash. "Do I get to choose colours and designs?"

"As long as they're not beige!"

"I promise." Maggie's mind was in a whirl. She loved fabric and design. If wishes were fishes, design was the field she would have gone into. Ah well, they did say hindsight was 20/20 vision and she loved her girls – wouldn't trade them for the world.

"I don't know what kind of money we'd be talking about." Finn intended to sell her wedding and engagement rings. She needed more money than the small amount she was receiving from the estate. She wanted to stop counting pennies for a while.

"I don't either." Maggie had never made clothes for someone other than herself and her family. "Let me have a look at what you've got. We can figure something out." If she could get a few outfits made before Christmas, any money earned would go into her Santa fund.

"Right – follow me." Finn sighed – she didn't even want to look at the beige outfits she'd stuffed any old how into one of the attic wardrobes.

Maggie grabbed her glass and followed along. "I've always been curious about this house. I've asked Angie to put me on one of the teams she uses to clean it. It never happened. This place is like a slice of the past sitting right in the middle of the modern buildings around it."

"You can come over some day and walk all around if you want." Finn didn't mind having people look around the place. There was a lot to see.

"I'd love to." Maggie looked from side to side, running her hand along the glossy handrails as they climbed. What would it be like to live in a house like this?

"This house was built in a time when servants were plentiful," Finn said almost in answer to Maggie's thoughts. "It's not much fun trying to keep the place running when you are just one person. I can't imagine having a butler and housekeeper with a team of servants to order about and take all the responsibility off of my shoulders. I quite fancy having a silver bell to ring for a maid." Finn laughed at the thought. "I'm trying to convince my father and his partner to live here. They like to entertain and have the money needed for the upkeep of this place."

"It would make a great B&B." Maggie was almost panting

by now and having difficulty preventing her glass from slopping wine over its side. How many stairs did this place have?

"I would hate the work involved." Finn was having no problem running up the stairs. She stood at the top of the attic stairs, waiting for Maggie to join her.

"Jesus, I need air and gas after that!" Maggie put her glass on the floor and almost fell onto a tapestry chair against one of the attic walls.

"I don't want to even look at this lot." Finn pushed damp hands down the sides of her jeans. "I don't want to remember the woman I was when I wore them."

"Life's a bitch." Maggie leaned back and looked around. The attic was bigger than her house. It was free of dust but the thought of having to keep the house clean hadn't really occurred to her before. It would take all day every day to keep it polished and shining – she wouldn't fancy it. "I'll need to see you wearing them – get an idea of the fit."

"We'll need to be quick – Angie should be here soon." Finn kicked off the crocs she wore around the house. She pushed her jeans down her legs and stepped out of them, pulled her T-shirt over her head, and without checking pulled the first thing she touched out of one of the plastic bags. It was a dress. She pulled it over her head and waited.

"My mother wouldn't wear that." Maggie pushed to her feet. "It looks like it was designed to make you disappear." She pulled at the side seams. "It doesn't fit you properly. Is this a good example of everything that's in those bags?" She kicked at one of the stuffed black plastic bags.

"Pretty much. I have skirts, blouses, suits, tailored pants, jackets and dresses – all in beige and all deeply unflattering."

"Why on earth did you wear them?" Maggie stopped Finn from pulling more beige stuff from the bags. "You needn't bother." She'd seen enough with that one dress. She'd think of the items as fabric only. She'd take everything apart before dyeing the pieces and starting over.

"I didn't know any better." She'd never taken time to examine her own image. She had always been so intent on providing whatever service her men needed that she'd ignored her own.

"I'll take one bag away with me this evening. I need to see what I can do with the fabric before we can even think about making it up into anything." She wasn't too confident but she'd try.

"That will be Angie," Finn said when a bell rang loudly through the house. "I'll run ahead – you can take your time coming down." She grabbed one of the black plastic bags by the neck and took it with her.

"Took you long enough," Angie said when Finn unlocked and pulled open the door in the curtain wall.

"I was up in the attic with Maggie – showing her my old wardrobe – sorry." Finn shot the bolts behind them.

"That must be a pain." Angie indicated the door she'd stepped through.

"I'm learning to live with it." Finn led the way. "I had the gates put back up. We always left them open before so it was easy to step in and around them. I was glad of them this afternoon."

"I heard about Patrick and Miss Green."

Maggie was waiting for them in the hall.

"Hello, Angie."

Angie stared at her. "I tell you what," she said. "Here we are, three women without a man between them. The twenty-year-old –" she pointed at Maggie, "the woman entering her forties," she pointed at Finn, "and the one in her sixties," pointing to her own chest. "We look like an ad for laxatives or something."

"Trust you to think of something like that, Angie!" Maggie raised her almost empty glass to her boss.

"I see yez have hit the booze without me."

"I needed something to give me the courage to show Maggie my beige wardrobe." Finn led her guests into one of the drawing rooms. She illuminated the fireplace screen which showed a log-burning fire. It was pretty but it would never beat a real fire in her opinion. "Grab a pew!" She pointed to the green leather seats set around the fireplace. "I'll get some nibbles." She left them together.

"Why was she showing you her old clothes?" Angie lowered

herself into one of the chairs she'd admired and polished for years.

"Finn wants me to dye and update her beige wardrobe." Maggie took the chair across from Angie.

"High time if you ask me!"

Finn returned with a tray of nibbles, two glasses and a newly opened bottle of wine. She put the tray with its dips, cheese, fruit and crackers onto a coffee table and poured wine for Angie. With her own glass in hand she sat down to join her company. It was the first time she had ever invited friends of her own to her home, she'd realised while she was fetching the food and drink.

"What have you heard from the boys?" Angie asked.

"Not a lot." Finn grimaced. "They appear to be having a great time. I learn more from Pieter when he telephones. My sons are having too good a time to keep their mother up to date."

"Who is Pieter?" Maggie asked.

"Ah, now you've opened a can of worms." Angie laughed and settled back to listen to Finn explain once again how she'd got started in life.

"Jesus," Maggie was wide-eyed when Finn stopped talking. "It's like something out of the films."

"It's the only life I've ever known." Finn was going to have to stop drinking – her head was muzzy and she still had a meal to serve. "Let's go into the dining room and I'll serve the meal."

"Thank God – I'm starving." Angie stood.

"I always love a meal I don't have to prepare." Maggie didn't care what she ate. It was nice to be out of the house and in adult company. Her ma was babysitting this evening – there was football on the telly – her ma had been glad to get away from that.

Chapter 32

Finn stood in line at the bank, trying not to catch the eye of anyone in the queue. She was going to deposit Dare Lawrence's cheque – not the first one either. She couldn't believe how much money he was paying her for her nutjobs. The number of zeros on this cheque had made her dizzy.

Patrick was still bemoaning his lot every weekday on his radio programme. He'd had the cheek to give out her address live on air. She'd been forced to call the police to move women along who stopped to scream abuse at her from the street. He told everyone who would listen of his heartbreak at being kicked out of the 'family' home. It was almost the end of February – why couldn't he just let it go! The listening public seemed to be completely on his side.

She clutched her deposit slip tightly, fighting the urge to dance in the aisle. That would give the old biddies something to talk about!

Dare had made the first payment by bank transfer but at her request he now sent bank cheques. When Finn had seen the bank charges on that credit transfer she'd screamed. It had cost her hundreds of pounds as the money seemed to travel around the world and each bank took a slice of the total amount. They should be wearing a mask and carrying a gun – highway robbery.

* * *

Finn stood back to examine the row of microwave and freezer-safe plates on the kitchen island. She'd discovered she didn't like cooking for one. She stuck her tongue between her teeth and continued to pipe creamed potatoes around the rims of the plates. She'd decided to experiment with preparing and freezing meals for one. She was so tired of eating sandwiches and, when she did cook a meal, she had the darn thing for days. Maggie told her she was spoiled but she liked her meals to look and taste a certain way – if that was spoiled, well, she'd put up her hand. She carefully arranged the delicious-looking segments of Dijon rabbit in the middle of the plates over the colourful vegetables.

"I can have a delicious meal now and pull an individual meal out of the freezer when I want. Win-win no matter which way you look at it."

Before she could sit to her lonely meal the phone rang. She jumped to answer. She'd heard so little from her sons. They seemed to think a quick message telling her they were having a great time was enough information for her. She wanted details, darn it.

"Dare! How lovely to hear from you. I was just at the bank depositing your cheque. I'm still having a hard time believing you are willing to pay so much hard cash for my nutjobs. But don't stop." She slammed her mouth shut. She was gushing – how embarrassing.

"I'm glad to hear the cheque arrived safely. Christmas and the New Year caused me nothing but headaches as far as the mail is concerned. I had a lot of gifts to mail off." He had asked an art appraiser to give him a figure for the things he'd bought from Finn. He hoped she was pleased with the result. The price wasn't as high as it would be if she were a household name but it wasn't shabby either.

"It's called the post here, Yank," she said with a laugh.

"It seems I'll have to relearn the language when I'm finally able to return home to live."

"Still having problems making your children understand your desire to return home?" She'd heard a lot from Dare over the last few months.

"Yeah …" His sigh travelled over the line. "But that's not the reason I called." He didn't want to talk about his problems again. Finn was too good a listener. He'd telephoned over the Christmas holiday, thinking she'd be alone and lonely. Not so – she'd been so positive he'd been ashamed of his own depressed state. She became a good long-distance friend over the last few difficult months.

"Have you seen the articles about Tim Liner the movie star who wants to buy your work?" He had his fingers crossed. He wasn't sure how she'd react.

"My sons brought it to my attention." She laughed with genuine pleasure at the absurdity. "Rubbish."

"I'm afraid it's not." A deep sigh came over the line. "It's all my fault." He didn't know why he was apologising – any artist would be thrilled with the recognition – but not Finn – not yet anyway. "His current wife is a friend of mine. I gave her one of your nutjobs as a thank-you for all of her support of me and my kids."

The world-famous actor had offered him a mouth-watering sum for the large male figure he'd bought for his own enjoyment. He'd refused and the man continued to up the amount, unable to believe he couldn't buy what he wanted. Dare had no intention of selling the figure. He was in the fortunate position of not needing the money. Who knew a lad from a Dublin Corporation housing estate would ever be able to say that, let alone think it?

"You mean he really liked my tinkering?"

"*Will you for God's sake stop calling it that, woman!*" Dare bit out between clenched teeth. "It is art – *art* – can you try and remember that, you stubborn redhead!"

"But … it's just …"

"*Art!*" he shouted, not allowing her to denigrate her own talent in his hearing.

"Whatever." She couldn't be bothered arguing – every eye formed its own beauty.

"Listen," he said. "I have something to tell you – I –"

"Hold on a minute – there's someone at the gate." She switched views on the screen and saw Angie and Maggie standing outside. What on earth were they doing here? "I have to let your mother in – hold on."

She ran through and out of the house.

"Come in quick!" She pulled the door in the curtain wall open. "Lock the door at your backs! I have Dare hanging on in the kitchen." She ran back into the house.

"Sounds kinky." Maggie nudged Angie with her elbow.

"Hush up, you!" Angie pushed home the bolts on the door. "God, gates and bolts – I couldn't be doing with this malarkey every time someone wants to drop by for a cup of tea."

"She's lucky she has a big wall and locked gates around her house now," Maggie said. "That Patrick Brennan has a lot to answer for – imagine giving out his wife's details to the public. She should sue him. Although the women who have turned up here shouting abuse need their ears boxed. Where is the female support, I ask you?"

The two women followed Finn in, Maggie pulling a shopping trolley behind her. They paused to hang their coats on the coat stand in the hallway.

"*Morning, Mother!*" Dare shouted at Angie. Finn had told him she'd put him on speakerphone.

"It's afternoon here, son."

"It's an ungodly hour of the morning here," Dare responded. "Look, Mother, you know what I want you to do?"

"Yes, but I haven't had a chance to talk to Finn about it yet. I'm doing nothing without her permission."

"You can do that later." He pushed a hand down his tired face. "I have to get some sleep. Finn, I'm sorry – I wanted to talk to you before my mother arrived. I'm afraid I weakened and gave your telephone number to Tim Liner, the actor. He goes to the studio at an ungodly hour and is planning to get in touch with you on the way there this morning. You have about four hours before he gets in touch. Sorry. My mother can explain." Dare shut down his side of the connection – he'd opened the lines of communication. It was up to them now. He was tired and going to bed – no doubt he'd hear all about it when he woke up.

"I'm staying." Maggie pulled forward her polka-dot shopping trolley. Gone were the days when she travelled at the wheel of a Mercedes, feeling like queen of the road. "The kids are at school." She started pulling items from the trolley. "I'll get my parents to pick them up if yer man runs late."

"Would someone please explain to me what is going on?" Finn began to put the congealing food on her kitchen island into freezer bags. No use letting good food go to waste. This pair would tell her what had brought them to her door – eventually.

"Are you having a party, Finn?" Angie was looking at all the food.

"I'm going to freeze this lot."

"I'll give you a hand!" Angie knew her way around this kitchen. It took them no time at all to cover the plates and put them into the giant box freezer in the mudroom.

"You would not believe the fun I have had dyeing your old clothes." Maggie was putting the items she'd pulled from her trolley, neatly folded, onto a section of the long kitchen work surface. "My kids have begun to think their mother is a witch." She was nervous about presenting the clothing she'd prepared. She'd never charged for updating old clothes before. Would Finn like what she'd done?

"I'll put the kettle on." Angie pushed Finn into a chair.

The bell on the gate sounded. Finn looked to see who else was calling on her today. If it was more of Patrick's crazed fans, she was calling the Garda.

"Name of God, what are Paul and Scott doing here?"

She sat and simply stared at the image of the two men on her kitchen computer screen.

"I'll let them in." Maggie ran out of the kitchen.

"Are you ever going to tell me what's going on, Angie?" Finn asked.

"I am so excited!" Paul almost bounced into the kitchen. "I couldn't sleep last night after you called me, Angie." He clasped two hands to his chest. "Tim Liner. This is the ult!" He turned to beam at Finn. "I'm doing your make-up, sweetie."

"I'm doing your hair." Scott followed his partner into the kitchen.

"If someone doesn't tell me what's going on soon, I won't be responsible for my actions!" Finn almost shouted over the excited babble of the others.

"Hang on a minute and I'll tell yeh." Angie began to bring mugs of tea over to the island.

A minute later they were settled down, sipping tea.

"Diarmuid called me last night," Angie began. "He told me that actor fella is determined to buy some of your work. He'll not take no for an answer. He has my poor Diarmuid motheaten, demanding he sell him one of the pieces my Diarmuid picked out for himself."

Finn was looking bemused.

"Angie called me," Maggie said. "I suggested she call Paul and Scott."

"We were delighted to agree to attend to you personally," Paul said soberly but spoiled it when he screamed *"Tim Liner!"* aloud and threw his arms in the air. "I can't believe someone I know is going to talk to and meet the great man – God," once more the hands were clutched to his chest, "I almost had a heart attack at the very thought."

"Please!" Finn dropped her head onto the table.

"It's like this." Maggie took control. "That actor could be the making of you. If he buys one of your nutjobs, everyone in the world is going to want one." She waited to see if Finn would say anything but when she remained mute continued with her explanation. "Dare let it drop that your man does nothing without sending in 'his people' to check out the situation. Your friends got together," she waved a hand around the company, "and we decided you couldn't talk to your man's 'people' wearing your sons' castoffs and without a touch of make-up. So, here we are. We are going to find your look – your fashionable artist look – and it will be great. All you will have to do is talk to the man."

"It's all about presentation, dear," Paul said.

"Even if the man himself can't see you," Scott put in. "How you feel about yourself when you speak with him could be all important. We want to help."

There was silence as everyone waited for her to react.

"Are yez all mad? I'm not going to talk to the man. I won't accept his call." She went to push back her chair.

"Oh yes, you will, if I have to tie you to the bloody chair myself." Angie reached over and pushed Finn back into her seat.

It was madness. Finn was pushed, pulled and poked around.

Her opinion wasn't asked or needed. She was ordered to shower, wash and condition her hair and, with Scott and Maggie waiting outside her bathroom door, she obeyed.

Downstairs, Angie was reading the instructions her son had sent her aloud to Paul and the list of nutjobs he thought would appeal to the actor.

"I know where most of those should be," Paul said. "We might have some trouble finding all of them. Emmet and Rolf have moved a lot of Finn's stuff out to Bray." He stopped to think for a moment. "If we don't find the ones Dare asked for, I'll select others. God knows Finn has twenty years of producing her little wonders stored in that shed out the back. Who knows what we'll find when we root around?" He'd been wanting a chance to pull that shed apart for years.

"How do you know about them? I didn't think Finn ever showed her work to anyone." She'd thought Finn kept her tinkering secret.

"That's how we met. She was having trouble with elbows and knees, she told me. I thought she was crazy until she explained. I've been giving her lessons in welding for some time." He'd been forced to train as a welder in his youth. "We've been getting together for years and letting our hair down while we create. It's been a lot of fun." He'd never thought of turning his welding skills to anything like Finn's artwork.

"Right." Angie had run a cloth over the kitchen surfaces. "We'll have to dust and polish the items we want. We can't bring them into the kitchen covered in cobwebs."

"Perish the thought," said Paul.

"Come on," said Angie. "Follow me. She's given me the key."

Paul followed her out.

They carried the little sculptures they found into the mudroom first. They were unable to find some that Dare had asked to be displayed. That didn't bother them and Paul had a great time choosing his own favourites.

Finn came out of her bathroom in a towelling robe, a towel around her head.

"I'd better trim your hair in the bathroom." Scott snapped

his scissors. "You don't want to spend weeks getting hair out of your bedroom carpet."

"I want to show you what I've done." Maggie had carried all of the items she'd taken from her trolley into the bedroom. She put everything on the bed.

"Follow along, Maggie." Scott pushed Finn in front of him back into her bathroom. "You can talk while I snip."

"OK." Maggie grabbed an item and followed as ordered. "I dyed several pairs of your trousers black." She held the trousers up so Finn could view it in the bathroom mirror. "I'll need to check the fit but for the moment you can get away with wearing them – I hope."

"Just move your eyes, sweetie, not your head!" Scott barked.

"You can never have enough black trousers," said Maggie.

She left the bathroom and re-entered holding a sweater up.

"That's a fabulous shade of green." Scott leaned slightly towards the mirror. "Matches her eyes."

"You would not believe the colours available in modern dyes." Maggie had shopped like a fool. She'd picked up so many different colours – always with Finn in mind – and played around with hot and cold dyes. She'd loved every minute of it.

"Black and green are great together," Scott was snipping at Finn's hair and talking directly to Maggie, "but trousers and a sweater – kind of boring for an important outfit, don't you think?"

"I have a special outfit in mind." Maggie bit her lip. "I'll show it to you both when her hair is finished." She left the bathroom to display the outfit across the bedspread, glad no one could see her knees knocking.

"I'll go help Paul." Scott had cut and dried Finn's hair into a flattering feathery cloud around her head. He stopped with his hand on the bedroom doorknob. "If you'll take my advice, Maggie – I'd have Finn put on her underwear then have her close her eyes – put the outfit on before you ask her opinion." He'd seen the outfit spread over the bed. It was unusual but fabulous.

"Can we do that?" Maggie stood in the bathroom door, looking in at Finn with worried brown eyes.

"Why not?" Finn stared into her own green eyes, wondering

how she had lost control of the situation. Lost control, she thought, staring at herself – did you ever have it?

She went out to the bedroom, put on her underwear and then stood, eyes closed, while Maggie dressed her and turned her around, presumably to face the full-length mirror.

"You can open your eyes now."

Finn opened her eyes and stared at her image.

Maggie was standing behind her, holding her breath.

"I love it," Finn said.

Maggie rushed into speech. "I noticed you seem to like to wear the boys' sleeveless ski jackets. I made the sleeveless jacket out of two old-dear dresses you had."

"With the weather we have and the work I do, sleeveless jackets are a blessing." Finn was surprised to hear she had a style of dressing. She'd fallen into the habit of grabbing the most comfortable thing she could find to wear. She shrugged and began swinging around, watching the ankle-length jacket swirl around her body. She was wearing basic black slacks and a black V-neck sweater. The jacket was the main attraction. "How did you manage to find two shades of the same colour?" The jacket was panelled in shades of aubergine. It was stunning and turned a basic outfit into a work of art.

"I didn't." Maggie was almost collapsing in relief. "It's the fabric – the dye turns out a different colour on different fabric – it's a joy to work with."

"*Are you nearly ready?*" Paul shouted up the stairs. He still had to do her make-up. He'd do it in the kitchen – the worktops and bright light made the place ideal for his needs – he couldn't wait to get started. "*I have to turn you into a vision of loveliness!*"

"Would that involve surgery?" Finn walked to the top of the stairs. She was wearing black boots to complete the outfit. "I don't know what all this fuss is about. It's not like the bloody man is even going to see me."

"Just my skill." Paul ignored her complaints. He gave Maggie a nod of admiration. The outfit looked great on Finn's tall body.

Back in the kitchen, Angie didn't have time to admire Finn's image. "Finn, we couldn't find four of the figures Dare wants put in place here." She described the ones they couldn't locate.

"But Paul has chosen substitutes. Is that OK?"

"The jug-eared boy is definitely not here – Rolf wanted that for himself – and I guess he took the other three away too. But I don't understand – he won't be able to see the figures so why set them up?"

"Dare wants you to describe these particular ones if yer man asks what you have on offer," said Angie.

"Sit down." Paul pushed Finn into a chair. He had his cosmetics laid out and ready.

"Give us a hand, Maggie," Angie said. "Scott, put the kettle on again."

"We'll step into the mudroom when he calls you," Scott said when Paul had completed Finn's make-up. "Be sure to press record on your phone – you'll probably be all flustered and forget half of what he says."

The make-up was among Paul's best efforts. Finn's green eyes looked enormous, her generous lips were moist and inviting, her skin glowed like a pearl – yet it all looked natural.

"This is ridiculous!" Finn wailed. "I'm going to be so nervous I won't be able to speak and I don't know why I'm all dolled up like the dog's dinner just to take a phone call." She'd never be able to force words past her lips at this rate. "I'm starving. I never got to eat the meal I'd prepared."

"Dear God, you can't eat before you speak to the great man!" Paul gasped. "Not with your make-up done! My work would be ruined!"

Scott pulled her into the mudroom and, with his hands on her shoulders, forced her to face her image in the long mirror attached to the wall there.

"Look, this is the image you should present to the world. You can't keep going around in your sons' cast-offs trying to be the invisible woman. Enough! We are in the year 1999 heading towards 2000 and doesn't that sound like science fiction – anyway, you want to be a new woman. Well, that starts now."

They stood gazing into the mirror.

"The way you feel about yourself will come across in your voice," Scott went on. "You want to sound calm and efficient – not apologetic. You are an artist. Your work is in demand. You have to sound like that when you speak to this man. This is too important to fuck up!"

"See why I love him?" Paul with Angie and Maggie behind stood in the doorway of the mudroom. "The man could get a job as an agony aunt!"

"OK."

The ringing of the telephone had all five of them scattering.

Finn took a deep breath before picking up the phone. She pressed record before answering. She'd feel a right fool if it was just someone trying to sell her something.

"Ms. Emerson?"

Oh, sweet Baby Jesus! It was him! She'd recognise that voice anywhere.

"Hello," said Finn. "Diarmuid Lawrence wa – told me you'd be calling." She bit back the word *warned* just in time. She hoped he hadn't noticed.

"Who – oh sure – Dare."

There was a pause for a moment and Finn frantically wondered if she was supposed to say more.

"So, you know why I'm calling – that's good. I'll cut right to the chase – I want one of them nutjobs – one just like the one Dare has – that kettle makes me laugh every time I see it."

"I'm sorry – I don't recreate my work." Finn tried to keep her eyes away from the terrible foursome who were gripping each other in horror at her words. "I design original figures. I never repeat a design." She heard her own words and thought she sounded like a pompous twit – her work – her design – who did she think she was?

"That's a shame – I don't suppose you could change your mind – just this once?"

She could practically see his world-famous wide beaming grin. He made his living from the charm of his smile and handsome face.

"Sorry, that would be impossible." Finn had been married to a man just like him. She wasn't about to crumble. Besides – it was hard to get those old kettles that she'd used in the nutjob Dare loved so much. She made whatever the metal suggested to her. She wouldn't know how to recreate her own work.

"That little figure Dare gave to my wife sure is cute but I'd like something bigger." He wasn't going to let Dare have a bigger figure than him.

"Mr. Liner –"

"Call me Tim, no need to stand on dignity."

"Tim." She could see Paul almost swooning in Scott's arms – the ham. "I don't make a great many large figures. I have some on hand at the moment but really – I let the material I'm using – I suppose you could say I let it talk to me. I don't make to order."

"I'm almost at the studio and I've lines to learn." His voice became all business. "Look – I have to be in London in a few weeks to pick up a BAFTA – those good folks are giving me a special award." He paused, perhaps waiting for her to gush, but then continued. "If I pop over to Ireland – would you be able to show me your work then?"

"I suppose I could." Finn grabbed the back of a chair pushed under the island in a white-knuckled grip.

"Good. Got to go – you have a nice day. I'll have my assistant get in touch with details nearer to the day. Good talking to you." He broke the connection.

"He wants to come to Ireland and see my work for himself," she said in a daze staring at the phone in her hand.

Finn's kitchen exploded with shouts of surprise – exclamations of delight – and basic hysteria. It all went over Finn's head. She was too busy trying to catch her breath. She dropped into a chair, let the phone fall to the surface, and moved her hands towards her face.

"*Stop!*" Paul screamed. "Do not dare mess up my make-up before I've taken a photograph."

She leaned against the chairback with her eyes closed but didn't touch her face. She didn't dare.

"God, Finn," Angie dropped into a chair across from her, "you talked to him just like he was human."

"As far as I know he is." Finn didn't open her eyes.

"You know what I mean."

"I'd have been a nervous wreck." Scott too dropped into a chair.

Maggie put the kettle on.

Chapter 33

Finn picked up the handles of her red wheelbarrow, ready to get out of the house and scour the local markets. The first months of the year were a great time for scrap metal. People had bought or received gifts of pots, pans and cutlery over the Christmas period. They always dumped what they didn't want, much to her delight.

She walked around the local flea market, making like a bandit. There was so much on offer. Patrick had stopped her line of credit and repossessed her little car. She missed it. Thanks to the money Dare had put in her account she had enough for a healthy deposit on a car but the thought of going into debt – needing to make regular payments – frightened her. She couldn't bank on selling more of her nutjobs.

She'd had to sell her engagement and wedding rings for scrap value only. The jeweller told her the diamonds were inferior. It was funny but painful. She'd paid Maggie for all of the work done so far on her old clothes. Maggie told her that she'd passed the best Christmas in years – not because she'd spent madly – it was knowing she had money in the bank if needed that made it good.

She wanted to try painting some of her nutjobs. Maggie's almost manic delight at dyeing fabric had given her the idea.

"You'll not get much more on there."

"Think of the devil!" Finn looked up at Maggie in surprise. "You going home?"

"I'll have to clear out this lot and come back." Finn straightened her back painfully.

"I have something for you." Maggie held up one of her patchwork shopping bags.

"I'll be glad of a break."

The two women walked slowly back to Finn's home.

"Before I show you this, I want to say …" Maggie held closed her bag, "if you don't like it I won't be insulted."

"I've loved everything you've produced for me so far." Finn put the kettle on – she was gasping for a cup of tea.

"I thought," Maggie still didn't open the bag, "if you are going to be known as a big-time artist," she held up her hand and shushed Finn when she looked like objecting, "you should have a signature look." She pulled a long black garment from the bag and shook it open, displaying another long sleeveless jacket. "I've embroidered it with flowers and birds using the colours of the dyes I've used on your clothing. If you hang it behind the kitchen door – you can grab it and cover whatever you're wearing at the time. You know in case members of the press or a famous actor drop in. The colours in this jacket will match anything you wear." She looked up nervously. "It's only machine embroidery – no big deal."

"Maggie!" Finn spread open the folds of the garment. "It's magnificent – a work of art."

"It is not." Maggie blushed. "Don't be silly."

Finn froze for a moment and looked at her friend. "My God, is that how I sound when I talk about my nutjobs? To my eyes this," she gently shook the jacket, "should be framed and on my wall."

"I loved making it." Maggie shrugged. "It's so easy for me and so much pleasure – it seems wrong to charge for it."

"We, my friend – are going to have to work on our attitude." Finn would take time to think about this moment later. "Sit down. I'll make us something to eat. I want to go back to the markets and see what else I can find before someone gets there before me."

The street bell sounded.

Finn pushed a button to check the screen. Then she stood frozen, her hands pressed to her mouth, tears starting to her eyes.

Maggie was determined to protect her friend. She ran for the door. She'd send whoever was there away with a flea in their ear.

"Young woman, who are you? What are you doing?" a strong male voice demanded.

The sight that met Finn's eyes had her laughing aloud. Maggie was trying to keep Emmet Emerson from stepping over the threshold.

"*Da!*" Finn rushed to the door.

Maggie beat a hasty retreat to the kitchen.

Finn threw herself at him. She knew her da would catch her. The feel of his strong familiar arms closing around her was blissful.

"Da, what are you doing here? Why didn't you tell me you were coming?" Finn was kissing her father's cheek and squeezing the daylights out of him.

"Would you let me in before you question me to death, woman?" Emmet pushed Finn away from him to stare into her face. She looked wonderful – happy and full of life. He'd been worried about her but his daughter looked better than she had in years, he was delighted to see.

"Come on in." Finn wiped tears from her eyes and pulled at her father's hand. "Want a cup of tea?"

"Does a dog bark?"

Emmet allowed Finn to pull him through the house into the kitchen where she introduced him to her friend. He grinned, thinking he'd have to call Rolf and tell him their girl was making friends. Rolf worried Finn was spending too much time alone.

The conversation became general with Maggie asking Emmet about his travels. Finn loved to listen to her da entertain people. He enjoyed talking about the places he'd been.

"Daughter, my stomach thinks me throat's been cut," Emmet finally groaned. "I'm starving. I can't talk with me taste buds dripping."

"I should leave," Maggie said. "Let you two talk."

"Oh no, Maggie, stay!"

"Don't leave on my account," Emmet said.

"I'll have lunch with Finn another time. You two enjoy your visit. I'll get along."

"I really am starving, Finn – can we go get something to eat?" Emmet said when Finn returned from showing her friend out.

"I was going to defrost meals I've prepared," Finn offered.

"I'll pass on that, thanks. I fancy some pub grub. Is there a decent place around here somewhere?"

"OK, Da, fess up." Finn demanded as soon as they were seated at a window table in a local pub. The menu was written on a blackboard. They could decide what they wanted to eat from where they were. "What's going on, why are you here without Rolf?"

"That brother of Rolf's, Dolph – he's a big noise in German television. I'm not sure what, director of programmes or something like that. Anyway, he has Rolf booked on chat shows talking about the cottages and showing his photographs. Ronan and Oisín have found roles as guest stars in some kind of vampire thing that's been running for years on German television. They have taken the place by storm. Your sons are turning into minor heartthrobs on German daytime television." Emmet examined the menu.

"My sons?" They'd never mentioned anything about this in the few short missives home.

"The very same." Emmet ordered Guinness stew and a bottle of red wine from the waitress.

Finn ordered stew too. She hardly cared what she ate – she needed to hear about her boys.

"Da? Tell me more."

"Your sons, daughter, are having the time of their lives. Ronan is drowning in family. The boy spends hours comparing every little feature of his that matches his cousins. What is it with that boy and family?" Emmet shook his head. "Oisín plans to spend every spare minute he has behind the wheel of my camper van. That boy has wanderlust."

"So I gave birth to one son for Rolf and one for you – nice to be useful."

"There is that."

"Did you give Oisín money, Da?"

"Nope." Emmet waggled his eyebrows. "I didn't have to. The lads earned a tidy bundle taking their shirts off and oiling their manly chests. Ronan lapped it up. Oisín is taking the money but I don't think his heart is in it – he's got a good head on his shoulders. He knows the kind of money they are offering him now might never come his way again."

Finn waited while the waitress served their food and poured the wine.

"What about Rolf, Da? What's he planning?"

"Finn, for the first time in years I haven't a clue." Emmet ran fingers over his face. "The man is having the time of his life being a minor celebrity in his own country. His family are around all the time. Ingrid is playing Queen to his King. I left before I said something I shouldn't."

"Da, are you and Rolf having problems?" Finn had never seen her father without Rolf by his side.

"No, nothing like that – we love each other, this is just a bump in the road." Emmet sighed and dug into his food.

"You're sure there is nothing wrong between you and Rolf?"

"Everything is fine." Emmet poured more wine. "Tell me how things are going with you?" He didn't want to talk about his private life.

"I'm getting there one day at a time."

"I've a feeling Pieter and his family want to spend time with you. He really enjoyed meeting you and can't stop talking about his visit to meet his Irish sister. How do you feel about that?"

"I talk to Pieter on the phone a lot. We're getting to know each other."

"Glad to hear it."

"Here you go, Da." Finn had made him a hot whiskey as soon as they reached home.

He took the mug from her hand. Now he was in out of the cold he felt great. The brisk walk, fresh air and wind had really got his system moving. He checked his phone for messages.

"I missed a few calls while we were out. I don't know if I love or hate these bloomin' phones."

"Anything important?" She checked her own phone.

"Patrick, it's Finn."

"Nuala, it's about time you came to your senses." Patrick had been confident this call would come. It might have taken longer than he'd expected but it was happening now. Nuala wasn't fit to live alone. She needed someone to guide her. He'd go softly with her – now the call had come he could afford to be magnanimous. He was mentally kissing goodbye to this one-bedroom flat. He'd had enough of living in this tiny space that cost a small fortune to rent.

She refused to comment on his asinine assumption. "Patrick, the reason I called –"

"There's no need to go into that now, darling." Patrick was almost purring with satisfaction. "I know you've made some mistakes but we can put all of that behind us. Why don't I come home? I want things to return to the way they were. You can cook me one of your special meals and we'll talk."

"Patrick, the reason I called," Finn repeated from between clenched teeth, "is that the first of the boys' German television appearances has been shown. There will be clips on Irish television this afternoon." The frantic phone calls from Germany had been to tell her to tune in. It was a feature section of a regular program covering Irish success abroad.

"I know, darling. I'm so proud of the sons you gave me." Patrick waited for her to beg him to come back home.

"I'm glad." She hung up. She had nothing to add.

"Sugar, come back to bed."

Patrick had completely forgotten the woman he'd left languishing in his bed. He'd carried his mobile phone into the tiny lounge for privacy. What was her name again?

"Coming, dear!"

Perhaps he should get rid of whatever her name was, call Nuala and invite her out for a meal. It would make good copy for him to be seen taking his wife out for an intimate evening. He needed to do something about his image. The reporters were paying too much attention to the women in his life. He could tip off a few reporters he knew. He could take time to discuss a possible reconciliation on his radio programme. That should add to the numbers. The radio programme was his bread and butter now he'd learned he'd lost the chance of presenting that current affairs programme on TV.

"How did it go?" Emmet asked when Finn rejoined him in the kitchen.

"The man's a fool but I did what I thought was right." She shrugged off the depression that wanted to sit on her shoulders. She was surviving – building a new life – she would not wallow in regrets.

"So Pieter and his truck will be here any day now with your belated Christmas gift from the family in Germany."

The flurry of phone calls from Germany had been to inform them of that as well as the boys' television appearance.

"I'm going to spend a few days with Harry Bailey," he added, "so you'll have the place to yourself."

"Running away, Da?"

"To a certain extent." He'd had enough of family for a while.

Pieter was driving one of his company's rigs over – must be a bloody big gift – he was glad for Finn.

Chapter 34

"The problem with being the boss," Pieter grunted with effort, "is you never get to do the fun things you love to do. I can't tell you how much I'm enjoying doing this work with you."

A sixteen-wheeler truck bearing the name of Pieter's company was parked on Finn's driveway. The truck was a travelling workshop. The back of the cab was a living area for the driver. Finn had spent time with the driver Heinrich, exploring the interior of the truck. It was fascinating to see the efficient use of space. Every tool Pieter could possibly need was at hand.

"It's an amazing gift." Finn sat back on her heels, admiring the flow of natural light around her through the glass roof panels Pieter had fitted to her work shed. She was enjoying working with this man but it was the videos of her sons that he'd brought with him that she truly cherished.

"The gift is not solely from me," Pieter reminded her. He was walking on eggshells around this self-contained sister of his. She'd refused all invitations to visit her family in Germany.

"I didn't know tough glass roof panels like this were on the market."

"You have told me how much you admire the houses my company builds, *ja?*"

"I've seen your buildings featured on British television programmes." Finn had recorded the programmes to drool over at her leisure.

"Rolf suggested putting one of my small module houses here." Pieter pointed out the open door of the workshop. "He worries that if he and Emmet move into the house you will not want to stay with them."

"Wow, Pieter, that's a lot for me to think about."

"You are building a new life for yourself, *ja?*" Pieter knew Finn's husband was living in a luxury bachelor apartment. "You need new surroundings."

"*Vater*, are we to visit this place you talk about?" The driver of the truck appeared in the garden, speaking in English for the first time in Finn's hearing. "I want to see these pubs."

"*Vater?*" Finn looked at Pieter with raised eyebrows. "Father?"

"Heinrich, you are a trial to your parent." Pieter should have known that allowing his son to drive the truck to Ireland was asking for trouble, but Heinrich had been eaten alive with curiosity about this Irish aunt he'd never met. "Finn, meet my disobedient son Heinrich." Pieter had allowed his son to accompany him on the strict understanding that he would keep their relationship private. He did not want to damage the delicate relationship he was building with his sister by introducing relatives without her permission.

"I must say, Heinrich, you've developed an amazing knowledge of English overnight." Finn had spent days picking this young man's brain for information about building and the tools stashed in the truck. "You watched me struggle to find the German word for every work tool in that truck."

"I needed the time it took you to find the right word." Heinrich grinned. "While you tried to find a word in German I tried to remember the use for each tool. It was lucky my *vater* had trained me well."

Why had she never noticed how familiar that cheeky grin was?

"So, it would appear I've been allowing my own nephew to sleep on my driveway."

Finn wasn't aware this was the first time she'd claimed any relationship to Pieter and his family but Pieter was very aware of the step forward.

"I didn't mind – it was fun." Heinrich pushed his hands into his jeans and stood grinning at his father and aunt. "So, what do you say? Are we going to visit Temple Bar or this Bray?"

"I suppose Eddie Coyle never took you to Temple Bar?" Finn crossed her arms and stared at the young man with the earnest blue eyes. "I find that hard to believe." Finn had asked Ronan's friend Eddie to take the German driver around Dublin. She'd thought Eddie would appreciate the chance to practise his German, a language he was studying at college.

"He did, yes, of course." Heinrich nodded his head. "But I prefer to spend my parents' money. We visited the pubs but I would like to visit some of the restaurants."

"Heinrich, I despair!" said Pieter.

"Grab your bags, Heinrich, and come into the house," Finn said.

"I have been trying to talk Finn into putting one of our custom-designed modules in her garden," Pieter said when all three had walked over what felt to Finn like every inch of the house.

"Good idea," said Heinrich.

They were sitting in the lounge drinking coffee.

"So, Heinrich, are you studying business at university?" Finn asked.

"No," Heinrich replied. "I'm studying Media."

"Didn't you want to go into the family business?" Finn was surprised. He'd been a mine of information when she'd questioned him about it.

"We are a large family. We have many fingers in the pie – that is how you say it, yes? Media is also the family business."

"Really?" Finn was astonished.

Pieter laughed. "Yes, our family have been leaders in the field of television and film for generations."

Finn envied Heinrich his choices. She had no qualifications. She'd thought about returning to school but had no idea what she wanted to study

"Please, I am curious," Heinrich said. "What is the reason for the shelving going around the house under the ceilings?" He'd been examining it but couldn't understand its function.

"I'll show you." Finn didn't know how they'd react nor did she care. "I'll be a minute." She'd set up command central in her kitchen, where else?

The sound of a train whistle echoed and a tiny train puffed into view, speeding along the rails hidden on the shelving under the ceiling. The men jumped to their feet.

"A steam train!" Pieter almost ran after the little train. "Finn, this is *wonderbar!*" Pieter and Heinrich watched the train run all around the downstairs and up the stairs across the upstairs hall and back down the stairway to continue its journey around the house.

"The train was a childhood gift for my boys." She laughed. "Well, it was for my boys but really it was something I had always dreamed of having."

She'd wanted to put up this train set when the boys were young, but Patrick had been horrified by the idea. His gentle hints and sorrowful headshakes had convinced Finn it would be inappropriate to have a train running around her house. She'd put the shelving up over Christmas.

"I didn't have enough track to cover the house. Then I found a load of track for sale at the market." She'd been unable to believe her eyes when she'd seen it and so reasonably priced. It was her Christmas gift to herself. "I was lucky enough to buy more carriages and rolling stock to add on to my original train. I'm keeping a look-out for hardware to complement the set." She wanted to put in train stations and bridges eventually.

They continued to watch the train, delighted by the steam whistle that rang out on each bend in the track. Heinrich's face felt sore his grin was so wide. What an amazing woman this unknown aunt of his was turning out to be! He couldn't wait to tell his brother and sisters about this.

"*Vater* – we need to film this."

Pieter turned in place. "The camera!" He slapped his forehead. "I am cursed by a family that must record every little thing. Rolf hasn't seen this, has he? There would be hours of film if he had."

"I haven't finished it yet." Finn was pleased her train set was being admired.

"Can you stop it, please, Finn?" Pieter smiled. "I would love to examine it. Do you have a set of steps? I will need them, I think. I can bring in the set from my truck if I need to."

"No need for steps," Finn said. "I set up the central train station in one of my kitchen wall cupboards." The men almost ran after her into the kitchen.

Finn leaned against her kitchen counter, watching the males examine her train set-up. She grinned with pleasure when Heinrich and Pieter began to plan making little additions to her railroad, wondering what they might have in the truck to cobble together stations. She loved to share her pleasure in the train.

Eventually they settled down at the kitchen island with more coffee.

"If we leave Bray till tomorrow we can spend the day there," Finn said, "but tonight my da is taking his fiddle and joining in a session in one of the local pubs." She'd take them out on the DART. She was finding her lack of a car embarrassing.

"You will have to wrap up well, Heinrich," Pieter said. "The wind would slice you in two."

"Yes, let us wait to visit Bray tomorrow," Heinrich said. "It will be pleasant to listen to Emmet and his music."

"Is anyone hungry?" Finn wouldn't mind a snack. She had a ham hock and split-pea soup ready to serve.

"I could eat." Pieter wondered how soon his children would demand he put a train set in their home. He'd seen the longing in Heinrich's eyes.

The sudden ringing of the telephone sounded loud in the kitchen.

"Do you need us to leave?" Pieter stood and stretched.

"There is no need." Finn picked up her phone. "Mr. Atkinson." Finn's eyes almost crossed when she recognised her caller. The man was driving her insane. You would think he was trying to organise the Second Coming of Christ the way he continued to find problems. "What can I do for you?" She put the phone on speaker so she could continue to prepare a meal. He'd be blethering for ages.

239

"I am concerned, Ms. Emerson." The noise of paper rattling came over the line – the man was obviously consulting notes. "You do not appear to appreciate the great compliment being paid to you. It is not usual for a star of …" He hesitated to even mention his client's name – who knew who might be listening? – but in the end he had no choice. "Of Mr Liner's magnitude to arrange private visits like this – I need to be reassured that you will do everything in your power to see that the great man is extended every courtesy."

"I have already told you – on several occasions – that I will treat the man as a guest to my home. That is all I can promise. I am unaccustomed to visits of this magnitude." Tongue in cheek, she added, "No one can quite appreciate the wonder of a visit from such a personage."

The sarcasm went right over the man's head. He continued to drone on about all the minutia he insisted must be in place. Finn didn't listen, just let him waffle. She'd heard it all before. She wasn't going to lay out the red carpet for the man. She hadn't invited him to visit.

"Are you listening to me, Ms. Emerson?"

"I'm hanging on your every word, Mr. Atkinson,"

"I'll call again nearer to the date." The man snapped the connection off.

"Finn!"

She spun around in surprise. "Oh, I'd forgotten you were there." She threw her hands up in the air. "That man frustrates me so. I'd like to box his ears. Who the hell does he think he is? He calls day and night." It was only when she focused on father and son that she noticed that both had tears running down their faces. "Is something wrong?"

It was as if she had let the air out of a balloon – both exploded in red-faced laughter.

She stood with her hands on her hips, staring at the other two. They were clutching each other – every time they looked at Finn they went off into fresh gales of laughter – it was beginning to annoy her.

"I'm sorry." Pieter wiped the tears from his face with a pristine handkerchief he pulled from his trouser pocket.

"Me too," Heinrich pulled the cloth from his father's hand and used it on his own face.

"Care to explain?"

"You have no idea –" Heinrich tried to explain but got the hiccups.

"My Uncle Dolph," Pieter calmed enough to say, "would crawl on his hands and knees from Germany to America for the chance of a word with that man." He pointed at the phone as if the officious Mr. Atkinson was sitting there.

"The man he says is coming to visit you – Tim Liner." Heinrich was trying to hold his breath to stop the hiccups. "Do you have any idea of his power in the film industry? His name alone is a guarantee of success."

"I don't really care how powerful the man is." Finn turned her attention back to her meal preparation. "He's a large pain in my arse, that's all."

To her horror the other two were off again. She left them to it. She didn't understand what was causing so much mirth nor did she care.

"Why don't you two shower and change?" she suggested. "The soup can wait."

She listened to them laugh and joke while walking upstairs. She sighed with relief – she needed a moment to herself. She bit back a curse when the phone rang again. She was tempted to ignore it – but her curiosity would kill her.

"Hello, Mum, how's it going?" Oisín said.

"Oisín!" Finn wanted to kiss the phone. She missed her sons so much.

"Did you watch the videos Uncle Pieter brought over, Mum?"

"I did." About a hundred times. One of the videos had been shot in the almost derelict kitchen of one of the Bray houses. A fire burned in the black range. "I couldn't believe my eyes when I saw you and Ronan wearing Aran sweaters and tweed hats. You two wouldn't wear something like that without a gun pointed at your chest."

"That, Mum, is Uncle Rolf's impression of an old-fashioned Irish pub." Oisín's laugh sounded sweet in her ear. "Granda gave Rolf a description of an old shebeen. The two of them got all the neighbours on the Parade involved."

"This is the movie you lot made while you were in Bray?" While she'd been busy trying to end her marriage with as much dignity as possible – embroiled in lawyers and paperwork? But she'd been glad Rolf was keeping her sons busy playing at making movies, being Steven Spielberg.

"There is more, Mum." He knew she hated to be taken by surprise. He didn't think she had a clue what she was in for. "You need to talk to Grandfather and, if Pieter is still there, ask him about his Uncle Dolph – that family can sure pick names, can't they?" He was surprised by how much he missed his mother. He wished he could hug her. "Rolf sent that footage to his brother Dolph, and Dolph used it to make computer-generated images or CGI as it's called in the trade."

"Smart Alec – get you!"

"Pieter's daughter Frieda is a popular child star. She needs to make the transition to young adult."

"Jayzus, Oisín, what have they done to you? I don't understand a word you're saying."

"Rolf's family have been heavily involved in the development of German television for generations." Oisín tried to explain the juggernaut that was going to descend on her soon. "Dolph is considered a pioneer in his field. Think the Attenboroughs and the BBC. The Reutgars – Rolf's family, are television royalty."

"What has this to do with you two wearing 'Oirish' outfits?"

"Dolph's looking for something Frieda could star in. When he received the footage from Rolf he got a Eureka moment." Oisín wished to God someone else had explained this to his mother. "He doctored the footage using CGI as I've mentioned. He's made a vampire – reincarnation – ghost-story pilot. It's promising to be a huge success. The Americans have been sniffing around talking about buying the storyline. Everyone is really excited about the possibilities. Dolph has been given an enormous budget to 'sex' up the storyline."

"Is that why my sons were running around half naked?"

"We're big boys now, Mum." Oisín wanted to crawl away.

What was it about a mother's opinion? His mum had seen him without his shirt before.

Finn had watched Ronan – his white hair thick with extensions running down his almost naked body to his ankles – bite a buxom female on the neck. She hoped they weren't planning to make him fight with hair like that – his enemy could hang him with his own hair.

"So Ronan and me are Irish vampires. Frieda's character has been having vivid dreams of old Ireland using the footage Rolf provided."

"Why didn't they fiddle with your hair?"

"I'll have you know they love my hair. The red really burns under the lights." Oisín hadn't known what to expect from his mum. "The storyline has Frieda coming to Ireland to research the dreams she's been having."

"So you and Ronan will be coming home?" She almost danced on the spot – her boys were coming back!

"Dolph has been in talks with RTÉ about the use of their facilities."

"What about my da's camper van – he left it with you, didn't he?" Finn wanted to demand the exact date and time Oisín was coming home but bit her tongue.

"Grandfather had the good taste to buy a German-manufactured camper van. Good old Dolph wants to write off some of the expense of the trip to Ireland by getting a sponsorship from the manufacturers of that particular camper van. He's trying to sell the story of a trip to Ireland, staring me as an inept camper, to the Travel Department."

"Did you know Emmet is here?" She wasn't going to get into her father's private business with her son.

"Yeah."

"We're going to a session. Your grandda is performing."

"Go, Granda!"

Chapter 35

"Honest to God, Da, me nerves are shot!" Finn was sitting at the kitchen table, watching Emmet make breakfast. She had to almost sit on her hands to stop herself interfering. "The man won't be here till this afternoon. What am I supposed to do in the meantime? I can't settle to anything."

"He's human like the rest of us." Emmet cracked eggs one-handed to make omelettes. "Show him your nutjobs – be polite – and hopefully take his money." He looked at her downcast head, longing to box her ears. This visit could be the making of her. He bit his tongue. She'd had over twenty years of that prick Brennan telling her she was useless. He couldn't expect her to shake off that conditioning overnight.

"That can't be him!" Finn jumped to her feet when the doorbell rang. She pulled her phone from her pocket and ordered the kitchen screen to show the outside camera. "I'm being invaded!" she wailed, running towards the door.

Emmet checked the screen to see what was happening. He laughed aloud, watching Finn try to hold back the group that pushed her in front of them back into the house.

"*Should I crack more eggs, daughter?*" he shouted.

"*I want you to crack heads!*" Finn led the way into the kitchen. "You already know Angie and Maggie – meet Paul and Scott."

"Morning!" Emmet began to crack more eggs. "I've met the two lads at the pub sessions."

"Emmet," Paul shook his head sadly, "we can't let your daughter meet the big man looking like a bag lady." He waved his hand in Finn's direction. "Look at the state of her! Honest to God, anyone else would have been titivating for weeks but not your daughter."

"I was going to shower and change before he came."

"Your hair needs a trim and a good conditioning." Scott grabbed the hair on Finn's head in ungentle hands. "Honest to God, woman, would it kill you to come into the salon now and again? Thank God your own colour has grown in and you don't need to dye it anymore."

"What's the order of business, folks?" Emmet asked.

"I'll take care of her hair first," Scott said.

"Don't dry it." Paul pulled at Finn's hair. "This needs a deep conditioning – you do that and I'll moisturise her skin while the hair rests."

Finn allowed herself to be treated like a doll, told where to go – what to do – what to wear.

"How come you lot could come here?" Finn sat at the kitchen island wearing her bathrobe, her hair with deep oil conditioner under a towel, her face and hands glistening with moisturiser.

"We had no appointments booked." Scott leaned back to allow Emmet to put a ham-and-cheese omelette on the kitchen island in front of him. "We put a sign on the door. If we miss walk-ins – well, they can just come back." He picked up his fork.

"I knew you would need my help with your make-up." Paul waited for his food to be served.

"I came to check what you plan to wear." Maggie was already eating her omelette.

"I'm just nosey," Angie said.

"I hope that man Atkinson is not with him," Finn said.

"Relax." Emmet was nervous enough for both of them. He stared across the length of the high iron gates at his daughter.

Her friends had done a wonderful job of presenting her.

"If any of those reporters are hanging around, they're going to know something is going on." Finn eased the cramps in her hands. "The pair of us standing here ready to pull open these gates is a dead giveaway."

"Well, the driver was good enough to call and tell us they were almost here." Looking through the openings in the design of the gates he saw a luxury car turn slowly into the street. "Heads up – here he comes!"

The pair jumped to unlock and open the double gates – pulling them back to allow the car to pass through. Then they shut and locked the gates as soon as the car had cleared them.

"I'll take the driver in for a cup of something." Emmet walked over to the car to be introduced. No need to be rude. He'd have done the same for anyone.

"Blue balls!" The famous man examined the figure standing under one of the glass panels in the workshop roof. "I want that one."

"I'm experimenting with colour." Finn was enjoying his company. He was not a bit stuck up – nothing like that man Atkinson. "You admired Dare's figure and when I found this old kettle I thought I'd try something different." She pointed to the spout of the kettle. "The spout on this is significantly smaller."

"So it is, but you can almost feel the cold coming off him. I live in California – on hot days, looking at this poor guy will cool me down."

Finn tried not to point out what she saw as defects in the figure. She'd used another exhaust system and had the figure bent with its arms across its chest. She'd achieved the effect she wanted – you could almost see the figure shiver.

"Fair enough – this one." She turned to walk out of her workshop.

"Whoa, lady! I'm not finished." Tim put his hand on her shoulder to hold her in place. "You sure don't try and force sales. I've come all this way to see your work. I'm not about to walk away without seeing everything."

Finn hoped the smile on her face didn't look as sickly as it felt. She accompanied him around her workshop, answering his questions.

"I want this one." He took the small figure of a boy from high on the shelves. "I had ears like this poor guy before they pinned them back."

"That's one of the first I ever made." Finn took the figure from his hands. She had ignored the top shelves because she considered the items of interest to no one but herself. The figures were experiments to her mind, not finished items – but who was she to argue with the great man! She'd used the half-moon handles of a pot to make the ears that stood well away from the figure's head.

"I want this one."

Finn was beginning to panic. How much was she supposed to charge? She'd thought he'd buy one large figure and she'd agreed a price for those with Dare. This man was like a child. He wanted everything he looked at.

"You're not going to faint on me, are you?" Tim was standing at her side and she'd never noticed him move.

"I'm sorry." Finn smiled at him. "It has nothing to do with you. I hate parting with my nutjobs." She could hardly tell him she thought he was crazy for wanting to pay good money for scrap metal.

"I love that name – nutjobs." He flashed his famous teeth. "I'm buying your stuff because I love it but," he looked away for a moment, "I'm also buying it as an investment. I believe your work will increase in value – so does Dare – I have a famous face and body but I'll get old like everyone else. I don't want to end up with my mouth pulled back to my ears trying to stay young. So, while I have the money, I'm investing, but only in things that please me. No point in being surrounded by things you find ugly, is there? Hey, is that a turf fire?"

Her da had called that one right – and he'd insisted she have turf on the fire for this visit. She looked at this man wearing jeans and a sweater. He made her think of her sons but she knew for a fact that he was older than her.

A delighted smile lit up his face. "May I put some turf on the fire?"

"Don't burn yourself!" She hurried over to join him. She stood back and instructed him.

"Thanks." He stood watching the soft brown lumps of turf ignite. He looked at his hands and grimaced. "Anywhere I can wash up?"

She pointed to her little sink, almost laughing at the clean white towel hanging on a hook. She'd never seen it before – Angie's touch, she supposed.

He washed his hands, looking over his shoulder at her. "I want to make sure I haven't missed anything."

She didn't see how he could have. He'd poked his nose into every corner of her workshop. The items he wanted to buy were standing in a group to the side of the doors. She watched him add another two figures to the group.

"I'll have Atkinson call you about payment and delivery." He picked up the big-eared boy. "This one I'm taking with me." He laughed. "It will keep me humble. I've had a great time."

"My da's making Irish coffee – would you like some?" She led the way. "In spite of the fire it's cold out here." She'd noticed him shiver. He wasn't wearing enough clothes for this weather.

"Is that different from American coffee?"

"It has whiskey in it." She opened the door to the mudroom, pointing out the facilities. She left him to it, stepping from the mudroom into the kitchen.

"Irish coffee, daughter." Emmet was dying to ask her how it went but was very aware of the driver sitting drinking coffee at the kitchen island.

"I'd love some, Da. It's brass-monkey weather out there." She blew on her hands.

"I was showing Mick here your train." Emmet had the glasses, coffee, cream, sugar and whiskey ready. "The man is a volunteer on a steam railway."

"I love those." Finn smiled at the man. "I've been on several. It was a great day out when the boys were young. Have you seen the steam train sets that some shops are putting in?"

"What am I missing?" Tim Liner stepped into the kitchen. He looked around taking everything in – he couldn't be too careful – hidden cameras could be anywhere. This woman had told Atkinson about her security cameras and promised to shut down the system while he was here. "Is that the Irish coffee?"

"Would you like one?" Emmet asked. "It has alcohol if that's a problem." You couldn't be too careful.

"Not a problem." He watched the glass being filled. He didn't take much cream but he was willing to try new things. "What were you talking about – if you don't mind me asking?"

"Mike here volunteers on a steam railway. I was showing him my daughter's set-up." Emmet nodded towards the driver while carefully adding the cream to the whiskey-laced coffee. The cream swirled and floated beautifully on top. The train had been a way to pass the time. He'd had no idea how long this visit would last and he'd had to talk to the man about something.

"It's a little corker." Mike thought he should say something.

"Show the man, Finn," Emmet prompted.

"Oh, I'm sure ..."

"I'd love to see it," said Tim.

Finn opened what she thought of as her train cupboard, conscious of Tim coming to look over her shoulder. He began to pepper her with questions. He wanted to know all about it. She set the controls and, with glasses in hand, they went out of the kitchen and into the hallway where they stood watching the little train run around the house. When it had completed a full circle they returned to the kitchen and she shut the system down.

"I'd love one of those trains." Tim sipped his drink, enjoying time spent in company that didn't appear to be in awe of him. "How would you like to come to California? You could pick the spots for your nutjobs and set up one of those trains for me?" He waited for her to jump at the offer. He didn't invite many people to his home. "Course, I'd like it bigger."

"I was just starting to tell Mike about a company that puts train systems into shops," Finn said. "They are fabulous but far more expensive than anything I can afford. I'll look up the name and pass it on to your man Atkinson if you're really serious, Tim." She ignored his comment about visiting his home, sure he was joking.

"You do that." He hid his small smile behind the glass. She was a strange woman. He'd expected her to fawn all over him. He was giving her the kind of boost to her career that most artists could only dream of – he'd come to her, for goodness' sake – then she refused an invitation to his home. He liked it.

Chapter 36

"I have got to take control of my life." Finn was beating an empty bean can into the shape of a dog's head. "It's been nine months since my birthday. You can have a baby in that time. What have I done?" She gave the metal a particularly vicious bang. "I've been inching along – coasting – hoping everything will turn out right – allowing life to happen to me. It's not good enough. I need to do more. I'm still waiting to hear about my legal separation." A hefty bang accompanied the words. "My sons are running around the place naked for public consumption." The long snout of a dachshund began to appear in the metal. She'd already made tiny paws and a tail for one of the car suspension springs she had on hand. "I've met a man who wants to be my brother and his son." The two German men had been a delight to meet and get to know – but still. She was glad to have met them but equally glad they had returned to Germany. "I have an almost ex-husband pontificating about his troubles to the world. I have reporters following me about. I never asked for any of this. I've two sons I only see if I care to watch them on screen. I have movie stars talking about me in interviews."

She'd almost swallowed her tongue when her name was mentioned on TV. The darn man had carried the little jug-eared figure onto the set with him – shouldn't she have been consulted about that?

"I'm afraid to answer my own phone. The world and its mother seem to want one of my nutjobs. Then I have one da running around the place like a swinging single and the other one is missing."

She stepped away from the work bench. She'd destroy her work if she didn't calm down.

"All of that is outside my control."

She put the hammer she'd been using carefully on to the bench – she wanted to fling it at something. She was almost panting, she was so frustrated with herself. "I can't keep reacting to what other people do – it's me time – I have got to take control."

She stepped out of her workshop into the first blush of dawn.

Thank heaven she had no near neighbours next to her workshop or she'd have them complaining about the noise she made. You couldn't hear her noise over the road that ran outside the curtain wall and the public walkway that surrounded her place. She'd been unable to sleep, her mind running in never-ending circles. She'd come out to her workshop to try and quiet her mind.

She stood listening to the dawn chorus – birds greeted the rising sun in frantic song.

"I need a pot of tea and a pad and pencil. I'll write my worries down and see if I can drag myself out of the mire."

"I need to divorce the house." Sitting in a soft chair in her lounge, she stared down at the long list she'd made. "I'm buried under household chores. I have to get myself away from here or I'm always going to be jumping to complete the maintenance and care of this place." She fought the urge to nestle down and sleep – escape her own thoughts. "I really have been married to a house."

The bouncing of her phone on a nearby coffee table made her jump. She rolled out of the chair and made a mad dash to answer it. It must be a problem at this hour of the morning.

"Emmet, Da, wake up!" Finn kicked the bedroom door. She was carrying a piping hot mug of tea to her father.

"For the love of God, daughter, if this house isn't on fire,"

Emmet pushed his grey head out from under the bedcovers, "I'm going to kill you."

"Have some tea." Finn put the mug close to the bed before turning to pull the curtains open, wide.

"How did I ever end up with a kid who gets out of bed before the bloody lark?"

"Da, come on, wake up!" Finn came and shook Emmet's shoulders. "We're being invaded."

"Huh?"

"I had a phone call from some assistant to an assistant. Oisín and a film crew will be here this morning."

"*Huh?*"

"Da, *will yeh for God's sake wake up! We're about to be invaded!*"

"Finn, go away – I'll be out in a while." He sipped at the tea, his eyes still half closed. "I promise I'll be awake enough to listen to you then but for now, go *away!*" The last was said with a muted roar.

Finn hurried from the room, satisfied that she'd got her da moving.

"Angie, morning, it's Finn!" She needed help. "I need someone to make beds and tidy up. I'm being invaded by hordes of people from Germany. Today. I have at least six beds that need to be made up and rooms to be freshened."

"Maggie needs the money." Angie was awake and at her desk. She had crews out. "I'll send her and Joan Porter over to you. If it looks like an all-day job for two – get back to me."

"You're a star, Angie, thanks."

They hung up, each knowing what needed to be done.

"By God, daughter, does everyone you know get up before the sun?" Emmet entered the kitchen, wearing grey sweatpants. "I hope there's more of that tea, then you're going to sit down and tell me exactly what's going on."

"I got a phone call. It seems half of Germany is on its way here."

"Here?" Emmet pointed at the floor.

"Oisín left Germany ten days ago but forgot to tell me. He is being followed by a film crew. They're all about to descend on

Ireland today. They're recording the trip apparently, some kind of exchange with the tourism board or television station. They're all going to stop here."

"Jayzeus."

"My sentiments exactly." Finn stood to put the kettle on again. There wasn't enough tea in Ireland to make her able to face this day. "And that's not all."

"No? What else?"

"That fella Dolph is flying Ingrid, along with Rolf and Ronan, over to join in the fun." In over forty years Ingrid, to her knowledge, never made any attempt to contact her. Now suddenly she was coming to Ireland in person. "They'll be here today."

"I'm leaving." Emmet almost jumped from the kitchen chair.

"You are not deserting me, Da." Finn grabbed his arm and hauled him back into the chair.

Emmet gave in. "What needs to be done?" He couldn't run out the door if Ingrid was about to barge into Finn's life.

"Thanks, Da." She gave his hand a gentle squeeze. "I didn't think to ask the assistant to the assistant how many people were in the crew." She'd been shocked rigid by the news – hadn't thought to demand details. "My heart stood still when I heard Oisín would be arriving today. I've missed him, Da."

"Why didn't Rolf ring me?"

"It seems we two were the last to know." Finn was worried about her two da's. They had never been apart for this long as far as she knew – what was going on with them? "Do you think I'll have to feed them?"

"It wouldn't do any harm to call the butcher and order breakfast meats." Emmet hadn't any advice to give – he didn't know what was going on either. "If we have half a pig in the fridge it won't go to waste. You know the two boys will want a full Irish breakfast as soon as their feet hit their home soil."

"I have Maggie coming in to get the bedrooms ready. She'll do yours too – put fresh linen on the bed. She'll stay the morning and then we'll see what's what."

"Good enough. I'll throw a few loaves of soda bread in the oven to go with the meat. We'll need more eggs and I'm not cleaning the kitchen afterwards."

"Fair enough. My sons can get their lily-white hands wet. They are the ones who invited this crowd." She was silent for a minute, thinking. "I'll have to ask the butcher to deliver – I've no car." She lowered her eyes for a moment. "Do you think it's wrong to resent all of this, Da?"

"No, I don't." Emmet was upset on her behalf. "It was ignorant of them not to inform you."

"I did the same thing to you and Rolf – just turned up."

"That was only one person and a delightful surprise. This is different."

"Do you think they'll want to film me greeting Oisín?" Finn cringed at the thought. "You know, like those reality shows, where people expose their private life to the world and his brother?" She didn't have to think about it. "I won't do it, Da."

"They will have to take us as they find us." Emmet hugged her close for a moment. "Rolf and your sons deserve to be greeted with love – the rest of them, they can like it or lump it." He finished his tea and stood. "I'm going to get dressed. We'll have to wait and see what we will see."

Finn stood at the window on the top landing overlooking the street. She was waiting for Oisín who had texted that they were almost there. She would resist the urge to run out and strangle him with hugs. She was trying to respect that her sons were grown men. She didn't want to embarrass him in front of his company.

The beds in all of the rooms had been made and fresh towels set out. The house had been buffed and polished, thanks to Maggie and Joan.

She watched a stretch limousine followed by a studio van and her da's familiar camper van turn into her street. Oisín put his head out the driver's window of the camper van and tooted the horn.

Finn ran down the stars and through the house. She watched the vehicles, holding her breath as the drivers parked on her lawn. She waited while the cameras rolled, filming her son's arrival home. It wasn't until the large cameras were put back into the van that she ran out the kitchen door into the back garden. She pulled Oisín into her arms, wanting to examine him from head to toe. She wanted to clutch him to her and never let go.

Dolph had left Ronan, Rolf and Ingrid off to enter the house by the front door. He wanted to be introduced to Finn. He'd been astonished by the story his nephew Pieter had recounted to him. How could his sister Ingrid have done such a thing, to give away her own child?

Finn was introduced to Dolph, then Pieter's daughter Frieda. The young woman was a blue-eyed blonde ball of bouncing energy. She'd travelled with Oisín and appeared on screen as his camping companion – she'd loved every moment of it, she said.

Emmet wandered over to speak with the camera crew. Surely they weren't expecting to stay with his daughter?

"Mum, Dolph has booked a hotel in Bray for the actors and film crew but can Frieda and her family stay with us?" Oisín asked. It was so good to be home.

"Of course," Finn said through gritted teeth.

This was exactly what she'd been worried about. The men in her life never seemed to think about the amount of work involved in taking care of a home. That was all going to change. She'd talk to Angie about staffing the house. She'd be sure Oisín got the bill for the service. She was no one's on-the-spot maid – not anymore.

"Mum, I need to talk to you." Oisín put his arm around her shoulders and led her towards the front of the house. Finn was surprised to see the front door standing open but allowed herself to be led inside. "Oh, shit!"

He halted abruptly and stood with his mother, watching Ingrid run a finger over the mantelpiece in the main lounge. The woman was barking demands at Maggie.

Finn stared at the woman – she knew who she was. Her resemblance to Rolf was remarkable. She was stylishly dressed all in black, her greying blond hair pulled back from her face.

"Ah, daughter, at last, I wish to speak with you." Ingrid reached up to pat Oisín's cheek. "Hurry away, Ohseen – your brother and mine have gone to the kitchen."

She mangled the pronunciation of his name, giving Finn a cheap feeling of satisfaction.

Ingrid clicked her fingers at Maggie. "Coffee now." She didn't wait to see if her orders were carried out but turned to Finn.

"Come, child. I want to look at you. You are tall. This is good. Sit, I wish to see the woman you have become."

"I am presuming you are Ingrid?" Finn was grateful Maggie had insisted she change and fuss with her hair and make-up. She didn't know how she was supposed to react to this woman. She had never felt the lack of her in her life.

"Who else would I be? Have you not longed to meet me? My brothers were coming to Ireland. Should I not have availed of the opportunity to see the child that was torn from my arms so long ago?"

"Why are you here?" Finn was wary of the woman ordering her around in her own home. Her da couldn't stand her and he was one of the easiest-going men she knew.

"You are a mother yourself with two fine sons. Can you not imagine the pain of a mother who has been denied her child?"

"Ingrid, you entered into a business agreement with your brother – an agreement you instigated," Finn said. "I can admire that. You have known where I was all of my life but never made any effort to contact me. Let us not pretend that this is some great Greek tragedy." Finn could not see any sign of painful longing about this woman. She'd missed her sons so much in the months they'd been away. It had been a constant pain in her heart. The woman sitting across from her wasn't even looking in her direction. The pale blue eyes were examining every detail of the room.

"Is that what you have been told." Ingrid smirked and patted her hair. "Your father has long fought his feelings for me."

Oh Christ, Finn thought, completely shocked by this unexpected declaration. Ingrid wouldn't be the first woman to fall for her da.

"Your coffee." Maggie came into the room, carrying a white coffee pot, milk, sugar and mugs on a tray.

"I will call if I have further need." Ingrid didn't even look at Maggie.

Maggie rolled her eyes at Finn as she withdrew.

Ingrid waited for Finn to pour the coffee. "You have no curiosity about your own mother. How is this possible?"

"Ingrid, you are my mother's sister." She sipped the coffee she didn't want. "You are a complete stranger to me."

"You are hard-hearted." Tears began to well in the blue eyes.

"That might work with the men in your life, Ingrid. Tears are not quite so effective when facing another woman."

"I cannot believe I gave birth to such an unnatural female." Ingrid sat straight in her chair and glared.

"Ingrid, you were a woman in a difficult situation – you found a way of providing for your young sons and protecting their inheritance – hats off to you. You are welcome under my roof as Rolf's sister. If you will excuse me. I want to see my sons." She rose and walked out of the room.

She found her father, two sons, Rolf, Frieda, Maggie, Joan, and Dolph in the kitchen.

"Ronan, let me look at you." Finn pulled her son into her arms and smothered him in kisses. She was amazed to feel him pull her close. He rocked her gently from side to side. "I'm glad you didn't leave in those silly hair extensions."

"I've missed you, Mum." He pressed a kiss into her hair.

"You have met your mother?" Rolf's gentle voice came from behind her.

"I met my mother's sister." Finn turned to throw herself into Rolf's arms. She pulled back, shocked. "Da-ma, why have you lost so much weight?" The words escaped unchecked from her lips. He looked dreadful. "Have you missed Da's cooking that much?" Finn hugged the only mother she had ever needed.

"I have picked up a bug." Rolf shrugged. "I needed to lose weight, sweetling."

"Not this fast." Finn bit back the rest of her words.

"Where is everyone?" Ingrid walked into the kitchen. "I thought we were going out for breakfast."

"I have food in," Finn said. "I'll cook. I've been looking forward to it." She turned to her son. "Oisín, show the lady to the green bedroom. I'm sure she would like to freshen up."

Ingrid left the kitchen, snapping at Maggie to follow.

With a cheeky grin and a roll of her eyes behind the woman's back, Maggie followed, prepared to be entertained.

"Ronan, set the table in the dining room. We'll put the food on the sideboard and everyone can serve themselves."

Ronan jumped to obey.

"Rolf, if you would squeeze oranges, please. Da, check the

bread and get the grills started."

The butcher had sent his eldest son over with the meat. She had everything she needed to hand.

"Da, here's the meat." Finn dumped the heavy, brown-paper-wrapped packages on the table. She pushed a pad on her work surface, showing Rolf the electric fruit press when it appeared. "The oranges are in a crate there."

"I should check on your mother," Rolf fretted. "She was so nervous about meeting you."

"Da-ma, I don't want to be rude to you. I love and respect you." Finn hugged Rolf, kissing his sagging cheek. "But Ingrid is not my mother. You are. I will not have you give her the title you so richly deserve. Is that understood?" She shook him gently. "Is that understood?" She repeated when it looked as if Rolf would disagree.

"*Ja*, sweetling, I understand." Rolf had tears in his eyes.

"Finn," Dolph said, "I have left my film crews in Bray but my son and grandson are in the camera van outside. They wish to come inside. Will this be a problem?"

"Not at all."

Finn organised everyone and everything. She was introduced to Dolph's son Max and his grandson Franz and sent them off with Joan to freshen up.

Shouting out orders, she was soon serving a full Irish breakfast to ten people. The smells were mouth-watering.

They were all sitting with laden plates in front of them when Finn appeared from the kitchen with tea and coffee. Joan and Maggie had started on the kitchen clean-up. They would keep the tea and coffee coming.

"Ronan, why are you sitting in my place?"

"Just keeping it warm for you." Ronan didn't mention that he had prevented Ingrid from trying to sit across the table from Emmet at the head of the table. He didn't know what was going on between Ingrid and his mother but the seat at the head of the table belonged to his mum.

Finn served tea and coffee before shifting her son from her place.

"You should see the footage we have shot!" Frieda said when everyone was seated.

"No talk of work at the table," Ingrid bit out.

Her brothers and German grandchildren hunched their shoulders.

The only sounds after that were murmurs of appreciation for the cook and the Irish cuisine.

Finn looked around the table, astonished to be surrounded by so many people who shared blood ties with her. It was a strange situation.

The food disappeared faster than she would have believed possible. When everyone at last leaned back in their chairs, she turned to Rolf.

"Da-ma, you go take a nap. My sons will clean up here. They ate most of the food anyway. Ronan, see that fresh tea and coffee are served."

She watched Rolf leave the room without a word of protest.

"Da, something is wrong with Rolf," Finn said when chairs were pushed back and fresh coffee and tea were being served. "I don't like how he looks."

"Nor do I." Emmet was fascinated by the Amazon across the table from him. She was a far cry from the timid mouse who had turned up in Deauville.

"I'm going to check Rolf has everything he needs," Finn excused herself to the company.

She ran up the stairs and tapped lightly on the master bedroom door. She opened the door.

Rolf was lying on top of the bedclothes, his eyes closed. Finn crawled onto the bed with him. She put her arm around him and laid her head on his shoulder.

"You have to tell me what is upsetting you," Finn whispered softly.

"I am fine."

"Don't deny it. I know you. I love you. Something is very wrong in your world. Tell me what is going on?" Finn rose up on her elbow to stare down at Rolf.

"It is nothing."

"Nothing is not making you look so unhappy. You have always been there for me. Let me help you, please."

"It is not a subject for your ears."

"My ears are here." Finn kissed his cheek. "Let me help."

260

"I am an old man." Rolf sighed. "Fat and tired. I cannot keep up with Emmet. He is vigorous and vital. I am holding him back."

"That is about the silliest thing I have ever heard you say."

"Emmet left me in Germany without a backward look."

"Rolf, Da was not happy without you. He believed you wanted to stay in Germany. He didn't want to keep you from doing something he thought made you happy."

"How could he believe I would be happy without him?"

"I'll get Da." She left the room before he could object.

"Da, Rolf needs you." Finn waited until her father had left the room before taking her seat.

"Mum," Ronan, a pile of dirty plates in his hands, said, "you don't seem to understand. We are sex symbols. We shouldn't be doing dishes." There was a dimple in his cheek she hadn't seen in a long time.

"Tell that to someone who hasn't changed your nappy."

"You tell him, girl!" Maggie walked around the table refilling the coffee mugs.

"*Am I the only one working?*" Oisín put his head out of the kitchen to shout.

"Have you two made up?" Finn demanded of her parents that evening when the crowd of people were relaxing in the lounge. She could see from Rolf's beaming smile that they had.

"Yes, nosy parker," Emmet said with a grin.

"Da, I couldn't let me ma and da fall out," Finn said in a broad Dublin accent.

"Rolf mentioned he is putting his affairs in order," Emmet said in Gaelic under the noise of the company. "Ingrid suggested it. She also suggested he might care to live with her now that I was tired of him and he had no home to go to." Emmet was furious and trying to handle it without exploding.

"*Bitch!*" Finn exploded in English.

"Oh, yeah."

"She's his sister so we'll say nothing," Finn decided. "We'll make sure he knows we love and want him."

Chapter 37

Finn leaned against the trunk of an apple tree in her garden. She looked at the old wall around the garden, feeling as if she'd run headlong into its unforgiving surface. So many people, so much to think about – what was she meant to be feeling? She heard the noise from the house but didn't move – they could call if they needed her.

Oisín watched his mother from his bedroom window. He'd set his alarm, he wanted time with her. He watched his mother straighten her shoulders, take a deep breath and step away from the tree. He half expected to hear her give a battle cry.

"Oisín!" Finn opened her arms when her son stepped into the garden. She pulled him into a tight embrace. She climbed onto a low wall that bordered the flowers so she could stand above him. She was his mother, she was meant to be taller. She put her arms around his strong young shoulders and rocked gently, amazed that he allowed her. He was almost nestling into her.

"What's wrong, Oisín?" Finn ran her hand down the waterfall of red-gold hair.

"An awful lot has happened, Mum." Oisín closed his eyes, feeling like a little boy again.

"I got that impression."

"Anything to eat, Mum?" Oisín raised his head and grinned.

"Why did I miss you?" Finn tapped his cheek lightly. "I'm having fruit and yogurt, want some?"

"That my only choice?" He pretended to gag.

"Come on, cheeky. I suppose I can find something for you to eat. This once."

"I missed you, Mum."

Oisín sat at the kitchen island watching his mother bustle around the family kitchen. He was home. He almost buried his face in the plate of food his mother put in front of him, trying to suck up the smell of a full Irish breakfast. He'd tried to get something similar in his travels but nothing came close.

"I missed you too, son." Finn spooned yogurt watching her son. He seemed so serious – what had she missed?

"I don't know how to say what I want to say."

"Just spit it out."

"It's Ronan, Mom." Oisín felt like a snitch but it was only fair to warn his mother. "He is madly in love with what he calls his German family. He particularly thinks it is amazing to have such a lovely German grandmother. He almost melts with pity at how his poor little grandma was treated." He didn't like Ingrid that much himself – she pulled strings and expected them to dance – his bro couldn't see that. He'd been happy to see Ronan protecting their mother a little yesterday.

"He'll learn." Finn had noticed Ronan dance attendance on Ingrid. What was she supposed to do about it?

"Ronan is really enjoying being a sex symbol." Oisín smiled. "I think being out from under Patrick's shadow has done him a power of good as you old folks would say."

"Less of the old, son of mine."

"In Germany we were two Irish lads with no connection to a famous father. It felt good. We got to be ourselves. But you should have seen Ronan with all of the uncles and cousins – honest to God, Mom, he practically compared the hairs on their heads."

"What about you – did you enjoy meeting these people?"

"I did but I was just curious – Ronan was desperate – I never realised how much he wanted family connections."

"And you don't?"

"It's interesting but I never thought part of me was missing – Ronan did." He stood to get coffee. "You met Cousin Frieda. This trip to Ireland and all of the people waiting for us in Bray are here because of her. Ronan is really buzzed about helping his family as he sees it." He was making a mess of this. "Mum, you might want to give this first trip to Bray a miss."

"Why?" She'd had no intention of travelling out to Bray but she was curious now.

"Patrick is sure to be there. Dolph has arranged for television coverage of the 'event'." Oisín hated having to choose between his parents. Patrick courted publicity, his mother never had. She had the right to decide what she wanted to do. "Dolph has been in talks with RTÉ and Ardmore Studios about the use of their facilities while he's here. Father will most likely be excited about the 'exposure' he can get from this. You know how he is."

"I hadn't planned on going out to Bray today." She wasn't going to make her sons chose between their parents. If Patrick wanted to use his sons, there was little she could do about it. Besides, she was busy trying to suppress her resentment of the way Rolf's family seemed to have completely taken over the Bray cottages.

"Morning all – what's the story for today?" Emmet walked into the kitchen. He put the kettle on to make a fresh pot of tea though the coffee pot was full and scenting the air. He joined Oisín at the kitchen island.

"The action will all be taking place in Bray today," said Oisín. "Ronan has already left with some of the people who stayed here. You were out in the garden when they left, Mum. We get a very early start in the film world. I now have to get ready to go and show my 'sexy' self in Bray to greet my fellow vampires."

"Jayzus," Emmet laughed, "I won't know where to put myself if my grandsons are going to be running around the place naked."

"You can take Ingrid and Rolf out to join them, Granda. Get them out from under my mum's feet." Oisín stood with a sigh.

He didn't enjoy this but he liked the money so he'd shut up and do what was asked.

"Before you run away," Finn put out a hand to stop him leaving, "am I supposed to have food on hand to feed these people when they return here?"

"Having snacks on hand would be appreciated, I'm sure." Oisín hadn't really given it any thought.

"I can take care of getting something in if you like," Emmet offered.

"Thanks, Da. I suppose it wouldn't do any harm to have the ingredients for a fry-up in the fridge. God knows it won't go to waste. Mr Walsh the pork butcher is going to want to erect a statue to me if I buy any more meat from him."

"Got to go, Mum." Oisín pressed a kiss into her hair and left the room.

Finn sat in her lounge, angry at herself. She was fighting the need to cry. The bedrooms and bathrooms in the house had been left as if this was a flaming hotel. Why should she have to pick up after all those people? Did none of them know how to make a bed or hang up a towel? Her sons were as guilty as everyone else. The master bedroom had been pristine – at least her fathers knew how to pick up after themselves. They had trained her to do the same thing. She flat out refused to be the maid of all work.

"I want to call Angie and order a daily cleaner – two would be better – but if I do that who is picking up the bill?" She put her head on her bent knees, refusing to let the tears fall. If this crowd continued to treat the house like a B&B she'd start charging them. "You talk tough, Finn, but you're chicken," she whispered aloud. She took a deep breath and tried to find her courage. "I'm doing it – I'm calling Angie – if the bill remains unpaid, I'll pay it out of my own money – but the bill will be presented."

She took her phone from her pocket and started tapping numbers.

"Angie, it's Finn, are you home?"

"I've just walked in the door. I'd tell you I'm in my office but you would know I'm sitting in my kitchen." Angie's kitchen had a square marked off to serve as her office. She liked it. She was handy to the tea and telephone – what more could you want?

"I need cleaners, Angie, ASAP. You would not believe the state my sons' guests left the place in." Finn was determined her voice wouldn't shake. "I've already put one load of towels in the washing machine and I have to tell you I used language that would put you to the blush. I am so very tired of being taken for granted."

"Not a problem." Angie turned on the small TV she kept in her kitchen for company.

"I want you to print up bills with Ronan and Oisín's names on them." She and Angie never needed printed bills. Finn paid for the work as soon as it was done. "I want to be able to hand my sons the bills and demand they pay you. I need to do this, Angie. If for any reason the bills aren't paid, you know I'm good for the money." It would have to come out of her own account which she resented.

"I'll have the women ... sweet Jesus, Finn ... put the TV on." Angie was staring at her own small screen in open-mouthed horror.

"What – why?" Finn used the remote to give the command for a screen to rise over the fireplace.

Angie remained silent, knowing it would take Finn a few minutes to get one of her TV's to appear.

"Well, that's no surprise." Finn said when the image of Patrick Brennan holding a microphone appeared. "I think my boys were expecting their father to cash in on their fame. Do I even want to turn on the sound?"

"You had better, I think," Angie said. "It's as well to know what you're dealing with."

"Is this going out live, do you know?"

"It must be – it wasn't advertised for a slot on this programme." Angie was familiar with the programme format. She was a regular viewer.

"This is Patrick Brennan in Bray. I am at this moment watching a German television crew set up for filming – join me after the break – I'll share the story with you – I know you're going to love it."

"Angie, send those cleaners around as soon as you can." Finn's broke the connection with Angie.

"Oisín!" Ronan was trapped in one of the production trailers, having his hair done. He'd been stuck in this chair for hours having extensions added. The darn things took so long to attach – he hated them. "Oisín, for God's sake, where are you?"

"What's wrong?" Frieda in the next chair asked.

"*Someone find my brother!*" Ronan shouted in English and then in German.

"What's all the noise?" Oisín, oiled and groomed, came to stand at his brother's back. He leaned over and met his eyes in the mirror. "What are you roaring about, oh mighty sex symbol?"

"Shut the fuck up!" Ronan met his brother's eyes and in Gaelic told him their mother had telephoned. "God knows what Patrick is up to but Dolph won't be pleased if Father messes up his planned publicity and schedule. You need to get out there!" He waved a hand covered by a black hairdressing cape in the general direction of the exterior. "How long more will I be?" he asked the hair stylist in German – all this changing of languages gave you an unmerciful headache.

"*Fertig* – finished!" The stylist threw his hands high and stepped away with a sigh of relief. It was no fun for him either spending hours weaving all of that hair into place.

"*Come on!*" Ronan jumped to his feet, pulling the cape off. He didn't care if he was covered in hair. "Someone needs to find Dolph and we need to find out what Patrick has planned."

He grabbed his brother by the shoulder and both shirtless young men jumped from the production trailer. They hit the ground at a run.

Finn sat watching her television screen. She knew nothing about publicity. She'd phoned Ronan to tell him his father was on site with an outside broadcast crew. Did he need permission for this? The commercial break ended and the screen revealed Patrick's smiling face.

The camera suddenly swung away from Patrick. Finn

watched her two sons almost explode out of what she had assumed was a giant truck parked on the Parade. The pair of shirtless young men began to run in the direction of the camera.

The shrill excited voiceover of a young woman replaced Patrick's measured tones while the camera zoomed in for a close-up of what the woman told viewers were the German stars of the show. Finn almost felt sorry for Patrick – his big chance – and he'd blown it.

She leaned forward when the boys reached the camera crew. She watched Oisín approach the young woman with the microphone while Ronan peeled off to talk to his father. She'd never seen that expression on Ronan's face before – not when in his father's company anyway. She tried to read his lips. She'd love to know what he was saying but was glad his comments were not being broadcast to the world and its mother.

"Is this your first time in Ireland?" the young woman shouted in fractured German. The microphone visibly shook in her hands. It seemed there was more than one person in Bray hoping for their big break. "Why was this area chosen?"

"Why are you talking to me in German, love?" Oisín stepped through the newly erected gates that now protected each end of the parade and over to the reporter. "I'm from Dublin."

The gasps from the crew could be heard over the air.

Finn didn't know where to look. In the background of the shot Ronan had his father by the elbow as he led him away. It looked friendly but you could see Patrick was struggling to break away.

Oisín was charming the drawers off the young female reporter. The wind blew his long hair back from his chiselled face. The poor woman was almost panting. It wasn't a comfortable thing for a mother to see.

Dolph arrived on the screen and Finn relaxed. Everything seemed to be in hand now. Perhaps she'd panicked when she didn't need to. She was not under the impression that Dolph had expected television cameras not his own on his set.

Chapter 38

Finn stood in her workshop heating and stretching one of the car suspension springs she had on hand. In her mind's eye she could see a cat's arching back. She beat the metal using her shoulder to wipe away the tears that fell from her eyes from time to time. She was so sick of herself. She seemed to be constantly taking one step forward and two steps back.

She wanted to stand in the gently falling rain and scream. Just stand outside screaming and screaming. She wanted to pull at her hair and wail. The only thing stopping her was fear of the men in their white coats. She didn't need to be locked up as a lunatic – but, dear Lord, it was tempting.

She'd left the doors of her workshop open, glad of the gentle rain-laden breeze that blew.

"*Finn, are you about?*" Angie's voice came over the noise of the hammer. Someone must have left the gates unlocked – again.

"*Finn, we want to talk to you!*" Maggie shouted.

"I'll be out in a minute, ladies – the back door is open – one of yez put the kettle on – I'm spitting feathers." Finn continued to shape the spring in her hands. She had the metal at a perfect heat. She couldn't stop now.

"What's going on?" Finn walked into the kitchen after locking the gates, to see Maggie and Angie sitting at the kitchen island, a pot of tea simmering on the range, the island top set for tea and two large yellow notepads sitting open.

"Here," Angie stood to pour Finn's tea, "sit down we have something we want to talk to you about."

"I've been poking my nose into your business." Maggie had left the twins asleep in bed, a young neighbour babysitting. "I'm afraid you'll be offended but I can't watch you spinning around in circles anymore." She pulled the notepad she'd set out over closer to her.

"It's because we care, Finn." Angie was terrified Finn would be insulted by their interference in her life.

"Why don't you two tell me what you've been up to?" Finn sipped her tea and waited.

"It's like this," Maggie gulped nervously. "I met a woman through the single parents group I belong to. She gave a lecture at one of our meetings." She glanced down at her notebook. "This woman lives in the middle of nowhere – her husband found religion – he was born again if you can believe it. Anyway, his new church claims he has never been married to her and therefore has no responsibility for their children. She's fighting it but in the meantime she's left with a big house and no income."

"Convenient," Finn prompted when Maggie seemed to be struggling to find words.

"I telephoned her earlier. I needed information. She was left with a large house – three children – and no income. She had to learn to survive. She and her children spend the summer in a little camper van at the bottom of the garden while she rents the house out to French fishermen." Maggie mentioned a weekly sum of money that made Finn gasp. "She does all the care and maintenance of the house herself. The money she makes in summer supports the family for the rest of the year."

"Maggie called me," Angie said when Maggie seemed to have finished talking. "You know I clean for estate agents? I got in touch with them and asked – hypothetically – what a house like this in this area would fetch in rent. I described your house, Finn, and this is the figure I got from more than one estate agent." She pushed the yellow pad across the island, tapping the figure of over ten thousand she'd written down. "They were almost hyperventilating at the thought of renting out a place like yours."

Finn looked at the figure on the pad until black dots danced in front of her eyes. She had to count the zeros. "That's Monopoly money, Angie," she pushed the pad back. "Why would anyone pay that amount of money to rent a place? That's more than most people pay in mortgage."

"My contact gave me figures for self-catering holidays and catered. There's a big difference there but it's a lot of work to cater to people who want to come and go as they please." Maggie too pushed her pad across to Finn.

"I thought the money Dare paid me for my nutjobs was crazy," Finn pushed the pad back, "but this is outrageous. Who would have that kind of money?"

"Lots of people it would seem." Maggie too had been amazed when the woman she'd contacted gave her the figures.

"So." Finn looked between her friends. "If I pitch a tent in the garden, the house can pay for itself – that's what you're saying?"

"You're getting experience at the job anyway with that shower from the film company." Angie had teams in this house daily.

"You're being paid regularly – right?" Finn worried about paying what must be a very large bill by now.

"The film company are picking up the tab," Angie said. "The bill is paid directly into my bank account. The thing is," she leaned forward to stare into Finn's green eyes, "you should be charging them a room rent as well. They would have had to stay in a hotel and pay for security if they weren't staying in your house."

"They're Rolf's relations." Finn dropped her head into her hands. "I couldn't charge them for staying here – besides, the house belongs to my father."

"You need to sit them all down and have a talk with them, Finn," Angie insisted. "You can't go on like this."

"It's hard to talk to them." She'd tried. "They leave really early in the morning and are gone all day. I'm in bed by the time they get back from Bray."

"They have Sundays off." Angie knew the routine, thanks to the women she employed to work in this house.

"My sons turn into tour guides and take everyone out and about on Sunday." Finn wasn't putting obstacles in her own way. She had tried to set up a family meal where they could talk but it was shrugged off as not important. "My da is supplying the background music for the sections being shot in Bray – even Judge Bailey is involved on copyrights and so on – I'm whistling in the wind trying to get them to listen to me."

"You have to put yourself first, Finn," Maggie stated.

"She's right." Angie slapped the island top. "You can become the invisible woman waiting on your men to have time for you – *or* – you can take matters into your own hands. It's your choice."

"It sounds easy." Finn tried not to wail.

"I'll leave you my notes." Maggie tore out the pages of notes she'd taken and pushed them across to Finn.

"You can have mine too." Angie too tore out her pages of notes and added them to Maggie's. "It's something to consider." She kept her hand on top of the papers and stared at Finn. "You can't keep waiting for someone else to do something. You have to stand up and be counted."

"Finn?"

Finn pushed herself up onto her elbow. She was lying across the foot of the big bed in the master bedroom.

"Jayzus, Finn, what are you doing still up?" Emmet pushed the bedroom door closed at his back. The loud voices coming from downstairs were slightly muted.

"I need to talk to you."

"If it's about Patrick again ..."

"It's not." Finn yawned widely and forced her tired body to stand. She had never been a night owl. "I need to talk to you about your long-term plans for this house. I'm serious, Da. I can't go on like this not knowing what the hell is going on."

"Where did I get you from?" Emmet took her swaying figure

in his arms. "You could never just go from one day to the next. Always wanted to know what was over the hill." He rested his bristled chin on her head. "This house will pass from me to you to Ronan – there is a little matter of death to decide the matter."

"You would have a great deal of money if you sold it."

"That was never an option." Emmet kicked off his shoes and with Finn in his arms fell onto the bed. He was knackered. These film people kept unholy hours. "I was always going to pass it on to you." He pressed a kiss onto her forehead. "Only not while Patrick Brennan could benefit from it." He'd been determined that Finn's husband would never be able to lay his hands on the Emerson family property. He'd never thought the marriage would last as long as it did. Finn had kept her eyes closed and her mouth shut for longer than he thought humanly possible.

"All very well, Da, but the place costs a fortune in taxes and upkeep." She told him about her friends' suggestions. "I need to know if you are ready to settle down, Da, or if I'm turning this house into a high-market rental property. I can't keep going day to day waiting for you to make a decision."

"Finn," he shook her gently, "I don't want to make any firm decisions about this house right now. I have a lot of thinking to do. But you should go ahead and plan your own future. You are related to the man whose company claims it can put a house up anywhere in the world in five days. Why the fuck would you think of putting a tent in the garden?"

"I never said anything to you about a tent, you old rogue! Those modules you're talking about don't come cheap." She'd drooled over them on the TV often enough to know. The actual house was built to the customer's design in a factory. It was delivered complete to the site.

"So, borrow money on the house." Emmet yawned widely. He wanted to sleep not solve the problems of the world. "If you do it in your own name that will start that credit history you've been moaning you lack."

"*Was ist das?*" Rolf came into the room. He'd left his noisy family downstairs.

"Miss Moan-a-Lot has been asking me of our plans for the house." Emmet patted the bed on the other side of Finn. Lord knows the bed was big enough to hold a football team.

"A Finn sandwich, my favourite," Rolf, after kicking off his shoes, lay down tiredly on the bed.

"I don't want to be married to this house anymore." Finn wanted to make that very clear. She would protect the family's heritage but she wanted to be free to live her own life. "I will oversee the property but that is all I am willing to do." She snuggled down and fell asleep as the last word left her lips.

"She never could stay up late." Rolf looked over at his partner. "I will talk to Pieter about a house for her. Our Finn would never be happy with a camper van at the bottom of the garden."

"It makes sense that she should have her own place." Emmet settled down. He'd been going to take a shower but the bed was so soft and his favourite people were with him. He pulled the leather belt from his trousers and undid the top button. "Finn must be allowed to work on her art."

"We have done well with our child." Rolf was getting too old to keep up with the young people. "I will book a flight for Ingrid in the morning." It was time for his sister to return to her farm.

"Thanks be to God," Emmet didn't know why she'd bothered coming to Ireland. She'd spent no time with Finn, seeming to want to be with him and Rolf all the time. It had become bloody uncomfortable for him.

Chapter 39

"We can never be friends ..."

Finn laughed. It was so nice to sit in her home office first thing in the morning and talk to Dare. It was late at night in California.

"I'm a night owl and you're an early bird." His voice was amused.

"I love the view from your deck." He'd sent her photographs at her request.

"You can come see it in real life any time you like."

It wasn't the first time he'd invited her. They had fallen into the habit of chatting from time to time. Dare sat out on his deck most evenings, making calls while his children slept.

"Me ma tells me you got a car?" he said when it looked like she was going to ignore his invitation yet again.

"I did." Her smile was bright and happy. "Barry, my mechanic, found me a lovely second-hand car. It's fire-engine red and bigger than my old one. I'll be able to fit more scrap metal into it – which is a relief – I haven't been able to move much with the wheelbarrow." She sipped her tea. She'd prepared a pot before she'd put the call through. Dare always telephoned her to set up a time to talk. It was very convenient for both of them.

"I thought my aul' ma was losing her mind when she told me what she was getting you for a birthday gift." He laughed.

"I love it." Her smile disappeared when she looked at the painted figure of the beige woman hanging on her office wall. She mentally shook herself. "What's happening with you? You're beating about the bush about something – spit it out."

"I want to come home, Finn." Dare raised the long-neck bottle of beer he held loosely in his hand to his lips. "I told you that when I was last over." He shifted around in his deck chair. "I'm at a loose end – don't know what to do with myself. I'm too young for retirement." They had become close during these chats. They were both in the same position – trying to find the next step in their life's journey.

"Are your children still horrified by the thought of living in Ireland?" Finn had listened to him pour out his troubles before. "Have you explained to them that you won't be selling the Malibu house?"

"Yeah," he sighed. "You were right. They were scared of losing the memories of their mom that are in this house. I don't need to sell up. I have enough money. Who would have thought a lad from a Dublin Corporation housing estate would be sitting on a deck in Malibu talking about his money?" His laugh held no humour.

"I have a suggestion." She'd given this matter a great deal of thought. She hoped she wasn't about to damage their growing friendship. "If you don't like it – tell me – I won't be insulted." She knew Dare had more money than he could ever spend thanks to the computer chip he'd invented that was used extensively in computer-generated images. He'd sold his own computer software company for a fortune, wanting to be home with his wife in what turned out to be the last days of her life.

"It's your turn to spit it out." Dare sat forward. "I'll accept any advice gratefully."

"I showed you around my house when you were last here." She gave herself a mental kick. "Your mother suggested I rent it out – make the place pay for itself."

"She told me about the film crew you have there at the moment," Dare prompted when she seemed to be struggling for words.

276

"Yes." Finn let out a breath, blowing the red hair from her brow. "I thought of offering to rent the place to you – at a reduced rate – your children would have time to get to know your family and I'd get a feel for what is involved. What do you think?"

"Are you serious?" Dare tried not to get his hopes up. It was difficult to travel as a single parent with four children at your heels. It was too much to expect family to put all of them up together. His children didn't want to be separated from him and spend time with what were essentially strangers to them even though they were his family.

"I thought you could be my first paying guest."

"Finn," he sat forward, his mind whirling at this opportunity, "if you're seriously thinking of renting out your house – it would be an answer to my prayers. I could rent it for a couple of months this summer. The kids are off school and it would give them a chance to get to know my family better." The house was close to all of his brothers and sisters – their kids could hang out with his kids. That house and garden were big enough.

"I'm serious but I haven't had time to check everything out yet." She'd been running around thinking and planning in an abstract way. If Dare was going to rent the house it changed everything – put the boot in so to speak.

"I'd need someone to look after us."

"Your Auntie Mabel is a widow with no children," Finn put in quickly. She had no intention of becoming a housekeeper and carer. Not even for Dare. "I hardly know the woman but surely as your mother's sister she'd be as efficient as Angie?" It didn't necessarily follow but there was no harm in asking.

"Good idea – you've given me a lot to think about." He looked off into the distance. "One of my kids is up. I have to go. I'll talk to you about this again."

Finn snapped off the connection on her side. The sounds from outside her office door had been increasing while she'd been talking to Dare. The visitors were up and about. She used her office screen to check on her house guests. She sighed deeply and stood – time to face the mayhem that ensued every morning at this ungodly hour.

"Morning, daughter!"

"*Guten Morgen*, sweetling."

Emmet and Rolf were in the kitchen when Finn entered, bustling around preparing breakfast and beaming. The noise of scraping cutlery and rattling dishes came from the dining room where the visitors were eating breakfast. The hosts with the most – it was a role her fathers seemed born for.

"I've left a list of foodstuffs I need you to order." Emmet pointed to the kitchen notice board with his spatula. "Your yogurt and fruit are in the fridge. The tea is fresh."

"Angie's crew will change the beds today." Rolf, a brimming coffee pot in hand, went towards the dining room.

Finn took her tea and yogurt out to the patio. She'd learned it was better to get out of the way and let them get on with it.

"Finn," Max, Dolph's son, a loaded plate and mug of coffee in hand came through the kitchen door to join her, "I need your bank details." He put his plate and mug on the table. "I may join you?"

"Please." She waved at a vacant chair. What else could she do? "Why do you need my bank details?"

"You are my cousin." He waved a hand to stop her making any disclaimers. "I will not see you taken advantage of." He gulped at his coffee, closing his eyes at the first taste. He pulled his plate of food towards him and began eating. "I have taken the liberty of sending an invoice in your name to the film company." He waved his sausage-laden fork in the air. "They must pay for the use of your home."

"I –"

"No. You are too nice. They have big money. Let them spend it." He moved to take a piece of paper from his trouser pocket and passed it to her. "This is the amount you will be paid for the time already spent." He pointed to the figures on the paper. "The second will be a weekly payment."

She looked at the figures, wondering if she was going to faint. They couldn't be right – surely? She looked at the top of Max's head. He was busy forking food into his mouth. She looked at the paper again. Three thousand pound a week! Were they insane! What was it Elizabeth Taylor had said when she was asked about the first million-dollar movie contract offered to her? Oh, yes – *'If they are stupid enough to offer millions, I'm not stupid enough to refuse.'* She'd do the same. It wasn't millions but it felt like it to her.

"This Irish breakfast is so good," Max said. "We are being spoiled." He pushed his empty plate away. "I must call my office today. I have been away longer than I thought." He took a deep breath. "The filming here will be finished soon. Ingrid has been saying many nasty things about you to your German family." Max looked down the garden. He had hoped to spend time with Finn but it seemed someone else always needed his attention and this woman – his cousin – she liked to disappear into the background, very unlike his family. "She is not a nice woman. I am sorry." A shout from the house pulled him to his feet. "The bank details." He took a pen from his pocket and waited while she provided the details. He would not see her cheated. The film company could afford to pay for their stars' living accommodation. The shout came again. He shoved the paper with Finn's bank details into his pocket and ran back into the house, shouting goodbye over his shoulder.

Finn picked up his dirty dishes and carried them into the kitchen. She looked at the mess and had to force herself not to touch it. Angie's crew would be here shortly.

"Bye, Mum," Ronan put his head into the kitchen to say. A shout of his name had him running out, not waiting for her response.

"Bye, Mum – you should come out to Bray to see what we're doing!" Oisín shouted without appearing.

She had tried going out to Bray, wanting to be part of the action. She had been very much in the way although everyone had been polite to her.

"Daughter – there you are." Emmet stepped into the kitchen, freshly showered and shaved. He drove his own car to Bray so had a degree of independence.

"You have told her?" Rolf joined them.

"Give us a minute." Emmet put the kettle on – his Finn

always thought better with a cup of tea in her hand. "The film crew will be finishing up soon." He turned and leaned on the untidy kitchen counter by the kettle. "We two," he waved to where Rolf stood, "we are going to spend the summer in the camper van. It will be our last long journey. We want to say goodbye to some of our favourite places." He turned when the electric kettle at his back switched off. "You are getting your way, daughter. We are coming home to live." He looked over his shoulder with a smile before turning back to making the tea. "We will have to talk more about the nitty-gritty but that can wait. We have to go – give the tea a few minutes to brew."

They turned to leave a stunned Finn staring after them.

"*Don't forget to order the food!*" was a parting shout.

"What just happened?" Finn dropped into a chair, feeling as if she'd just been run over by a steamroller.

Chapter 40

"Happy Birthday, Finn, you're looking good!"

Finn tipped her glass at her image in the mirror, grinning like an idiot. She was wearing an outfit Maggie created as a birthday gift. She wouldn't be serving tea this morning. She was getting ready to 'grow old' disgracefully. She'd been a 'good girl' for the first forty years of her life. She intended to do as she pleased from this day onward.

"I love this look!"

She sipped a Mimosa while admiring the woman in the mirror. She'd spent very little time in her life looking at herself. The outfit, palazzo trousers in a soft white material decorated with red and blue birds in flight, thrilled her. The wide twisted straps of the summer top, in the same blue as the birds, hid any hint of strap from her push-up bra. A scarlet leather belt cinched her slim waist. The weight she'd lost in the last year gave Finn a long, lean, elegant look. The open-toe scarlet shoes pushed her height to almost six feet. She looked bloody good if she did say so herself. The phoenix earrings that were Angie's birthday gift finished the look.

"Right, stop admiring yourself. You have to get ready for your company." She'd invited Maggie and Angie for brunch.

She walked slowly along the long hallway. The steam train

she'd put in motion whistled merrily as it chugged along. The house felt different – no longer an enormous weight on her shoulders. It felt – if she wasn't being too woo-hoo about it – the house felt happier. She admired the dust-free surfaces and highly polished furniture. Angie's cleaning team had a full-time job here now. The German film crew were paying her a very handsome retainer to keep the house available for visiting staff. They hadn't finished with the houses in Bray. She didn't care – she got paid even when the house stood empty.

She walked into her kitchen with a pleased smile on her face. She had the waffle irons out and sitting on the work surface. The measured ingredients for the waffles were ready and needed only to be mixed. She'd squeezed orange juice to add to the champagne she'd opened to make Mimosas. The strawberries gleamed red and moist. The blueberries and fresh fruit salad looked delicious. The cream was whipped. She'd been up and about since early getting everything ready. All she had to do now was assemble the ingredients. She pulled on an apron to protect her outfit – it might not be glamorous but she didn't want anything to spill on her lovely clothes.

She wanted to laugh out loud. It didn't matter that her family had forgotten her birthday again. Her sons were in Germany getting on with their own lives. She heard from them when they had a moment to spare. Emmet and Rolf were spending the summer touring favourite sites for the last time. They would return and take charge of the house in the autumn. It would have been nice to get a card but she didn't feel like sitting and crying because everyone had forgotten her birthday. She'd finally realised that the only person's acknowledgement she needed in life was her own.

Finn belted out show tunes while mixing ingredients for the waffles.

The doorbell interrupted her. She checked the kitchen screen, smiling when she saw Angie and Maggie almost dancing impatiently on the street outside the curtain wall. She hurried to let her guests into her home.

"I don't know what's going on." Angie shoved Finn out of her way and dragged Maggie by the hand through the gate. "Be sure to lock that and turn off your bell quick."

"There are news vans all over Rathmines asking after you." Angie was breathless. "They're asking for Finn Emerson, so that should slow them down – most everyone still calls you Mrs Brennan." She'd run out of church and hadn't stopped running since. If there was a just God she should have lost a stone in weight with the workout she'd just had.

"What in heaven's name is going on?" Finn stared at her two gasping friends.

"I need something to drink." Angie wanted to collapse onto a flat surface.

"Come into the kitchen." Finn practically carried the gasping Angie into her kitchen. She poured a glass of fresh orange juice that Angie swallowed at a gulp. She filled a fluted glass with Mimosa and put it on the island surface. She had thought of serving brunch in the dining room but these were her friends and it was easier to be in the kitchen watching the waffle irons. She preferred eating in the kitchen anyway. "Sip that."

"Give!" Maggie accepted a tapered glass of Mimosa. Her girls were with their father. She could do as she pleased today.

"I was sitting in the back of the church." Angie had wanted a quiet moment to say a few prayers. She'd been minding her own business until she heard Finn's name being shouted. "A news van was sitting in the parking lot shouting questions at people as they left the church. They wanted to know where Finn Emerson lived." She sipped her drink slowly, enjoying the refreshing taste. "In minutes the street was filled with vans and reporters shouting questions. I grabbed Maggie and we slipped away. We saw vans driving slowly around the place. There are loads of them, Finn."

"What on earth do they want with me?" Finn was completely at a loss.

"They could be here any minute, Finn." Angie wondered if this had anything to do with the garden her granddaughter had designed for the Bloom festival. The garden had won several awards and Finn's nutjobs had been a great success. That wouldn't bring this kind of attention though, she didn't think.

"Well, I have no idea what they want." Finn shrugged.

"We'll have our brunch and see what happens." She took a moment to turn the image on the kitchen screen to the street outside her house. She'd keep an eye on the goings-on outside.

"Aren't you scared?" Maggie was thrilled to see Finn wearing the outfit she'd made. It looked fabulous.

"I don't know what they want with me and until I find out there's not a great deal I can do about it." Today she felt she could handle anything life threw at her. "Thanks for the warning, ladies."

"Give me another glass of that stuff." Angie held out her empty glass.

Maggie immediately finished her drink and held out her glass for a refill.

"You look incredible, Finn. Where did you get that outfit?" To Angie's eyes Finn belonged on the cover of a magazine, not wearing an apron beating batter.

"It was a birthday gift from my personal designer." Finn mixed the drinks while nodding at Maggie.

"It's amazing, Maggie, could you make me something?" Angie knew she couldn't wear anything as fitted as Finn's outfit but she'd love something as original in her own wardrobe. She'd feel like a film star if she didn't look in the mirror for too long.

"Of course I could. I'd be delighted." Maggie smiled. "We'll talk about that later but first we need to know what has reporters after our Finn."

"Have you received any calls about this?" Angie jerked her head in the direction of the street. She kept expecting to see the news vans suddenly appear on the kitchen screen.

"I haven't checked my messages today." Today belonged to her. She'd do whatever the heck she liked. The wants and needs of others could wait.

"Where's your phone? I'll check." Maggie was consumed with curiosity. What on earth had Finn done that had the paparazzi after her?

"I left it on the desk in my office." Finn poured waffle batter into the hot waffle irons while Maggie hurried away.

"You're taking all this very calmly." Angie was a nervous

wreck. She'd only ever seen people being shouted at by reporters and the paparazzi on television. It had never looked like a pleasant experience. Now she knew for a fact it was scary and they weren't even looking for her!

"There's not a lot I can do." Finn took the cooked waffles from the irons and poured fresh batter into the steaming irons.

"Finn, when did you turn off your phones?" Maggie came back into the kitchen carrying Finn's mobile. "The red light is flashing on your landline and you've missed what seems like a hundred calls on your mobile." The sound of air brakes being applied almost drowned out her words.

"I don't know what the hell is going on but I am not letting anything interfere with my birthday brunch." Finn stared at the kitchen screen for a moment, watching as vehicles tried to find a place to park in the street outside her home. "The world can wait on me today."

Angie and Maggie shrugged and allowed Finn to serve them the hot waffles. She had a tray of delicious toppings for them to choose from. The Mimosas disappeared at a fast rate as the women tried to ignore the noise from outside the house.

"Finn, I'm sorry. I can't stand it." Maggie pushed her half-eaten waffle away. She'd had too many of the delicious treats already. If she thought she could manage to make them she'd get the recipe from Finn – her girls would love them. "I have to know what's going on. Can I please check your messages?"

"Go ahead." Finn calmly continued eating. The waffle irons were turned off and cooling.

"You have at least twenty calls from Charles Upton." Maggie stared at the phone. Patrick had to be behind these calls.

"Your ex?" Angie stared at Maggie. "It couldn't be anything to do with your children, could it?"

"He doesn't even know I know Finn. He'd never try to call me using her number." Maggie was certain of that. She examined her own phone just in case.

"See what he wants." Finn couldn't be bothered.

"He wants to talk to you rather desperately by the sounds of things." Maggie could hear the tension in the voice messages

Charles left with Finn's answering service.

"Want to call and ask what he wants?" Finn offered with a grin. "Introduce yourself as my personal assistant and tell him Mizzz Emerson says no."

"Payback is a bitch," Angie sniggered.

"Payback by a bitch this time." Finn winked. "Go ahead, Maggie, go into my office and call using the landline – enjoy yourself." The Mimosa gave Finn a nice little buzz. "I'll freshen my make-up and see what those fellows shouting in the street want. Coming, Angie?"

"Couldn't you wait for me?" Maggie didn't want to miss any of the action.

"Sure, I'll make tea and coffee while we're waiting. I'm ever so slightly drunk."

"You better put our name on the coffee pot," Angie said. "Maggie and I are feeling no pain at the moment."

The kitchen was cleaned, the tea and coffee brewing, when Maggie returned a look of dazed astonishment on her face.

"What did he want?" Finn asked more out of politeness than anything else.

"Finn, thank you. You are my God." Maggie was buzzing, refusing Charles the opportunity for the media scoop of the century had done more for her than all the lawyers in the world could.

"What's happening?" Angie wondered if they should try and sober Finn up. It wasn't natural to be this calm.

"The television station in Germany broadcast previews of the upcoming new show. It went out on some kind of entertainment news programme Thursday evening. Finn Emerson was lauded for her artwork as worn by the stars. The 'nutjobs' apparently featured heavily in the Irish scenes shown to the German public. The telephone lines into the station crashed with viewers demanding the name of the artist." Maggie did a little hip-boogie. "The world is demanding the name of the genius who managed to capture ... let me get this right ..." Maggie consulted her notes, "The *pathos of the human condition*' and set the art world on its ear."

"What?" Finn croaked, collapsing onto a stool. She'd been

sure it was something to do with her son's sudden fame as sex symbols or some scam of Patrick's. She'd never thought it had anything to do with her personally. "Jayzeus."

"Yes, it seems the world and its sister are going crazy over your 'nutjobs', Finn. Everyone wants one." Maggie laughed in delight. "You're going to be rich and famous, Finn."

"I wouldn't mind being rich but I draw the line at famous!" Finn wailed. She didn't want to be famous. Her 'nutjobs' had saved her sanity through the lonely years of her marriage. How could they do this to her? "How did they find out my name and where I live?" What in the world was going on? How could this have happened? She was losing her mind. That had to be the answer. She'd been busy planning to make money for her 'old age' from the house. She'd been ready to get dug in arranging planning permission and permits for a new building to be built in the garden. She'd measured out the footprint for the foundation. She wasn't ready for any of this.

"I suppose they could have asked one of your sons." Maggie wondered if Finn would allow her to put the television screen on in the kitchen. She looked at Finn's pale face and decided not to ask. She was still tingling from the sheer thrill of telling her ex to take a hike – her friend, Finn Emerson, wanted nothing to do with him or his programme. The thought of his frustration would keep her warm on cold nights.

"We need to get out of here." Finn didn't intend to be kept prisoner in her own home – it was her birthday, darn it. She was going to kick up her heels and enjoy herself. "It's a shame I didn't know about this before I drank all of those Mimosas. I'm not fit to drive."

Maggie didn't know how Finn was sitting there calmly ignoring the mayhem outside her house. The screen in the kitchen continued to show more reporters trying to gain entrance. She wondered when a bold one would try to climb the curtain wall.

"How were you planning to get past that lot in front of your house?" Angie asked. The street was blocked with news vans and cars. Reporters were everywhere talking to curious neighbours and anyone they thought might have information.

"Look, isn't that your German brother Pieter?" Maggie pointed to the man pushing his way to the front of the crowd.

"What in the name of God is he doing here?" Finn turned on the sound. "I wasn't told to expect anyone." The film company usually informed her of arrivals.

"*Sister, sister, I have my car! I have come to take you out for the day*." The heavily accented voice echoed through the kitchen.

"I thought he was in Germany," Angie gaped.

"So did I." Finn frantically wondered how she was going to let Pieter in without the reporters pushing in behind him. That lot didn't look like they had any manners.

"Angie, you let him in, please. I'll turn everything off and lock up. We'll grab what we need then we're getting out of here for the day, ladies. That lot will lose interest when they see us leave." She hoped.

Finn and Maggie bustled about, getting ready to leave.

"Finn, I did not call your name because it is you they wish to see. I hope you don't mind me naming you sister." Pieter arrived in the kitchen, grinning like a bandit. They had been told about the crowd outside Finn's house. He'd come to help. It wasn't every day he charged to the rescue of a damsel in distress.

"You can call me Bodiddley if you can get us out of here." Finn was almost past surprise at this stage. "Then you can explain what you are doing here."

"You ladies will have to walk past them, I'm afraid. I could not get the van up the road." Pieter smiled. "You look wonderful, Finn."

"Thanks." Finn would never be ready to face the horde outside – but it had to be done. She sucked in a deep breath and forced a smile, looking around at her friends. "Let's do this," She walked towards her front door with her head high. "Up the women," she muttered under her breath.

They were almost blinded by the flash of light that exploded as soon as she stepped into the street. She couldn't make out what everyone was shouting, it was all a crazy jumble. She was pushed forward by Pieter while Maggie and Angie cried 'No *comment!*'. The crowd of reporters shoved and pushed forward, terrifying Finn. She couldn't breathe. Pieter was almost carrying her as he pushed his way through the crowd to where the van sat, engine idling.

"Get us out of here, Dolph!" Pieter snapped as soon as he'd pulled the side door of the van closed. They inched forward, watching reporters run to their cars and vans ready to give chase.

Finn was shaking. She never wanted to experience anything like that again. "How are we going to get away from them?" Her plans for the day were ruined and her two friends were being jostled around like loose luggage in the back of a van. This was not how she'd wanted to spend her birthday.

"We are accustomed to this. We have a plan." Dolph, at the wheel of the van, grinned over his shoulder. He could not have bought this kind of publicity for his new show. He was delighted. He drove slowly, letting the media get a good look at the van, before he jerked on the wheel and pulled the van into the private parking space behind the butcher's shop.

"When did you get here?" Finn wondered if this was how Alice felt when she fell down the rabbit hole to Wonderland.

"All will be explained. Your butcher Mr. Walsh has been very helpful. He was only too happy to offer help to one of his best customers."

Dolph pulled the van over to an idling limousine. The three women were quickly removed from the van and into the back of the stretch limousine. The van, with two of Dolph's crew inside, took off. They allowed the media vans to see them and the chase was on.

"Have some champagne, ladies!" Dolph invited.

He and Pieter had joined the ladies in the rear of the limo. They were grinning and slapping each other's backs in manly delight. Finn wanted to kick them – she didn't know how but she was sure this was all their fault.

"Gentlemen, allow me to tell you that you are still breathing only because it would be illegal for me to *kill you!*" Finn shouted the last two words.

"But this is wonderful!" Dolph exclaimed.

"For whom?" Finn took the glass of champagne Pieter passed to her. Who needed to be sober on a day like today?

"Why, for everyone!" Dolph was rubbing his hands together in glee. The reaction of the public to his footage astonished him. The media frenzy guaranteed the success of his new series. He could name his price. The sky was the limit. The fact that the woman – the artist – was his newly discovered niece and the mother of the two male stars of his new show was a licence to print money. He wanted to throw back his head and howl in delight.

"No, Dolph!" Finn snapped. "This is wonderful for everyone else. I am not enjoying this."

"But I don't understand." Dolph couldn't see any downside to this explosion of interest in his family's enterprise.

"Why don't we sit back and enjoy the ride," Maggie suggested, sipping her champagne, looking at the luxurious comforts all around her. She wanted to remember this ride for the rest of her life. "There is a lot for Finn to take in. Why don't we allow her to process some of the sh–stuff that hit her this morning?"

"Where are you taking us?" Angie couldn't care less. She was in the back of a limo sipping champagne, not a hardship. They could drive around all day as far as she was concerned.

"We are putting the finishing touches to some things in Bray." Dolph shrugged. "We will go there unless you object, Finn."

"Bray is fine."

"Settle back and enjoy the trip, ladies." Dolph couldn't stop beaming. "Would you like some chocolates to go with your champagne?"

Chapter 41

"*Dolph!*" Ronan shouted and started running when he saw the limo come to a stop outside the gates guarding the Parade.

"Angie, Maggie, am I seeing my own son or have I fallen into an alcoholic coma?"

"That's your boy." Angie bounced on the seat. She was having the time of her life.

"The other one is strolling along with your father and Rolf if I'm not mistaken." Maggie waved.

"Happy Birthday, Finn!" – "Mom!" – "Sweetling!"

The voices echoed around her as she was pulled from the car and hugged to within an inch of her life. She finally found herself standing free with a swimming head and no idea what was going on. The buzz of everyone trying to speak at once confused her.

"*Yoo-hoo, Finn!* Good to see you!" Nellie McGinn's voice broke through her haze. The woman held a covered tray in her hands.

There was no sign of the media here at least.

"It's about time you folk got here!" Mick Carr, one of the men living in the Parade, shouted while pushing a barrel of Guinness in front of him. Breda Carr his wife was laden down with her own burdens. People were pouring out of their houses.

Everyone was carrying something or other.

Finn stared around her. She was way past confused.

"*Right – now, people!*" Nellie McGinn shouted and clapped her hands. "Let's get organised. Where is Emmet? Someone go get that man." Nellie was in her element. "Finn, you and your friends grab yourselves a seat. Where's that charming father of yours? He can play a bit of music while we get organised here."

"What's going on?" Angie looked around at the hustling crowd.

The three women gazed along the row of long white-cloth-covered tables sitting in a line along the Parade.

"Who on earth knows? I thought all my men were in Germany yet here they are. Nobody tells me anything." Finn was simply going to go along with whatever happened. "They must be planning some kind of a 'street party' – nice of them to make room for us."

"Nuala, could I have your attention?"

Patrick Brennan glared at Angie and Maggie, expecting them to move. The two women ignored him, remaining close to Finn.

"What do you want, Patrick?" Finn wasn't really surprised to see Patrick here. Their sons would have told their father what was going on – she wished someone had told her.

"I want to talk to you about doing an interview for my morning programme. I'm planning a human-interest story covering your reunion with your birth mother Ingrid," Patrick said as if he were granting her a great honour. He'd already taped Ingrid's piece. The sudden interest in his wife would send his audience share soaring. "I've asked Charles Upton, my researcher, to approach RTÉ about televising the piece. We may even be able to sell the story to the German media."

"I don't consider Ingrid anything other than a surrogate, Patrick. The fact that my mother has a penis bothers you but no one else. Rolf is the only mother I've ever needed. Your idea doesn't interest me at all. I only do things that interest me these days."

"You don't understand, Nuala. I'm offering to allow you to appear on my show. I'll be on hand to guide you through the televised interview. Having your husband close will set you at ease. We might even be able to work in a mention of your little hobby."

"I don't consider you my husband. I don't want to talk about my 'hobby' and my name is Finn."

"I think you need to think about this, sweetheart." Patrick gave Finn one of his patented smiles, guaranteed to melt every female within range.

She was thrilled to notice it made her want to laugh.

"Not interested." Finn wanted nothing to do with his idea.

"Are you Patrick Brennan?" Nellie had noticed the famous Irish presenter in their midst. "The one who thinks he has the right to tell us how to think and act?"

"Excuse me." Finn pulled her two friends away, leaving Patrick to the tender mercies of Nellie.

The three women walked down the Parade and mingled with the crowd getting ready to party.

"How come you two didn't tell me you were coming home?" Finn demanded, standing in front of Emmet and Rolf, her hands on her hips. "Do yez know what's going on around here?" She looked around at the smiling crowd – some she knew – some strangers. Her two sons were much in demand.

"Would you just enjoy yourself for once, Finn?" Emmet grinned, pulling her into a tight embrace. "You look fabulous by the way."

Rolf kissed his fingers and blew a kiss to Finn.

"Make way there." Mr. Walsh, Finn's butcher, and two of his sons carrying a roasted pig were trying to push through the crowd onto the Parade. Where had they come from?

Finn stood back and watched. The Parade was lined with tables. Food and drink appeared from all directions.

"*Right, are we all here? Someone do a head count!*" Breda Carr shouted. "*Where's Larry Jameson, he's supposed to be here?*"

The residents of the Parade were having a ball. They were film stars and when it got dark they were going to show the film with the people from the Parade in it. This was the most excitement they'd ever had in their lives.

"Coming, missus." Larry with a group of his 'lads' in their Sunday best appeared, carrying yet another table.

"Nellie, Nellie McGinn, are you going to do this or shall I?" Breda Carr was flushed and happy. She'd been a vampire's victim and her face had been shown on German television. Imagine.

"*I'll do it!*" Nellie McGinn shouted. "*It was my idea!*"

She waved at one of the German cameramen to follow along. She could have been a film director herself if she'd been born later in life, she thought, as everyone jumped to obey her commands.

Nellie stationed herself in the middle of the Parade. "We're going to do this the old-fashioned way. We promised our German visitors an Irish hooley and that's what they're going to get. Now, where is Finn? Finn Emerson, front and centre woman, yer holding things up!"

Nellie examined Finn as she walked towards her. The girl was suitably dressed for once.

Finn looked at the smiling faces that surrounded her.

Nellie swung into action, issuing orders to everyone. She put the men in Finn's life in a circle on a bare piece of the Parade they'd marked out as a dance floor. When she went to include Patrick Brennan, Angie quietly stepped in with a whispered "Not that one". Nellie nodded. She'd guessed as much.

"Jim Kelly, play something beautiful. A waltz if you would." Nellie looked to where Jim Kelly sat on a kitchen chair pulled close to his own front door, his accordion across his chest ready for action. The man gave a nod and with lively fingers and much smiling began to produce beautiful music from his squeeze box.

"Now, Finn, you dance with your father first," Nellie ordered while Jim played a waltz by Strauss.

Emmet took his daughter in his arms and waltzed her skilfully around the impromptu dance floor. He kissed her then passed her into Rolf's arms. Finn was taller than Rolf but it didn't matter. He danced her around, beaming, before passing her to Ronan.

Ronan did a passable waltz, whispering to his mum that she

looked fabulous before dancing her over to Oisín.

Oisín picked Finn up and swung her around, shouting that he had the sexiest mother in the world.

Finn was flattered but mortified by the attention.

When Oisín stopped moving Nellie gave the signal and everyone started to sing. They roared out a vigorous rendition of '*Happy Birthday to Finn*'.

Finn was hugged and kissed to within an inch of her life. Everyone wanted to give her personal good wishes. She was passed laughing from one pair of arms to another.

Emmet brought out the crate of champagne he'd hidden. Mick Carr cracked open the Guinness and the party got started. It was a good old Irish hooley with everyone performing their 'party piece'. The German crew ran around recording everything. Angie's Irish dancing stole the show. The woman was a wonder to watch – her knees lifting – feet kicking – skirt flying. The audience clapped along and cheered.

The partygoers showed no sign of tiring. The Irish weather for once was co-operating. The summer evening closed in slowly. Tall garden candles were pushed into soft earth and lit to add a hint of glamour to the gathering.

"*Riverdance* has a lot to answer for," Angie gasped, dropping onto a chair beside Finn. She put out a hand for the glass of water Finn held. She needed it. She'd been whirled around the place by countless young men. "Very different from your birthday last year, isn't it?" she whispered.

"It couldn't be more different." Finn looked around for more bottled water. They were going to need it. "I noticed you teaching the younger visitors a little Irish dancing."

"Did you see your two, Ronan and Oisín – I remember you dragging them kicking and screaming to dance classes." Angie grabbed the bottle of water Finn passed to her and guzzled it down.

"They've discovered the advantages of being Oirish in their travels." Finn watched her family. She hadn't had time to talk to them yet but she didn't care. They were here and that was all that mattered at the moment.

"Patrick is desperately trying to impress the visiting

executives, have you noticed?" Maggie dropped into a nearby chair, panting from her dash around the Parade in Larry Jameson's arms. The man had stamina, she'd say that for him. She'd telephoned to check on her children. They were having a great time with their father's latest woman friend. She was free to enjoy herself.

"Nope." Finn shrugged. "I've been busy."

"Busy being the new, improved and very popular Finn Emerson?" Maggie accepted a bottle of water with relief. "Good for you."

"Good for everyone!" Angie chinked her water bottle against Finn's and Maggie's. Dare had told her he planned to rent Finn's house. She hadn't mentioned it to Finn. She reckoned it was none of her business. It would be lovely to see her grandchildren. She'd be free to enjoy them without worrying about entertaining and feeding them all. She couldn't wait.

"You and Larry Jameson seem to be enjoying yourselves, Maggie?" Finn said.

"The man can dance," Maggie said. "It's always a pleasure to meet a man who can waltz you off your feet."

"Look at Pieter and Gerta dancing cheek to cheek, lost in the music – you'd never believe they had four teenage kids." Finn was thrilled Pieter had brought his wife with him on this trip. She believed she and Gerta could become good friends. She'd be glad to get to know them all. "Paul and Scott seem to be much in demand."

"Have you thought about it?" Angie leaned in to say.

"Thought about what?" Finn laughed aloud at the antics of the crowd around her.

"Last year for your birthday you gave a party and no one came. This year – just one short year later – you didn't bother with a party yet everyone came." She waved her hands around at the laughing people.

"I suppose you're right." Finn had a lot more family around her than she knew what to do with. Thank God Ingrid, according to Gerta, had refused to travel to Ireland again. The woman had been in a foul mood since her return so they said.

Gerta thought Rolf and his sister had had a falling-out. "It's a shame we don't have street parties anymore."

"You have had an amazing year, Finn." Angie smiled at Rolf walking over to them. He was smiling and happier looking then she'd seen him in a while. It would do the man good to be able to stay in one place for a while. She wouldn't fancy being on the move all the time. Although, she wouldn't say no to the odd trip abroad.

"Angie, you have not danced with me." Rolf offered his hand to Angie who jumped to her feet.

"Well, daughter, will you dance with your old man?" Emmet held out his hand to Finn. They took to the dance floor under the smiling gazes of the crowd. "Before I forget and while it's only the two of us – I think Rolf is finally seeing his sister for what she really is. That will make our settling down here a lot easier. I wasn't looking forward to having Ingrid as a regular visitor."

"Da, we can handle whatever that woman chooses to dish out," Finn said. "The two of us will protect Rolf. What do you know about Dolph and his plans for me and mine? He seems awfully willing to throw me to the wolves."

"He'd be a good man to have in your corner." Emmet swung her away from him before drawing her back close to his chest. He was enjoying this slice of a disappearing part of Irish life. Maybe he'd try and start having the odd hooley when he was once more living in the family home. "He's a powerful man in Germany. He could help you push your career along. The man loves your artwork and featured it heavily in the indoor scenes in his new programme."

"We'll see how things go. I like Pieter's wife." Finn put her head on her father's chest. The evening air was so soft and the music being created by fiddle and squeeze box suited it somehow. "She has invited me to visit them in Germany. I'm thinking about it."

"Enough of this – it's your birthday." Emmet kissed her. "Jim, take a break. I have my fiddle here somewhere." He looked for one of his grandsons. They'd know where his fiddle was. He spotted Oisín and waved, then mimed fiddle-playing. A minute later a smiling Oisín was carrying his fiddle case towards him.

Finn sat on a windowsill while her father played dance music and the crowd whispered and moved around them. Oisín and Ronan came to lean on either side of her. She saw the studio photographer going crazy taking pictures. She'd have to get a copy. It wasn't every day a woman of her years sat with a sex symbol standing guard on each side like bookends.

"Dolph is thinking of having Frieda's character in the show discover a love of metalwork." Ronan sniggered and nudged his mother gently with his elbow. He ignored the young girls trying to catch his eye. He'd missed his mother and wanted to spend a little time with her.

"The man is planning to put the poor girl in a leather bikini while she works on her 'models'." Oisín's shoulders shook with silent laughter. "It will certainly catch the eye."

"Well, it is what every sane woman wears when there's burning hot metal flying around." Finn lifted her nose in the air and grinned facetiously. "Think how useful the open flame will be for fighting vampires."

The three of them held onto each other and giggled like lunatics.

Finn stared around her at the crowd, wishing she could trap this moment in a bottle. There was a small mountain of presents waiting to be opened by her. They could wait – it hadn't been presents she'd wanted for her big day last year. She'd needed an acknowledgment of her worth as a human being. She'd learned her own worth through her own efforts this year. She knew who she was. She liked herself.

She was determined to keep going forward. No one knew what tomorrow would bring but she would greet it on her own terms. She'd been in charge of her own life for a year. Looking around at the smiling faces, surrounded by the men she loved, she decided she hadn't done a half bad job. She'd keep it up.

Epilogue

Present Day

"Dad, are you ready to leave?" Finn had been searching for her father. He'd found a seat almost hidden from sight of the wedding party.

"Don't annoy me, daughter. We haven't heard Ronan perform yet." Emmet patted the seat beside him. "Sit down here, you've been running around like a blue-arse fly since we got here."

"Paul and Scott look so happy." Finn was glad to sit down – get the weight off her feet. She sat beside her father, staring around at the happy crowd gathered in the hotel ballroom.

"I never thought I'd live to see the day two men could exchange marriage vows – it's a wonderful thing." Emmet took a hankie from his pocket and blew his nose vigorously.

"The happy couple are glad you're here. They didn't expect you to attend. It hasn't been that long since we lost Rolf." Finn fought the tears that came to her eyes.

"We didn't lose him, for feck's sake, Finn!" Emmet snapped. "He died. I hate those mealy-mouthed expressions. We lost him, he slipped away, he's gone. He's past. Rolf died." He fought for breath. "He died in my arms."

"I know, Da." Finn put her head on his shoulder. "I was there."

"Now's not the time to be talking about such things, daughter. Look at Paul and Scott there. The pair of them are beaming." He moved his shoulder, shaking her head. "Speaking of happy days," he pointed towards Dare Lawrence, "when are you going to marry that man?"

Patrick Brennan had been dead for over five years. Finn was free to marry but was dragging her feet about committing to Dare.

"You'd better be quick about it," Emmet said. "I haven't that many days left meself."

"Now who's being depressing?" Finn sat up and glared. She'd lost her da-ma – she wasn't ready to lose her da.

"We are all going to die, daughter." Emmet felt like a day didn't pass without him hearing of the death of another friend. He was one of the few left breathing as far as he could see. "It's not something to be feared, you know. It happens to all of us will we or nill we."

"I don't want to think about it."

"I thought we'd cured you of hiding your head in the sand."

"This is not the time to be thinking sad thoughts." Finn looked around at the laughing happy people.

"It's hard not to think about the people who aren't here." Emmet too looked at the crowd. So many familiar faces missing. "You know, I think I feel sadder at a wedding than I do at a good Irish wake. You can have a few good laughs at a funeral!"

"Honest to God, Da, it's worse you're getting."

"What are you two doing over here all on your own?" Oisín knelt down in front of the pair. "I've saved you seats in the front of the room. Ronan will be performing soon. It's not every day people get to see a renowned singer-songwriter perform live. Everyone wants to be near the stage. So, come on," he stood, offering both hands to pull them from their seats. "Let's be having yeh."

Emmet waved the proffered hands away.

"Good lad, you found them." Dare joined them. "I'll be forced to throw me body over those seats if you don't move. The crowd is beginning to mill around the stage – hoping to catch a glimpse of the star."

"I'm fine where I am," Emmet said. "I can't be doing with all those iphones or whatnot flashing and wagging in the air. Does no one just enjoy the experience anymore? They'll be fighting to record Ronan and be the first to send him over the net, I've no doubt. I can't be arsed with all of that – sorry. I'll stay here and enjoy the music."

"If that's the way you feel," Dare said, "I'll grab a chair and join yez."

"I'll leave you old fogies to it." Oisín wished he could join them. He didn't enjoy the mania that surrounded his brother's performances. But he'd promised his wife he'd find seats close to the stage for them. "I'll see yez later." He left them to enjoy their little hideaway.

"Is it just me or are weddings a great deal of work? I've a pain in my face from smiling." Dare sank into the chair he'd carried over.

"I've just been saying I enjoy a good wake more meself." Emmet slapped Dare on the back.

"Me ma's was certainly a party to end all parties." Dare shook his head, remembering the wake they had held for his mother. Angie had died in her sleep, shocking everyone who knew her. It was the first time the woman had ever done anything quietly.

"Someone remind me to get a copy of the official video of the wedding for Maggie." Finn didn't want to think about Angie and her passing. "She was sad she couldn't get away to attend the wedding." Maggie lived in America – LA. She'd made a name for herself in costume design.

"So many changes," Emmet said sadly. "What is it about weddings that makes you count the passing of the years? I don't get to see my grandsons unless there is a wedding or a funeral." He blew his nose loudly. "Rolf loved that Ronan married a German woman and settled in Germany. Then there is Oisín running around the world filming nature documentaries." He shook his head and sighed. "Still, I suppose it's not a bad legacy for an old man to leave behind him. Two talented grandsons, five great-grandchildren. I can die happy knowing I've left something of myself behind me."

"Don't talk to me about grandchildren." Dare could see Finn was getting upset. "I've lost count of the number my kids have presented me with."

"Do you ever think, daughter," Emmet waved a hand towards the stage, "that it was your little nutjobs that started all of this!"

"In the name of God, Da, how do you figure that?"

"Paul made his fortune teaching people to weld bits of metal." Emmet sucked his lips as he thought. "He has all those millions of followers on YouTube now. Maggie got ahead because you introduced her to Tim Liner – and you met him because of your nutjobs. Your two sons were catapulted to fame because they were seen on screen wearing your nutjobs and the world went crazy." The jewellery arm of Finn's business made a fortune. Finn designed and made the original items before they were sent out to factories to mass produce. "Dare has a job keeping up with the demands for your designs. Yes," Emmet nudged her gently, "the more I think about it, the more I believe none of us would be where we are today if it wasn't for your nutjobs."

"Would you whist, old man!" Finn didn't want to talk about it. "The star is on the stage."

The End

Printed in Great Britain
by Amazon